FAREWELL COMPANIONS

And when he walked to school it was a journey through the multiple tiers of a society where tuppence ha'penny looked down on tuppence, while tuppence in turn was a cut above three ha'pence. Iveagh Hostel offered a casual night's shelter to the destitute. So too did the Morning Star Hostel down by the river. The tenements were for those who had not so utterly given up. Crowded cottages without gardens and corporation houses with tiny ones were a step higher. Respectability fringed the South Circular Road, modestly in cottages, more assuredly in two-storey houses. In Harrington Street there were even hints of residential splendour. What your father did for a livelihood was of importance.

JAMES PLUNKETT

Farewell Companions

Gainsborough Press

To the memory of my Father

This edition published in 1996 by Gainsborough Press
An imprint of Leopard
20 Vauxhall Bridge Road, London SW1V 2SA

First published by Hutchinson & Co. (Publishers) Ltd 1977
Arrow edition 1978
© James Plunkett 1977

Printed and bound in Great Britain by
Cox & Wyman Ltd, Reading, Berkshire

ISBN 0 752 90404 3

Contents

ONE · The Standing Circle

> Ancient Ireland, indeed! I was reared by her bedside,
> The rune and the chant, evil eye and averted head
> Formorian fierceness of family and local feud.
> Gaunt figures of fear and of friendliness,
> For years they trespassed on my dreams
> Until once, in a standing circle of stones
> I felt their shadows pass
>
> Into that dark permanence of ancient forms.

JOHN MONTAGUE

The photograph album on the table beside the window lay on a brown velvet cloth and was the inseparable companion of the geranium. On its leather binding, which was blue, a peacock with real feathers in its tail and a bright red bead for an eye glared at everyone who drew near and dared them to open it. Much to its surprise, they sometimes did. Beyond the lace curtains of the window were the railings surrounding the basement area and across the cobbled street another row of tall, Georgian houses. From time to time, though not very frequently, for they were away from the main thoroughfare, the clip-clop of horses' hooves drew the eyes. Occasionally it was the post-office parcels van with its two enormous horses. It made such a heavy trundling sound and moved so slowly that when he heard it there was always time to run to the window, in case it would draw to a halt at the hall door steps. If his mother had saved and sent off enough cocoa coupons for one of the free gifts offered by Bournville or Frys or Van Houtens he would watch out for it each evening for days on end.

It was on such occasions, or simply when there was nothing else to do, that he brooded over the photographs in the album, often until the light went, or the rain clouds darkened the skies outside, making the geranium give off its sad, clayey smell. Sometimes his mother stopped in the middle of her scrubbing or polishing or meal making, or singing songs like:

> 'If ever you marry a nice young man
> Don't give it away in a joke
> That ever you slept in a sentry box
> Wrapped up in a soldier's cloak'

and sat down beside him for a while to identify the photographs for him, saying your Uncle James, your Uncle Hugh, Grand

Aunt Ellen God be good to her, your father's pal Bob Fitzpatrick. At times she would exclaim, O Mother of Mercy will
you look at the get-up of Mollie Longmore in that stickyback
we got took in Lloyd's of Grafton Street – will you look at the
hat, and then there was no more to be got out of her because
she had lost her wits with laughing. It was true of course. It was
like ten hats.

The women stood surrounded by trellis work and trailing
roses or sat on sofas reading letters; the men occupied straight-
backed chairs with their legs crossed and their elbows resting on
a side table, or stood in twos or threes with watch chains across
their waistcoats and their arms on each other's shoulders. There
were postcards, too, some with funny pictures, some with small
greeting cards in little silk envelopes, embroidered with the
names of regiments and countries and their coloured flags. There
were war photographs: Germans with spiked helmets, French
and Belgians with helmets like dish covers, British with helmets
like basins. There were teams of horses dragging guns through
the mud; Tommies in trenches; his father in camp; his father
standing beside an army lorry; his father with medals on his
breast and sergeant stripes and service stripes on his sleeve. Open
the album and there, to be puzzled over, was a world that had
been going about its business before he was born. That was a
mystery, the first of many.

Where had he come from? From God, his mother said.
Where had he been before he was born? In heaven. If so he had
no memory of it, although already there were many memories
stuffed into his head, such a crowd of them that it too was a
kind of album. There was the time he woke frightened because
shots were going off somewhere in the remote darkness; there
was his mother lighting the lamp and himself sitting in his
nightshirt at the brass fender by the blazing fire and the wind
making its storm noises in the chimney; there were the Christmas
decorations running in red and green chains to each corner of
the room from the red and green Christmas bell in the centre;
there was his little sister eating porridge one morning in her
nightdress and her face breaking out in red blotches before his

eyes; there was the funeral one night from the cottages by the river with a torchlight procession and a flag and the wailing of women; there was the steamer with clockwork propellers his grandmother had bought him; all these. But none of heaven. Not a single memory of God. Try as he would all recollection of God and heaven eluded him. He tried hard. He tried in vain. But he believed he would remember later. When he was older, perhaps.

World, he knew already, is not sudden. World is very slow. Creak, creak. Rock, rock. A little and a little. Long hours of nothing at all. Eat up din-din to make you grow big. Bless yourself. Go to sleepies. Peep, I see you. Warm olive oil on cotton wool for an earache. For a cold or a toothache an eggcup of punch. How to tie laces. How to comb hair. How to say a song; clap hands till Daddy comes home or ding-dong bell.

> Ding dong bell
> Pussy's in the well
> Who pushed her in?
> Little Johnny Thin
> Who'll pull her out
> Little Johnny Stout

Cruel Johnny Thin. Good Johnny Stout.

Of course he was beyond all that now, this long time. He could feed the ducks from a paper bag and swing on the iron chains that bordered in spiky loops the pathway's edge all the way around St Stephen's Green. He could go to a football match in Shelbourne Park, walking beside his father all the way to Baggot Street and sitting listening to the hissing of the trolley on the open-air deck of the tram.

'You're getting as big as a house,' the milkman remarked. 'You must be eating up your porridge.'

'I am,' he agreed, holding out the jug, 'every day.'

'I can see that. And twice of a Sunday.'

The milkman filled the measure from the can and emptied it into the jug

'Do you know what I'm going to tell you?' The milkman assured him, 'You'll be as strong as Jack Dempsey if you keep it up.'

He scooped a little more milk into the measure and poured that into the jug too.

'That's a tilly for yourself,' he said. Then he did the same thing once again. 'And a tilly for the cat.'

Then, if Mrs Curtis had left her can in readiness, beside the iron rail which was for wiping the mud from your boots, he filled that too. The churns with their brass hoops and taps rattled and bounced as the milkman drove off so that everybody for doors down knew he was making his rounds on his horse and cart.

The world composed itself about him in this way: the houses the streets the trams the green with its bandstand flowered walks ducks on the pond waterfall and pavilion the humped bridge over the canal the tree-lined bank the locks niagarous the barges drawn by horses Fitzwilliam Square the tennis court and smells of dogs' number one and number two. Then the sky with heaven immediately above, purgatory slightly to the left and limbo to the right behind blue curtains; underneath his feet hell long corridors the devil doomed souls smoke fire iron gates and a sign: ABANDON HOPE ALL YE THAT ENTER HERE. Purgatory up above was a place of flame and smoke too but the souls there suffered only for a time while arms outstretched eyes looking down from the left-hand corner of the sky they begged continuously for the prayers of the living. Remember me, remember me at least you, my friend. There was a picture of them like that on the classroom wall.

Sister Aloysius Gonzaga instructed them in catechism and prepared them for first Holy Communion.

Who made the world?

God made the world.

Who is God?

God is the creator and sovereign Lord of Heaven and Earth and of all things.

To receive communion worthily you must be in a state of sanctifying grace that is without stain of mortal sin and you must have fasted from the previous midnight. Anyone who received unworthily ate and drank his own damnation.

She told them a story.

Once there was a little boy who was about to receive his first Holy Communion. The night before his mother laid out his new shirt and tie, his new cap and suit, his new shoes and stockings, his first communion medal in its white rosette and the new mother-of-pearl prayer book which was to be his present for the happiest occasion of his life. He had been to confession and he said his prayers carefully, and then his mother kissed him good-night and tucked him into bed. But during the night he woke up very thirsty, and he went to the kitchen for a drink of water and was so sleepy he had swallowed some before he remembered what was to happen the next day. In the morning he was afraid to say that he had broken his fast, so he put on all his new things and was brought to the church, and when the time came he went up to the altar rails with the other children. The priest placed the consecrated host on his tongue and the boy rose and walked back to his seat with the rest. But as he hid his face in his hands and swallowed the communion particle, which was now the very flesh and blood of Our Lord Jesus Christ, he was so terrified by the enormity of his sin that his heart stood still, and he collapsed and died in an instant. That little boy, she said, went straight down to hell. That little boy was at this very moment burning in flames, and would so burn for ever and ever.

The school was down Quinn's Lane, divided from the grounds of the nearby hospital by a high stone wall, in which there was a door. This was the morgue where the dead bodies were left. They opened it sometimes on their way home to peer inside. On one occasion he was pushed in and the door slammed shut. Four bodies lay on slabs. One had a yellow face and spiky hairs curling from thin, sharp, upturned nostrils. Somewhere else, he thought, one of the bodies moaned softly. The others began to move, not while he looked at them, but whenever he turned his back. So he stared at them for some seconds, then turned to hammer on the door and shout for help, then turned swiftly to stare at them again to keep them from moving, and then again he would risk turning his back on them to hammer on the door. After about twenty minutes a man wearing a rubber apron came and let him out. The apron had a strong hospital smell. A carbolic smell. Several times afterwards he woke from his sleep at night to find that same smell staining faintly the darkness of his bedroom.

Mr and Mrs Curtis lived at the very top of the house. On each landing a window bordered with coloured glass looked out first at the gardens and their derelict coach-houses but later over roofs and chimneys and last of all, when you reached the landing outside their door, at the trees in the green and the spires of churches.

Almost always there was a pot simmering on the gas stove when you went in, the warm air smelled of treacle and spices, saucepans of homemade jam or trays of homemade sweets cooled on the window ledge. In its cage the bird, no longer interested in hopping from perch to perch, tucked its head into its shoulder to eavesdrop on all that was said. From the gilt frame on the mantelpiece the pictures of their two sons looked on in silence. Both were in uniform and both had been killed in France. There were no other children. An artificial poppy separated the two pictures. Underneath it was a couplet in ornate script:

> In Flanders fields the poppies blow
> Between the crosses, row on row . . .

Mr Curtis, who sat in a chair at the window, would sometimes leave down his book and his magnifying glass to talk about such things as the principles of steam locomotion or why a magnet could pick up a nail; or to borrow a bowl from Mrs Curtis to show that when a spoon was placed in the water it seemed to bend and the reason for this.

His bookshop on the quays was looked after now by a relation while he himself worked at home, and sometimes the pile of books on his table grew so high that he had to remove half a dozen of them to make a hole to talk through it. If he called you over you had to pick your steps among the others that lay around him on the floor. Mr Curtis spoke at length about the cultural associations of the immediate neighbourhood. The family of

Bernard Shaw, he said, had occupied the house at the corner of Hatch Street, a distance of some fifty yards. The writer George Moore and the poet and surgeon Oliver St John Gogarty lived the space of a few gardens away in Ely Place, which had connections also with John Millington Synge, whose prose was beyond praise though his plays were in questionable taste. Senator W. B. Yeats, the poet, lived near at hand also. Almost next door there was a Miss Hone, whose work in stained glass was very highly regarded. She herself, he thought, was somewhat overbearing. When Mrs Curtis begged him to remember that he was talking to a child of seven, not an old man of seventy, he said that a young imagination which was fed on the singular and the curious, however imperfectly understood, could be expected to grow in freshness and originality. It was a mistake to talk down to children. Understanding, like a flower, reached upwards. Then for recreation he told the story of Hans Clodhopper who, ungifted though he was, was interested in everything and won the hand of the king's daughter.

'Stories,' Mrs Curtis complained when he had finished. 'There's no surer encouragement to idleness than a head stuffed with stories.'

'If there were no stories there would be few books,' Mr Curtis said, 'and if that were the case you and I might beg for our bread.'

Mr Curtis led him out to the landing, where the coloured glass that bordered the window burned in the evening sun. If it were an hour to sunset, could he guess approximately where was the west? Having done that, could he point to the east? To the north and the south? What were the landmarks? This spire, that chimney? During the rebellion of 1916, he said, Mrs Curtis and he had stood watching the glow in the sky as the houses burning along the length of O'Connell Street threatened the rest of the city. He had felt Pembroke Street would escape because of the open space of St Stephen's Green in between. But what of their bookshop on the quays? They had both stood for some time, the landing in darkness except for the reflection from the fierce glow in the sky beyond, listening to the sound of bullets and the crash of shells from the British gunboat in the river Liffey, until Mrs Curtis said to him: 'Here we are worrying about a shop and a few shelves of books, but not a thought for our unfortunate fellow creatures caught in the middle of it all,' so that night they had asked God's mercy on Dublin city, not alone on the innocent civilians or on the forces of the Crown who were fighting bravely to restore law and order, but on the rebels in the General Post Office as well. They were rebels, but educated men; poets, professors, schoolteachers. He had known some of them personally because sometimes they had come to his bookshop. If the British government had used compassion instead of executing them, Britain would not have lost Ireland.

Mr and Mrs Curtis were Protestants. They were in favour of the King and the Union Jack and were in the British Legion. His father and mother were Catholics and their flag was green, white and orange, but on Remembrance Day his mother bought a poppy from Mrs Curtis because his father had fought in the war and one of his uncles had been killed in France and another came home wounded only to die. Another uncle was shot dead in Dublin fighting for the Republicans. Their mass cards with black borders and a little photograph were all together in his mother's prayerbook. His father had not been fighting for the King, he said, but for little Belgium and the freedom of small nations. On Remembrance Day his father marched wearing his medals, and his mother wore her poppy and stood looking on. The war had ended at eleven o'clock on the eleventh day of November 1918, and so at eleven o'clock on that day each year the bugles sounded the last post, the crowds stood to attention, and while people thought of those who had been killed, everyone was silent for two minutes except the Republicans. The Republicans let off fireworks and shouted 'Up the Republic' and burned the offices of the British Legion. They wore lilies and one of them snatched the poppy from his mother's coat as they were going home. He tried to kick at the man but he was too small and the man laughed at him.

'Never mind him,' his mother said, 'he's only one of de Valera's cornerboys, reared on robbery and loot.'

When they got home she told him a song to cheer him up:

'Oul de Valera has a shop down in hell
He's selling ammunition and he's doing very well
Sixpence for a rifle, a ha'penny for a shell
Oul de Valera has a shop down in hell.'

They had a laugh together at that. But only a little while later, as she was lighting the gas for their meal and he was shouting out the song for the umpteenth time, he looked at her and forgot to finish it. She was in tears.

The greatest occasion in this life, Sister Aloysius assured them, something ever afterwards remembered by a good Catholic child, is that moment when Christ under the appearance of bread but truly and wholly present in His Divinity and His Body and Blood, becomes the guest of the soul for the very first time. A guest, Sister Aloysius further explained, for whom every last preparation must be made.

They had all seen what happened at home when an important guest was expected. There was a general spring cleaning. The floors were swept, the windows cleaned, the table spread with the finest linen and the best tableware. In the guest room the pictures on the walls were thoroughly dusted and fresh flowers were arranged in the vases. All the dark corners were gone over. Nothing was left to chance.

They, too, in preparing for first Holy Communion, must think of the heart as a mansion to be scrubbed and polished and set in order for the expected Visitor. Good deeds were the bright pictures they would hang on the walls, little prayers, frequently said, would be flowers to fill the vases. They would cleanse the mansion with sanctifying grace through repentance and confession. But first they must have sorrow for their sins. Being seven years of age, they had reached the age of reason. Therefore they should begin the practice of frequent examinations of conscience, so that they would know their sins to tell to the priest.

His mother bought him a navy blue serge suit, a white shirt, a blue silk tie, black shoes and grey stockings, and a new school

cap. She got him out of bed early. She watched like a hawk
while he was washing in case he swallowed any water. For the
same reason she thought it better he should not clean his teeth.
When he was fully dressed she pinned his communion medal
and white rosette on his lapel. He was starving by that time
and wished he could have his breakfast and make his first
communion some other day. In case that was a sinful thought,
he made an act of contrition and then tried hard not to think
at all. The result was that thoughts weltered and darted about
his head like a legion of devils. The other children had assembled
at the convent. They were marched in ranks of two to the church.

It was not a great success. Distractions beset him on his way
to the altar rails. As the priest distributing the host moved
nearer, he wondered would he see in it, as in a medallion, a tiny
image of Christ. Not a sign. When he got back to his seat his
mouth was so dry the wafer glued itself firmly to the roof.
Instead of praying he spent several minutes convinced it was
stuck there forever. It would be a sacrilege to use his fingers.
He had been instructed to avoid even contact with his teeth.
Through agonizing minutes, his face buried devoutly in his
hands, he worked desperately to peel it away with his tongue.
Beyond his predicament the mass was drawing to its conclusion.
Barely in time, it seemed, the wafer softened and became un-
stuck. He swallowed it. By then sweat had glued the new shirt
to his back.

Deciding on sins for his first confession had been an ordeal
too, although Sister Aloysius helped with suggestions of
possible offences. Had they been disobedient, irreverent? Most
children were from time to time. Had they taken the Lord's
name in vain? Perhaps they had told lies? Or stolen things?
Apples from an orchard, or sugar or jam from the cupboard.
Neglected morning or evening prayers? Or more serious
offences still? They must go over their behaviour carefully. They
must hold nothing back from the priest.

He made a careful note of these and would have confessed
readily to all of them if that would have disposed of the matter.
But it would not. If he confessed anything that came into his

head he would be telling lies to the Holy Ghost and that, he knew, was one of the worst sins of all, so he took precautions against committing a sacrilege. In the weeks beforehand he stole a few spoons of sugar from the press and a couple of times he took a few mouthfuls from the milk jug before bringing it in to his mother, though he hated milk except in tea or on his porridge. He made sure to tell a few blatant lies and made a note of the number of times. He repeated a parody of the Confiteor to his younger sister:

> 'I confess to Almighty God,
> To Blessed Mary ever a virgin
> To Blessed Michael the dark Angel,
> To Blessed John the Blacksmith.'

He asked her what means 'Amen' and then gave her an answer he had heard from one of the big boys:

> 'Amen means so be it
> Half a loaf and a threepenny bit.'

That looked after irreverence.

Then he fitted it all into the formula he had been taught, rehearsed it day after day and had it word perfect by the time he entered the confession box to receive the sacrament of penance for the first time. When he knelt down the grill was about a foot above his head. The slide clicked open. There was silence. He could hear the priest breathing. With the door closed it was very dark. An interval passed.

'Is there somebody there?' the priest asked.

'Yes, Father,' he said.

The priest leaned forward until his nose was against the grill.

'Have you fallen down a hole, child?' the priest asked.

'No, Father.'

'Surely Sister Aloysius told you to stand up.'

'I forgot, Father.'

'Stand up, like a good boy,' the priest said wearily. And after a pause, 'Well . . . my child.'

He crossed himself and said, 'Bless me, Father, for I have sinned. Father, this is my first confession and I accuse myself of my sins: Father . . . I stole the sugar on my mother twice; I drank the milk twice; I told lies three times, I said an irreverent thing twice; I said God's name in vain three times . . . and for these and all my sins I am sorry.'

The priest said he must be a truthful boy in future and told him to recite for his penance three Our Fathers, three Hail Marys and three Glory be to the Fathers, and now to make a good act of contrition. When he had received absolution he groped about in the darkness, found the crucifix which hung on the side panel and kissed the wounded feet in gratitude and submission as Sister Aloysius had advised them. First confession was over.

Now first communion was over too. Both forever. The glimpse of irretrievability disturbed him. Was it never possible, under any circumstances, to have two first anythings? The question strove for his attention while the group photographs were taken and again while they waited for tea and sandwiches, buns and lemonade in the private grounds of the convent, an occasional privilege. The answer, in the end, seemed to be no, though he caught tantalizing glimpses of a possible affirmative. He tucked the matter away for later consideration.

'I'll have to bring him in to Mrs Tuite in the basement,' his mother said at lunchtime, 'and to the Kielys next door, I suppose. But what about the Curtises?'

The rest of the day would be devoted to ritual visits to friends and relatives who, despite his mother's spurious protests, would insist on giving him money for his pocket in honour of the occasion. In case it would be regarded as avarice, he pretended not to listen.

'Why not?' his father asked.

'Because the Catholic way isn't the Protestant way,' she said, 'and it might be bad manners to make a parade of it.'

'I suppose it might,' his father said. 'On the other hand they may feel slighted if you don't.'

'It's hard to know,' she agreed. Then leaving it to one side, she said, 'I suppose you wouldn't think of taking him to your Aunt Emily yourself?'

'And get de Valera and Shin Fain awahn for the length and breadth of the visit,' his father said, 'no bloody fear.'

'She puts years on me too,' his mother admitted, 'all that diehard republicanism.'

'Mother Erin in person,' his father said; 'she's like a gramophone record. Why go near her at all?'

'Because she'd be that mortally offended I'd never hear the end of it if I didn't.'

His father agreed, by way of compensation, to look after all the visits after tea.

Mrs Tuite said, wasn't he lovely God bless his innocence he was like an angel, and rooted at last in her bag but could only find sixpence. He did better in Kielys: half-a-crown from missus and a shilling each from her two sons who were on their half day from the drapery business. In the street an old gentleman, seeing his white rosette, remarked the great occasion, patted him on the head, praised his mother until she blushed and raised him a further two shillings. Another thirteen and he would have enough to exchange for a whole pound note. It was beginning to feel like what he had been told: the happiest day of his life.

They climbed the creaking stairs beyond the side door to the rooms above the greengrocer's shop, leaving behind the smells of onions, potatoes, cabbages and clay. The parlour was close and over-furnished, the unopened window looked out at the sunlit sky above the spire of St Patrick's Cathedral. It seemed a long way off. A nondescript plant in a wicker basket drooped by his elbow and pined for air. He sat decorously between his mother and Aunt Emily, oppressed by faint bodily odours, hemmed in by knick-knacks and beaded hangings, finding it difficult to stay awake. They were talking across him of family news: who had died, who was getting married, the kind of match it was, who was in ill-health, who was prospering, some circumstance or other that shocked his mother.

'I'd never have suspected it,' she said.

'You'd want to be blind,' Aunt Emily said.

'I always knew he was fond of the bottle.'

'He gave that up when she got the priest on to him,' Aunt
Emily said, 'and worse followed. I could tell you stories.'

The two daughters, pale from incarceration, were sent to
make tea. Aunt Emily felt freed.

'There are two homes to be catered for now.'

'You're not serious.'

'A fancy woman he's picked up with that lives in Exchequer
Street.'

'But there's a houseful of children.'

'Five,' Aunt Emily said, 'and the eldest no more than fourteen.
That's the carry on in this so-called Irish Catholic city of ours
and no one lifting their little finger. She'd go to his employer
only the little she manages to get out of him would stop altogether if she did. I met her coming one day from the pawn-
shop . . .'

'Mother of Jesus,' his mother exclaimed, deeply shocked.

'She was in such straits I made up my mind to go to the
parish priest myself on her behalf. It opened my eyes, I can tell
you, the attitude of the same clergy.'

He found his mother's glance ordering him out of earshot.
It was difficult in so crowded a room, but he left his chair and
began exploring. There were ornaments made of seashells,
highly breakable. There was a sewing machine and spools of
coloured thread. On the wall above it a picture of Patrick
Pearse in profile complemented another of de Valera. On parch-
ment near them a poem was set out under a title decorated on
the left by the tricolour and the right by a Golden Harp on a
green background.

IN AN ENGLISH PRISON

To Eire of the clean, true hearts
My blessing swiftly speeds;
For Eire's hopes, for Eire's dreams
I tell my loved brown beads;
For every hand that tries to lift
Our Mother's load of care
Here in my narrow prison cell

> Each morn I breathe a prayer
> My heart cries out to Mary's Son
> In every prayer I pray:
> 'Dear God, remember Eire's night,
> And speed her cloudless day.'

Although it took him a long time to read it through, they were still whispering when he had finished. A copy of *The Messenger of The Sacred Heart* provided a limited distraction, but there were no pictures and he could make very little of the text. Unobtrusively he found his way to the window. The sky above St Patrick's was still full of sunlight, with high white clouds drifting slowly at great distances, setting the spire journeying with a floating motion like the mast of a boat. A seagull landed on a nearby roof, reminding him of the descent of the Holy Ghost in his penny catechism. Sometimes He descended in the form of a bird, or as a mighty wind. Other times He looked like a tapering flame. He was the Third Person of the Blessed Trinity. St Patrick's was a Protestant cathedral. Cromwell took it from the Catholics and burned the crozier of St Patrick. I'll bet he's sorry now, he remarked silently to the seagull, there being nobody else who was interested.

He heard the chink of Delft and turned to find the daughters passing round tea.

'Do you like milk in first?' one of them asked him.

'I don't know,' he said.

She looked at her sister, and they giggled together. He paid no attention. They were only girls, uninteresting, not even pretty. He took a slice of currant loaf and wondered why at home they called it spotted dog. It was not at all like a dog; it was more like a game of dominoes. Still more, it was like a card of football studs.

'He's lost his tongue,' he heard Aunt Emily saying. The four of them were staring at him.

'I like his suit,' one of the sisters remarked.

'Isn't his tie lovely,' the other said.

'It's such an unusual shade, so refined.'

'My son Freddie, God rest him, and his father made their first

Holy Communion together. We used to have a photograph of it somewhere,' Aunt Emily said.

'It's among his things in his room,' one of the daughters told her.

'It could be,' Aunt Emily admitted. 'I haven't disturbed a single item since he died.' She gave him her whole attention. 'I hope you said a prayer for your Uncle Freddie this morning.'

' I had him well tutored on that,' his mother put in quickly. 'He had the names of all of us that's gone.'

'Your Uncle Freddie died for Ireland,' Aunt Emily told him, a little colour creeping for a moment into her face, 'and to their sin and shame he died at the hands of his own, in the belief that they could give away Ireland to her enemies without hindrance. But their hour is passing, whether they know it or not.'

'Do you think de Valera will do well in the elections?' His mother's tone pretended to be neutral.

'There's no doubt of it,' Aunt Emily said.

'I can't see him taking the oath.'

'It won't arise,' Aunt Emily said. 'With his new party he'll be strong enough to abolish it altogether. And when that's attended to, we'll settle with Sir James Craig. No oath and no border.'

'And bring the English back on top of us. Or another civil war,' his mother answered in a quiet tone.

'England's star is in decline,' Aunt Emily said. 'She can't find work for her own, never mind taking up arms for black Orangemen. And if she does, we proved a match for her before. It's not England but our own would-be Free State government are our worst enemies; Cosgrave with his Public Safety Act and O'Higgins with the blood of decent republican boys on his hands. Legal murderers. But they'll meet their fate.'

'God forbid,' his mother said. Her voice was grave, but it was clear she was yielding no ground. It was clear also, in the politest possible way, that she had no love of either de Valera or extreme republicanism.

After that exchange he reckoned his chances of collecting anything from Aunt Emily were negligible, but when he was leaving she gave him five shillings. The girls presented him with a mother-of-pearl rosary in a small leather purse with 'Made in Ireland' stamped on it. As a bonus they gave him some apples and oranges from the shop below. It was adequate recompense. But perhaps they were unaware that his mother was one of the poppy wearers.

'Why are they all for de Valera?' he asked on the way home.

'They're all Shinners on that side of the family,' his mother said, 'and they don't want the treaty or partition or the oath of allegiance to the King. They say de Valera is the real president of Ireland and they refuse to recognize the Free State government. The only thing that seems to please them is burning police stations and destroying property and shooting those of us who don't see fit to agree with them. To my mind they do Ireland more harm than a whole regiment of kings.'

Nevertheless the visit to Aunt Emily entertained his father and mother at teatime. Then he was washed and tidied again and set off on his round of evening visits with his father. The subject still worried him.

'Does Aunt Emily shoot people?' he asked.

'Not personally,' his father said. 'It wouldn't be ladylike.'

'Did Uncle Freddie?'

'Your Uncle Freddie regarded it as a sort of duty.'

'Isn't it a sin,' he asked, 'if you kill people?'

'It depends,' his father said. 'To Aunt Emily's way of thinking if you shoot a policeman or a Free State soldier you're a hero striking a blow for Irish freedom. On the other hand, if you're caught and hanged or shot for it, that's regarded as brutal and legalized murder.'

'When you were in the war, did you shoot people?'

'I suppose I did.'

'Why?'

'If I hadn't,' his father said, 'they'd have shot me. You wouldn't have liked that, would you?'

He would not. Not his father. To lie stiff and still. To have a yellow face and spiky hairs curling from thin nostrils. That was death.

Yet so it would be. It would happen to his father. It would happen to his mother. Later, at some infinitely remote and unknowable distance in time, though inescapably there nevertheless, it would happen also to him. That threat lurked in everything, even as he held his father's hand and walked in love beside him. It lurked in the declining of the day's heat which lay as an afterthought on the dusty streets, in the long yellow bars of evening on the skies above them, in the stillness of the trees along the canal bank, the smell of decaying matter where the torrents poured through the lockgates, in the silence and dusky glitter of undisturbed water between. Not for the first time he was aware of its presence. There had always been, beyond negotiable space, beyond the circle of firelight, aspects of reality undefinable until language began to supply a vague vocabulary. Death was one of them. With immensity and infinity it beleaguered the world, surrounding the geranium and the album as they existed in his mind when suddenly he thought of them; it brooded in the silence of the room where his mother was sewing perhaps or reading in the carpet rocking chair by the window. The incomprehensibility of a universe without a beginning and the measurable passing of Time were further worries. After that it became somewhat easier. The existence of God accounted for a lot; the creation of the world by Him in seven days was clear-cut and acceptable, though not its alleged roundness, about which he continued to be sceptical, thinking of the dilemma of the unfortunate Australians, condemned by geographical ill-chance to spend their lives walking upside down. Without falling off, as obviously they ought. After that babies were almost the only problem, wherever they came from. People said the doctor brought them. It might well be. But where did the doctor get them?

'In a few weeks' time,' his father said, 'when you get your holidays, you'll be finished with the nuns. No more Sister Aloysius whatever-the-rest-of-her-name is. You'll be glad of that, I expect.'

He might. It depended.

'Where will I be going?'

'To the Christian Brothers, I hope, though it isn't easy to get in. I mustn't forget to ask your Uncle Hugh about it. He knows the right people.'

Uncle Hugh, and his aunts and Grandfather Keenan were all waiting to admire him when he arrived in the house that had once been his mother's home. It stood with its back to the sea and its hall door looking across the cobbled street at the grocery shop, the sweet shop and Madden's public house.

Aunt Kate said he was a real swank. Aunt Ellen said she heard he was going to bring his sweetheart to the pictures on Saturday with all the money he had collected. Aunt Kate said she would die of jealousy if she thought for a moment he had another sweetheart besides her. Uncle Hugh said not to mind them, they were a couple of men-mad females with sweethearts on the brain.

'Listen to Ramon Novarro,' Aunt Ellen said.

Uncle Hugh's Sam Browne belt was hanging on the hook on the hall door with his Free State Army cap and his tunic. On rare occasions a heavy black revolver in its leather holster was there too, but not today.

'Did you have a party after mass?' Aunt Kate asked.

He said they had it in the convent grounds.

'What did they give you?'

'Lemonade and cake. And a bag of sweets.'

'He wouldn't get fat on what the nuns would provide,' Aunt Ellen said. 'They're not very givish.'

'Never mind. As soon as school closes, tell your mother, you must come and stay for the holidays.'

He said he would.

He liked staying with his aunts. The sea and the strand were a few minutes' walk away and as well as that they often went cycling in the country and had picnics. In winter the waves beat over the sea wall and flooded the road. When there were storms the house shuddered and the wind roared in the chimney. Once, when he was much smaller, he would sit on his Uncle Hugh's knee and watch him drawing trains all night, carriages with windows, wheels with four spokes each, a tender with coal. The cat looked on too from her stool at the fire, licked her whiskers, opened and closed her eyes, a lemon in each. At Christmas his aunts used to help him to write to Santa Claus. In the beginning he was satisfied to put the letters up the chimney, where Santa sometimes listened to hear if he was being a good boy or a bad boy. Later he insisted on the more sensible procedure of dropping them like ordinary letters in the pillar box on the street corner near the front door.

> Santa Claus Esq.
> Toy Land
> The North Pole
> The Arctic Circle

The pillar box was red, but one day a post-office man came along and painted it green. It caused quite a stir. His grandmother and a group of neighbours gathered to watch him at work and to make jokes about it. Afterwards the man sat at the kitchen table having tea and bread and butter. He remembered that very well because a little while later, quite unexpectedly, his grandmother was dead. She lay on a bed which had been put up in the parlour, a table beside it with holy water and a sprig of palm for sprinkling, a crucifix and two wax candles. They had dressed her in a brown habit and drawn the blinds. There was black crape on the hall door when they brought him down to say good-bye. Saying good-bye meant blessing himself at the bedside and touching her forehead with his hand. It was cold. Nothing in the world could have been so cold. That must have been in winter. On the day of her funeral when all had gone off, and the house was empty except for the neighbouring women who came in to keep the fires going and look after the cooking, he walked on his own by the sea wall. The world was desolate. Housefronts and streets were blackened with rain, salt spray drenched the windows, for miles out to sea the white spume drove in tormented drills across the black and heaving waters. A gull which unwisely attempted the air was flung backwards by the wind and screeched its anger. He looked up. It had gone. But the disembodied cry transfixed him. He closed his eyes tightly to deny the daylight, to shut out the world, to swathe himself in impenetrable blackness. Burial was the crunch of carriage wheels, the strong smell of horses.

Uncle Hugh and his father went across to Maddens' but returned uncharacteristically in less than half an hour.

'I've to get him to the mother's,' his father said, 'and then to the Fitzpatricks'.'

'You'll have your work cut out,' Aunt Kate told him.

'I'll get on to the Brothers during the week,' Uncle Hugh said. 'There may be a little bit of an entrance test. Arithmetic, Irish, that sort of thing, but I'm sure there's nothing to worry about.'

'So you'll be a big boy very soon,' Aunt Kate said to him, 'a Christian Brothers' boy with the school colours on your scarf and CBS on your cap.'

They all gave him money and Uncle Hugh said to his father, 'Watch yourself.'

'I know,' his father said, 'a long bit of a tour.' They laughed.

In his grandmother's house they depressed him again by going on about it, especially Uncle Charles.

'The Brothers will fill the bill for him right enough,' Uncle Charles said. 'The Brothers is great men. No bloody lawdedaw nonsense about them, for a start. None of your cricket or hockey carry-on with tea and ham sandwiches at half time. And no rugby either.'

'What's wrong with rugby?' Uncle Christy asked.

'Snobocracy,' Uncle Charles said, 'lawyers and dentists with ascendency accents on their way to building up a practice with flashy-looking flappers on the sideline wrapped in rugs and the club scarf, shouting good for you Ernest when one of them trips over himself. Of course I needn't tell you what brings them lassies to rugby matches in the first place.'

'Nor in the second place,' Uncle James put in. He was grinning at something. Uncle James was always grinning at something.

'Now, now,' his father warned, 'ears are listening.' Uncle Charles looked surprised.

'I would hope the meaning is still a mile above his head.'

'I would hope so too,' his father said, 'so we'll do our best to see it stays there.'

'Nothing wrong with a flapper or two,' Uncle James said. They looked at him very sternly.

'They ban soccer football too, the same Christian Brothers,' Uncle Christy said. 'What's the sense in banning a game every kid in Dublin starts playing the minute you lift him out of his cradle?'

'Prejudice,' Uncle James explained. 'They're nearly all countrymen so they want Gaelic football and hurling, as played in oul God's time by Finn McCool or Little Setanta wherever they could find a dry patch in the bog. Soccer is regarded as a foreign game, a British garrison influence. They've a narrow view of the world, the same brothers.'

'That's my point,' Uncle Christy told him.

'They turn out the goods just the same,' his father insisted.

Uncle Charles seized his chance to recover lost ground.

'No question about it,' he said stoutly. 'Coax it into them or beat it into them, but do the bloody job – that's the motto of the Brothers. And I'll say this for them, it works.'

He gave the arm of his chair a ferocious blow. The sound made his grandmother angry. She stopped her tidying to include them all. Do you want to frighten the wits out of the child?' she asked. 'Is that what you want – do you want to turn him against the new school before he sets foot in it at all? Have you no sense or understanding?'

But they had lost the habit of ever listening to her.

Uncle Christy's eye went to the clock. 'Who's for up the road?' he asked.

'A quick one,' his father agreed.

'I'll move the adjournment,' said Uncle James.

'Is Granny very rich?' he asked his father later.

'I think she has a bit in the stocking all right,' his father said. 'Why?'

'She gave me a ten-shilling note.'

His father seemed impressed.

'Do you know what I'm thinking? Any day now you'll be buying up shares in Guinness's,' he predicted.

Among back streets lit by gas lamps and breathing smells of butchers' shops and vegetable stalls they found the house of his father's wartime friend. At the hall door he felt his father's hand on his shoulder.

'Remember what I told you?'

'Yes,' he answered.

The bottom floor was an eating house for working men, spread with tables and benches. There were salt cellars and sauce bottles on the sideboard. They climbed the stairs to the living room and, when he was being introduced, he walked over to the chair as he had been told to do. Mr Fitzpatrick, who was blind, took his face gently in his hands. After a moment he said, 'He's like yourself?'

'Not as good-looking, they tell me,' his father answered.

Mr Fitzpatrick smiled and said to the big man who was sitting near him, 'Would you agree, O'Sheehan?'

'In the matter of comeliness,' Mr O'Sheehan said, in a voice measured and rich, 'I would give the palm to the boy.'

He shook hands also.

'And how old are you, my son?'

'Seven and a bit.'

'The age of reason; wisdom may follow. It is cumulative, if at all. What book are you in?'

'First book.'

'We all begin at the beginning. Next year it will be Book the Second. Will you be going to the masters or the Brothers or the clergy?'

'The Brothers, I hope,' his father said.

'*Facere et Docere* is their motto – to form and to teach. Despite the Latin they are sturdy champions of the Gaelic mode of life.'

Mrs Fitzpatrick intervened to hand Mr O'Sheehan a bottle of Guinness, which he accepted with elaborate courtesy.

'Dear lady,' he said to her, 'you are generosity itself.'

They asked him questions about school and learning his catechism. Mrs Fitzpatrick admired his suit. Then the men talked about politics and Mr O'Sheehan predicted that the new Intoxicating Liquor Act would cost the government the election.

'The publicans of the country are men of money and influence. Their sons are prominent among the clergy and have all the best parishes. The largest dowries the convents get are from the daughters of publicans and many of them are Mother Superiors. Have you ever been offered a drink in a convent?'

'I don't move in elevated circles,' his father said.

'The best stuff in the country, bar none. Better than in a bishop's palace. I heard the Governor General had sharp words with the Minister about it. Called him a stubborn, self-willed fool.'

'Self-willed, perhaps,' Mr Fitzpatrick said, 'but Kevin O'Higgins is no fool.'

'I don't agree,' his father said. 'Mind you, closing the pubs on Christmas Day is understandable enough. It's a day for the home and a barman is entitled to be with his family. And I don't quarrel with keeping them under lock and key on Good Friday either. If there's any day in the year it won't kill a man to forgo his pleasures, then that's the day I'd name myself. But St Patrick's Day – that takes the biscuit. The politician who tells the Irish electorate that in future the pubs are to be barred and bolted for the duration of Patrick's Day, and does it on the eve of an election, isn't overburdened with sagacity. Are we honouring the patron saint, or having a day of national mourning?'

'There were abuses, just the same,' Mr Fitzpatrick said, 'you must admit it.'

'Did you know,' Mr O'Sheehan asked them, 'even if you have lodgings in a licensed premises, the publican daren't serve you a drink on those particular days, except with a meal.'

'It depends, I suppose,' his father answered, 'on what constitutes a meal.'

'It must be substantial,' Mr O'Sheehan told him. 'Apart from the curtailment of opening hours, the publicans see a big threat to business in the restaurants and the railway buffets. And of course, the theatre bars.'

'I'm thinking of myself,' his father said, 'not the publicans. They're the boyos well able to look after Number One. We'll never need a flagday for distressed publicans.'

'There are stalwart men among them, nevertheless. Men of principle. I have in mind, for example, Cornelius Moloney of High Street. A good friend. And skilled at chess.'

'Con is a decent man, I grant you that. Con I would accept,' his father conceded. 'I notice he's going in for the greyhounds recently. A couple of times I've seen him out on the bicycle, with two or three of the brutes trotting behind him on enormous-looking leads.'

'Greyhound racing is the coming thing,' Mr O'Sheehan pronounced. 'There is money to be made in it if you have animals that are carefully bred and skilfully trained.'

'So that's what he's up to,' his father observed.

'Ever since the opening of the track at Shelbourne Park. Cornelius has been in touch with principals in White City and Celtic Park. At present he's coaxing the animals into their best fettle.'

'Trust a Tipperary man,' his father said.

Mr Fitzpatrick, who had been looking straight in front of him while they talked, raised his hands to gather their attention and told them he would remember one thing to Cornelius Moloney above all else, and that was that when Jim Larkin returned to Ireland in 1924 and there was trouble between him and the executive, Cornelius had given practical help to the men from the gas company who went on strike without union funds.

'The result was they were able to pay the men and after a while the butchers and the dockers and carters came over. It was the time the Transport Union was advising them to accept a ten-shillings wage cut.'

'I remember it,' his father said. 'A novel line for the champions of the worker.'

Mrs Fitzpatrick brought tea, but Mr O'Sheehan begged to be excused. He had some private study to do before bedtime.

'Your man O'Sheehan,' his father said when Mr O'Sheehan

had gone. 'Is there a slate loose there, would you say?'

'A little bit odd, but the full shilling just the same,' Mr Fitzpatrick explained. 'I've heard it said he claims to be an old Fenian, and I can believe it. He has their grandiloquent style.'

'Stiff and straight in the back too, you'll have noticed.'

'I wouldn't know that. I only met him after Mary opened this place. He was among the first customers.'

His father coloured slightly and was silent. Then he said, 'Sorry about that, Fitz.'

'Nothing to be sorry about, Paddy,' Mr Fitzpatrick said, easily. 'You should know me well enough.'

'That's true, God knows,' his father agreed. 'Haven't I His Majesty's certificate to prove it, thanking the two of us for the way we won the war.'

He was reminded of something.

'I met a mutual acquaintance the other day – Jeremiah McGibbon.'

'Gloves McGibbon,' Mr Fitzpatrick remembered, 'that was another eloquent Dempsey. He had a peculiar addiction, hadn't he, to some medicine or other?'

'Venos lightning cough cure,' his father confirmed. 'He knocked it back by the bottle. In a quiet, gentlemanly kind of way he used to get plastered on it, whatever was in it.'

For a while, taking care to conceal his interest, he listened as they talked about old times, until the lateness of the hour and the wealth in his pocket tempted him to pretend he was already grown up and leaning back in his chair like them, smoking cigarettes and drinking bottles of stout. There would be no school. He would wear long trousers. In the mornings he would lather his face before the mirror and sharpen the razor on its strop. But it was all far away. It would only come about in another lifetime, at the end of uncountable years that moved hardly at all, so inconceivable in length that sleep began to creep over him. Their voices receded into its immensity and became the low sound of a summer sea. Far away, where candles flickered on an altar, a priest held up the host and beckoned to him to come and receive. He rose uncertainly.

His feet made no sound, and though he walked and walked, the distance between the beckoning priest and himself remained unchanged.

A hand fell on his shoulder. 'We were forgetting about you altogether,' his father's voice said, 'and you're nearly asleep.'

'What time is it?' Mr Fitzpatrick asked.

'Nearly half past ten,' his father said, 'time for barracks.'

Mr Fitzpatrick called his wife. She had money set aside on the mantelpiece and gave it to him and they both shook his hand and said God would bless him and guide him through life. Poor child, they said, he had the long walk home ahead of him.

'We'll take a cab,' his father decided. 'It'll mark the occasion.'

They said that was a very sensible decision.

Gas lamps on the bridge shed streaks of light on the river that made him think of tears. They wavered gently with the movement of the water which the full tide had swollen so that it almost filled the arches and smelled like the sea. They stopped a cab which was returning from King's Bridge Railway Station and climbed in. The jingle of harness and the horse smell reminded him of his grandmother's funeral. There had been times since when he thought he had glimpsed her in the street. If He wanted to, God could put the dead back again on earth. The arrangement would work so long as He saw to it that they would never meet anyone who had known them in their previous life, an easy matter for God in so crowded a world.

'Can there be two first anythings?' he asked his father, the puzzle returning.

'What do you mean?'

'Could you have two first communions?'

'Hardly,' his father said.

'Why?'

'Because the first is the first, isn't it? After that it has to be the second. Then the third. And so on.'

'Then how can Granny do nine first Fridays?'

His father pondered for a while. Then he said, 'I'll put it to you this way, son. Each month of the year has a number of Fridays in it, one of which is the first in that particular month.

But there was only one Friday in all the Fridays since time began that was the first; the one during the first week of Creation, when God was getting round to making Adam and Eve, or whatever He was up to. That was a while before your granny's day.'

The explanation, as so often, was more perplexing than the question. He felt the buttons on the leather panels against his cheek as he leaned to look through the window. Under successive lamps the chains bordering the pathway around St Stephen's Green gleamed black and the leaves above stirred faintly in little pools of brightness. It had been a long day. There would not be such a day ever again in the whole of life, because there could be one first of anything only. His father had said so. That was that.

The clip-clop of hooves echoed and faded away among the tall houses as they climbed the steps. The hall door groaned heavily, objecting to being disturbed. A lamp burning on the hall stand cast nervous shadows on its marble top.

'Did I hear a cab?' his mother asked.

'We came home in style,' his father confessed.

'I thought you were both lost. Mr Curtis called in to see him. I said I'd send him up when you got back, but it's far too late now.'

'We were wrong then,' his father said, 'well, it can't be helped. Is there a bottle in the house?'

'You've had your share, I'd say.'

'Now, now. Don't take the good out of it.'

She got two bottles from the press. His father took a Baby Power from his pocket and put it on the table.

'There. I didn't forget you.'

'Paddy – whiskey at this hour. How will I get up in the morning.'

But she got a glass for herself and sat down, just the same. He began to unload the money from his pocket, putting it a handful at a time on the table, until his mother begged him to get into his pyjamas first. He did so with reluctance. Then he began counting it while his mother made sounds of disbelief.

He found he had three pounds and seventeen shillings.

'I bet that beats the convent record,' his father said.

'Now put it away,' his mother begged him, 'and off with you to bed.'

He began to obey. But very slowly. He no longer felt sleepy. Moments of the day were returning in vivid and confusing flashes, demanding to be marshalled into some kind of order. While he was trying to do so, a knock on the door, low and gentle, surprised them. It was Mr Curtis. He would only come in for a moment.

'I heard the cab and guessed aright,' he said. He put a book on the table, apologizing as he did so for intruding.

'To mark the great day. I could have left it, of course. But I remembered wondering, the night he was born, if any of us would live to see him out of petticoats, and I was determined to have the satisfaction of conveying my good wishes in person.'

His mother was moved.

'It's too kind of you. Such trouble.'

Mr Curtis refused a bottle of Guinness because of the lateness of the hour. Instead he shook hands and wished him a prosperous career.

'We'll talk another time,' he promised. And in spite of their protests, he left.

'It's no wonder he'd remember the night you were born,' his mother said. 'There was shooting and Black and Tans everywhere and Mr Curtis went to fetch the doctor. It was one of the worst nights of the troubles, and it was after curfew and your father hadn't come in. We thought he was taken up or shot.'

'No thanks to certain parties I wasn't,' his father said, pouring the second bottle. 'I often think of that. Our own quite ready to shoot me, while a decent Protestant risks his neck to get the doctor. I'll not forget it to old Curtis.'

His mother picked up the book and handed it to him and said, 'Say good-night now, like a good boy, and take the book in with you.'

He did so. There was an oil lamp burning on the table by his bedside. Its funnel cast a bright circle on the ceiling imme-

diately above it. Sometimes it wavered in the draught. Tonight
it remained absolutely still. He lay watching it, thinking of it
no longer as a toy sun, but the host which the priest had placed
on his tongue that morning. Was it still in his belly? When he
died would he go to heaven or to hell? It would be a long time
yet. He had to grow up first and then grow old. Unless there
was an accident or God decided to bring the world to an end.
As He might. There was no way of knowing. Why did people
sin? They were fools. He would stay good himself. He would
not commit sins. It was too risky.

There were pictures in the book. One was Pegasus, the winged
horse. One was Midas, the king whose touch turned everything
to gold. You would be very rich if you could do that. You
could touch, say, the buttons on your pyjamas and you would
have one, two, three, four, five round gold pieces. He did so
slowly, but they remained just ordinary pyjama buttons.
Opposite the picture on the front just inside the cover, Mr
Curtis had written something. He read it word by word:

From N. CURTIS

to

his young friend

TIMOTHY McDONAGH

Wishing him a very prosperous career

2nd June 1927

The white circle on the ceiling drew his eyes once more. Not
a stir. It was like the Blessed Host. It was like a toy sun. It was
like the light shining in droplets on black painted chains. Or
droplets on bright leaves or a hoop touched by Midas or a toy
sun and the rocking horse with wings was soaring and soaring
and would float through it into a strange land with people and
houses you could hold in your hand. The book wedged itself
between his cheek and the pillow. He barely noticed.

Throughout the years the inscription was to remain bold and
clear, surviving all that crumbled and disappeared, whether

predictably or surprisingly, bearing witness at unexpected intervals to the reality of such a day and such an hour long after the invisible flood had pilfered away its trappings and its pilgrim players; including the milkman and his dancing churns, the insolent peacock, Mr and Mrs Curtis and their listening bird in its cage.

But that was not yet.

I

By twenty past seven every morning with the exception of Sundays, when he could lie on a bit longer, Paddy McDonagh had finished shaving and was ready to begin the ritual of cleaning and packing his razor, an open one, clumsy in appearance, delicate to handle. Although an easygoing man, he took meticulous care of his few personal possessions, as though at any moment someone might spring a kit inspection. He wore his hair short, using a little oil for tidyness, but washing it frequently for cleanliness. To keep his trousers smartly creased he stored them between the mattress and the base of the bed. In his carriage too and in the set of his shoulders, his years in the army had left their stamp. The mirror he used was a war souvenir also, with nothing except sentiment to recommend it. In size it was eight and a half by four and a half inches (approximately), framed in wood with a cheap varnish, regular British Army issue of the 1914–18 period. But it had been with him from the day he got it, surviving miraculously through years of hazard; active service in France; Black and Tan raids during the troubles on his return to Dublin; a civil war which, when it followed, threatened to destroy the new Irish State and his already rather slim prospects of a livelihood. Paddy McDonagh, shaving before it morning after morning in an onflowing sequence of situations and places, pondered at times on the detached head it obligingly reflected for him and contemplated the face which from long habit he assumed to be his. It was changing, presumably, but so far imperceptibly. Behind the eyes that peered through the thick lather like those of a snowman lurked that unique and essential being imprisoned within him from birth, masquerading exteriorly now as a raw volunteer on the plains of Shrewsbury, now as a trained transport driver in the Army Service Corps, decisive, sometimes foul of mouth, shifting supplies and munitions along cratered roads and through shattered towns, who then and since hardly ever watched a sunset or moonrise without the thought that it might well be his last. Or again as a young married man on his honeymoon in Bray, where the hotel was a little too grand and the shaving mirror (he had packed it automatically) a source of embarrassment to his bride. Paddy dear, she had implored him, take it off the mantelpiece and don't make a show of us before all those stuck-up maids. He had done so without complaint. She could not know and it would have been difficult to explain, that there had been times when the reappearance in it of that same old face was welcomed by him as the confirmation of a near miracle. Habits of peace rendered those occasions less frequent, but the underlying notion persisted. Life's utter dependence on whim, or fate, or whatever it was struck home on the day he embarked for service and remained firmly lodged ever afterwards. The troopship was moving slowly down river between long-familiar quays. The waving crowd and valedictory band were both out of earshot. He took a cigarette from its package, found he had no matches, approached a soldier who was leaning on the rail.

'Got a match?'

The two of them smoked together while the coalyards, the idle cranes, the squat gasometers slid gently past.

'Funny feeling – isn't it?' he said.

The other nodded.

'My name is Paddy McDonagh.'

'Bob Fitzpatrick,' the other reciprocated.

The accent was Dublin, a comfort, in its way. When they had cleared the quays and could see the railings of Ringsend Park, a small knot of people began to wave to them. Their faces were indistinguishable, but some of the shapes were familiar and after a little while he began to recognize them. Then a voice cried out. It was unmistakable and his heart jumped. He waved hard as the sound drifted across the water and died. It was at that moment, while waving in response to the voice, that he saw with incandescent clarity that life hung on the frailest of threads.

A voice beside him asked: 'Wife or sweetheart?' It was sympathetic.

'I'm not married. One of her sisters.' Then he added, to hide the sudden weight of pain inside him, 'They were all up at the mother's place last night. We'd a hell of a party. Drink and Come-all-yehs. And Tom Moore, need I say.'

'That's Dublin,' Fitz said, 'I don't think I ever went to a Dublin party without getting tears and Tom Moore at some stage of the proceedings. Usually the "Last Rose of Summer" and "Has Sorrow thy Young Days Shaded".'

'We had those,' Paddy confessed, 'and "Oft In the Stilly Night" for good measure. It's Joe's party piece, and the mother's favourite.' He tried to smile and repeated, hearing his own voice as from a distance.

> 'The smiles, the tears of boyhood's years
> The words of love then spoken
> The eyes that shone, now dimmed and gone
> The cheerful hearts now broken.'

They could see now the Martello tower and the houses along Sandymount Strand. Further inland the mountains encircled the bay. They seemed to float between sea and sunlight. They were multi-coloured. At the Black Lighthouse the ship cleared the river, swinging out into the bay as bells tinkled remotely. It was too much. He excused himself and pushed his way through a press of uniforms until he found a corner to sit in below deck. The cry was still in his ears, disembodied, a bird skimming the water. He searched the inside pocket of his greatcoat for the postcard which had been there since his period of training on The Curragh and when he had found it he wrote in copying ink pencil the first of many quickly scribbled messages to those at home.

Dear Nora

Have just seen Ellen and Katie at the Wall when we were passing. I hope you got home all right last night. Thank your mother for the parcel and also say good-bye to your father and Hugh for me. I mustn't try to explain how I am feeling after leaving you and all at home. However, I hope it will not be for long. Letter follows tomorrow. Good-bye and all my love, Paddy.

PS Don't worry about me, I will be all right.

He had little or no belief in the postscript as he attached it, but it worked out that way. Four years or so in fields of death and mutilation left him unscathed by bayonet or bullet, though once a gas attack almost killed him because of a faulty mask. He seldom spoke of what he had seen, except for two incidents, by no means the most terrible, which seemed to linger more vividly than the rest. One was during the shelling of a village when, unable to brake and pull up in time, he had driven his lorry over the bodies of an old peasant couple and their mule. All three were already dead, but the experience upset him profoundly. The other was a night when he and a companion were carrying between them a large billy from the rear kitchens to the trenches across open ground. The ground was difficult and the billy was heavy and when a shell exploded above them and the billy sagged against his leg he grumbled at his companion: 'Lift the bloody thing, will you.'

A Very light soared into the sky and lit their surroundings. When he glanced across to complain again about the billy, the body by his side was buckling at the knees and had no head. It had kept walking beside in that condition for some paces after the shell had exploded. Or so he was convinced. Whenever he had a little more than enough to drink he had a compulsion to rehearse both incidents to the company. His family and friends indulged it. It was a minor fault in one who was usually the best of company.

By 1916 he was on active service, first at Verdun and later, without respite, in the first battle of the Somme, remote from the uprising in Dublin where his close friend and cousin Freddie Lindon joined those who took up arms against British rule and fought beside Connolly and Pearse in the General Post Office. Though rumours percolated, it meant very little until he returned on leave to find Dublin's principal streets in ruins. He was used to devastation on an incomparably larger scale, yet the sight shocked him. Men who wore the same uniform as himself had done it and their government had executed the leaders. He was fighting in France, he had been assured, for the freedom of small nations and for Home Rule for Ireland which was on the Statute Book and only waited the end of the war. O'Connell Street in ruins and sixteen executed Irishmen struck him as a strange form of down payment. But his predicament was that of nearly two hundred thousand other Irishmen who had volunteered for service in the British forces and there seemed nothing much that could be done except wait and see. He was still waiting when, in May 1920, the dilemma took another form. It was the day on which his first son was born.

His working day had ended like the rest with minor servicing to the couple of lorries in the company's Stephen's Street garage, then the hosing and cleaning of the directors' private car, which he occasionally drove. It was already six o'clock and he was anxious to get home. Military raids had been building in intensity since March, and in a few hours the Black and Tan lorries would begin the nightly searches for IRA suspects. He wanted to be with his wife just in case Upper Pembroke Street was on the list. Nevertheless he did his work meticulously. It was a new job in a city where they were hard to come by. He was only one of a multitude.

When he had finished polishing he mopped the skin of water from the floor, removed his long rubber boots and overalls and washed under the hose tap. He checked that the large gates were locked, slamming the wicket as he stepped into the street. It was warmer out in the air, though tall houses blocked the sunlight from the cobbled lanes. They were narrow and devious, but as far as he could he kept to them. Aungier Street, the main thoroughfare, had seen so many ambushes that it was known popularly by now as The Dardanelles. There was no sense in dying before his time because of a Black and Tan bullet or an IRA bomb. The walk through Stephen's Green was pleasanter, with the sun warming its open spaces. He stopped to light a cigarette.

'The very man,' a hand fell on his shoulder and he looked around. It was his cousin Freddie.

'Freddie.'

Freddie Lindon indicated his companion and said: 'This one here is Willie Mulhall. The same profession, if you follow me. We were on our way to have a word with you.'

'Then come along.'

'Not to call in. The idea was to ask you to have a drink. We have a place in mind.'

'Nora is expecting. I ought to be with her.'

'We won't delay you. Say twenty minutes or so, but it's essential we talk to you, Paddy.'

Paddy hesitated.

'If we loiter around here there's every chance we'll be picked up,' Freddie urged. That was true enough.

'Is it far?'

'Only a few minutes from your own place.'

He went with them reluctantly. The public house occupied the corner of a laneway, which gave access to a line of derelict stables and coachhouses. They went by a passageway to a store-room at the back. It was within a few hundred yards of his home, as they had said, but it belonged to a different world. Barrels and packing cases lay about, usefully near if the need to block off an entrance arose. A ladder gave access to a loft above. A glass slit high in one wall was almost totally lost in accumulated grime and mouldering cobwebs. Willie Mulhall lit a candle while Freddie found a bottle of whiskey and glasses. He pushed one into Paddy McDonagh's hand.

'I'm not a whiskey man, Freddie, you should know that.'

Nevertheless Freddie poured.

'Make an exception. We'll celebrate the birth – in advance.'

Paddy smiled but said: 'That mightn't be lucky.'

'Willie, when you're picking up the stuff from the man inside, bring a couple of stout for Paddy here.' Willie went off.

'Is Nora well otherwise?'

'She's in good shape. My worry is these Black and Tan raids.'

'The bastards enjoy destroying a place,' Freddie agreed, 'whether it's loyalist or nationalist makes no difference. It suits us, of course, because then everybody hates them. But it isn't so good for a woman near her time.'

Willie Mulhall returned with two bottles of stout.

'Thanks,' Paddy McDonagh said, 'that's more my style.'

'Part of the service,' Willie said. Then he took two revolvers from his pockets, examined them and gave one to Freddie.

'With the compliments of the man inside.'

'Happy to have them off the premises,' Freddie said. 'I understand his feelings. Well – good luck.'

They drank together.

'How's the new job going?'

'Gameball,' Paddy said, 'and the right time to have it.'

'I've seen you driving around from time to time,' Freddie remarked pleasantly, 'and it looks nice and comfortable. I mean when you put on the chauffeur's regimentals to ferry one or other of the directors about his business. Very smart.'

'Very servile too,' Willie Mulhall added.

Paddy McDonagh thought that unnecessary and said: 'It's that kind of world, isn't it?'

'Don't misunderstand me, comrade,' Willie explained, 'We're all on the same side. When the Workers' Republic is established there'll be only one class: the working class. Here's to it.'

He raised his glass and drank.

'Willie here is a follower of James Connolly,' Freddie explained, 'so he talks a bit like a manifesto. They like flying the Starry Plough instead of the green-white-and-orange, and they end all their meetings by sending off telegrams of congratulation to Soviet Russia about this thing and that. Then they all sing the "Red Flag" together. No harm in that, I suppose, but I like things to be simpler. British Out is my own slogan. Shoot the arse off them until it occurs to them that they're unwelcome. I suppose you never considered coming in with us?'

'I'm not ambitious,' Paddy McDonagh said. 'France put me off shooting, somehow.'

'You were on the wrong side.'

'That's what they say now. When we enlisted, though, we were fighting for Ireland and Home Rule. Or so John Redmond and the Irish party told us.'

'Home Rule is a dead duck, as dead as John Redmond,' Freddie said. 'It's got to be a thirty-two-county republic now, that or nothing. Which brings me to what we have in mind.'

He finished the whiskey in his glass and poured again, a small amount this time.

'It's got to do with that directors' car we were talking about, the one you keep in the Stephen's Street garage. We've been admiring it for some time.'

'You mean you want to commandeer it?'

'It's just the thing: dark glass in the windows, very polished up and important looking, a uniformed driver; not likely to be searched by army patrols or some ignorant sod of a policeman. We could use it.'

'When?'

'Tonight.'

Paddy McDonagh felt a little sick inside. But cars were disposable. He had no impulse to lay down his life for one.

'Well, it's there for you,' he said, 'all spick and span. What do you propose?'

'We'll hold you up somewhere and you hand over the key. In Stephen's Green, shall we say?'

'Anywhere that suits. You'll want the garage keys and the ignition key. Which of you will drive?'

Freddie hesitated.

'This is the unpleasant part, Paddy,' he said. 'We want you to do that.'

'You're out of your mind,' Paddy McDonagh told him.

'We need your help.'

'Not a hope. The keys you can have anytime. After that you're on your own.'

He stood up. Freddie put his hand lightly on his arm.

'Hold on a while.'

Willie Mulhall moved away a little bit.

'You said twenty minutes, Freddie. I have Nora to think of.'

Freddie said, in a voice no longer friendly: 'I have to insist.'

Willie Mulhall now guarded the door and held a revolver. He was their hostage. To dispel any lingering ambiguity, Freddie began to spell it out:

'We have orders, Paddy, so we'd better understand each other. First of all, that gun isn't for ornament. You co-operate, or Willie uses it. If for any reason, now or later, it becomes necessary and he can't, I'll use my own. Second, don't entertain any doubts about it. We haven't any choice and won't hesitate. Two simple points. Keep them before your mind and you won't get hurt.'

Paddy McDonagh looked at his cousin as though for the first time. They had grown up as friends. His mother's household had sheltered Freddie not once but many times, and at the peril of their own lives. It was a betrayal so fundamental there could be nothing left to which to appeal. Neither declining nor consenting he stood up and waited for the next move.

'Let's go,' Freddie said.

At the garage he was ordered to change into the chauffeur's uniform. He had done so many times without a thought. Now it was a deep and bitter humiliation. Freddie, perhaps realizing that, or simply as a precautionary measure, spent the time examining the car while he did so. He fiddled with windows and door locks to check how they worked. He stood in a couple of places on the running board, testing for grip and balance.

'The caretaker makes his next round at half past eight, right?'

'Right,' Willie Mulhall said. He had the gun in his hand again.

'And if the car has been taken out in the meanwhile,' Freddie continued, 'the procedure is to leave a note of the time and the reason. That had better be done too.'

Paddy made a number of drafts until he found one that satisfied them. They decided to go. Both of them sat in the back.

'Take her out towards Naas,' Freddie instructed.

Paddy McDonagh secured the garage gates and they set off. As they found the canal road and followed it, Willie rested his revolver on the top of the back seat. The nozzle pressing between the shoulderblades was irksome at first and then unbearable.

'You don't have to push it through my bloody back,' Paddy protested.

'He's right. Take it away,' Freddie ordered, 'and stop showing off.'

They avoided the main road and continued deviously by lanes which served the outlying townlands, disturbing nothing except occasional, wandering hens and dogs dozing at gates. The pace was painfully slow.

'If I knew where we're supposed to be going,' Paddy complained, 'it would be a help.'

'It's a cottage where we pick up some gelignite,' Freddie said, 'and it's to the north beyond Naas. Work around towards Robertstown.'

They reached it just after dusk, a low thatched cottage in a flat countryside where small roads ran parallel with the canal for brief intervals before hiding themselves again between high and overgrown hedges. There were ten at least in the bare kitchen. It was lit by a single oil lamp, and a blazing fire.

'Our driver,' Freddie said, when two of the men stepped forward. 'Gentle treatment.'

They brought Paddy to an adjoining room. A camp bed and a couple of chairs furnished it. One of his guards was a mere boy, pale-faced but strongly built, with nothing at all to say. The other was pleasant and offered a cigarette.

'Thanks.'

They lit it for him and then lit a candle with the same match.

'We won't be starting for about an hour,' he was told. 'You might as well sit down.'

He sat on the bed. While they watched him there was activity in the yard. He heard cans being moved and guessed it was paraffin oil. They were probably loading the car. He could have saved himself all that hosing and polishing.

'You were in France, I'm told,' the conversational one said. 'What outfit was it?'

'Motor Transport, ASC,' Paddy answered. 'I was there for the duration.'

'A brother of my own was with the Seventh Dublin. He was killed at Kislah Dagh. On the nineteenth of August. I remember the date.'

'I had a cousin in the Dublin's,' Paddy told him. 'He died at Gallipoli too. From what I've heard about the Turks, better that than fall into their hands.'

'I've heard the same,' the other agreed, 'they have barbarous customs.'

It was over the hour before he was led back to the kitchen again. The men who had been there earlier had gone. Only Freddie and Willie Mulhall remained. They ordered him to the car and got in with him. It was night by now. The pleasanter of the guards joined them as a guide.

'You've gelignite and paraffin aboard, so take it gently,' Freddie warned.

Their destination, as he had rightly guessed, was a police barracks. It had been evacuated some weeks previously. So had several others which proved too isolated, as the resistance developed, to be any longer defensible. The length of a small field separated it from the road and a narrow boreen gave access, but when he attempted to drive along it the jolting became severe and he was told to stop. Figures emerged from the darkness to surround them. He recognized some of the men from the cottage.

'We'll move the stuff from here by hand,' Freddie decided.

In a while the barracks crawled with men. They worked swiftly, some scattering paraffin inside, others using sledge hammers on the roof to lash the oil through gaping holes to the rafters. Some of the gelignite was wrapped in yellow clay, so that when thrown it would adhere to walls and slates. When all was ready they fired the interior and withdrew to watch while it took hold. Places where it showed signs of failing or that were slow to take were bombarded with gelignite. Its heat spread through the air about them. Their faces became visible to each other. The flames inside licked upwards through the shattered windows and leaped through the holes in the roof. Soon they engulfed everything. Freddie watched with growing satisfaction.

'Next time,' he said to those near him, 'the peelers will be inside.'

They burned the car before leaving. Paddy McDonagh watched silently, wondering why. Why not keep it? For its usefulness, which was obvious. For the craftsmanship that had been lavished on it, its precision and complexity, its pleasing elegance. Who would benefit? Freddie filled in the time with a short address of congratulation to the men. For some of them, he said, it was the first taste of active service. The old hands would agree that it had been a bit of a cakewalk. Nevertheless it was experience. They had assembled the stuff successfully; they had put up the roadblocks and dug trenches under campaign conditions and that would stand to them in the near future, as the war to push the British out of Ireland built up. They were sworn to fight for that day and to die for it, if so it must be. They would be faithful, that he knew. Their warrant was that night's work. God speed Freedom's hour.

'God save Ireland,' Willie Mulhall responded for them.

When they were assembled on the roadway to await formal dismissal he said to Willie Mulhall:

'You can let Paddy go.'

Two men led him to the centre of the road. He was to remain standing with his back to the assembled men.

'Dublin is somewhere in front of you,' Willie told him. 'Start walking that way on the order to march. Don't look back at any stage. If you do, we'll shoot.'

He was left standing for some time, listening to the movements and low voices of men he could no longer see, wondering if it was a trick to keep him quiet until the moment came to shoot him from behind. The chauffeur's cap felt so incongruous that in spite of the risk he took it off. Now that the light of the fires had died, the surrounding darkness seemed deeper than ever. Aware of his isolation, he stood with his feet apart and his hands clasped behind his back, at ease in the army way, using the military formality of it as a shield against the humiliation they were inflicting, until at last the command rang out.

'Right. Forward march.'

He came automatically to attention, his heels clicking as they met. Then he strode forward. He had no desire whatever to look back. His cousin's betrayal left no room for curiosity.

Despite the curfew he travelled all night. In the early morning the driver of a wagon carrying milk churns believed his story that his car had broken down and took him several miles of the journey. When he got home at last his first child had been born. He decided to eat something before reporting to his employers and to the police. In telling Nora what had happened he decided against any mention of Freddie having been involved. It would upset her, for a start. He withheld it from the police too. The men who held him up, he said, were complete strangers.

No one suspected otherwise. The event was commonplace, the details of no importance in that first year of Paddy McDonagh's new role of father of a family. Law had broken down throughout the country. A general strike forced the government to free eighty political prisoners who were on hunger strike in Mountjoy. The Liverpool dockers secured the release of Irish hunger strikers in Wormwood Scrubs by threatening sympathetic action. Ships carrying munitions for the British forces in Ireland were blacked by Dublin dockers and the railmen refused to work the trains for the same reason. Dismissing them made matters worse. It helped to speed the collapse by starting a long campaign of passive resistance by the transport workers. Among the first victims were the Irish Loyalists in Dublin Castle who were responsible for the country's affairs. They found themselves replaced by administrators sent over from Britain. In a world where even the élite were vulnerable, Paddy McDonagh went about his business and managed most of the time to look on the bright side. Whatever else was happening he still had his job. In a world of ambushes, street executions, military harassment and the ever present risk of innocent death, many had not even that. Nor in England. One evening he read out to Nora an item from his newspaper reporting that an advertisement which had offered ten jobs managing street coffee stalls at a couple of pounds a week to ex-officers had been answered by five thousand applicants. He had only been a sergeant, but his new job was a lot better than that. Nora thought so too. She persuaded him to go with her to Glenns of Grafton Street to have a photograph taken of the two of them with the baby. He even agreed to hold the baby while it was being taken, though he was inclined to regret it when she had it framed in gilt and set it on the mantelpiece.

'I must have been a right gobdaw,' he admitted, whenever people made fun of him about it. Beside it, similarly framed, she put the photograph of him in his army uniform with his sergeant's stripes and service bars on the sleeves. If the Black and Tans broke in, she thought, it might act as a protection. He had grave doubts but the raids and searches were spreading such terror everywhere he pretended to believe so too. Raids and arrests were now part of everyday life. People kept indoors in the evenings. By the hour of curfew the thoroughfares were empty and the searches began. Armoured cars and lorries roared through darkened streets, searchlights blazed, boots kicked at closed doors. They saw people across the road from them herded downstairs and into the street by uniformed men with bayonets fixed. Night after night they sat in their darkened room listening to distant knocking or sudden rifle fire, wondering if their own area was to be next. One morning in winter, on their way to early mass together because it was the first Friday of the month, they found the body of a man blocking the alleyway at the back of the house. A card hung about the neck bore a now familiar message: 'Informers, take warning'. On their own it might have been easier to accept and get used to; other people seemed to manage. But the presence of so young a child magnified the dangers and kept them constantly anxious. In November Nora decided the photograph would be more effective still if she pinned a poppy above it. The next day the poppy had gone.

'What happened the poppy?' she asked, when she noticed.

'I took it down,' Paddy said. 'I didn't like it there.'

'You wear one on Armistice Day.'

'For remembrance,' he said, 'not to placate the bloody Black and Tans.'

The whole population, including the loyalists, were beginning to feel the same way.

II

The nursing brother knocked on the door of the Father Prior's office and was admitted. It was a May morning in 1921, early still, with birds making their music over freshly green fields. The countryside, though more murder-haunted than ever, shone with an unconcerned and misleading innocence. Inside the office sunlight streamed through the large windows, scattering pools of light on the bare, polished floor and the oaken desk, reflecting back from the white Dominican habit with a dazzling brightness. Outside, the hawthorn blossom radiated whiteness too and wore a plume of vapour after the night's rain. A black crucifix with its alabaster victim leaned from the panelling and seemed to peer over the Father Prior's shoulder at what he was writing. He looked up after a moment.

'Is he conscious?'

'He came to a few minutes ago.'

'Did he give any information?'

'Nothing I could make sense of. He seems to think he fell off his horse.'

'In our grounds?'

'That's what he said. Some workmen were trying to lift

something. He leaned from his saddle to help them and fell. He's rambling a bit, I think.'

'Did he give his name?'

'O'Sheehan, I think he said. It sounded like O'Sheehan, but he seemed very confused and I decided not to delay – your instruction –'

'Quite,' the Father Prior said. 'I'll go to him.'

They walked together down bare corridors that magnified the creaking of leather.

'You disposed of the . . .' the Father Prior stopped himself long enough to dissociate his office from the word '. . . the rifle?'

'We did. Father Barrington concealed it very cleverly. He put it –'

'Enough,' Father Prior said. 'I am not curious.'

The brother, holding his peace, opened the infirmary door and led his superior to the bedside of the man who had been found unconscious in the priory grounds. A fresh bandage about his head hid the wound which had been made, the Prior was privately certain, by a bullet grazing the scalp. There had been a lot of shooting during the night – an ambush, some might think. The Father Prior declined to speculate. He was an instrument of God's Will, not a listening post. The fellow was conscious.

'Feeling better now?' the Prior asked.

As he seated himself by the bedside his disciplined bearing relaxed and his face, which had delicate bones and pale but fine skin, expressed a natural gentleness.

'Where is this?' the injured man asked.

The nursing brother looked surprised.

'I had already told him,' he whispered to his superior who bent to listen, and then said: 'This is the priory of Tibradden.'

'Another monastery. You are followers of Patrick?'

The usage was odd. It was even archaic.

'Only in the most general way,' the Prior said. 'We are Dominicans. Have you any idea how you got here?'

'A puzzle,' the other said, 'I can't make it out. There's a sort of darkness in here.'

He touched his head and seemed surprised to feel the bandage.

'What's this?'

'We dressed your wound this morning,' the brother told him.

'You were found unconscious just inside the boundary wall,' the Prior explained, 'your clothes were wet through and you had obviously been lying there all night. There is a scalp wound of some kind. Can you not remember?'

'I remember falling from my horse.'

'You mean it flung you and you landed in the grounds?' It sounded unlikely.

'No, no – a long time back. The bellyband broke.'

'But where did this happen?'

'Somewhere in the mountains. I lived there a while among them. An insignificant people.'

'And you can remember nothing further?'

'I remember monks. The country was alive with them. You couldn't hear your ears for bells.'

The Prior looked at the nursing brother. It seemed pointless to continue.

'Has he had breakfast?'

'Not yet.'

'Tell the kitchen to prepare it.'

He turned his attention to the patient again.

'You are a Mr O'Sheehan, I understand. Is that your name?'

'It will do,' the other said.

'Good. You must rest now. Breakfast will be ready shortly. I doubt you will be strong enough to leave for a few days at least, but have no fear. You will be looked after and it will be . . . how shall I say it . . . you will be quite safe. Do you understand?'

The other nodded.

'Good. Very good.'

The Prior transferred his attention to a pair of boots lying beside the locker.

'Those are his, I presume. Where are the rest of his clothes?'

'They are being dried and aired.'

'I see. Well, come with me.'

As they walked to the office together the Prior spoke what was in his mind.

'There was no horse.'

'I would find it hard to believe.'

'You have only to look at the state of his boots. The dye has been washed away and the leather about the toecaps has worn white. That man has been wandering mountain and bog for some days.'

'With a flying column, I'd say.'

The Father Prior was displeased.

'To say is not our business. If you wish to surmise, do so silently. The problem is he may be here for some time so, for various reasons, he had better be one of us. A gardener or kitchen help, perhaps. Or a lay brother. That's probably best. For the time being, he is Brother O'Sheehan. Do you follow me?'

'I think so, Father Prior.'

'And the rifle which was lying beside him. Did he refer to it at all?'

'I mentioned it but he seems to know nothing about it.'

'Very strange.'

His hand on the doorknob, the Prior paused. It would be as well, he felt, to explain himself a little.

'These are troubled and confused times, Brother. Unusual situations – contingencies, arise. A lay brother's habit would serve O'Sheehan while his clothes are being seen to; indeed, until he is well enough to leave. He will feel less conspicuous; I hope you fully understand me?'

'Fully, Father Prior. I'll have it seen to at once.'

'And, of course, the other little detail. A matter of . . . conforming.'

'I beg your pardon . . . ?'

The Father Prior was a fair man. God sometimes denied the gift of imagination.

'Shave off his moustache,' he said patiently, by way of dismissal.

He had reason to be glad of his foresight. Sometime after lunch the throbbing of motor engines penetrated his office and continued so persistently that he went over to the windows. What he saw shocked him, though he had anticipated the possibility. Parties of uniformed men were searching the grounds. Their vehicles he could not see, but the sound seemed to come from the main driveway. He summoned the nursing brother. He also sent for Father Barrington. They had even graver news. An army officer, accompanied by the local police sergeant, was in the reception room requesting permission to search the monastery. In some buried recess of himself the Prior felt a sting of medieval outrage. His monastery was part of God's city, extra-territorial, inviolate. But there were practical considerations.

'What about Brother O'Sheehan?'

'He's much recovered.'

'Not his health. Has he been provided for?'

'As you instructed. His clothes were still drying when he got out of bed after lunch so I had to draw from stock anyway. He agreed about the moustache.'

'And the bandage. That may be a difficulty.'

'He has only to wear his cowl. It covers it completely.'

The Prior looked relieved.

'I had better meet this officer. In the meanwhile, on so beautiful an afternoon, and in the unusual circumstances, I think we could allow a period for perambulation and meditation. In pairs. Will you see to it, Father?'

'Immediately.'

'You, Brother, will be O'Sheehan's companion. All he has to do is to walk quietly. Explain to him as best you can, though I doubt it will be necessary. And don't let him out of your sight.'

'Yes, Father Prior.'

They went about their business. The Prior followed. As he strode towards the reception room he assumed his gait of office, walking erect, his hands hidden in his wide sleeves, his thought bent inwards. The policeman was well known to him, an elderly, godfearing man who seemed convinced already that his duty was leading him into sacrilege and hell's flames.

'Sergeant Durcan. Is it true that you have come to invade us?'

'Not me, your reverence,' the sergeant said unhappily, 'the officer here. I'm only a go-between, so to speak. 'Tis way and beyond my control.'

He introduced the officer, who was apologetic also.

'An unpleasant duty,' he said, 'but there were several ambushes during the night, one on the road just outside. We have reason to believe some of them may be hiding here, and we wish to search.'

'Your men are already searching the grounds – without notification, may I point out.'

'A military necessity.'

'And to search a house of the religious, is that also a military necessity?'

'I'm afraid it is. I very much regret it.'

'If you insist I have no means of stopping it. But I am bringing it to your attention, and Sergeant Durcan here is a witness to it, that this is a Dominican priory, and I will protest strongly to the authorities.'

'We will cause as little inconvenience as possible,' the officer said, in a tone that made it clear he was not to be deterred. His departure left the sergeant on his own and intensified his embarrassment.

'Everything will be quiet and orderly,' he explained. 'They're regular army, not Black and Tans, thanks be to God.'

'If the authorities are condoning the searching of religious houses, they will condone anything.'

'The IRA have taken over the Custom House and set it alight. It's burning away and nothing will save it, I'm told. They do a thorough job, the same boyos.'

'When did you hear this?'

'On the station telephone, barely an hour ago. It's the sort of thing makes these young fellows jumpy. But don't fret at all. He's very British and very gentlemanly, your reverence, and not much harm in him. If he ever has the misfortune to find the IRA they'll serve him up for breakfast.'

'He won't find them here,' the Prior said.

'That's what I told them. But you might as well talk to the

wall there. For all their posh accents the English is hopelessly ignorant when it comes to religion. What the missus will say if she hears I had hand, act or part in this, hardly bears thinking about.'

The Prior relented. He was also anxious to keep the sergeant out of the search.

'You're not to blame. Take a seat while I see what is happening.'

'Maybe I should join the young officer.'

'Leave the officer to us. I'll have a cup of tea sent in to you. Just remain where you are.'

He left the sergeant in the company of the only picture in the lounge, a large portrait in oils of one of his predecessors, and went to survey whatever was happening. Father Barrington had acted quickly. In the grounds the friars were already perambulating in pairs, walking silently and contemplatively in the sunshine. Others were moving through the corridors on their way to the open air. The nursing brother and Mr O'Sheehan were among them. He scrutinized them closely. O'Sheehan had shaved. The friar's hood hid the bandage completely. He had his hands folded in his sleeves. Father Barrington had taken charge of the young officer and his search party. The Prior decided to retire to his study. As he awaited the outcome he wondered if, in fact, he was harbouring an IRA gunman. It seemed more than likely. Was he, then, in breach of the law? Technically, yes. Could he answer satisfactorily if so accused? He could. The things that were Caesar's he would render to Caesar, but not a man's life which was the gift of God and God's only. The State's right to hang or shoot its enemy was questionable, whereas the exercise of mercy was not. It was the prerogative of the Church to give sanctuary. And if one of the English were in a similar plight, would he do the same? He would. With equal enthusiasm? Possibly not, but it was irrelevant anyway. The act was what was in question, not the measure of his emotional involvement.

The search dragged on through the afternoon. When it had ended Father Barrington reported that another body had been found among the bushes, a dead one this time, that of a young IRA man who had been shot through the head. The army had allowed the last rites to be administered before removing it. They had left the grounds and O'Sheehan was safe.

'Thank you, Father,' the Prior said.

'They damaged nothing inside, I'm glad to say. I don't know about the grounds.'

'I'll take a walk there myself,' the Prior decided. It was an excuse, he knew, to leave his study for a while. The death of the young man weighed on him. He had grown restless.

There was no real damage there either, though shrubs and bushes showed traces of their activity. That in itself was strange enough. For a brief moment the world had burst through the gates, disorderly, indiscriminate, loudly trampling a place where tranquillity and order were habitual presences. For what? The corpse of a youth – their spoils of war. It was a serious matter, nevertheless. The secular Power had deliberately crossed the line, setting custom aside and planting, however unconsciously, a seed of anarchy. If they wanted to lose Ireland they were going the right way about it. Perhaps they knew they had lost it already. If they could ever be said to have possessed it.

Its produce and its wealth, yes. Never its people. The British had never wished to be at one with any other people. Master Race, deriding whatever was beyond its comprehension, with no inkling of the rich labyrinth God made of His Truth when He hid it piecemeal in the multi-cultures of his peoples. The Anglo-Normans had been wiser conquerors. They grabbed the cream, then intermarried and integrated. *Hiberniores Hibernicis ipsis*, Cambrensis complained about them: more Irish than the Irish themselves – when they were installed in all the top places, of course.

His own father had been a Fenian. There was a family story, he remembered, that he had gone to Tallaght to take part in the rising of 1867 but had been prevented by a ruse of his brother, who offered overnight accommodation and then locked and barricaded the bedroom door. It was never told openly. Under lamplight at family parties, uncles with lavish bellies and red faces, and pockets never lacking the jingle of a few sovereigns, would listen to his father reciting patriotic verses.

> On far foreign fields from Dunkirk to Belgrade
> Lie the soldiers and chiefs of the Irish Brigade

And if he patted you on the head and said: son, we fought every nation's battle but our own: you knew he had a sup taken. What had shocked his mother was the savagery of the Catholic hierarchy. 'Hell is not hot enough nor eternity long enough to roast a Fenian' one of them announced. Dogmatic machine gunners. Poor woman. She was too pious to understand that bishops, like anyone else, were prone to occupational illnesses. Galloping infallibility was one of them. It was better to be a friar, engaged in the more fruitful search; the search for God-in-me; an unceasing and companionable exploration.

While he was formulating his protest, listing mentally those who should be consulted and those whose advice he could well do without, he came unexpectedly on the spot where the dead youth had lain. It brought him to a standstill. The undergrowth had been crushed and hollowed by his weight, little globules of blood were strung like a red dew along bent blades of grass. Emptiness and silence hung about it. This, then, was the reality of Ireland. Always in revolt, always being defeated, always paying in blood for the crime of being weaker than its neighbour. Little sense in it and the end so predictable. A young man gave his life and nothing at all was changed. The sun above the grounds still shone, the day continued to smile. It had been so, time and again, for hundreds of years. The thought pressed down on him, a physical weight, and refused to be disciplined. He put duty aside for a while. There was no option. Later on he would reassume his role of Father Prior.

Tibradden Priory rested among the foothills beyond Dublin city. An Anglo-Norman knight had built his tower there in the thirteenth century, his men-at-arms close about him, his look-out posts regularly manned against forays from the clans of O'Byrne and O'Toole in the higher fastnesses of the Wicklow mountains.

His descendants, though they put themselves in constant jeopardy by refusing the Reformation and clinging to Catholicism, managed to make themselves more comfortable by stages, building a small manor house in the sixteenth century and a larger one in the eighteenth. It was at a time when in the city whose spires they could see below them Jonathan Swift from the Deanery of St Patrick's was inflaming the populace against base money. It was a time also when the rewards for the head of a popish priest and a wolf had attained parity at five pounds for either, so they prudently incorporated a secret room, to be used as a chapel for the celebration of mass and as a refuge for hunted religious. If their powerful connections failed at any time to sustain a delicately balanced toleration, it would provide the same service for themselves. The Dominicans took over in turn and for the sake of its hallowed associations kept the room intact. They also kept it secret, finding it ideal for safeguarding their small store of treasures. So it was that throughout his stay and for long after he had gone, O'Sheehan's rifle had for its nearest companions a silver cross of the seventeenth century and a pewter chalice, simple and functional, a relic of penal times.

Though the Prior had his movements kept under observation at first to see if he made any attempt to search for it, he gave no sign of thinking about it at all, but took on odd jobs to occupy himself, one of them being to help Father Felim in the library, where it was discovered that he already had formal training as a librarian. Another surprise was his command of Gaelic and Latin. Father Felim, whose knowledge of librarianship was limited to making the key available to clients who wanted it and seeing it was returned when they had finished, was greatly impressed. O'Sheehan was soon indexing and cataloguing on his own and had virtually taken over.

'He's doing a grand job,' Father Felim reported to the Prior, 'and he works all the time. He certainly knows the ropes.'

'I wonder where he was trained. Has he said?'

'Never directly. From what he tells me he may have worked for a period with a professor of Celtic studies – a German, I imagine,' Father Felim said, 'but I couldn't be sure. O'Sheehan is a man who has information to impart on everything conceivable, except himself.'

'What do you make of him?'

'Highly educated. Very grandiloquent too, when he gets steam up. But a bit of a puzzle. There could well be a slate loose, in a harmless sort of way. He goes on at times about falling off his horse.'

'That was the story he told when he first arrived,' the Prior said, 'and highly unlikely. Perhaps he imagines it. Do you find his general conduct satisfactory?'

'Impeccable. A decent and sober man. I'd be sorry to see him go.'

'Then why not encourage him to stay. Discuss some form of remuneration with him.'

'In the circumstances,' Father Felim remarked drily, 'he's unlikely to venture out to spend it.'

'Nevertheless, it puts the affair on a business footing.'

'It does. That's true. I'll suggest an arrangement.'

The terms suited O'Sheehan very well. He settled down, working in the library by day and reading or talking to the friars in the evenings. He found it pleasant to walk in the grounds where he could be safe and content in a world of order and certainty, while beyond the walls the new State of Northern Ireland was brought into being by Act of the British Parliament and celebrated its triumph by driving Catholics from their jobs and then burning them out of their houses. In the South, where Sinn Fein laid claim to be the lawful government of the whole of Ireland the IRA were gutting the stately homes of the gentry. The British forces, deciding the best answer was official acts of reprisal, began to burn down the homesteads of struggling farmers. With arson as commonplace as murder it was a world that could well be let go by. O'Sheehan did so quite happily until sometime in July when desperation drove both sides into signing an armed truce so that they could at least sit down together to search out a solution. A temporary amnesty allowed wanted republicans to show themselves freely. The Prior consulted O'Sheehan.

'It seems to offer you the opportunity to leave here in safety.'

'I like the work I'm doing,' O'Sheehan said, 'I'd rather stay and finish it.'

'To have the work completed would suit us here very well. But is it best – in your own interest?'

'I think so.'

'If you do, then very good,' the Prior said, pleased.

His conversation with Father Felim was also on his mind.

'When you first came here you were injured. You seemed to be concussed. Do you remember the circumstances?'

'In a general way.'

'And have you recovered fully, or do you still experience difficulty in recalling the past?'

O'Sheehan appeared reluctant to answer. His expression became guarded. The silence grew embarrassing.

'Perhaps you have difficulty in speaking of it,' the Prior hinted gently.

After a pause O'Sheehan said: 'No. Difficulty in being believed.'

The tone was sad, not offensive. Behind O'Sheehan's eyes, the Prior thought, he caught a brief glimpse of something lonely and astray. It would be better for the present to let the matter rest.

'In the new circumstances, it will be quite understandable if you decide to see a little of the outside world on your free evenings,' he said, 'so feel at liberty to come and go provided it fits in reasonably with our routine.'

But the exchange preoccupied him. He mentioned it to Father Felim a few weeks later. Father Felim's view was by then unambiguous.

'The man is deranged,' he said baldly.

'That seems excessive.'

'I mean in a nice gentlemanly way. He thinks he's Oisin.'

'But he is O'Sheehan, presumably.'

'Not O'Sheehan,' Father Felim said. 'We misheard him. He meant Oisin, the son of Finn McCool in the old Fianna cycle, the one who returned to Ireland after several hundred years in

the Land of the Ever Young and became an old man when he
fell from his horse.'

'Has he told you this?'

'No. I've simply put two and two together. But he goes on
about falling from his horse.'

'I don't believe he fell from his horse myself,' the Prior said,
'but Oisin is hardly unique in the matter.'

'He talks at length of the old sagas, when he gets wound up,'
Father Felim explained, 'and when he does there is something
not quite sane about him. I've no doubt at all he worked for
some Celtic scholar and picked it all up as he did so. He's
convinced he remembers falling from his horse. My own belief
is he probably fell off his librarian's ladder on his head and
woke up thinking he was Oisin.'

As a theory of O'Sheehan's eccentricities and odd answers, it
had possibilities.

'If he does, it seems harmless enough,' the Prior conceded,
'but it's an interesting lead. I must renew my acquaintance with
Gaelic mythology.'

'Consult O'Sheehan,' Father Felim advised. 'He's a walking
encyclopaedia.'

The lanes about Tibradden Priory dipped down in gentle
gradients to green pastureland and tiny villages. They were
heavy with summer odours as O'Sheehan freewheeled down
them for the first time on a battered bicycle that belonged to no
one in particular. His chief concern was to buy himself a hat.
Without one he felt exposed and uneasy, a man deprived of his
due dignity. It marred his pleasure in his new-found freedom.
It reduced the satisfaction he felt at being once again in his own
suit of clothes. What was worse, he suspected none of the nearby
villages would be able to supply his want. 'When the hat is on
the house is thatched' was a traditional expression he had heard
many a time without finding it in any way remarkable. Now,
in his nakedness, he understood its deep truth.

He explored the village with diminishing hope. Its main
street offered only a police station and a post office. The market

square was better. A string of shops on one side looked across at the squat church and its flanking gravestones on the other. There was a dairy, a bakery, a butcher and a mixed business which combined groceries, snuff, tobacco and clay pipes, with an attempt at haberdashery, but kept nothing in the way of hats. He was advised to try the public house. His journey took him past a harness maker's and the village forge. The swing door of the public house was set between symmetrical plate-glass windows which seemed bent in the middle and elongated by the downward pressure of the stones above. Inside, flitches of bacon and bags of flour, only dimly visible because the evening sunshine hovered at the windows but refused to enter, mingled their smells with the reek of porter. A figure seated on a barrel of salted pork greeted O'Sheehan and thumped at a partition to summon attendance.

'A grand evening,' he said.

'Thanks be to God,' O'Sheehan replied.

Storm lanterns and farming implements hung from the ceiling. There was no sign of hats. Footsteps across the ceiling above and the creaking of stairs signalled someone's approach. A man in his middle forties with a white apron arrived in due course, blinked at him for some moments and then with dawning recognition exclaimed, 'O'Sheehan – on my soul.'

O'Sheehan recognized an old friend, who by right ought to have been a hundred miles away in his native Tipperary.

'Cornelius Moloney – by all the powers.'

'What takes a man like yourself to a place like this?' Cornelius asked.

'I might pose the same question,' O'Sheehan countered.

'By God, then, you might,' Cornelius conceded, 'you might well. And where the hell is your moustache – I hardly knew you.' He scooped aside a group of derelict glasses and swung open the counter door. 'Come inside with you and we'll both answer. Mind your head on the beam above.'

The back parlour was brighter. O'Sheehan noticed a bunch of flowers on the little table and a spray of cape gooseberry adorning the empty hearth. That was another surprise. A woman's hand. There was much to be caught up with. Cornelius took a bottle of whiskey and glasses to the table and poured for his guest and for himself.

'You have as heavy a hand as ever,' O'Sheehan told him, apprehensive of the liberal measure.

'A taste of water will take the sting out of it,' Cornelius said. He filled a small jug from the kitchen tap, and put it on the table.

'And when did you leave Tipperary?' O'Sheehan asked, after he had drunk his host's good health.

'A long story,' Cornelius told him. 'It began shortly after I last saw you. With the anti-conscription campaign and the Sinn Fein elections of 1918 I was in the thick of it.'

'I know your feelings on that score,' O'Sheehan conceded.

'The movement found a warm welcome in Cornelius Maloney's public house and of course the authorities knew it. Well and good. I was doing my bit and prepared to put up with the harassment. But then I married a wife and a year ago we had our first child. It was the worst time it could happen, the beginning of the Black and Tan reprisals. I was warned a few times they had a mind to put the premises up in flames – wife and baby included, though I had the right side of the local RIC which was a measure of protection. Howsomever, we had a visit from a fella from Dublin, a Vice-Commandant Mulhall; you've heard of him, maybe?'

'No,' O'Sheehan said.

'You're as well off. A young pup more interested in trade unions than the cause of Ireland and full of the social question.'

'There are some like that,' O'Sheehan agreed, 'the Fenians were much afflicted by it. Fellows who attacked private ownership and the like. I remember it alienated the American interest.'

'It turns the clergy against us too,' Cornelius added. 'But what could I do? He came with written recommendations from some of the top Sinn Feiners in Dublin – on the military side too – and I had to agree to give him one of the rooms over the pub. He was a bit of a mystery for the first few weeks until one fine morning we woke up to the news that the local RIC

Barracks had been burnt down during the night. It was the worst thing could happen, because there were decent men in it who were friendly to us. After that I knew it was only a question of time before my own place went up in smoke. It was a well-known rendezvous.'

'They burnt you out?'

Cornelius held up his hand.

'Not so fast. They intended to burn me out. But Cornelius Moloney knows as much and a little more than the Black and Tans. I sold the place and bought this one, in the wife's maiden name, of course. Only just in time. A fortnight later the place in Tipperary was burned over the new man's head.'

O'Sheehan expressed astonishment.

'Of course,' Cornelius added, 'this place is only to mark time while I look around a bit, though it isn't bad. We have the market-day custom and a good weekend trade from the city because they bring out the wife and kids for a trip on the steam tram which passes there below the main street. But I have my eye on Dublin; a nice little place in High Street. That's where the money is.'

'And you've a wife and child since I saw you last,' O'Sheehan said, 'that's a full enough schedule. Is it a boy or a girl?'

'A boy of twelve months. We called him Brian.'

'A kingly name.'

'The greatest in our history. He gave Cashel to the Church. And what about yourself. What brings you this direction?'

'Like yours, a long story. My immediate quest is for a hat.'

It was Cornelius's turn to be astonished.

'I think I may have misheard you,' he said.

'I was looking to buy a hat for myself and was told you might have such a thing here.'

'Not unless they've started to bottle them,' Cornelius said, 'but if you're in the extremes of need I can lend you one of my own to tide you over.'

'I'd be greatly obliged.'

'Hold on, then.' He went upstairs again.

O'Sheehan sipped his whiskey. It was a luxury unobtainable

in the Priory except in special circumstances and the yellow liquid with its smoky bouquet filled him with the contentment of the secular life. Beyond the small window was a white-washed yard where crates and barrels lay about in friendly disorder. The stillness of summer had settled on it, bathing it in a late evening warmth. Now that chance had led him to it he could look forward to further pleasant evenings in the company of his friend. Cornelius returned with the promised hat. It was to O'Sheehan's taste and fitted well enough.

'And so you still play the chess?' Cornelius asked.

'Whenever I can, though the times we live in are no encouragement.'

'If Ireland ever lost the chess,' Cornelius pronounced, 'it would be like losing her language – the end of nationhood. What was it they wrote in the bygone days about the heroes and poets of the gael?'

O'Sheehan looked at the ceiling in grave recollection.

> 'Good they are at man-slaying
> Melodious in the ale house
> Masterly at making songs
> Skilled at playing chess.'

'That was it. The great men of old. You'll have another taste of whiskey.'

'Not now. I have to be away.'

'Are you staying near at hand?'

'Near enough. You'll have to let me tell you more about that another day.'

Cornelius understood the times and the need, on occasion, to be discreet.

'Next time you come I'll have the board and the pieces to hand.'

'I'll look forward to that.'

'And you'll meet the missus and the boy. They're out at present. Don't leave it too long.'

O'Sheehan promised not to. He felt a new man in the hat and faced the road with a will, though this time it was mostly uphill and he had to wheel the bicycle. But with twilight the air was cooler and the exercise pleasant. The hedges were thick and scented. In the flowering weeds beneath them a multitude of small creatures found shelter and concealment. From time to time they stirred as he passed and betrayed their presence. It pleased him. He felt in many ways kin to them and was moved by their company.

III

'This truce,' Freddie said, 'do you notice anything remarkable about it?'

He was stretched full length on the bed, his hands behind his head. Willie Mulhall sat at the window looking down at the railway line below. The parallel tracks gleamed in the sunshine with a steely brightness.

'The whole thing is remarkable,' he answered. 'Have you anything in particular in mind?'

'Weddings,' Freddie said. 'Do you know how many from our own crowd have got hitched since the cease-fire? Fifteen. If it's the same with other brigades, the new National Anthem will be "Haste to the Wedding".'

'Better than that bloody "Soldier's Song",' Willie said. 'Anything but that.'

'Think of the cradles of Ireland nine months from now. Full of good republicans.'

'Or the gaols. That was your forecast yesterday.'

'Both. And just to make it nice and handy for John Bull when the talks break down and he wants to round them up, they've been having their wedding pictures took by Bobs of Henry Street.'

'We may get what we want.'

'Not a hope,' Freddie said. 'Can you see Lloyd George recognizing an Irish Republic, or telling Craig and the Unionists Partition was a mistake and must be dismantled? I can't. Craig has got what he wants and Lloyd George can't take it back. So the war will go on.'

'It suits me. Hanging around doing nothing is a wash-out.'

'You could be learning Irish. Or working out your social theories.'

'Fintan Lalor did that a long time ago,' Willie said, 'Ownership of Ireland for the people of Ireland, from the sun down to the centre.'

'It's a tall order.'

'The Russians succeeded.'

'A different problem. They only had to dispossess the capitalist class. In Ireland when the British have been rooted out you'll still have the native capitalists, and who's going to discommode them? Not Dev or Griffith. If Connolly hadn't been executed you might have had a chance, though I doubt it. The Irish people aren't interested.'

'If I believed that,' Willie said, 'I'd no longer know what I was fighting for.'

'Yes, you would. It's straightforward. No king. No empire. Irish freedom.'

'In a slum in Chandler's Court,' Willie said, 'thanking God and some employer or other whenever you succeed in having enough to eat? That's not my idea of freedom.'

'It'll do – for a start.'

Freddie, unconcerned, let it rest. Social structures and systems had no relevance, at least until the immediate struggle was won. The ideal must be national freedom, pure, uncomplicated, singleminded. After that it would be the politicians' turn. They could fight it out among themselves.

Telegram from His Holiness Pius X to His Majesty George V of England, 19th October 1921.

'WE REJOICE AT THE RESUMPTION OF THE ANGLO-IRISH NEGOTIATIONS AND PRAY TO THE LORD, WITH ALL OUR HEART, THAT HE MAY BLESS THEM AND GRANT TO YOUR MAJESTY THE GREAT JOY AND IMPERISHABLE GLORY OF BRINGING TO AN END THE AGE LONG DISSENSION,'

Telegram from His Majesty George V to His Holiness Pius X.

'I HAVE RECEIVED THE MESSAGE OF YOUR HOLINESS WITH
MUCH PLEASURE AND WITH ALL MY HEART I JOIN IN
YOUR PRAYERS THAT THE CONFERENCE NOW SITTING IN
LONDON, MAY ACHIEVE A PERMANENT SETTLEMENT OF
THE TROUBLES IN IRELAND AND MAY INDICATE A NEW
ERA OF PEACE AND HAPPINESS FOR MY PEOPLE.'

Telegram from Eamon de Valera to His Holiness Pius X.

'THE PEOPLE OF IRELAND HAVE READ THE MESSAGE SENT
BY YOUR HOLINESS TO THE KING OF GREAT BRITAIN AND
APPRECIATE THE KINDLY INTEREST IN THEIR WELFARE AND
THE PATERNAL REGARD WHICH SUGGESTED IT. I TENDER
YOUR HOLINESS THEIR GRATITUDE. THEY ARE CONFIDENT
THAT THE AMBIGUITIES IN THE REPLY SENT IN THE NAME
OF KING GEORGE V WILL NOT MISLEAD YOU, AS THEY MAY
THE UNINFORMED, INTO BELIEVING THAT THE TROUBLES
ARE "IN" IRELAND OR THAT THE PEOPLE OF IRELAND OWE
ALLEGIANCE TO THE BRITISH KING.... THE TROUBLE IS
BETWEEN IRELAND AND BRITAIN AND ITS SOURCE THAT
THE RULERS OF BRITAIN HAVE SOUGHT TO IMPOSE THEIR
WILL UPON IRELAND AND BY BRUTAL FORCE HAVE
ENDEAVOURED TO ROB HER PEOPLE OF THE LIBERTY
WHICH IS THEIR NATURAL RIGHT AND HERITAGE.'

The telegrams caused a stir. Cornelius Moloney consulted
O'Sheehan's assessment of the exchange.

'Unimpeachable sentiments,' O'Sheehan conceded. His tone,
however, was not very enthusiastic.

'But less than respectful to the Holy Father?' Cornelius
suggested.

'Some might so regard it.'

'That was my own conclusion.'

'Ill judged, perhaps.'

'Just so,' said Cornelius. He was displeased.

Chandler's Court, its windows open to the unexpected
warmth of the September afternoon, exhaled the smell of age.
Willie Mulhall hardly noticed. He had grown up with it. The

games the children played in the street were those of his own childhood, the rhymes they chanted he still knew by heart, the lamp-posts they swung from had once borne his own weight and made his head reel. If it had changed in his eighteen months of absence it was only to advance that much further on the road to dissolution. His visit was against Freddie's advice. They would note his movements for use when the truce had ended. But he wanted to see his mother. It was not enough just to write or send her money from time to time. She was all on her own and growing old. If she were to die Freddie's reasons would seem less than adequate.

He climbed the stairs, remembering as he passed each landing that the neighbours he had grown up with were no longer there. Strikes and labour troubles once drew them close together; a world war and a national uprising had scattered them. Only the poverty and deprivation remained, the shattered fanlights, the broken windows stuffed with cardboard, the bare and malodorous hallways. Whatever else changed, these were the constants of the world he belonged to, as predictably there as the key of his mother's door which he groped for automatically and found as usual in the recess on the left-hand side. He inserted it and stepped into the room. It was silent. At first he thought she was out. Then he saw her hand on the armrest of the rocking chair which stood at the window with its back to him. When he went over he found she was asleep. The beads in her lap, large and brown, were no surprise. She used prayer almost as an occupation, in the way younger women worked at knitting. He drew over a chair and sat quietly beside her, waiting for her to waken. She looked worn and unguarded. He thought he could see age at its feeding, an appetite satisfying itself stealthily, crumb by crumb. It was sad and inevitable and better not dwelt on. There were things which you deliberately excluded in order to buttress up the will to act. The onset of age was one of them. It crept up on you too soon, while the work of revolution still remained unfinished. What if revolution proved too slow? What if Freddie were right and the people apathetic and disinterested?

On the pavement below, among the games chalked out by the children, someone had written the current slogan: 'Up The Rebels'. It made his point. Defiance radiated from it as it had from the banners his father marched under during the great trade union battles of 1913. He was leaning forward to search it out when his mother awoke and saw him. It took her a while to accept he was truly there.

'I was dreaming about you,' she said. He embraced her.

'What were you dreaming?'

'I was sitting here with your father and we were watching you playing in the street. It was a Sunday afternoon.'

'That's a long time ago,' he said.

'You were with young Quinn and he had a new bicycle, wherever he got it, but you had a better-looking suit than he had. So I remarked it to your father. If we could lay out two shillings a week, I said to him, we could get you a bike like that. I was thinking of you riding round the neighbourhood on it and using it for going to school.'

'It's a far cry now to the schoolgoing days,' he said, on his guard against sentiment.

'And where would we get two bob a week, your father said to me. But after a minute or so he said: I suppose I could go off the drink for Lent. Well, I said to him, that would be no great catastrophe. He was sitting where you are now and laughing and I looked around at him and saw yourself.'

She groped for the beads and put them in her apron pocket. 'You look thin,' she said, surveying him critically.

'I'm kept going,' he said. He gave her a bag of toffees he had bought on his way, knowing she liked them.

She put them in with the beads.

'Now I'll make you a cup of tea.'

As she busied herself he thought of her dream and his father. His father's presence was everywhere in the room; in the chair he used to sit in which was still by the fireside; a nail on the wall where he always hung his working gear; the closed door leading into the little room in which he had died. They imprisoned a world past, completed, unalterable. After so prolonged an absence, they exercised a perilous magnetism. He closed his mind against them. They, too, sapped the will.

'Will you stay tonight?' she asked him.

'If it's all right.'

'Your bed is made up.'

It always was, though in five years he had used it perhaps a dozen times. After the Rising of 1916 he had been in prison, then released, then on the run. The latest fiction was he had got a job travelling. As they drank he wondered if she believed it.

'Do you remember the Fitzpatricks?'

He did.

'I had a visit from her not long ago.'

'Where are they living now?'

'On the quays somewhere. They opened some kind of eating house there with his disablement money.'

'Do you mean Bob Fitzpatrick. What disablement?'

'He got some hurt in the war that cost him his eyesight, the poor chap. I thought you knew that.'

He had not. But he remembered Fitzpatrick as the good friend of his father and it was a shock.

'You always said the best are the ones that suffer,' he said to her. 'I knew nothing about that.'

Later, when she had cleaned up and they had been sitting together for some time, she said:

'You're still in the movement. Don't deny it. I know it's so.'

He nodded.

'And it's that that keeps you on the go, not the job you pretended about.'

'There was a sort of a job,' he said, 'but that was only for a short while. It was a long time ago.'

'And you're here because the truce gave you the chance?'

'That's true.'

Useless to deny it.

'And what's going to happen. Will they reach an agreement, do you think?'

'I imagine so. Things is looking very rosy, anyway,' he lied.

'It would be a great ease to many a woman's mind,' she said.

That too, was a hazard of visiting home. You saw that others suffered.

He went out to explore the streets. They were grim enough, but that was only one side of it. The people who lived in them might be despised, but they had formidable power. In his own memory Larkin had organized them to paralyze the system. And whatever Freddie might say they showed it again when they left military supplies for the British Army lying at the quaysides and the railway stations. Freddie believed in the gun and thought it sufficient. It was not. Without the sympathy of the people military resistance would last no time at all. They harboured you and fed you. If you were being hunted they were a great forest to screen you. Of course the gun was essential. It cut a road through all the fancy stuff. It had the Pope scattering telegrams and Lloyd George saying why can't we sit down together like men of sense and talk this over.

Someone on a bicycle hailed him from across the street. It was Dick Quinn. A strange thing. He could tell his mother her dream was out. On the other hand he might not. She might see in it some ill omen.

'Is it yourself,' Dick said, dismounting.

'Yours truly. Not at work?'

'No,' Dick said. 'We're slack at Doggets. A spell of fine weather and no one buys coal.'

'It was the same in father's time. I suppose the union can do nothing.'

'It can see you're laid off according to service and not how you rank as a pal of the gaffer. It's not much, but it's better than old times.'

As they went together down the street Willie remembered something and remarked:

'Kids are peculiar. I remember when my own father was idle now and then in the summer season, it set the mother pinching and scraping and worrying. But for me it meant jaunts to the Park on the crossbar of his bike or going swimming with him, usually at Williamstown or Blackrock. Those are the happiest memories I have.'

It was a long time since he had walked in the company of someone who knew his world, someone who was a touchstone. Freddie and his kind venerated patriotic phantoms. Dick Quinn understood the daily miseries of flesh and blood. He knew freedom was the pay you earned, the rent you paid, a job you had to work in. He had once seen Chandler's Court stepping out on the road to that kind of freedom, carrying banners and torches to mass rallies. Now it had joined the spectators again, its future in abeyance while the national struggle was being waged.

'It's thirsty weather and I'm carrying,' he said when they were near Cotter's public house. 'Let me buy you a drink.'

They found Lamb Magee still shifting the crates and sweeping the sawdust. Cotter himself, his elbows on the counter, was engaged in an intellectual tussle with his newspaper.

'What is it?' Willie asked.

'Raspberry cordial will fit the bill.'

Willie showed surprise.

'Nothing stronger?'

'No, thanks. I'm trying to keep it at arm's length for a while.'

Cotter disengaged his attention for long enough to attend to their needs. The Lamb could be heard stacking bottles in the back store.

'When I've been off drink for a week I find it stops bothering me altogether,' Dick said, 'and that's the only comfortable way if you're idling around. But if I touch one at all I'm back where I started.'

Cotter overheard and looked up at them.

'Do either of you remember a docker some years back, a big man called Barreller Morgan?'

They did.

'Barreller's fare was usually whiskey or porter and he was a man to shift any available quantity of either. But every year come the holy season of Lent he'd promise the wife to give up drink for the duration. So instead of whiskey and porter he'd come in here and for further orders he'd drink pints of ale with a dash of raspberry cordial in them. He argued that the cordial took the harm out of it.'

'I wouldn't like to be making his case to Father Mathew,' Dick said.

'Nor I,' Cotter agreed. 'But a batthery of theologians wouldn't budge him. He was a stubborn man.'

He scrutinized Willie more closely and said: 'You're Barney Mulhall's son.'

'That's right,' Willie acknowledged.

Cotter's expression changed.

'Now we know where we stand,' he said. He took the information away with him to chew on it. When he returned he had decided it was in order to continue.

'I was reading that clatther of telegrams,' he began, 'you wouldn't get better at the Tivoli. Will the talks come to anything, do you think?'

'I wouldn't lay odds about it.'

'I differ with you,' Cotter said, 'I differ categorically.' He picked up the newspaper and struck it with the back of his hand. 'A few weeks back I was reading in this thing that the British had sixty thousand regular troops here plus about fifteen thousand Auxies and Black and Tans, enough to furnish a western front. And do you know what it is? Youse have the whole bloody bagful of them bet. That's what it is.'

He pushed the paper from him and shouted over his shoulder.

'Do you hear me, Lamb. Give over what you're at and come out and serve a couple of friends and myself with a drink.'

While they protested the Lamb arrived. There was elaborate ritual as he searched the shelves for a bottle of special whiskey.

'Not for me anyway,' Dick said, 'I'm on the wagon. Definitely.'

'We hadn't meant to delay,' Willie said.

'Nor are you expected to,' Cotter agreed. 'I know you're a man with heavy responsibilities. Have this drop for the journey.'

The Lamb poured for the two of them.

'Do you know who you've the honour of serving?'

'If it isn't his identical twin,' the Lamb said, 'it's young Willie Mulhall.'

'Here's to success,' Cotter said, 'and the Irish Republic.'

'Amen to that,' Willie answered.

But his manner was uneasy and after enough conversation to satisfy politeness he managed to get away.

'How does it feel to be a hero?' Dick asked when they went outside. Willie looked grim.

'That was a mistake,' he answered.

'Cotter's a safe man. I wouldn't worry.'

'Cotter's the best in the world maybe; but he's a talker. Oul gab is dangerous.'

'You gave him nothing to gab about.'

'I've started him off. He's known me and my family since I was a child. That's plenty to be going on with.'

'So have I,' Dick said.

'You don't run a public house.'

When they were parting Dick said:

'You mentioned Williamstown earlier. If you'll be around tomorrow, how about a swim there?'

'What time do you go?'

'Mornings if it's fine. Usually around ten.'

'I'll call over for you.'

Dick hesitated a moment. Then he said: 'It's funny I should have met you today. Eileen was talking about you only last night.'

'Was she?' Willie said. Now they were both unsure.

'How is she?'

'In good form. Eileen isn't one to talk a lot, usually.'

'She talked enough with me.'

'That's different, isn't it?'

'We had good times together. Tell her I was asking after her. Is she usually at home mornings?'

'If I tell her you're calling she will. She might come swimming with us.'

'Tell her wild dogs won't keep me away,' Willie said. For the first time in many months he smiled easily.

He spent the evening sitting in with his mother and went to bed early. In the morning as he was coming down the steps a youth whom he recognized as a Fianna Scout was parking his bicycle against the railings. It was a despatch. He read it while the boy waited.

'That's all right,' he said.

The truce, Freddie said, was to be used for intensive training. He was to report back immediately.

Before going up to tell his mother he struck a match and burned the despatch in the hallway. He cut short his farewell. The shock of grief in his mother's face was unbearable. He felt it too much to be able to call and explain to Dick Quinn. Or to Eileen. As he descended the steps a second time, the bells of St Brigids had begun pealing for ten o'clock mass. Even in Chandler's Court there was the faint smell of the sea. The morning was warm and cloudless.

Aloysius Hennessy's interest in the progress of the peace talks was personal and non-political. He was a timid man. On several occasions before the truce he had been on the point of giving up his job as night watchman in a highly flammable premises given over to the manufacture of confectionery. He found it almost unbearable being alone from eight at night until eight in the morning, surrounded at first by streets so utterly deserted because of the curfew that he felt like the last civilian left alive in the world, but which then filled up with army lorries, probing searchlights and military patrols so prone to shoot anything daring to breathe that they threatened nightly to deprive him even of that undesirable distinction. The owners, he well knew, were entrenched loyalists, a circumstance that did nothing to protect the premises from the Black and Tans and everything to attract the notice of the Rebels. There had been two attempts at arson, during one of which he was held at gun point by Black and Tans while the flames were already taking hold of a small storeroom. Only the good sense of an officer got him released in time to deal with the blaze and even then entirely ôn his own. Nobody thought it worthwhile to help him. On a number of occasions he had to lie on his stomach while bullets from a street ambush shattered the glass and whizzed above his head. But it was either that or stay at home listening to abuse from his wife, and he continued to stick it out.

The truce was a great relief. He confessed to a friend that he hardly knew himself and demonstrated the miraculous improvement in his nerves by drinking the pint in front of him without spilling it. When the evening papers of 6 December carried news of the signing of the treaty he made a diversion on his way to work to join the crowd who were cheering outside the Mansion House. It was understood that Mr de Valera was inside. What was not understood was that he was merely chairing a symposium in honour of the poet Dante. It was the six hundredth anniversary of his death.

If there was to be peace over Christmas, Hennessy considered, he could search for seasonal work for two of his eleven children, in the knowledge that they would not be in danger. They were aged fourteen and fifteen respectively. The youngest was just a year old. He mentioned it to his wife.

'Cotter used to take on extra help for the Christmas season,' she suggested.

'That's true,' he agreed, 'There might be a messenger boy needed or an extra hand in the stores.'

When his next free night came he put on the bowler hat that was on the big side and the overcoat that was too long. It was seldom he set off for a public house with his wife's encouragement and benediction. He found that Cotter too was affable and well disposed.

'I see few of the old neighbours these days,' he explained.

'The troubles, I suppose,' Hennessy said.

'That's what I thought. But it's been quiet this few months back and still I don't see them.'

'A lot of them has moved. I've moved myself.'

'Where are you now?'

'A little cottage off Grand Canal Street.'

'That's a step up in the world.'

'Things is better now,' Hennessy said; 'the two oldest can do a man's work and I'm watching regular myself.'

'And why not,' Cotter said, meaning he approved of Hennessy's bit of good fortune.

'But of course it's getting a bit crowded on us.'

'How many is there now?'

'Eleven,' Hennessy confessed.

Cotter looked astounded.

'Have you no shame at all,' he said.

'It's the will of God, I suppose,' Hennessy said, dissociating himself.

Cotter relented.

'Whosever will it is,' he acknowledged, 'it's a handful.'

It seemed to provide an opening, but Hennessy understood the courtesy of decent delay. He finished his drink while they talked of other things and waited until he had started his next before he took it up.

'Do you expect to be busy over the Christmas?'

'If it hasn't picked up by then,' Cotter predicted, 'I can put up the shutters.'

But his gloom was unjustified. The press hailed the treaty as a triumph for Ireland and Sinn Fein and the people at large were as welcoming as the headlines:

PEACE AT LAST
IRELAND A FREE STATE

Almost immediately there were signs that peace had come to stay. Batches of political prisoners were being welcomed at railway stations on their release from English gaols. British troops were already making preparations for their departure. Mr de Valera, of course, had published his disagreement with the treaty terms but his objections were having little impact. By day people went freely about their business. At night there was so much to talk about they filled the public houses. The Christmas trade became so good that when Hennessy got his next opportunity to visit Cotters he was able to sit down in the comforting knowledge that both his boys were earning by helping in the stores and doing errands.

'That's a change for the better,' he remarked to Cotter, noting the full bar.

'Like Christmas long ago,' Cotter agreed, wiping his hands

and face in his apron. He was a large man who sweated easily, with no time now to spread the elbows and squeeze the last bit of news from the daily paper. The Christmas orders required personal supervision. With some a seasonal bonus had to be included: here a free bottle of Tawny wine, there a naggin of whiskey or a couple of ounces of tobacco. Onerous judgments had to be made. Nevertheless he was pleased.

'A bright pair, the two boys,' he said.

Hennessy was happy to hear it.

'We'll be on the pig's back this Christmas,' he said.

'And a bit of peace for 1922, if it lasts.'

'Of course it'll last,' Hennessy said.

'I think so too,' Cotter agreed, 'and I'll tell you why. Every last man of the militants is out and about. I get a lot of them in here.'

'I got a lot of them myself at one time,' Hennessy said, remembering a number of ambushes, 'too bloody much, to tell you the truth.'

'One of the first of them was a one-time neighbour of yours, Willie Mulhall. I haven't seen him since.'

'Barney Mulhall's son. He was Citizen army, I thought?'

'What's the difference. They were all equally handy with the gun.'

'They were indeed.'

Hennessy reflected.

'There's peace and a proper government to be formed,' he added gravely. 'I trust they'll prove as efficient now with the plough as they were in the past with the sword.'

Cotter was impressed both by the style and the sentiment. Several customers to whom he subsequently retailed it praised its felicity.

Hennessy shared with his family the best Christmas dinner they could remember. He was even able to buy a few cheap toys for the younger children. And despite the growing split in Sinn Fein and the resignation of Mr de Valera as president, he continued to look forward to a new year of peace and progress. Later, when a body of the anti-treaty dissidents took over the

Four Courts he told himself it was merely a stunt. The Four Courts almost overlooked the confectionery premises so optimism was a necessity. His timidity demanded it.

'Come inside.' Cornelius Moloney said grimly, 'there's something I wanted to show you.'

Mr O'Sheehan, blinded from stepping from the May sunshine into the dimness of the shop, held the counter briefly while his eyes adjusted and said, 'You seem worried.'

'Too bloody true I'm worried,' said Cornelius, 'let me show you.'

He led O'Sheehan into the back parlour and sat him in a chair. 'Have a look at those.'

The parlour was brighter. O'Sheehan examined a bundle of pamphlets that had been thrust into his hands:

The New Traitors
On What Side Are You.
Craig, Collins, Churchill
or
Dev, Stack, Brugha
The Empire
or The Republic.

'When did you get these?'

'Yesterday. A group of them stamped in and slapped them down in front of me. Hand them round – or pack up, I was told.'

'They were in earnest, you think?'

Cornelius, who had an experienced eye for activists who meant precisely what they said, assured him they were.

'It's a nice prospect,' he said, 'to be bombed out or burned out by one side or the other. Me that gave shelter to the best of them when the fight was against the British.'

'We may have civil war.'

'If we do, the noble cause we so often conferred about has taken a strange turn.'

'We are going to be a show to the world,' O'Sheehan agreed. They both fell silent.

'I have asked you to come so that I could put some questions to you, if I may,' the Prior said.

'Certainly,' O'Sheehan replied.

They were seated together at the window. The Prior's study was familiar ground by now. They had sat often to talk of the library, the political and military situation, the literature of Ireland. The only subject never mentioned had been religion.

'You may find my questions too personal. If so . . .'

'Please ask what you wish.'

'Do you remember the circumstances in which you arrived here in the first instance?'

'Only vaguely.'

'There had been shooting during the night – an ambush. You were lying in the grounds, unconscious from a head injury. There was a rifle beside you. Does that help you?'

'No,' O'Sheehan said.

'You don't remember yet how it came about?'

'No.'

'That's what I've suspected. You are still suffering the effects of that head injury. Do you remember any earlier military engagement?'

'Many of them. I have always resisted the ancient enemy; as a Fenian, as a United man, as a follower of Sarsfield, in fact whenever the opportunity arose. Before the British it was the men from Scandinavia, the Fair Strangers we sometimes called them. I resisted them too.'

The Prior retained his composure. He asked gravely, 'You are speaking figuratively, I take it?'

'Not at all. Quite factually.'

'Are you telling me that you are a thousand years old?'

'More than that,' O'Sheehan said, 'nearer two, I imagine. It is very difficult to calculate.'

'It seems a great deal in excess of the allotted span,' the Prior suggested, still without any hint of scepticism.

'Greatly in excess. I have often wished it would end.'

'And you believe you can remember events over all that period?'

'From time to time,' O'Sheehan said.

'At this moment, what comes to mind?'

'The little cell of St Feichin, who had a blackbird to fetch him down apples which were on branches out of reach. I recall also a tower burning when Cromwell sacked Drogheda and a wretch who was trapped crying from the flames: "Christ damn me, I burn, I burn." '

'These could be things you have read about.'

'They could. But they are not.'

O'Sheehan spoke with unshakeable belief. The Prior, searching for the next question, hesitated.

'If you believe all this to be true, then who are you?'

'Oisin, son of Finn, Chief of the Fianna.'

'You believe that possible?'

'Whatever is, is possible. Let me recite the maxims of initiation:

If armed service be your ambition, be equable in your Lord's house, but surly in the narrow pass.

If he is not at fault, do not chastise your hound.

Do not censure one of grave repute; do not stand up to take part in a brawl; have nothing to do with a wicked man.

Be not violent to the lowly; show your gentleness to women and the little ones who creep the floor; to poets be gentle also. Avoid swaggering speech. Your lord do not forsake.

To a chief do not belittle his people, for that is unmannerly. Be no tale bearer. Utter no falsehoods. Be not talkative nor rashly censorious. Do not stir up strife. Be no frequenter of the ale house. Do not carp at the old. Have no dealings with a mean man. Dispense your meat freely. Have no niggard for your familiar. Stick to your gear. Hold fast to your arms until the stern fight with its weapon glitter is ended. Be more apt to give than to deny. Follow ever after gentleness.'

'These are good precepts,' the Prior said, 'but they can be got from a book.'

'Have you had them from a book, Father Prior?'

'No,' the Prior confessed.

'I had them myself from Finn, and heard him give them also to Geena, the son of Luga. It happened at Lough Lena, in Killarney.'

The Prior spread out his arms. It was as though he were about to invoke a blessing.

'If you say so,' he said.

He was acknowledging that there seemed to be nothing he could do. It made him sad. He had developed much affection for the large, grey-haired, dignified man who seemed at the moment to be lost in a trance. What age was he? His middle fifties perhaps. With a well, if oddly, stocked mind.

'You know so much about Ireland,' the Prior said. It was meant in admiration.

'In a way,' O'Sheehan conceded, 'I *am* Ireland.'

He was entirely serious.

IV

In June 1922 the leaders of the Four Courts garrison marched openly to the churchyard at Bodenstown to renew their Republican oath and to reassert their anti-treaty inflexibility. They laid wreaths, they observed a minute's silence. The birds of summer warbled unconcerned through their speeches, the sun shone, the long grasses and the heavy hedges absorbed the sunlight in drowsy silence. The country at large was unimpressed. When the elections were completed the poll was heavily pro-treaty. LABOUR AND THE TREATY SWEEP THE COUNTRY, the newspapers said. The newspapers, it was clear, approved. Hardly had they announced the results than another and sensational report demanded attention. Sir Henry Wilson, Chief of the Imperial General Staff, had been shot dead outside his London home. British anger exploded. Official Ireland made sounds of shock and condemnation. But the man in the street, unhampered by diplomatic obligation, knew Sir Henry had openly stirred up sectarian feeling in Belfast and found his assassination understandable. There were four thousand Catholic families already homeless as a result of the pogrom and thousands more were seeking refuge in the South. If there was dying to be done, no harm if Sir Henry did his share. He had died for his convictions. Humbler people were dying too, unconsoled by any conviction whatever.

'The trouble with the world we live in,' Cotter told a customer who had forecast a magnificent military funeral, 'is that we've too many military funerals, too many governments, too many bloody armies.'

He was having a bad run with the horses. It always affected his humour.

'One thing is certain now. They'll have to root them rebels out of the Four Courts. Or stand forever disgraced.'

A few days later it happened. Hennessy, taking an unofficial break from his watching duties at the factory nearby, jerked awake to the sound of the explosion and a shower of flaky dust from the ceiling. A second bang shattered a window. It was 4 a.m. on Wednesday, 28 June. The field guns across the river, he knew, had opened up on the Four Courts.

'Christ have mercy,' he begged and flung himself to the floor. It quivered under a third and fourth while his heart beat with a force that threatened to choke him. He lay as still as he could. The bombardment continued for over an hour. He could hear brickwork collapsing in the streets outside and the shattering of glass as he lay transfixed by fear until the first brief lull occurred. He would be safer, he thought, in the small office on the ground floor. As the silence continued he moved towards the stairs and descended on tiptoe as though the sound of a footstep would set the guns snarling about him again. The office was undisturbed. On the wooden table the remains of his nightly snack lay as he had left it, the slices of bread among scattered crumbs on the spread-out piece of newspaper, the box with a compartment at one end for tea and at the other for sugar, the can of condensed milk with dribbled bars like white paint down the sides. The clock on the wall told him it was almost six.

He crept to the window. Sunlight was filtering into the cobbled laneway. The smell of cordite and burning timber mingled with that of the river. There seemed to be nobody about. Until there was, he decided, he would stay put. He thought a cup of tea might steady his nerves and had just lit the gas ring when the guns opened up again. The match burned his fingers and he dropped it with a cry. But he had the presence of mind to switch off the gas before crouching in a corner.

Throughout the day the same pattern continued. Whenever there was a lull he moved about, made a cup of tea, finished the little food that had been left. When the firing resumed he retired to the protection of his corner. By nightfall he had lost all will to face the peril of the streets. When morning came again the heavy firing convinced him that to venture out of doors would still be madness. Hunger gave him the courage to make another cup of tea. He did so by re-stewing the dregs of the previous day. He had no bread left so he opened a box of bullseyes and settled down to breakfast off them. Their minty flavour mingled unpleasantly with the sour taste of tannic acid. But he was hungry. Beggars, he told his protesting stomach, could not be choosers.

Nobody reported for work. The deserted factory became a private world, a place of eerie silence during lulls, a quivering hermitage whenever the bombardment recommenced, dust floating where light poured through the windows, a sweet and treacly smell pervading every corner.

During the afternoon rifle fire replaced the heavy crash of shells for a period, then it too stopped. In the late evening he heard footsteps on the cobbles and peered cautiously through the windows, hoping they were those of civilians and that the streets were now safe to use. But the men who passed in small groups carried rifles and wore bandoliers. They were republican combatants. As he debated whether to call out to them for information, an explosion rocked the street once again. The sound of falling masonry and splintering glass sent him scurrying back to his corner. Were they getting out because the whole neighbourhood was going to be demolished? In desperation, despite the sounds of bombardment he went to the window again. A man with a bandolier and rifle was huddled in the gateway opposite and obviously in pain. Hennessy peered intently through the glass.

'Willie,' he shouted suddenly, 'Willie Mulhall.'

To see someone he knew after the long hours alone drove him almost frantic. He heaved at the lower frame of the window. It had not been opened for years and was wedged tight, but he succeeded in opening it.

'Willie Mulhall,' he yelled.

Explosions and rifle fire echoed through the laneway as Willie Mulhall flung himself across it and climbed through. The left sleeve of his jacket was ripped and bloodstained.

'You've been hit.'

'A bloody big piece of glass,' Willie said. 'I haven't had a chance to look at the damage.'

'Let me take off your jacket.'

Hennessy did so very gingerly. There was a deep, three-inch gash along the muscle. 'It's bad.'

'But nothing fatal,' Willie said, examining it.

'It's bleeding a lot.'

'You'll find a bandage and cotton wool somewhere,' Willie said, indicating the discarded bandolier. Hennessy searched inexpertly but with eventual success. He began to attend to the wound.

'Stuff the cotton wool into it,' Willie said. 'Go on. Well in. I don't want to bleed to death.'

Hennessy, reluctantly, did as he was told. Then he wound the bandage tight about it. Willie's face screwed up as he did so.

'Jesus,' he said, 'it bloody hurts.'

He sat down and struggled to control the pain. His face was grimy and unshaven. When the wound became easier he stared at Hennessy and said: 'I should know you.'

'Aloysius Hennessy. From Chandler's Court. I knew your father.'

'So you did,' Willie said. He looked about him. 'What are you doing here?'

'I'm the night watchman. I've been trapped here since Wednesday.'

'You did well to stay put. The Free Staters have two eighteen pounders on the far bank. They've been lobbing shells at us at close range. With the compliments of Winston Churchill. The British Army supplied them.'

Hennessy made no comment. In a shooting war he was strictly non-partisan. They could decide it between them. Willie noticed the gas ring and the condensed milk.

'A cup of tea would be no bad man,' he suggested.

'There's none left.'

'You'll find some where you found the bandage.'

Hennessy searched again. He unearthed a tin with two compartments like his own and something that looked like a tobacco tin.

'What's this?' he asked.

'A collapsible mug.'

'How does it work?.

'Take off the lid and pull the rest upwards.

Hennessey did so. A series of metal rings interlocked to form a cup. Its ingenuity took his attention momentarily from the peril about him.

'Wonderful,' he said.

'Like a melodeon,' Willie commented. 'Is there anything to eat?'

'Only these,' Hennessy said, showing him the tin of bullseyes.

'Is that what you've been living on?'

'There may be some chocolate upstairs,' Hennessy said, 'but I haven't the nerve to go up and see.'

'Chocolate would fill the bill,' Willie said. 'Whereabouts?'

Hennessy pointed the way. When Willie had gone he put the kettle on to boil. By the time he returned the tea was made. He had unearthed a box packed with bars of chocolate. They sat down to eat. The chocolate was a great improvement on the bullseyes.

'I remember you well now,' Willie said. 'Are you still in Chandler's Court?'

'No. We moved.'

'I thought you might have word of my mother,' Willie explained. 'I haven't seen her in months.'

He pushed the collapsible mug aside.

'I could do with some sleep. Will you keep watch?'

Hennessy nodded.

'Can I trust you?'

'Your father would have.'

'I think I can. Sooner or later we'll have to find our way out of here. I'll do it better after a few hours' sleep.'

'How long?'

'Three hours will do. If nothing happens meanwhile.'

'I'll keep watch,' Hennessy assured him. Willie put his jacket under his head and stretched out on the floor. For a while the throbbing of the wound kept him awake. Then fatigue won and his eyes closed.

Hennessy remained in his corner, alert and watchful, but less frightened now that he had companionship. The room grew dusky about him as the long summer evening deepened into night. At intervals the bombardment was renewed and then died away. Spasmodic rifle shots filled the gaps. The sky beyond the laneway glowed with fire and the smell of burning became heavier. He lit the small candle and wondered, when three hours had gone by, if he should waken Willie or let him sleep on. He was breathing easily and lightly and deep in sleep like a child. Yet this man would kill another without a second's thought. For what? For Mother Ireland, of course. But where did he find the nerve to face British soldiers and Black and Tans, to lie in ambush on mountain roads or to snipe from roof-tops that were likely to be blown from under him? The Free State soldiers who had been bombarding the Four Courts were once his comrades-in-arms. Did that mean civil war was a reality? Was the country to be devastated yet again because de Valera and a few like him found the Oath of Allegiance too bitter a pill to swallow? The people had voted for the treaty. Did that not count? Michael Collins was for the treaty. So was Arthur Griffith. If the Republicans won the British would return in a week. Where would that leave things? Back to Act One.

At four hours he shook Willie gently by the shoulder.

'I don't like to disturb you, but it's four hours since you popped off.'

'What time is it?'

'Just gone four.'

'Nothing out of the way?'

'No. The guns is still at it.'

'We'll have a cup of tea.'

Hennessy set about preparing it. Morning light was creeping into the room once more. By the time the tea was ready the candle had become pale and redundant. Hennessy blew it out.

'Here you are,' he said, intrigued again by the ingenuity of the collapsible mug. Willie propped his back against the wall and drank in silence.

'Our lads will surrender today,' he said at last, 'they're only holding on to let the rest of us get clear. Is there a way to the roof?'

'There is, but I wouldn't chance it.

'We'll have a look later on. Then I'll try to pick up with the rest. I remember you better now. You lived in the top flat.'

'Just under the roof. It used to let in. Rashers Tierney lived in the basement.'

'A man with a limp.'

'He played the tin whistle.'

'And starved to death. I remember it.'

So did Hennessy. He had found the body. He pushed the recollection from his mind.

'With a little more help from the British TUC,' Willie said, 'my father and others would have changed all that.'

'The British were never our friends,' Hennessy said. It was a safe and diplomatic sentiment, he thought.

'The British working class were our friends,' Willie contradicted. 'No better to be found. The working classes of the world are all friends of each other. Or ought to be. Capitalism keeps them apart. Have you a cigarette?'

Hennessy explored his waistcoat pockets and unearthed a handful of butts.

'That's the extent of it,' he said, showing the assortment. Willie selected one and Hennessy lit it for him. He inhaled deeply.

'I once hoped for a Workers' Republic,' Willie confessed, 'it's no go now. The Free Staters don't want it. Neither do the Republicans. Only a handful care a damn about it. So what am I risking my neck for?'

'For principle,' Hennessy suggested.

'For my father,' Willie said. 'My father was a great man.'

'You should sleep again,' Hennessy told him. 'I'll keep watch in case of trouble.'

'I'd appreciate that. There wasn't much of it doing in the Fourt Courts.'

He stretched out again. Hennessy waited until he was deeply in slumber before tidying away.

Hennessy, watching the morning strengthen, wondered if he would ever see home again. There was none of the usual noises; no traffic, no footsteps, no one shouting to another, no children playing. If this was Irish freedom, the new Irish Free State, it was a shaky start. He examined the tea situation. Enough for two last cups, he calculated, if he mixed the few fresh leaves that remained with the dregs left in the pot. There was any god's amount of chocolate, for what it was worth. The smell of it was now enough to put him off. They were mean enough to charge him for what had been eaten. Stop it from his wages. If the factory wasn't blown to pieces before the finish.

At ten o'clock he wakened Willie again. Over the stewed tea Willie asked him, 'Can you use a needle and thread?'

'I'm no tailor,' Hennessy confessed, 'but I can put in a stitch.'

'I want you to tack up that rip in my jacket. It's a giveaway if I run into any Free Staters.'

'Are you going to chance the streets?'

'We can't stay here forever. You ought to do the same.'

'I don't think I can face it.'

'Stick with me. You'll be all right.'

'Where's the needle and thread?'

'Where you got the other stuff.'

Hennessy found it. 'You travel prepared, I'll say that.'

'You have to eat and you have to look after this and that,' Willie said. 'Revolution is only five per cent shooting.'

Hennessy carefully stitched the rip in the sleeve. The jacket was dark serge and the thread black so the stitching was only visible on close scrutiny. Even then it was unexceptional, the kind of job any housewife would make of repairing a husband's coat. Hennessy helped him to put it on.

'Now we'll have a look at the roof,' Willie decided. His words were drowned in a sudden and intensive renewal of the bombardment. Hennessy dived for the corner. Willie moved close to the wall. Masonry and glass seemed to be tumbling incessantly. To Hennessy it lasted uncountable hours. When it stopped and they were able to talk again Willie said, 'Christ – that was some pasting.'

Before Hennessy could answer another explosion rocked the office. It was unlike the preceding ones. It had a different sound.

'What was that?'

Willie said grimly: 'We had stuff in the Four Courts with us. If I'm any judge the whole bloody lot has gone up. Which way to the roof?'

Hennessy led him to the top landing and pointed out the access door. They went through. Out towards the river, above a jumble of roofs, a great black cloud of smoke billowed towards the sky. The guns had fallen silent.

'That's that,' Willie said. They returned to the office, where Willie shaved and told Hennessy to do likewise. The result satisfied him.

'That's better,' he said. 'You're a civilian, but with that growth on you, you didn't look like it. Now let's go.'

He pushed the rifle and bandolier behind a press.

'I can't,' Hennessy said.

'If you stay on here you're likely to be caught up in street fighting or blown sky high.'

'Jesus help us.'

'Amen,' Willie said. 'Come on.'

They followed the laneway to the river wall but had to dodge into a doorway as Free State troops streamed down the main thoroughfare.

'We'll double back,' Willie said.

They passed the factory again and began to work their way towards O'Connell Street.

'Our crowd will be in occupation of the hotels there,' Willie told him, 'but it should be quiet enough for the present. If it isn't, I'll try to find a way through for you.'

Near O'Connell Bridge shooting recommenced, then began to spread out on all sides. Telling Hennessy to remain in cover, Willie went forward to investigate. He was gone a long time. When he returned he said, 'O'Connell Bridge is impassable. I don't know about the lower quays. We'll bear up north of the Pillar and see what happens.'

They followed laneways at the rear of O'Connell Street, a narrow, tortuous maze where slaughter houses smelled of offal and the flotsam of vegetable stores lay scattered along the cobbles. As they worked their way south again the firing came nearer and nearer. Eventually Willie stopped.

'I have to report to the Hamman Hotel. Try getting across Butt Bridge.'

'Supposing it's under fire.'

'Then you'll have to swim,' Willie said, half smiling, 'because you'll have run out of bridges.'

'I'll stay where I am.' Hennessy looked white and sick. He was on the border of panic.

'If you hang about here, you're just as likely to come to harm.'

He waited for Hennessy to move. Instead he lay back against the wall and closed his eyes. He was surrendering to whatever might happen. It was the surest way, Willie knew, to sudden death. Of all deaths it would be the humblest and least noticed. To Free Staters and Republicans alike, or most of them, Hennessy was entirely dispensable. Then what was the revolution about?

Willie reached out his hand and shook Hennessy.

'Come on,' he said gently, 'we'll go together.'

They explored cautiously. Gardiner Street and Marlborough Street were raked by fire. So too was Talbot Street but if they were to make it to the river it had to be crossed.

'Walk,' Willie said, 'don't run. When we get across, take cover.'

They waited for a lull. Willie took Hennessy by the arm.

'Now,' he said.

They stepped out from the corner and started to cross. Hennessy was aware of bright sunlight, a street that was empty and seemed immeasurably wide. And Silence. The silence was unbearable. He wanted to cry out to break it. He began to tremble.

'Steady,' Willie said.

A single shot rang out.

'It's all right,' he said, tightening his grip on the trembling arm. 'It's not for us.'

Walking slowly, they reached the far pavement at last. Willie pushed Hennessy into a doorway and waited for him to recover. There were beads of sweat on his own forehead which he brushed away.

'That's the worst part over.'

He said it to reassure Hennessy, but so it turned out. They negotiated the laneway behind Liberty Hall without incident and found Butt Bridge uninvolved and passable. Turning eastwards they followed the quayside for a while, then relinquished it, out of long habit, by way of Chandler's Court.

'Nothing happening this side. You'll be all right from here on.'

'I will,' Hennessy said. 'I don't know how to thank you.'

'You could buy me a box of bullseyes sometime.'

'God,' Hennessy said, 'that's a diet I won't easily forget.

They shook hands.

'Safe home,' Willie said.

When Hennessy had gone he began to assess his own position. It would be difficult to find a way to get back to Hamman's Hotel. However, the wound was a legitimate excuse. It still needed attention. The best course would be to have it attended to at a hospital, then present himself at Battalion Headquarters in York Street. On his way back from the hospital he could call in briefly on his mother. Meanwhile a drink would do no harm.

Cotter was surprised to see him.

'That's terrible work in the centre of town,' he said. 'You do well to keep out of it.'

Willie took his drink to avoid answering. The misunderstanding was convenient.

'I'm told the crowd in the Four Courts surrendered.'

'They hadn't much alternative. The Free Staters were using British field pieces,' Willie told him.

'And what were the Four Courts gang using – German rifles. I don't see that the nationality of the gun matters. The people spoke through the ballot box. Is that not enough? Is there to be no respect for the voice of the people? If Dev didn't want the treaty why didn't he go over himself to do the negotiating, instead of sending Griffith and Collins?'

'It's a good question,' Willie said, 'but Dev is no longer involved.'

'Are you joking me? Didn't he call for support for the crowd in the Four Courts?'

'I didn't see that.'

Cotter looked astonished.

'Then you haven't been reading the papers. He's been encouraging the civil war and now he has it – with a vengeance. Brother against brother. What's that but bloody cannibalism.'

It was. That was the part that made the heart sick.

'There was a time,' Willie said, 'when both sides wanted a republic. Some won't settle for less.'

'And some think we got a hell of a lot more than we ever hoped for. The elections answered that one.'

'The people have no right to do wrong.'

'And who's to be the judge of what's right or what's wrong – some fellow with a gun, is it?'

'Are you satisfied with the Free State?'

'I was satisfied with a bit of peace,' Cotter said. 'Now we're worse off than ever.'

'We're bad enough,' Willie agreed. Quite suddenly he had grown weak and tired. The wound was throbbing again. He had no savour for argument, no hope in the future, no interest even in the outcome. He thought the drink might be to blame and pushed it from him unfinished. Cotter noticed.

'Are you offended?' he asked.

'No, not a bit,' Willie said, 'I've remembered something I should be doing.'

At the hospital he had his wound attended to and began to feel better. There was little traffic about but the sound of distant firing had increased. It seemed to be concentrated still about the city centre. As he turned again into Chandler's Court, his thoughts on what he should say to his mother, a voice close to him said:

'Willie Mulhall, you're a black stranger.'

He turned. It was Eileen Quinn. She was smiling but unsure, remembering, he knew, his failure to call. It was a failure that had bothered himself on and off for a long time.

'I haven't been around,' he said. 'It must be a year now.'

'It is,' she said. 'You met Dick.'

'I was to call around to see you and go for a swim. I haven't forgotten. It didn't work out.'

'Nothing ever does, these times.'

'I got called back.'

She knew what he meant.

'Are you mixed up in it this time as well?'

He hesitated. Her face was open and concerned. He felt, as always with Eileen, the tug of confidence and sympathy.

'I was in the Four Courts but got out in time.'

'I hope you'll have the sense to leave it at that.'

'How can I? Do you think I'd desert the lads?'

'I think you should all have your heads examined,' she told him.

He smiled at her.

'I suppose we should.'

'Will it spread?'

'Not to Chandler's Court. A few stray bullets would bring

it down about your ears. Public buildings and hotels are safe.'

'Are you calling on your mother?'

'For half an hour. Then back into harness.'

'You look worn out,' Eileen said.

He heard the noise of a lorry approaching from behind him and saw Eileen's face stiffen.

'Free Staters,' he said, 'don't turn around.'

As the noise came nearer she linked her arm through his and led him away. She pressed close to him.

'Look as though you're walking me out,' she suggested.

They strolled slowly together until the lorry had passed. It slackened speed as it came abreast of them but rounded the corner without stopping. As they turned back again Eileen continued to link him.

'Just in case,' she said.

He had time to be aware of her closeness. It was more than merely pleasant and agreeable.

'Thanks for what you did just now.'

'Would they have picked you up?'

'If they recognized me, it's on the cards, but they've probably more on their minds at present.'

They walked in silence, their arms still linked.

'This is old times,' he remarked.

'That's what I was thinking.'

'Some day or other, we'll be able to have that swim.'

'If you manage to remember. Or don't get called away.'

'You're a persuasive argument against dying for the republic.'

She stopped.

'Don't say things like that.'

He had upset her.

'Never mind,' he offered. An apology. At his mother's house they stopped to part.

'Well. Take care of yourself,' she said.

'Remember our swim.'

As she went down the street she paused to turn round and smile at him. Again he felt the little stab of pain and happiness. He waved.

When she had gone he turned to climb the steps but paused at the distant sound of a lorry. He concentrated closely, trying to chart its direction. He became certain it was approaching. If it did and there was anyone in it who might recognize him, the last place to be would be in front of his mother's house. Instead of climbing the steps he decided to resume his walk along the street. He had only begun to do so when it rounded the corner, slowed down and pulled in just ahead of him. He backed against the railings as they clambered out to surround him.

'Just as I thought,' the officer said.

He recognized Joe Maher, a colleague he had campaigned with when the fight was against the British.

'I felt it was you first time round,' Maher told him, 'so we doubled back to make sure.'

Heads were beginning to appear at the windows of Chandler's Court.

'You were in the Four Courts, Willie,' Maher continued, 'Have you opted out?'

'No. I'll keep my Republican Oath.'

'By sniping at old pals.'

'By fighting until we have a republic.'

'You're a long way from the action.'

'I wouldn't think so,' Willie said, looking pointedly at the ring of rifles and Free State uniforms.

'Are you armed?'

'Find out.'

More windows were opening and people were gathering at hall doors. Willie wondered if his mother was watching. He resisted the temptation to find out by looking around him. Her sight was hardly good enough to recognize him at such a distance.

'All right – search him.'

They took the revolver from his pocket.

'I could have you shot here and now for this,' Maher said. They wouldn't, though. Too many people were watching. He turned the revolver over in his hand.

'Using it on your friends now, Willie?'

'All in the same cause.'

'We're the Irish government, Willie. The people said so.'

Willie said nothing. The gun was evidence enough. He was in grave trouble.

'Wheel him in,' Maher ordered.

When they gripped the wounded arm roughly Willie went white with pain.

'My arm is hurt,' he said.

'Take it easy,' Maher told them. They let him walk to the lorry. The people at the windows were calling to one another. He heard them as he climbed into the lorry but refused to look about him.

'We're taking you to Mountjoy,' Maher told him.

The lorry began to move.

'You can be executed for carrying arms,' Maher said, 'so be thinking about your defence.'

It was then he heard his mother's scream. Her voice rang out above the others and above the noise of the lorry. It filled the street.

'Jesus, Mary and Joseph,' it said, 'Willie. My son. Willie, Willie.'

He refused to look up. It was as though rough hands were tearing open his heart. As the lorry gathered speed and the engine noise rose higher the voice was obliterated. Bodies lurched against him when it turned the corner. They had left Chandler's Court and were travelling swiftly across the city where the now familiar smell filled the air. O'Connell Street was burning.

V

Cornelius Moloney finally took possession of the licensed premises at 144 High Street, Dublin, in October 1922, a week after the birth of his second child, a daughter. There had been times in the course of the affair when he wondered aloud to O'Sheehan if instead of buying the business he should spend the money having his head examined. His journeys to town took him through discouraging streets where burned and bullet-marked houses remained in the wake of open-street fighting that had ended in the collapse and withdrawal of the Republican forces. The war had changed to one of ambushes, reprisals, attacks on government ministers and their property. In August a cattle dealer he found himself dining with had assured him that the rest of the country was in the same plight.

'They're every bloody place you care to talk about,' he said.

In Clonmel he himself had been hauled out of his motor car by Free State troops searching for Republican leaders. A colleague had been shot dead in Carrick-on-Shannon by a Republican patrol who mistook him for a Free State officer. The unfortunate man left a widow and seven children. In Cork he had to edge along a mile of country road past Free Staters moving artillery forward for the attack on the city. The effect on the cattle trade was disastrous.

Cornelius knew it was likely to have the same consequences for the Society of Licensed Vintners. But he persisted. If he was to be ruined it might as well be in Dublin city as in a country village. One of his visits coincided with the funeral of the President, Arthur Griffith, who had died, many said, of a broken heart. Ten days later the city was at a standstill again as it paid its last respects to Michael Collins, shot in an ambush in his native county of Cork. The air of heartbreak and despair was unbelievable, he told O'Sheehan. A notice chalked on a wall in huge and uneven letters expressed the prevailing mood and pledged:

COLLINS STOOD BY US
WE'LL STAND BY HIM.

It was hard to read because his eyes misted over, Cornelius confessed. But he was able to describe the scene: the gun carriage drawn by six horses, the piled-up wreaths, the masses of troops moving at a slow pace, the bands playing a dead march or, when they stopped, the great drum keeping the rhythm steady with its sombre and muffled tap. Naturally, no business could be done that day.

'Where will it end?' was his despairing thought.

Nevertheless his instinct pushed him on. The site had advantages: part of a busy street which served as a shopping centre for the small cottages, the crowded tenements and flats that surrounded it. There was a trade union office and meeting rooms a few yards away and further down a large Roman Catholic church which would provide extra custom after Novenas, missions, retreats, weddings, funerals. If for nothing else, at least times were good for funerals.

'And for attendance at confessions too, I understand,' O'Sheehan added by way of enquiry. It was his first visit to the new premises. He had come to wish the venture well.

'A remarkable upsurge,' Cornelius agreed.

O'Sheehan was amused.

'There's nothing like the smell of sudden death for encouraging the conscientious practice of religion,' he said. 'I've often remarked it.'

'A man likes to be prepared,' Cornelius explained.

It was a subject on which they differed. O'Sheehan was non-practising. They were in the upper room, well away from the window which overlooked the street. The street lamps outside were glazed over by soft November rain, the tram wires a few feet below window level disputed at times with a passing trolley and threw out a crackle of blue flame. O'Sheehan had a question.

'This pastoral of the bishops condemning the Republicans,' he asked. 'Does it mean they're excommunicated?'

'I don't know if they're actually excommunicated – technically, that is,' Cornelius answered, 'but they're denied the sacraments. No absolution for sins, no access to Holy Communion, that sort of thing. It's a heavy penalty.'

'If they serve their country in conscience, they serve their God, whoever that God happens to be,' O'Sheehan asserted.

'Begod then, for a believing Catholic it's not as simple as that,' Cornelius objected. He jabbed a finger a few times in the direction of the floor at their feet. 'Let him get the bullet when he's defying the authority of his pastors and he's down in the book for a trip to the other place – in *secula seculorum*. It's a shocking prospect.'

'And the Fenians who were excommunicated. And the United Men before them? Are they all burning forever in the company of Lucifer?'

'God is Merciful too,' Cornelius said. 'We mustn't presume to know all His ways.' But he was uneasy. It was a thought that had troubled him from time to time.

'If the bishops are right,' O'Sheehan decided, 'hell could turn out a better St Patrick's Day parade than ever heaven could.'

'God protect us,' Cornelius answered. He was genuinely shocked. O'Sheehan might take the matter lightly. But there were young men in Mountjoy under sentence of death for carrying arms. Were they being refused absolution? He was a man of simple faith. The thought horrified him.

Outside Mountjoy Prison, oblivious of wet pavements and the biting wind of a December evening, people knelt and recited the rosary. There had been yet another execution that morning. There would be many more as the policy of government reprisal hardened. Inside the prison Willie Mulhall lay on his cell mattress and wondered if he might be the next to be awakened in the small hours by a hand laid on his shoulder and the voice of a warder repeating his name. They gave no warning. You were roused from sleep, told to dress and wash and led away. It had happened a dozen times already. He could hear the voices raised in prayer outside. If they led him out to die, would he accept the bishops' pastoral in return for the privilege of last confession and absolution? He thought not. Instead he would offer to God the young years he had sacrificed, the opportunities for happiness and enjoyment he had turned his back on. Eileen Quinn, for instance. It was a kind of celibacy being a guerilla fighter. If he was wrong, it was in good faith. He wanted freedom for his country, not for himself. More than that he wanted an end to the daily cruelties endured by the poor. God would hardly quarrel with that. The chaplain had explained that since they were shot and not hanged there was an element of hope. Death by hanging was practically instantaneous, but in shooting life lingered for some precious seconds in which the chaplain could dash forward to administer conditional absolution. He had intended it as a crumb of comfort, but its effects had been to put many of them off going to mass at all. Some were furious at his insensitivity. Some laughed at him. It filled Willie Mulhall with contempt for an outlook that reduced salvation to a game of snakes and ladders. He stayed away from mass. Nevertheless he prayed each morning and night. It was partly for love of God. Even more it was an innate loyalty to something inseparable from his concept of Ireland. Like the voices reciting the rosary outside. Later they would sing hymns and shout messages of comfort. That in itself was a rejection of the pastoral.

The rosary continued while the guards, heavily armed and alert for any change of mood, manned the walls and the gateways but made no move to interfere. Freddie Lindon was noting their disposition. He was on the fringe of the crowd and moved position casually from time to time, now mingling with passers-by, now stopping to join absentmindedly in the prayers. His object was to get to a house near the gaol. The crowd offered cover and safety. 'Easy does it', he said to his two companions. It was merely encouragement. They knew how to proceed. They had instructions to sink a shaft in the scullery in an effort to tunnel under the gaol. It would be a long assignment and not to his liking. Orders had also been issued for the assassination of nine members of the Free State government. That would have been more to his liking. It required alertness in the open streets, split-second timing, faultless co-ordination. He was a soldier, not a navvy. Nevertheless, it had to be done.

By the time the hymn singing started they were clear of the crowd and safe to continue their journey. But the vicinity was always dangerous and he peered ahead, assembling details of the darkened street.

'Road clear,' he said.

The terraced house was separated from a side wall of the

gaol only by the width of the roadway, dangerously close. It had to be so. An elderly man admitted them in silence, then disappeared while they went to examine the scullery. It was at the rear of the house with a door that gave access to a tiny yard with a high wall. They returned indoors to discuss it. Gallagher, the engineer, thought the yard ideal because of the height of the wall. It gave privacy.

'Until we have to get over it in a hurry,' Freddie said.

He turned to the other man, Ivory. 'Tell them we'll need a ladder.'

'They can send it with the props. A rope ladder I suppose.'

'That'd fill the bill fine. When can we start?'

'Tomorrow morning,' Gallagher said.

That was agreed. The yard was small but between it and the space inside the house there would be room enough, Gallagher reckoned, to store all the earth that would have to be moved.

'Christ,' Freddie groaned. He foresaw weeks of digging and removing the stuff.

'It takes all sort of things to make a war,' Ivory said cheerfully. He set about lighting the fire for them. Then he went off to make tea. He was small and stout, with black hair that curled over his forehead. He liked to keep busy.

'The way to think about it is,' Gallagher suggested, 'a lot of friends inside may owe their lives to this tunnel.'

'If it succeeds.'

'We can try.'

'We're too bloody close to the place. The guards have only to lean over to look in the windows.'

'You have to be as near as you can,' Gallagher said, 'and it has to be a safe house.'

'There's a particular butty of mine in there,' Freddie said. 'He's Willie Mulhall. Only for that I'd report that the plan is crazy.'

Ivory returned with the tea.

'Who's the bloke who let us in?'

'He's all right,' Freddie said. 'Guaranteed material. Don't worry.'

'He's reading a book in the kitchen and talked a bit to me in Irish. A decent soul. What happens to him if we're raided?'

'They'll shoot him out of hand, I imagine,' Freddie said. He was unconcerned.

'Couldn't we take him with us?'

'That could be a disaster. You have to think quickly.'

'He can climb a ladder, surely to God,' Ivory pressed. Gallagher came in with support.

'All it means is briefing him carefully and maybe a couple of rehearsals. Would you let the Staters get him?'

Freddie shrugged.

'If one of you cares to be responsible for him, go ahead.'

'I don't mind looking after him,' Ivory offered.

'Very well. When we're working out that bit count him in. I suppose he can take his chance.'

They brooded in silence on the possibilities.

'That fire makes a difference,' Ivory remarked. It was burning brightly.

'So does the tea,' Gallagher added.

'He's knacky about the house,' Freddie remarked.

Ivory was tolerant of jibes. He was younger and had to be.

'I like a job where you settle in for a while,' he said. 'It can be nice and cushy. The last time I had a house of my own was in the Tan war.'

Freddie was surprised.

'Were you in it then?'

'Only just,' Ivory said. 'I was in this one ambush and then the truce came. A job in the mountains at Tibradden. For weeks before it we were in the mountains. Then we commandeered this house. It was one of those old mansions miles from any-where, and when we took it over there was only this eccentric kind of bloke on his own. He was a secretary and the rest of the family were away. In Germany I think he said. We took him prisoner – house arrest. He did what he liked otherwise. In the day he worked in the library – the place was crammed with books. At night he taught us Irish. He was a bit of a Celtic scholar and said he had been a Fenian. In the end he took part in the ambush with us.'

'You took a hell of a chance,' Freddie said.

'The commandant didn't think so. The man took the oath. He was sworn in.'

'That's how informers are recruited,' Freddie said.

The incident irritated him. There were certain procedures. He liked things tidy.

'This was no informer,' Ivory said. 'He was killed in that ambush.'

'What was his name?'

'I think it was O'Sheehan but I can't be sure.'

'You must always remember a name,' Freddie said.

'We began to call him "The Professor" almost from the beginning and the name stuck. I think he liked it. Anyway we lived like lords for weeks, with plenty of drink in the cellar and nothing around us but the ornamental gardens and the Glenasmole mountains.'

'That's my kind of war too,' Gallagher agreed.

'On this one,' Freddie told them, 'we're strictly on the dry.'

'Understood,' Gallagher said.

'I didn't like the smell of it when it was put forward,' Freddie continued, 'and now I'm sitting here I still don't like the smell of it. There'll be constant security outside because we're too bloody close to the prison itself. They'll patrol the streets and the guards on the walls can see practically everything. They won't be able to get through with the stuff we need and when we've been sitting on our arses for weeks they'll wake up to the situation and call it off.'

He proved right. At the end of January, although they had the shaft sunk by then, word came that they were to withdraw without proceeding. The month had seen thirty-four more executions of Republican prisoners, among them Willie Mulhall. They gave him time to distribute small personal keepsakes and to write a last message to his mother. It was like countless others; telling her his love, asking her not to mourn but to be comforted in the knowledge that he was in the proud company of those who were called on to die for Ireland. Then they allowed him the chaplain who withheld absolution because he refused the formula of submission to the bishops' pastoral. In the end he was asked if he was sorry for any wrong he had ever done. He found he could in conscience say yes to that. The sacrament was administered. But the argument had held up the proceedings for almost an hour. They led him to the place of execution. He died cleanly. The squads by now were practised hands.

Freddie got the news as they were filling in the shaft, and left off work to go to the upper floor. From the windows there he could look across at the gaol. His impulse was to shoot blindly into it until the revolver chamber was empty. He resisted it with difficulty. There would be an opportunity, sometime, to take more effective revenge. Somebody would die for what had been done to Willie Mulhall, over and above any official reprisals that might be ordered. It was a personal debt owed out of friendship, owed too because of the failure, however predictable, of the contemptible tunnel. He made a solemn pact with himself and put the revolver away. But when he returned to the others his face was still white and terrible. They noticed. Neither cared to speak.

Instead of reporting for work Aloysius Hennessy put on the bowler hat and the long overcoat and asked the relief man to stand in for him for the night. Then he set off to convey his sympathy in person. He found Chandler's Court in mourning. Hall doors that had been open night and day for a quarter of a century were closed as a mark of respect. Blinds, where such things existed, were drawn. Children had been called in from the streets. A mourning card surrounded by black crape had been fixed to the hall door of No. 3. He pushed it inwards with as little noise as possible and went up the stairs. The woman who admitted him took his name in a whisper and led him over to Mrs Mulhall. She was in her chair by the window. A framed photograph of Willie had been placed on the table with two lighted candles on either side.

'Mr Hennessy,' she said when she recognized him, 'you're very good to call.'

'An old neighbour, ma'am,' he said, taking her hand. 'I'm sorry for your trouble.'

'I know that.' She looked around. 'Is there a seat for Mr Hennessy?'

Someone gave him one.

'You've come out of your way to visit me,' she said.

'What else would I do? I knew your husband as a friend and I owe more than the next to your son.'

'That's all I've left of him now,' she said, looking at the photograph, 'not even his body to wake in decency.'

'And did you see him, itself?'

'We advised her against it,' one of the women said.

Hennessy nodded.

'That was right,' he endorsed, 'you advised her well. I'm sure that was best.'

'He'll lie in Mountjoy gaol now,' Mrs Mulhall said, 'with no one to put a flower on his grave or say a few prayers over him.' She began to weep. He left her to do so for a while. Then, when it seemed the right moment to intervene, he spoke quietly, not to her but to the woman nearest to him.

'I must have been one of the last to see Willie on the day he was taken,' he said, 'and I can tell the world that I owe my life to his kindness.'

'Is that a fact?' the woman said. The rest turned their faces to him. He had their deep interest. Mrs Mulhall, hungry for any crumb of information or remembrance, dried her tears and turned to him also.

'I do indeed,' he said to them. He was glad to be able to acknowledge it. 'We were alone in each other's company for the length of three dangerous days, and only for his neighbourliness and courage I wouldn't be here tonight to tell the tale.'

He explained to them about the watching job and his hours of isolation and how Willie suddenly appeared in the opposite doorway. He gave them details of their vigil and even made them smile about the bullseyes. He told them of Willie's quip as

they parted and his own account to his wife and her deep
gratitude. When they had discussed it and remarked on it and a
decent interval had elapsed he took his leave. A neighbour saw
him to the door.

'You did her a world of good,' she whispered to him.

But the house reminded him so much of old times and old
friends that he was unable to answer and could only convey his
emotion by pressing her hands and shaking his head.

The street too, so quiet, so sombre in its sense of tragedy,
moved him unbearably. He stood surveying it from the steps,
the bowler hat which he had removed out of respect still in his
hands. As he went down into the street a man brushed close to
him and stopped to apologize.

'I beg your pardon,' the stranger said.

'Don't mention it,' Hennessy answered. But he was startled,
wondering where the stranger had come from. He returned the
bowler hat to his head and set off for Cotters. It would be full
that night, he knew. Chandler's Court made an occasion of its
griefs. Cotter greeted him above the buzz of conversation.

'I was thinking you'd be around.'

'A terrible occurrence.'

'The whole street is full of it,' Cotter confirmed.

'I've just been to see his mother.'

'And how is the poor woman taking it?'

'The way you would expect, God help her. But the neighbours is with her.'

'I'm glad to hear that,' Cotter said. Hennessy took his pint to
a table where some men had greeted him. Dick Quinn, who was
among them, introduced him where it was necessary.

'Sad occasion,' they all said, as they shook hands.

'You're a stranger these times,' Dick remarked. They insisted
on calling a drink for him. While it was being brought Hennessy
saw the stranger who had apologized to him earlier coming
through the door from the street. It surprised him. He had
moved off in the opposite direction. But the drink was put in
front of him and the company demanded his attention.

'You'll remember my sister Eileen,' Dick said. 'She was with

Willie only a few minutes before they picked him up. By the time she got back to the house the street was in a commotion and they were taking him away.'

'Joe Maher was the officer in charge,' one of the company told them. 'I was at school with him. A proper little bastard.'

'I knew two of the others,' Dick said. 'John Dixon and a bloke called Corrigan. Bunty Corrigan. Hard men.'

'I knew Corrigan,' someone else put in. 'He used to work in the Bottle House.'

'That's him.'

'No fear of them picking up de Valera,' another said, 'it's never the Brass Hats.'

'Wait a minute. What about Erskine Childers?'

'And Rory O'Connor. And Mellowes?'

'That was Kevin O'Higgins's doing,' the other answered. O'Higgins would execute his own mother.'

'If he could only find out who she is,' someone put in.

'Knowing Willie,' Dick said, 'I'm surprised he didn't shoot it out.'

Hennessy pushed his glass aside. His moment had come.

'He couldn't use the right arm,' he told them. 'There was a bad wound.' He pointed to his own arm. Just here. I dressed it for him.'

'You were with him?'

'For three solid days and up to a few hours before they caught him. Willie Mulhall saved my life. I was telling his mother only a while ago.'

Once again he was the centre of interest. They called another round and he recounted in detail all that had happened. His own role he slightly amended.

'The only way through was across Butt Bridge by way of Talbot Street. It was raked by fire but the thing had to be done.'

'Duck the head and run like hell,' one of them contributed.

'No, no,' Hennessy said, 'that's the surest way to get yourself killed. The trick is to walk. Take it nice and slow. No panic.'

'That takes a bit of nerve,' Dick suggested.

'I wouldn't wish to have to do it every day,' Hennessy conceded, 'but I said to myself: well – needs must. So we took it nice and cool and steady and, sure enough, we got across without stopping one.'

They were impressed by his self-control.

'I don't think I'd have chanced it,' one of them admitted.

'Of course, Willie was in charge. He knew the ropes,' Hennessy said. 'All I had to do was take it nice and cool and follow his advice. Then when we reached the street here we parted. It was the last I was to see of him.'

Cigarette smoke had thickened in the air and the groups spread around on the wooden benches had grown noisy. Someone began a Republican song but stopped when Cotter moved across to silence him. He joined Hennessy's group for a moment on his way back.

'That's the kind of thing that starts trouble,' he explained.

They agreed.

'The next thing is some Free State supporter objects.'

'And every right to.'

'In my personal opinion,' Cotter said, 'the people voted and the government is the government, but that's neither here nor there. The main thing at present is to keep politics out of this pub. If they want that let them take themselves elsewhere.'

They acknowledged his good sense. Hennessy insisted on calling a round. He made his way to the counter. As he picked a passage between drinking groups, he found the stranger in front of him once again.

'Are you Mr Hennessy?'

'That's correct.'

'I thought so earlier but I wasn't sure. Could we have a word privately?'

Hennessy hesitated.

'I'm calling drinks for the company,' he explained.

'When you've done so will do. It'll only take a couple of minutes. I've an important message.'

Hennessy stared at him.

'I think there must be a mistake.'

'No mistake. You'll understand when I have a chance to explain.'

'Very well,' Hennessy agreed, 'give me a few minutes.'

When he had brought the drinks to the others he asked the company to excuse him for a short while.

The street outside was dark. The wind, beating upriver, brought with it the smell of idle dockyards. He made to turn to face his companion and found that a gun was being pressed into his back. Freddie said:

'Take it easy and you won't come to harm.'

Hennessy, rigid with fear, managed to say:

'Who are you?'

'A friend of Willie Mulhall. Just like yourself.'

'How did you get my name?'

'I heard your friend introduce you.'

'You must have followed me?'

'That's right. I reckoned anyone calling at Willie's house tonight might have information. What you had to say inside there was interesting but not easy to hear. You were with him just before he was picked up?'

'A few hours before.'

'Who did the job? The officer's name was mentioned by a pal of yours.'

'He said it was someone called Joe Maher.'

'That's what I thought. I know Joe Maher. Two others were mentioned. Who were they?'

Hennessy searched his memory.

'A man called John Dixon. The other was Corrigan. I think it was Corrigan.'

'Bunty Corrigan,' Freddie said, 'that would be it. I know him. Do you know any of them yourself?'

'I never heard of them until tonight.'

Freddie regarded him closely. 'I believe you,' he said. 'Right. That's all I wanted to know.'

'Can I go back inside?'

'That wouldn't be desirable,' Freddie told him. 'I'd rather you went home. Turn around and keep on walking.'

Hennessy turned.

'Hold on,' Freddie said. 'Maher, Corrigan and Dixon. Does that check?'

'I beg your pardon?'

'The three that were mentioned.'

'Yes,' Hennessy said.

'Good. Very good.' Freddie said. 'Now get going. And don't look back.'

Hennessy started to walk. Remembering Willie's advice he tried to move at a normal gait. He could feel sweat on his forehead and his knees threatened at every step to buckle with fear. It seemed a lifetime before he reached the corner and could turn into the main thoroughfare. Despite the traffic and the pedestrians he still waited for a shot to ring out. He obeyed orders and never once looked back.

Cornelius took the oil lamp from the table and said he would let O'Sheehan out by the back stairs. The front was strewn with debris left by workmen who were extending the gas supply to the upstairs apartments. The back stairs were narrow and unsteady. As they turned on the last landing Cornelius, recollecting O'Sheehan's height, called out: 'Watch the head.'

But it was too late. He heard the crack of O'Sheehan's massive forehead against the overhanging beam and his profane ejaculation.

'That was a sore one,' he commiserated.

O'Sheehan shook his head several times to clear it of the sudden fireworks display.

'Damn it. I left it too late.'

'Never mind,' O'Sheehan said, 'I should have kept my eyes open.'

They promised to meet again within the fortnight and he set off on his bicycle. The night was cold and seemed to get darker as he journeyed. In a short while it was so dark he had to dismount to figure where he was. When the policeman found him he was holding his bicycle by one handlebar, immobilized and rigid to touch.

'I thought at first he was drunk,' he told the sergeant, 'but now I think he's sick.'

'What's his name?'

'I can't get a damn word out of him,' the policeman said, 'I don't think he either sees or hears me.'

'Let's have a look at him,' the sergeant suggested. He accompanied the policeman to the waiting room. After a close scrutiny of O'Sheehan's face he became alarmed.

'Get the ambulance,' he instructed, 'I don't like the look of this man at all.'

In the ambulance O'Sheehan said nothing either. At the hospital they got him to bed.

'It could be concussion,' the orderly said. 'It may be shock. I hope to Christ he isn't going to throw a fit or anything of that nature. We're short-staffed this few weeks past.'

O'Sheehan gave no trouble. While the life around him went on, they nursed him, fed him and changed his bed linen, he refused communication and lived only in himself. He was Oisin, son of Finn, son of Cumhal, son of Trenmor, content to play chess with Oscar in pleasant gardens under shady trees, or to listen to melodious staves in the companionship of the ale house. At times he floated on horseback high above a wine-red ocean, his arms about the waist of Niamh, his face pressed against her golden hair which was delicate and soft and aromatic. In that country the brown rivers were overhung with berried branches and the frothing pools under falls held abundance of trout and salmon. In that country the shapes of blue mountains trembled in the deeps of reedy lakes, and the boarhounds gave tongue on windy heights above echoing valleys. In that country were orchards and granaries and herds of kine and bee-loud pastures and bright pools after ebbtide on yellow strands; odour of salt air and wild garlic, eye-delighting yellow of gorse and purple of heather, murmur of minute flying things in leafy forests, moaning of wood pigeons under evening skies. In that country were kingly, white-walled residences, well fortified, well sentinelled, with golden-thatched roofs and great halls where the pillars were of cedarwood and the walls aglow with silken hangings. It was a world of sweet-tongued speech and happy birdsong, of hero contest and weapon glitter, of high deeds and hunting, feasting and poetry, harp music and genealogical pride and the delectation of females fervent and snowy-breasted. It was the bronze-bright world of the princely Gael.

Beyond the hospital windows, where winter remained impervious to every artifice of spring, the land was waterlogged under the biting winds and suffered the inconveniences of reality. When Kevin O'Higgins, Vice-President of the Executive and Minister for Home Affairs, walked on the roof of government buildings at night for the sake of the modicum of exercise and air it afforded, he had to remember not to light a cigarette because the flare of the match would attract a sniper's bullet. In the rooms below him his governmental colleagues and their wives and families who could no longer live in safety in their own homes were preparing to go to bed in improvised accommodation. In the mountains along the boundaries of Waterford and Tipperary Republican Army Headquarters shifted at short notice from one hide-out to another and argued hopeless strategies while their Commander refused to acknowledge defeat and Free State troops tightened the ring about their lines of retreat. Eamon de Valera, now on horseback, now on foot, with a long beard and an unreliable guide blundered through swollen streams and blinding rain in an effort to locate them and persuade them that surrender was inevitable. They were reluctant at first to admit him and when they did it was to refuse to listen to him. On his way back he had the good fortune to be unrecognized by a Free State patrol that stopped him for questioning and the bad luck to lose his way in inhospitable mountains on one of the darkest and wettest nights of the season. By the time he had settled back into hiding in Dublin the Republican chief of staff had been shot dead and the rest of headquarters scattered. He devoted himself to the composition of his message to the Republican rank and file, whom he addressed as Soldiers of the Republic, Legion of the Rearguard. It was the preliminary to surrender.

Cornelius Moloney searched everywhere for news, first in known haunts of O'Sheehan, then by undertaking a trip to the

Priory itself, something he had postponed doing out of reluctance to intrude on a religious and more or less enclosed world. But the Prior knew as little as he did himself. They established, however, that O'Sheehan had never returned from his visit to Cornelius.

'Has this happened before?' the Prior asked.

'I'm afraid it has,' Cornelius said.

'Does he simply wander off?'

'He could be walking the roads, or lying in hospital or making do with the doss-me-down or the workhouse. You wouldn't know.'

They tried the police who had no record of the name but an entry for the night in question which seemed to hold promise. At the hospital they were told a patient answering their description had discharged himself some weeks previously, very much against medical advice. He had left no information as to his intentions.

'That's that,' Cornelius said to Father Felim who had accompanied him. 'We can only wait to see if he turns up. At least we know he hasn't been ambushed or shot dead.'

'Indeed.'

'Which reminds me,' Cornelius resumed. 'The sergeant has been on to me a few times about the bicycle. He'd like it removed from the premises. My understanding is it belongs to the Priory.'

'If it does, what's the sergeant doing with it?'

'O'Sheehan was in the habit of borrowing it.'

'Oh. I see. Very well. I'll tell one of our students to collect it.'

They shook hands at the hospital entrance.

'The thought of that bicycle is oddly upsetting,' Father Felim confessed. 'I didn't know we possessed one. The library won't be the same. In fact we'll all miss him very much.'

'We will indeed,' Cornelius said. His heart was heavy. He had no closer friend.

Freddie Lindon might have lived but for two unforeseen happenings. The first was that Captain Joe Maher and his companion Bunty Corrigan, before entering the Liffeyside Billiard Saloon for their weekly session, stopped for cigarettes at a nearby shop. The second was that the army lorry which had dropped them off came to a standstill a short distance down the street to give right of way to two heavily laden horse-drawn floats which turned across its path on the way to the markets. This in itself might not have mattered but for a third element over which he had full control. He changed his mind. It was a breach of one of his own rigid and long-standing rules, and it sealed the outcome. He was not his usual, efficient self at the time. Neither Gallagher nor young Ivory would have anything to do with it. That angered him. It was a private vendetta however, without official sanction, so he had no authority to force them. On top of that the surrender had been ordered a couple of days before with a general instruction to cease fire and dump arms. Freddie had no intention of doing either until the job had been carried out. If it was to be done, though, it would have to be done quickly, if only because the effect of peace would be to change fixed routines.

When he found out about the billiard saloon he checked over the place in a number of visits. The toilets were to the back of the saloon, with entrance by way of a corridor and a window which gave access to backyards overlooked for the most part by seldom-tended storehouses. His plan was to watch their entry from the far side of the road, then to follow them in and do the job. The saloon was ideal for it. Hooded bulbs above each table threw light on the play but left the areas between in twilight. Two men with eyes and minds concentrated on contest would be easy targets. The job done, his line of retreat would be by the door to the corridor which he checked and which could be locked swiftly simply by depressing the button on the latch and then through the toilet window and out into the backyard.

It was a plan worth following, but something that had never seemed to be part of his make-up let him down when it came to carrying it out. He waited on the opposite side as planned. He saw the army lorry approaching and was in no way put out. Sometimes they came on foot, sometimes the lorry dropped them. To him it made little difference. But when, instead of leaving them outside the saloon the lorry came to a stop further up the street, he became uneasy. He saw them entering the shop and saw the lorry moving off. He remained concealed until it had passed. In a short while Maher and Corrigan reappeared and came slowly towards him. It was then that his confidence in his original plan faltered. They were close and vulnerable. If he shot now he could still get away through the saloon while those using it would be unaware of what had happened. He moved forward and fired.

The first bullet went high and struck Maher in the shoulder. The next missed Corrigan and shattered the shop window behind him. But the noise alerted the troops in the lorry which was idling while the two horse-drawn floats trundled slowly into the by-street and one of them, picking out Freddie, fired. He spun around and was trapped. Corrigan seized the opening and got him from behind. As he fell the troops in the lorry opened up in force. He had no chance. After an interval they swarmed down into the street and stood around him. Bullets had riddled his body and smashed his face, which was unrecognizable. They covered him with an army greatcoat until the ambulance came to take him to the city morgue.

Paddy McDonagh knocked off work when the message arrived and went home to change before accompanying his mother to the morgue. Identification was a formality. He restrained her when she reached out to draw back the face covering and did so himself so briefly that she was prevented from seeing anything.

'What about your Aunt Emily?' she asked him.

'Don't let her come.'

'That was my advice. We'll go across and see her. Will they take him into the church, would you think?'

'I don't know. A refusal would make it worse for her so I wouldn't try.'

'She can wake him at home, I suppose. But is he to be buried without priest at all?'

'One of the Franciscans might look after things. Or the

White Friars. The Orders are outside the bishop's jurisdiction, I understand. Anyway we can try.'

'Poor Freddie,' she said, beginning to weep. 'I remember him from when he was no size at all.'

He said nothing. When she recovered again she wondered silently at his lack of emotion.

Aunt Emily was dry-eyed and stony-faced. She had given a son to Ireland, she said. She would not grudge the giving. If others loved their country as Freddie had done, Ireland would soon be free of England. Paddy McDonagh, sensing a grief that seemed locked away in a block of granite, was sorry for her. She was suffering doubly by refusing to acknowledge her suffering. He saw, too, the source of that implacable purpose that had moulded Freddie into what he was. Violence he had experienced in plenty but without the fanaticism and devoid of hatred. In Ireland hatred saturated the air. It had the smell of evil and he recoiled from it.

The shop front was shuttered, the knot of black crape adorned the door, the blinds on the windows above were drawn. In the narrow street the sound of the band was magnified and thrown back on the procession. The coffin was draped in a tricolour flag, the torches in the hands of the advance guard swayed and were reflected in the glass panels of the hearse. The hooves of horses struck conflicting rhythms from the roadway and the wheels creaked and churned. Tim McDonagh, aged three, sat in the mourning coach between his father and his mother and listened. What it was all about he hardly knew and he was present only because the neighbour who was to have minded him had failed to turn up. He liked the music but feared the torches. He wondered why his mother had cried a little when the band first began to play and he was uneasy at the unusual gravity of his father. But he understood that his Uncle Freddie had died. He understood too, from a remark of his mother's, that the band and the torches and the coach and the plumed horses would eventually climb up into the sky and carry the coffin into heaven.

VI

At the entrance gate of a house in Cross Avenue, near the village of Blackrock, the policeman on duty saluted as the Minister for Justice and External Affairs left his home. Earlier he had made the few minutes' journey to swim in the sea. Now he was on his way to the Church of the Assumption in Booterstown. He was on foot and without his bodyguard, a circumtance that drew the policeman, when the Minister had gone a little distance, a few paces from the gateway to scrutinize the road ahead. He narrowed his eyes to search it and listened closely for some time, but there was nothing unusual. The avenue seemed empty, the ample gardens on either side, with their pebbled walks, their smooth croquet lawns, hummed harmlessly with summer insects. The noonday sun began to lean its weight on the shoulders of the policeman's blue serge uniform, warm and reassuring, a friendly arm. Finding no reason to do otherwise he withdrew again into the shaded entrance while the Minister, Mr Kevin O'Higgins, continued at an unhurried pace. He was thirty-five years of age and moulded already beyond change, a veteran of the State's struggle against armed dissent, aloof in his public bearing, immovable of will, particularly in his determination to establish and maintain the rule of law, a goal he had pursued single-mindedly and with marked success. He had endured the assassination of friends and colleagues and the slaying of his own father by political enemies through five years of violence. That his own chances of survival were slim, he had long accepted. It had made him fatalistic but by no means foolhardy. If from time to time he went unguarded, as he did now, it was because his sense of personal dignity demanded that he should occasionally assert the right of an elected representative to walk free. The well-disposed accepted him as a just man, courageous and meticulous in his devotion to public duty, if remote and cold of manner. His enemies saw in him only arrogance and ruthlessness. For the Minister himself it would soon cease to matter. He was about to be murdered.

It was the tenth day of July 1927, the very core of summer. High above Dublin, from the sea along its eastern boundary to the mountains behind and beyond it, the sky was blue and cloudless. Sunday's bells bombarded the houses, the streets echoed with mass-going feet. It would be a beautiful day, the mass-goers remarked to each other. After a decade of suffering they felt they deserved it a little better than most. Later they would marshal their children to trek in droves to the seaside or out to the mountains with shopping bags and sandwiches and teapots and blackened kettles. Meanwhile there was mass. The poor carried rosary beads or kept their hands in their pockets. The respectability of the better-off could be measured by the bulk of their prayerbooks.

In High Street at the heart of the old city, a distance of some six or seven miles from the Minister's residence, Cornelius Moloney, already at breakfast, was urging his son Brian to eat up his fried bread. There was nothing better in this world, he told him, for making the hair curly. Down the hill from him and nearer the river his friend O'Sheehan, restored after a period of mysterious absence to everyday society, relaxed at the window of his ramshackle room which overlooked Usher's Quay and allowed his attention to wander from the publication on his knee to the activity in the street below where balustraded parapets defined the breadth of the Liffey and the houses on either bank, old and neglected, leaned for support on each other in an effort to hold their own. Their inverted images wavered at him from the golden brown mirror of the water. If the images were pleasing, the bells were not. They disturbed the sunlit quiet and scattered his thoughts. They broadcast a brazen lie. Or so O'Sheehan believed. Exceptionally in that city he patronized no place of worship. He accepted no particular creed. That there was a mystery of sorts at the heart of human existence he was prepared to concede but not that any one of the several revealed explanations threw any light on it whatever. There were, of course, modes and planes of existence beyond the here and now, states of being and countries of insubstantiality where the heroes hunted and the kings continued to hold court and the salmon leaped in waters of celestial liquidity. These were not accessible however to the world of flesh and blood; and to the initiated only at moments of conjunction between the Dualities; as for instance daily at sunrise and sunset, or seasonally on May Eve when winter passed into summer and again when summer passed into winter on the eve of November, both powerful occasions of universal disorder and supernatural chaos and consequently perilous in the extreme. Conventional religion, for all its theological exactitudes and canvassed certainties, seemed either unwilling or unequipped to explore or explain such arcana and was consequently irrelevant. In the face of the Eternal Conundrum he found it sufficient simply to abide: to be born and to die, to wake and to sleep – the four corners of reality; and in between times to exist, which was its centre and fifth. In this he had long ago found a reassuring perceptual concord: all Truth being fivefold and all things divisible by five therefore perfect.

In the Church of the Assumption, Booterstown, which stood a few hundred yards from the corner of Cross Avenue and nearer again to the sea, the eleven-thirty mass had almost ended. The doors stood wide open because of the heat, the sun made magic-lantern slides of the scenes on the stained-glass windows. In silken thread along the borders of the High Altar cloth embroidered letters repeated three times the words, holy, holy, holy. Above these repetitions and the bowed head of the celebrant the red sanctuary lamp with its point of yellow flame proclaimed Christ's Living Presence. There was hardly a stir among the kneeling congregation. The warm air pressed heavily on them, the priest's voice was a far-off, summer murmur.

Cornelius Moloney wiped the grease from his lips and hands with an enormous red and yellow spotted handkerchief and pushed the empty plate away with the feeling of having done due honour to his God and the Sabbath. He had been to mass and Holy Communion. He had put away an enormous break-fast. It was now time to address his attention to his son Brian, who was aged seven.

'That's a fine healthy morning thanks be to God and there's nothing like a bit of exercise and a breath or two of fresh air for draining the poisons out of the ducts and the bloodstream,' he began, 'so would you like to come up to the Park with me? I'm thinking of taking the greyhounds out for a bit of a gallop.'

'Will there be polo?' his son asked.

'There will not,' he answered, 'and if there was itself you'll not hang about gawking at it.'

'Why can't I?'

'Because it's an Ascendancy affectation left behind from the days of the British,' he said severely, 'and that's not what we occupied the General Post Office for or fought the Black and Tans.'

'What can I look at, then?'

'Can't you look at the greyhounds?'

'I don't like the greyhounds.'

'First you won't eat your breakfast,' Cornelius complained, 'and now you don't like the greyhounds. Did your mother put you up to that – was it? What's wrong with the greyhounds?'

'One of them bit me.'

Cornelius looked astounded.

'Which of them? Was it Eileen Aroon?'

'I don't know. I can never tell which is which with grey-hounds.'

'If it was Slieve na Mon you must have been teasing her. I hope to God you were. Otherwise it could be the beginnings of distemper. Well, do you want to come?'

'If there's something to look at.'

'I'll tell you what you can look at,' Cornelius pronounced, 'you can look at decent Irish games played by Fontenoys or the peadar Mackens. That's what you can look at.'

'Where?'

'On the Forty Acres,' Cornelius continued, 'where young men that still has a few national ideals and aspirations wield the caman and talk in the Gaelic tongue as I did many a time myself when I was a gossoon in my father's house in Tipperary. Now go on in with you and get your mother to throw an eye over you and pass you as respectable while I put the dogs on the lead and pump up the bicycle. Ask her where did I leave the bicycle clips.'

As Brian slid off his chair his father found another reason for displeasure.

'And bless yourself before leaving the table or am I rearing a little heathen in my house or what?'

Cornelius, recollecting that an ounce of example was worth a hundredweight of exhortation, crossed himself, closed his eyes and went through his own grace-after-meals aloud, doing so with an excess of piety to enforce his point.

When Timothy McDonagh, also aged seven, descended the steps of his house the bells, one by one, were beginning to fall silent. He was on his way first to the house of his father's parents where he would have lunch and then to that of his mother's people where he would spend a week or two of his summer holidays. He followed Upper Leeson Street at first, then turned left at the bridge and went along the canal bank. Already the older boys were swimming and shouting to one another where the lock gates offered deep water, old men were reading their newspapers on the grassy verge, children fished for tiddlers from the towpath. Near Baggot Street the usual pair of goats, bearded and untrustworthy, scrutinized him wickedly as he passed. They were long-standing enemies. When there were no adults around they followed and menaced him. If there were they stood still but kept their eyes fixed on him, silently reminding him that their opportunity would be seized when it came. This morning there were plenty of adults. He had been confident there would be, for he too had received Holy Communion and felt as a consequence that God would ensure that nothing disagreeable would disturb anyone so stuffed with sanctifying grace. He had made a good confession in preparation and had told all about a halfpenny that ought to have but never actually did reach the Black Babies' collection box. The lifting of so grave a burden left soul and conscience so refreshed and contented that he got past the goats with something like confidence. He then crossed into Haddington Road. It was around that moment that, some miles away, the men stepped swiftly from the waiting car and gunned down the Minister for Justice as soon as he had turned the corner.

Cornelius Moloney, meanwhile, was negotiating with some difficulty the steep hill which ran down from High Street to the quays. He had over-inflated the bicycle tyres and the cobbles made steering a problem.

'Hold on tight, there,' he yelled over his shoulder to his son who was perched on the back carrier. Brian clenched his teeth and took a firmer grip on his father's coat tails. A few feet behind him, the tethered greyhounds trotted smartly.

As was his custom on Sundays, O'Sheehan levered himself from his chair at twelve-forty-five on the dot and a little later stepped from the hall into the sunshine. Down the street from him the congregation was leaving the Franciscan Church of Adam and Eve, so called not out of veneration for the Biblical begetters of the human race but, as he well knew, because in the bad times when Romish practices were suppressed, entrance to it had been through a public house of that name. He strolled eastwards to cross the river by the Ha'penny Bridge and lingered to watch the three-card-trick man who had set up his table by the Irish Woollen Company. It was illegal, and so, automatically popular. The usual tout sucked a butt on the fringe of the crowd and screwed up his eyes as he kept watch from under a peaked cap against any sudden descent of the police. At another corner a pitch-and-toss school was in session. Now that the mass-goers had dispersed there was little traffic. The gulls, after their morning's activity, were dozing along the river wall.

O'Sheehan occupied half an hour or so in successive scrutiny of the second-hand shops. He required a cast-off picture to cover a damp spot on the wall, something of adequate dimension, cheap yet tolerable to look at, since once hung in place he would be obliged to live with it, perhaps forever. The choice at the end seemed curtailed to a reproduction of 'The Dying Child', a battle scene with a bloody encounter between two war chargers in the foreground, or the patriotic alternatives of an inferior portrait of Robert Emmet or an even worse one of Wolfe Tone. There were others, however, indistinguishable and even concealed, which could be examined more closely on some week-day evening when the shops were open. Meanwhile he was almost due at the Fitzpatrick's Eating House for his Sunday dinner. Later, in all likelihood, he would take the train to Howth to visit the grave of Aideen, the faithful wife who died of grief when her husband had been slain in battle. It was possibly his favourite Sunday pilgrimage. She had been very dear to him, the lovely Aideen, as dear almost as her hero husband Oscar, Fenian warrior, his son.

The McDonaghs observed the rituals of Sunday lunch. Tim McDonagh, surrounded by uncles, knew it all by heart. Grandfather McDonagh was at the head of the table with a mug of porter beside him; Uncle Charles and Uncle Christy were to his right and left with bottles of stout each. His father and his Uncle Jim were next. He himself was at the bottom. They never sat differently. Grandmother McDonagh hovered about between table and kitchenette and for one who had so much to say on the subject of appetite took only bits and scraps herself.

'Is there another bottle of stout handy?' Uncle Christy asked her.

She made a disapproving face but nevertheless brought one.

'How about you, Paddy?' Uncle Christy asked.

'One's plenty, thanks,' his father answered.

'I never found it so,' Uncle Christy said, pouring. 'The last time I settled for a single bottle, I found myself walking to one side.'

'I wouldn't say no to another slice of that joint,' Uncle Jim said, 'the missus at home has been dishing up rabbit at a terrible rate. It's somewhere she gets them cheap.'

'I see nothing wrong with rabbit,' Uncle Charles said.

'You might if you got it three times a week two weeks running,' Uncle Jim told him.

'I wouldn't turn up my nose at a rabbit,' Uncle Charles said, 'I see no reason for that at all. The rabbit is the poor man's chicken. A nicely done rabbit is a dish I'd get up in the night to sample.'

'Did anyone ever have it with a rasher?' Uncle Christy enquired generally.

'I've had it in a stew,' Uncle Charles said. 'A few onions and bits of this and that, with the flesh falling away from the bone. By God, there's the rale McCoy for you; they'd pay a pound a go if they could get it in the Gresham.'

'I'm asking if you ever had it with a rasher?'

'How could you stew a rasher?'

'This is done in an oven.'

Uncle Charles left down his knife and fork.

'How could you do a rabbit in an oven?' he appealed generally. 'A rabbit isn't a thing you do in an oven. You stew a rabbit.'

'Wait now. This woman I was in digs with one time in the country. She always did a rabbit in the oven, but in some class of a dish or other. The rind of the rasher melts slowly through it. There's other odds and ends as well, of course. You never tasted the better of it.'

'It couldn't have been a rabbit,' Uncle Charles insisted, 'more likely it was some class of a fowl.'

'It was a rabbit,' Uncle Christy said, raising his voice.

'That's enough about bloody rabbits,' his grandfather put in.

His grandmother who was collecting plates from the table said:

'You're right. That pair can't eat together without raising dissension.' Then as she was leaving a thought of her own struck her which she delayed to give to them.

'The reason I never serve up rabbit myself,' she explained, 'is that I've always understood it can be very binding.'

'Christ,' Grandfather McDonagh said, looking up at the ceiling.

When they had finished eating they sat around smoking for a while and talking about the weekend race meetings. Grandfather McDonagh was highly satisfied.

'I had Musical Prince in the two-fifty at Lingfield,' he said, 'a comfortable win at five to one. Did you do any good yourself?'

'I only had the one bet,' his father said, 'Inky Boy in the three-fifty at the same meeting. Late last night they were still out with flashlamps looking for him.'

'A mug's game,' Uncle Charles put in from behind his newspaper.

'I'll have to give it up for a while,' his father agreed, 'the missus wants her pride-and-joy here to learn the violin. As well as that he has to be fitted out for his new school.'

'Is it to be the Brothers?' Uncle Charles enquired.

'I hope so. I'm expecting Uncle Hugh to have some definite word tonight. He was to see some party or other during the weekend.'

'The violin is a grand accomplishment,' Uncle Charles approved. 'Will he have the academic training, I mean scales and arpeggios and reading the music from staff notation, that sort of thing?'

'The full treatment,' his father confirmed.

'The main thing is to insist he plays all the time from the notes,' Uncle Charles advised. 'I believe what destroys the young student altogether is picking things out by ear. Of course, not everybody has the gift.'

'We can only wait and see,' his father said.

Uncle Charles turned around and said, 'Come here to me, Tim me lad, till I look at your hands.'

He went across dutifully. Uncle Charles took his hands in his and was greatly impressed.

'By God then,' he told them, 'he has the long fingers for it all right.'

He held up the hand for general inspection.

'Look at that,' he invited, 'not much good for a pick and shovel I grant you, but a musical hand, the hand of an artist.' He patted him on the head. 'You'll beat all before you.'

It was embarrassing and he looked down at the floor, but his father came to his rescue and said it was time for him to set off for grandfather Keenan's house.

'He may have the fiddle for you already,' he said. 'He was to see could he pick up one during the week. Tell them I'll be down for a while after tea.'

Out again at last in the air, the thought of the violin worried him a bit and the prospect of a new school more so. But both were in the far future. He would have maybe a whole fortnight near the sea with his grandfather and his aunts. Every nine strides he watched to keep his feet within the area of the flagstones and on each tenth he stepped deliberately on the line of demarcation.

Not for O'Sheehan, supine on the heathery heights of Howth, the vulgar disportations of the herd; the distracted parents blowing life into picnic fires and distributing cups and sandwiches; their children perilously climbing among red sandstone rocks; the entwined lovers nominally concealed but discovered unconsciously by an agitation of undergrowth or a foot protruding from a ferny bed. No. For O'Sheehan a world less coarsened by habit less worn by crude usage less vulnerable to chance and suffering. Sun on closed eyelids and birdsong all about were phenomena not merely warm, not simply melodious but an inner radiance and voices ancestral. Rock, fern, altitude, width of sky, blueness of sea, precipitous soaring of rose-red cliffs all penetrated and reassembled behind the closed eyelid to create from their intermingling essences an interior existence, an inhabiting wholeness in which all centuries, all chronicled high deeds co-existed as experienced realities. For example, the dolmen marking Aideen's grave, revisited within the past hour or so, but erected initially upon his own express command and under his supervision uncountable centuries before, a fact for which there was poetic witness:

> They heaved the stone; they heaped the cairn:
> Said Oisin, 'In a queenly grave
> We leave her 'mong her fields of fern
> Between the cliff and wave.

The cliff behind stands clear and bare
And bare, above, the heathery steep
Scales the clear heaven's expanse to where
The Danaan Druids sleep.

And all the sands that, left and right
The grassy isthmus-ridge confine
In yellow bars lie bare and bright
Among the sparkling brine.

So it had been long centuries before and so it remained still, except that with time the great capstone had slipped at one end from its supporting pillars to lie with one corner stabbing into the earth. That was an image to retain in the mind's eye, a symbol of a world long ruined which somehow and by strange arts of enchantment he had lost and must again find if he was to know at last the benison of death. On that sacred hill, by the Danes called Howth but by the Phoenicians Edor, he could breathe in its lingering presence. On that hill, the Danaan Druids rode in cloud shadows; Lugh, God of Light was near at hand; the heather stirred to invisible feet and it was Oscar who had passed, or it was Aideen:

Here far from camp and chase removed
Apart in Nature's quiet room
The music that alive she loved
Shall cheer her in her tomb.

The humming of the noontide bees
The lark's loud carol all day long
And, borne on evening's salted breeze
The clanking seabird's song.

He lay still in the sunlight and waited for the next verse to steal forward from the recess of memory. Later he would look on the harbour from which the white ship once set out for the kingdom of the Giolla Deacair and would pass on his way the rock against which the Pouka was transfixed for taking liberties with St Nessan when he was labouring to illuminate the Gospel of Howth. Meanwhile the bee, the lark, the clanking of seabirds, drifting sounds on a salted breeze under a blaze of sun, mingled harmoniously with verse and legendary recollections until at five o'clock or near enough a shiver roused him and he suddenly sat bolt upright. A cloud was clearing the sun. Balor, god of Darkness, had glided past.

Cornelius exercised the greyhounds for most of the afternoon, removing his jacket when the heat of the day became uncomfortable and revealing a broad pair of braces to which a cluster of holy medals had been stitched for protection against a range of undesirable contingencies. He praised the dogs' fettle to an unappreciative Brian.

'There's no finer sight than a couple of hounds in tip-top condition. I don't know what your mother keeps going on about.'

'She says they have the yard in a terrible state.'

'I can't see a hae'porth wrong with it.'

'There's an awful smell. Dogs' dirt and everything.'

Cornelius found this an excess of delicacy and effeminate.

'What's natural is decent,' he declared.

Brian mooned about while the rituals of training were gone through. There was no interruption except briefly, when a fellow publican stopped to comment about the Intoxicating Liquor Act and to urge the need for organized protest by the trade. Cornelius promised support, then went back to his dogs again, until the evening grew late and it was time to think of tea. He sent Brian off to kennel them while he himself went to wash. In the hot evening sun the yard was at its worst. Straw and excrement were littered about and the smell of urine was strong enough to make the eyes smart. A cow's head which Cornelius had got from one of the slaughterhouses for the dogs to worry stared hollowly at nothing and putrefied in the heat. Brian held his nose as he went about his work, got the hounds behind lock and key at last, and hurried away.

As the July day neared its end long bars of red streaked the sky behind the spire of Ringsend Church. From seaside and country the trippers were beginning the journey home, crowding into trams and trains with empty picnic bags and smoke-blackened pots dribbling their dregs of tea, or pedalling in groups with towels and togs wrapped about the handlebars of bicycles. Tim McDonagh was standing with his grandfather at the open hall door, where a neighbour delayed to remark on the weather.

It had been a day of some importance. Uncle Hugh had everything arranged and he would be accepted by the Christian Brothers in August when the school holidays came to an end. He pretended to be pleased. In secret he was apprehensive and unhappy. But his grandfather had got him the violin and the novelty of it occupied his attention. It had a deep red colour and the case smelled strangely of velvet lining and rosin. His grandfather had said if he was to learn music he must first be able to explain what music is. And what was music? He thought and said:

'Tunes.'

'But what are tunes?'

'Notes.'

'And how is it some notes become music and others remain just notes?'

That was too hard to answer.

'I'll tell you what music is,' his grandfather said. 'Music is a succession of sounds, pleasing to the ear and in satisfying order.'

He had repeated it aloud a number of times until it became fixed in his memory. As a result he was now able to reproduce it word for word when his grandfather requested it for the benefit of the conversational neighbour. His performance was admired.

'That's something I'd find difficult to memorize myself,' the neighbour confessed.

As they continued their talk he became aware of a voice, faint at first, calling out repetitively and urgently somewhere in the distance.

'What's that about?' his grandfather wondered when he too began to notice.

They waited in silence, straining to hear.

'It's a Stop Press,' the neighbour said.

'On a Sunday?' his grandfather questioned, unconvinced. But both their faces, Tim McDonagh noted, had become grave and anxious. When the newsboy rounded the corner at last his voice startled the street.

'Stop Press. . . . Stop Press.'

Doors opened and people began to gather about him. The neighbour joined them. After a delay he returned with the paper and its unbelievable news.

'What is it?' his grandfather asked.

'Kevin O'Higgins,' the neighbour said, 'shot dead this morning on his way to mass.'

His grandfather seized the paper to read the news for himself. He called down the hall.

'Hugh – come here.'

Uncle Hugh hurried out to read the news in turn.

'Bloody murderers,' he said.

Small and forgotten in the sudden confusion of voices as people began to call out to others and shock and revulsion charged the air of the street, Tim McDonagh looked up at the red bars of light in the evening sky as though to find an answer there to what it was all about. He thought of the body gunned down and bleeding to death on the roadway, of the killers speeding away with the unthinkable crime of murder blackening each of their souls. He pictured the hangman's rope and what their end would be when they were caught. The thought made him sick.

'Assassins,' he heard his grandfather saying, 'low, bloody-minded assassins, the dregs and the scum of Ireland.'

TWO · The Isle of the Blest

Like dolmens round my childhood, the old people.

JOHN MONTAGUE

I

In summer camp in Donegal in August in the sunshine
the wasps with yellow and black-hooped bodies buzzed all day
about the kitchen tent and drowned in scores in the jam. A
forest of pine trees dipped in grace to the edge of the lake and
behind it and above the mist of early morning trailed fingers
along the sides of mountains. There was the smell of pine and a
grassy smell near your pillow and a canvas smell from the
drying fabric of the tent. Canvas shoes became so soaked with
dew it was no longer cold when you stood in the lake to wash
and saw the image of sleepy face and tousled hair disappear in
ripples when your hands broke the water. Then there was no
smell but the smell of soap and there was the sore sweet sting
of sunburn. Then the whistles blowing cookhouse and corn-
flakes poured from a bag and some of them drifting away with
the breeze. Smoky tea, thick bread, yellow butter. Afterwards
scour the enamel mug with sand. Clean the shallow enamel plate.
Place it gently on the water and watch it fill slowly before
sinking slowly down to the bottom.

'Is there kit inspection this morning?'

'Yes – at ten o'clock.'

'Aw – sugar it.'

'If you ever listened, dopey, you'd hear these things. Do you
ever listen?'

Ignore him.

'Anyone any cigarettes?'

'Brian has. And Cunningham has a pipe.'

'God. Let's see it, Cunningham. Boy. What a wizard job.
And tobacco too.'

'I'll tell your oul' fella, Cunningham, honest to God.'

'Have you a licence for that, Cunningham?'

'Hey, chaps, Cunningham has a pipe.'

'Shut up shouting. Do you want Rorky to hear you?'

'He's right. Put a sock in it, O'Keeffe.'

Their voices travel clearly. That is because of the lake. Its surface becomes a reflector. Mr Curtis had so informed him. Take no part as yet. Roll up your sleeves and observe closely as you lift the plate from the bottom. It is a dark disc it is brown it is beautiful and golden it is cold and clean and white with a blue rim it is circular and shallow and capable of flight like a bird. So prove it then fling it then uphill inland miles high O Jesus into the air skimming above forest and mountains spinning and climbing swiftly and as swiftly descending, now aghastly likely to brain the sudden stout unwitting appearing figure. Christ. Rorky.

'Look out, sir.'

'Heads.'

It slices wickedly the empty air six inches above the startled brows. Trouble.

Later, on orderly duty out of turn for punishment, peeling potatoes, thousands of potatoes, while the rest are two opposing armies concealed about the mountain in a game of Snatch The Flag.

'Wish I was out there with them.'

'That's what you get for trying to decapitate Rorky.'

'Don't go on.'

'It's the third time. Why do you have to go slinging plates around?'

'I like the way they fly.'

'It could be serious.'

'I wouldn't count decapitating Rorky as very serious.'

'You're peeling too much off those potatoes.'

Brian Moloney, cookery expert. Tell him a riddle.

'What has eyes but can't see. Do you know?'

'Of course I know.'

Of course he did. He probably fell out of the cradle laughing at that one. How long ago? Same as himself. Nearly fourteen years.

'Here's another. If a man named Murphy loses all his money at the races, why is he like a peeled potato?'

No use. A pitying look. Better tell him.

'Because he's a skinned spud.'

'Very funny. You got me kept to cookhouse yesterday by being funny. Why don't you lay off?'

All right. Dry up, McDonagh. Peel the damn potatoes. There was a mountain of them, a self-multiplying mountain.

But later on they were friends again, going down to the farmhouse with cans for the milk supply. In the farmyard a bull was servicing one of the cows. They both stared, transfixed.

'My God,' Brian said, 'he has an enormous one.'

It was. And bright red. Men were supervising the bull's exertions and hooves clattered loudly on the cobbles.

'You've come for the milk I see,' the farmer called to them as though nothing extraordinary was going on at all. 'Knock on the door there and herself will fetch it for you.'

When they were cycling into the village later Brian told Cunningham and O'Keeffe all about it.

'And you both stood and watched?' O'Keeffe remarked.

'Free show,' Brian said.

'You'll have to tell it in confession.'

'Why? All I saw was meat being manufactured.'

Cunningham yelled out and nearly fell off his bike. When they came to a stop he took out the pipe.

'Wait until I have a few drags to compose myself,' he said.

'Rorky will smell it off your breath,' O'Keeffe said.

'Not if you eat peppermints afterwards,' Cunningham explained.

They had to stop again at the level crossing where the gates guarding the narrow-gauge railway were closed. It was late evening. Rooks were calling in chorus from the nearby wood and flax rotting in pits mingled with the faint smell of turf smoke. Above the flecks of mica gleaming on the rough road the hedges trailed red flowers like leaping flames. How many mountains, how many fields, how many habitations by empty roads all waiting for night to come in the vast spread of miles between this white gate and home?

'McDonagh is playing his violin in the village concert,'

Brian said, 'and Dillon is giving a recitation, the one about Fontenoy. You know it: "Thrice at the huts of Fontenoy the English columns failed, and Twice the lines of St Antoine the Dutch in vain assailed."'

'It's as long as today and tomorrow,' Tim observed.

'Better than the fiddle,' O'Keeffe said, whining through his nose. 'Saw, saw, scrape, scrape.'

'You shut up, O'Keeffe.'

Brian leaned his elbow on the top rung of the gate and his foot on the third to support his bicycle while he considered.

'O'Keeffe would like to be a bull,' he decided, 'wouldn't you, O'Keeffe?'

'I don't think this is a very good pipe,' Cunningham complained. 'It keeps getting full up with spit.'

'Bulls have it very handy when you think of it,' Brian continued. 'Cows all over the place for a start and then when they want food it's all around them. No trouble getting rid of it either. Just drop a pancake wherever you fancy.'

'McDonagh stepped in one yesterday right up to his socks,' O'Keeffe recalled. 'He never looks where he's walking.'

'You're saying that because Anne Fox got on the crossbar of his bicycle instead of on yours, O'Keeffe. Go on – own up,' Brian said.

'This pipe is definitely very peculiar,' said Cunningham. He was shaking it and examining it.

'You have to break them in,' O'Keeffe told him. Then he peered closely and said: 'Your face is looking a bit green, Cunningham. Hey, chaps, have a screw at Cunningham's face.'

But the tracks began to shudder and the labouring engine cut him short, deafening them with noise and filling the world with billowing smoke. They waved and shouted unheard remarks to the passengers.

In an idle moment in mid-morning he turned over a stone and there beneath it was the ants' nest. He squatted down to study it, thinking of himself as Gulliver, a giant brooding over a pigmy city. Among the streets and galleries and tunnelled entrances the insects worked in ordered frenzy. Some hurried to carry the white eggs to safety, others rounded up and herded grey lice like cattle, the guards patrolled the perimeter. An earwig blundering unwittingly into the middle of the activity was surrounded at once and attacked. Who would win? At first it seemed it would be the earwig. It shook off its attackers several times although it was held by the legs by others as it attempted to retreat. But it grew weaker and its case lost its glossy brown sheen and became dull and blackened. Slowly overmastering it the ants dragged it into one of the tunnels and out of sight. Others collected and removed the bodies of dead comrades. Should he have rescued it? It had not been the earwig's fault. But then neither had it been the fault of the ants. After a while the eggs had all disappeared, the streets and galleries were empty. Replacing the stone over the destroyed city he became conscious once more of warm sunlight and an infinity of sky. He was conscious too of a vague feeling of guilt, a deep and accusing hush all about him, as though the morning were disowning him. Was it, then, he himself who had been at fault? Had it been wrong that he, a passing stranger, a guest without rights in that remote place, had tampered with a stone which had rested undisturbed through a lifetime? The thought troubled him and brought him back at intervals to re-examine that hidden corner of the field.

The girls from the convent school were to take part in the concert with them, Rorky said, by kind permission of the Reverend Mother and the parish priest and he hoped, he said, that their behaviour would be that of gentlemen and in the best tradition of Catholic Scouting. At which the bigger fellows yelled out 'Yoo Hoo' and everybody clapped and made jeering noises. So there was a lot of clothes brushing and shoe polishing beforehand and a heavy demand for hair oil among the bigger fellows and then they set off in a bus which had to be hired to carry the props. Then the hall on the top floor of the Market Exchange in the centre of the village square had to have extra benches set along its side walls because it was going to be packed out. The girls' choir opened conducted by the teacher in charge and then the boys sang Scout choruses and then there were

sketches and individual items. Dillon's recitation took the
house down because it was about the Irish Brigade in Flanders
and their famous charge that won the victory for France against
the English and Dutch and Austrian allies. You could hear his
voice even above the hubbub in the dressing room and the way
he did it and the words themselves were super:

'Bright was their steel, 'tis bloody now, their guns are filled with
  gore
Through shattered ranks and severed files and trampled flags they
  tore.'

He knew from school of course that the officers and men of
the Irish Brigades on the continent were called the Wild Geese
because after the Jacobite wars the French ships that smuggled
brandies and wines and silks into hidden coves around the
coast took Irish recruits back with them and put them down in
the ship's log as so many wild geese. There was an historical
novel about it on their school course called *A Swordsman of the
Brigade* in which Piaras Gras of Kerry had to flee the country
and join Sheldon's Horse because he killed the English landlord
Sir Michael Sickles in a quarrel over a mare.

'That's a fine mare for a Papist beggar,' growled Sir Michael.
'No thanks to you for her fineness, you black hound,'
retorted Piaras.

If you had lived then you could have been one of them, a
feather in your hat and your trusty sword by your side, white
sails spread above you in the moonlight and the ship rolling in
a silver and black sea. You had to talk French a bit.

'Here is Monsieur le Capitaine Timothy McDonagh, milord.'
'*Ah – un brave Irlandais.*'
'At your service, Milord Marechal, Duc de Vendôme.'

Outside the recitation was coming to its close. Dillon's voice
rang through the attentive silence.

'Across the plain and far away passed on that hideous wrack
  While cavalier and fantassin dash in upon their track
  On Fontenoy, on Fontenoy, like eagles in the sun
  With bloody plumes the Irish stand, the field is fought and won.'

The dressing room shook with the thunder of their applause. It was warm and overcrowded there too and the air reeked of coconut butter, of cream and powder, of greasepaint and spirit gum. A powder-pollinated mirror with a gilt frame was peopled with their ghosts. When he opened the window to let in its cool stream of air the square below was deserted under a sky full of stars. The shapes of mountains gave it the air of an Alpine village. There was no light showing anywhere in the huddled houses. Knock thunderously on the door.

'Landlord, landlord, rouse up.'

'*Diable*. What is it you require at such an unseemly hour?'

'Lodging for myself and a stable for my horse. See to it, you villain.'

He sets before you cold meat and a stoup of wine and stirs the fire into a blaze. Carelessly you draw out an aromatic cigarro.

'Hey, dopey – you're next.'

The compère announced that assistant patrol leader Timothy McDonagh would render two violin solos: 'Largo' by G. F. Handel and 'Perpetuum Mobile' by H. E. Warner, accompanied on the piano by Miss Kitty Longmore. The piano was down in pitch and created a lot of difficulty, but they listened with good-natured respect, and when he had finished they were brightened considerably by the announcement that the next item would be a comedy sketch called 'A Cure for Nerves'. On his return he found the girls had just invaded the boys' dressing room.

'My God, they have everything,' the girls said.

'We're in to scrounge a bit of make-up,' Anne Fox told them. 'What sort?'

'Anything at all to glam up. Those lights out there make you look like something out of a morgue.'

'Did the school not fit you out?'

'It's the nuns. Are you mad? They think powder is a mortal sin.'

'Help yourselves,' the bigger fellows said.

'Hey, girls – lipstick.'

'Oh God, let me at it.'

They set to work slapping on powder and paint and helping

one another with pocket mirrors and advice. They let Anne Fox have first go at the large mirror because she was down to sing a song and she was dressed as a flower seller.

'I heard you playing and it was marvellous,' she told him. 'I meant to wish you luck before you went out but we were afraid to come near the dressing room while Miss Malone was hanging around. She blabs everything to Reverend Mother.

'Where is she now?'

'Gone off with her boyfriend. An awful stick. Are you going to listen to me? I'll probably die of fright so you could do your first-aid or something.'

If she really needed first-aid the bigger fellows would trample him to death. But he watched from the wings. She carried a basket on her arm and a spotlight followed her movements uncertainly as she sang in a voice which sounded remarkably beautiful to him.

> 'There are many, sad and weary
> In this pleasant world of ours
> Crying every night so dreary
> Won't you buy my pretty flowers?'

Beyond the footlights marshalled eyes gleamed in pairs from the darkness and the palpitating heat.

She took her curtain and stepped back into the wings.

'Was I awful?'

'Oh no. It was super.'

The space in the wings was confined. Her every movement engulfed him in great gusts of perfume.

'Here, you fry,' the stage manager looked at them, 'you're under my feet. Do your courting elsewhere.'

They hurried out of his way. She was mad with indignation.

'The cheek,' she said. 'He's really only the village butcher.'

They had tea and lemonade and cakes afterwards in a private house where the parish priest and Miss Malone, who had slipped back quietly before the end of the concert, kept a smiling and secure watch on the goings on. But the girls were allowed to walk with them to the bus.

'Why don't you come up to the camp tomorrow?' he invited.

'I don't think I can.'

'Lots of the other girls do.'

'They're the locals. I'm one of the boarders and they won't let you out of their sight. Nuns are the absolute limit.'

'What I can't understand,' he said, 'is why you're all not on summer holidays still.'

'It's the bloody Irish language,' she told him. 'They run a summer course every year for two weeks and you more or less have to come back for it. It's a bit much. I mean I wouldn't mind if it were one of the holiday schools where there's music and a bit of dancing and you can go out in boats and do some swimming. But here it's just the rotten old school all over again for two extra weeks.'

'That's a shame,' he said. 'I'd see them to blazes.'

'Not my father, you wouldn't,' she said. 'He spent ages away in America and now he's back he's mad about reviving Irish. He even talks it to the dog. What about yours?'

'The other way round. He thinks they're cracked.'

'So do I,' she said.

'You still have your make-up on.'

'I know. It's heaven. I can't bear to take it off.'

'Won't you get into trouble?'

'I don't care. Anyway I can wash as soon as I get back. The soap will soon get rid of the smell. It's in thick carbolic bars. The kind you scrub the floor with.'

'Well,' he said, upset that she should be less privileged than the others, 'do your best to come. Slip out if you can.'

'Not half. I'll use any old excuse. Say a prayer for me.'

He doubted that any of the saints he knew of would have very much sympathy. They were more likely to be on the side of the Reverend Mother.

'All aboard,' the assistant scoutmaster said. But they were all exchanging names and addresses and he had to wait. Then they hung out of the windows singing and calling funny remarks until the night swallowed up the waving girls. The smell of flax and turf smoke blew coolly through the open windows. Their lights gleamed on brown bog and pools of water. They sang above the churning of wheels and the labouring engine.

'Move over, O'Keeffe.'

'What?'

'I said move over. Take your big feet out of my face.'

'They're not my feet.'

'Are they yours, Cunningham?'

'What ones?'

'Those ones.'

'Oh. Hey.'

'I knew they were.'

'Silence in there. Lights out.'

Silence. A giggle. O'Keeffe whispers.

'Hanrahan's after the little girl in the farmhouse.'

'McDonagh's after a little girl too.'

'Where? In the post office?'

'No, in the convent.'

'Who?'

'Anna Vulpes.'

'Shut up, Cunningham.'

'Come again?'

'The little flower seller. The fair Anne Fox. Aren't you, Tim-tiddler?'

Do not answer. Pretend to be asleep. Keep her locked inside you. When all is quiet and they are curled in sleeping bags sleeping and oblivious she will turn her lovely face to you and smile. In the silence now, in the warmth of his sleeping bag a faint perfume lingered where her fingers had touched his arm.

'Monsieur – it is you.'

'Hush, not a sound. I have come to save you.'

They pass the sentry lying on the stone floor, his breathing heavy, his carbine beside him.

'Drugged beer, mademoiselle, he will sleep for hours.'

The walls of the convent are behind them and the horses are waiting. He wipes a trickle of blood from his cheek. He smiles through narrowed eyes.

'*Au revoir*, Monsieur le Butcher. You have paid, black villain, for your insult to a lady. . . .'

When you were on cookhouse there were only two others with you and the camp for most of the time was deserted. It was then you could sit preparing something in solitude and silence and think how deserted a deserted place could be, like the poem about Alexander Selkirk who had been the real Robinson Crusoe which went:

> 'I am monarch of all I survey
> My right there is none to dispute
> From the centre all round to the sea
> I am lord of the fowl and the brute.'

Survey once rhymed properly with sea because they used to pronounce it say. Country people did so still and the postman when he had finished the cup he had been offered said in praise of it by God then but that was the grand sup of tay. In the deserted camp the bell tents ringed you round and because they too were deserted seemed to have no meaning at all. But the lake however empty looking was always real. The water made busy sounds and slapped against stones or a fish would jump and leave a widening ring or a breeze you could hardly feel would cause a part of it to shadow over. The forest too was always real no matter how silent and so also were the mountains, their slopes and even shapes changing from moment to moment as cloud shadows moved across them or mist came down or dispersed or the wind pushed through heather or fern or the swampy patches which you knew from the green or grey colour of the reeds. They remained real because they continued to be themselves without any help from people or because in some peculiar way they continued to think all the time whereas bell tents and things people lived in or used for this or that were unable to be themselves or to think for themselves apart from people. But let a person walk through the camp or even the ginger cat which was wild come slinking around the guy ropes because it could smell food and immediately the tents were real and not things which you seemed only to imagine. On the other hand that was not true of the ruined cottages in the great valley below the slopes of the opposite mountain. A landlord had evicted a whole community so that he could enjoy the game shooting and although that was over a hundred years ago and storms had toppled the ruins and heather and fern had smothered them yet they were alive and never for a moment stopped thinking of what had happened. When you stood to look you could feel the waves of sad thoughts coming out and filling the air. That was because there was a story about them. The photograph album at home or a ticket which reminded you of a holiday that had passed remained real as well but that was for a different reason. They were real because of what you thought about them and not because they in some way like the lake and the mountains were able to think about themselves. Brother Hurley said that was a bit like Wordsworth Pantheism a pagan belief but he didn't seem to mind very much so it couldn't be seriously heretical.

Another thing of interest was the old blackened dixie boiled more quickly than the new one though they were both the same size. The reason was a dark surface absorbed heat while a light coloured one reflected it away. That was why people in hot countries should wear white clothes though why wear any at all. Also when the chaps down at the lake's edge were taking cock shots at a tin can you saw the can fall and roll first and a while later you heard the sound it made. Sound took that time to travel. Light took time too but not much. One day the ants ceased to crawl in the grass and sprouted wings and flew in dense clouds and always stuck together in pairs, which was the nuptial flight, after which the male would sink to the ground to die and most of the females too. The mayfly was the same; it would lie on the lake bottom for two years or so and then it would rise to the surface and take to the air and mate and after a very brief while it too would be dead. Butterflies were more or less the same. Butterflies were too beautiful to harm. When free like the rest you cycled into the village for bottles of lemonade and sweets when a postal order came from home. You learned how to make a bridge across the river with branches and ropes. You learned how to draw a map of the area to scale. You measured the height of a tree by reference to its shadow and a short stick stuck upright in the ground. For long hours you climbed in the mountains, the sweat trickling down your chest and belly. You were an explorer in uncharted lands searching for a lost city or scaling unconquered peaks. You were Cortez silent on a peak in Darien, who gazed about him in a wild surmise. Whatever you did or did not do, Time, the hardest thing of all to understand, kept on passing. Nothing could stop it. You got up and it was Monday and then it was Tuesday and then it was Wednesday and the holiday was being eaten up stealthily and unstoppably and school with its chalky air and interminable exercises was creeping nearer and again nearer.

On the last night of all there was a campfire. Father Fennell the troop chaplain came from Dublin for that and brought lemonade and cakes and sweets and ice cream in his car and the neighbouring people were invited, those who had helped them, the grocer, the farmer who owned the land and his family and others still and there was a singsong. Squat around the fire with your blanket about your shoulders and see in the red glow all those other faces grinning or looking thoughtful or listening but with hands also grasping the corners of blankets, and think of the pale lake below and the dark wood and always the out-lined height of mountains and the flag fluttering unseen on its high pole and sing ascending to the octave a line to each of the scale:

> 'I know a little pussy
> Her coat is soft and grey
> She lives out in a meadow
> Not very far away
> Although she is a pussy
> She'll never be a cat
> For she's a pussy willow
> Now what do you think of that?'

Then descend the eight notes again, getting louder all the time:

'Meaow, meaow, meaow, meaow, meaow, meaow, meaow, meaow – scat.'

Or don't sing at all but listen to the others with your blanket drawn tight and smelling of grass and woodsmoke and watch the sparks careering upwards against the tall pines and off into nothing underneath the high stars. Why is everything sad? Their voices in chorus these tiny sparks exploding flaring flying up to be lost in nothingness forever.

Dillon recites and Cunningham plays the mouth organ, 'Camptown Races' and then 'Way down upon the Swanee River'. They all join in:

> 'All the world am sad and weary
> Everywhere I roam
> That's why my heart is pining ever
> Far from the old folks at home.'

Last of all it is Father Fennell's turn, a chorus first in which all can join.

> 'The bear went over the mountain
> The bear went over the mountain
> The bear went over the mountain
> To see what he could see
>
> And what do you think he saw?
> And what do you think he saw?
> The other side of the mountain
> The other side of the mountain
> The other side of the mountain
> Was all that he could see.'

If that was all he saw he must have been blind. He would see other territories and further horizons. He would see yet another part of the world. There were other words to that air which you hummed softly to yourself in time with Father Fennell.

> 'O the cat she shat in the coalhole
> The cat she shat in the coalhole
> The cat she shat in the coalhole
> And covered it over with slack.'

'I thank you, one and all,' Father Fennell says when he has

finished, 'for having the patience to "bear" with me.' That was
a pun. He beams at them until the laughter and the groans die
away. He becomes solemn. 'The bear in that little song, my
dear boys, went all the way over the mountain to find only the
other side. All his searching after excitement and novelty left
him more or less where he had started. There is a moral there
for all of us and it suggests the song I will finish with, a simple
little song with an unchanging truth in it.'

He sings 'Home Sweet Home' and they listen respectfully and
applaud when it is over. It is now almost time to stand in a
circle clasping hands to sing 'Old Lang Syne'. So he clears his
throat and prepares to address them.

'My dear boys.' (They fix their eyes on the dying fire and
allow their thoughts to wander over the holiday.) 'Our Lord
Jesus Christ did not choose, as He might well have done, to
descend upon this world and begin His work of salvation as a
mature and adult man. No. It was His Holy Will instead to be
born a helpless babe, to grow up in the care of His Blessed
Mother and St Joseph and to dwell with them in deep filial
obedience. The Evangelists tell us little of His life in those early
years except that He dwelt with them in Nazareth and (this is
to be noted) "was subject to them". You can be sure that He
was a boy in the same way as all you gathered here are boys.
Indeed our Holy Mother the Church teaches us so when she
directs us to accept His full Humanity as well as His full Divinity.
For our Lord, the Church insists, was wholly human and at the
same time wholly divine. You may be sure He went walking
and swimming with the other children of the village; He took
part in their games; He studied at school with them and entered fully into all their pastimes and discussions. Now that is
how every boy should behave. He should love all that is clean
and healthy in boyhood. He should strive to be pure in mind and
strong in body, avoiding only those companions whose habits
may be evil and whose conversations are impure. He should
strive now to be as our Lord Jesus Christ was as a boy; just as in
later life, when time has brought with it the heavy responsibilities of maturity, he will strive to imitate Christ The Man. That

is what our dear Lord expects. And that is what our Scout movement tries to help you to do, especially in the last three rules of our Scout Code: to be brave, to be pure, to keep God's glory in mind, as the end of all our thoughts and all our actions. I am sure you are all good boys. And even if, now and then, one of us falls into carelessness, or even into sin, for the devil never rests in his efforts to turn the soul from God, then there is God's Church and there are God's sacraments to wash away every offence and make us again acceptable children of God.

'Your holiday is almost at its end. But the path to salvation knows no ending until the moment of death. Therefore, my dear boys, strive at all times to be good, to be pure, to be His children first, last and always. And for the rest, enjoy boyhood's great adventure, as Catholic boys, as Catholic scouts, as children of Christ Himself under the special protection of our Blessed Mother. And now we will conclude our little concert in the usual manner.'

Slip the blanket from your shoulders and shiver slightly as the night air seeps through the back of your shirt. Cross arms and clasp hands with each neighbour singing 'Old Lang Syne' all together, the fire now a circle of embers reddening and going dull again as the breeze lifts and falls. How many times will you sing it in a lifetime. How many hands to be clasped, how many journeys to end, how many partings to endure. Where would all these singing companions be in ten or twenty or thirty years to come? In what circumstances? In what strange lands? How happy or how sad?

The next morning they broke camp. Then the trek to the station. Then the long, long rail journey, the wheels pounding out a settled rhythm and everybody inclined to silence, everybody subdued.

II

The school playground, except for the ten minutes' break at eleven o'clock, was reserved for the primary kids. Once in secondary you were free at lunch hour to go home or wander the streets. You never wore a schoolbag but selected the books you needed by consulting the class schedule for that particular day and then you carried them in a strap. The primary kids wore their caps on the backs of their heads but a senior was expected to have one with a longer peak which he set straight above his eyes. Because of that in the poorer streets where school-going after the age of twelve was still a bit of a mystery you were sometimes mistaken for a Protestant. If it was cold you wore the school scarf with one tail hanging in front and the other looped over your shoulder the way they did in the pictures in *The Gem* or *The Magnet* and you never sneaked on another fellow and never cried when you got belted. If you brought sandwiches for lunch and Brother Gorman saw you throw any of the bread on the street he would pick it up, kiss it and place it in a scrap bin which he kept for birds and animals. He found it hard to stoop because he was as old as the hills. Brother Quinlan wore his hat all the time in class and carried on a personal crusade against company keeping. If he saw you with girls after school hours he announced it to the class next day.

'We have another recruit for the ranks of the love-lorn,' he would say, 'another precocious contender for the favours of the ladies. And who is it this time? Reynolds, stand up, boy, so that we can have a good view. There he is, boys, the latest young swain.'

When Reynolds had endured scrutiny for a time Brother Quinlan would make his next move.

'Now, Reynolds, up you go and add your name to the roll of honour.'

Reynolds would add his name to the sheet of paper pinned to the back of the door. It was headed in Brother Quinlan's perfect script: 'List of the Matrimonially Inclined'. But when Cunningham was caught he wrote down: *Eamon de Valera.*

'Christ, you'll be slaughtered,' they told him.

But Brother Quinlan never noticed and no one minded about the list any more because the joke was now on him.

Secondary school was makeshift, a row of Victorian houses converted into classrooms, their backs forming one wall of the school yard, their fronts overlooking wrought-iron railings and the street, which was quiet and tree-lined, a distraction if your desk was against the window and it was open to let in air on a sunny autumn morning. The sunlight and the silence and the changing colours of leaves drew the eye and then the mind.

'Continue, McDonagh.'

A sense of shock. A blank look.

'Wool-gathering again. Do you know where we were? Show him, Moloney.'

Brian pointed out the place and he stood up and began to read:

' "This universal passion for politics is gratified by daily gazettes, as with us in China. But as in ours the emperor endeavours to instruct his people, in theirs the people endeavour to instruct the administration. You must not, however, imagine that they who compile these papers have any actual knowledge of politics, or the government of a state: they only collect their materials from the oracle of some coffee house; which oracle has himself gathered them the night before from a beau at a gaming table, who has pillaged his knowledge from a great man's porter, who had his information from the great man's gentleman, who invented the whole story for his own amusement the night preceding. . . . " '

'Cunningham, can you tell us what "oracle" means?'

'Sir, a restless person.'

'Sit down, you godforsaken lump of a half-eejit. Tell him, McDonagh.'

'Someone who prophesies. A wise and discerning man, sir.'

'Do you think the *"oracle of some coffee house"* in what you've just read, would be such a person?'

'No, sir.'

'Then why does Goldsmith describe him as one?'

'Sir, he's using a mode of speech: verbal irony. He really means the opposite.'

'What literary style does Goldsmith use generally? Would you say it's the grand style or the sublime style, for instance?'

'Sir, the graceful style.'

'Good. All right, Moloney, continue.'

Brian stood up.

'By the way, McDonagh, Brother Cronin wants a word with you. Go and see him now.'

He found Fifth Year A in a deep tussle with Euclid. Brother Cronin had drawn the proposition on the blackboard and all their heads were bent over the task of solving it.

Brother Cronin regarded him sternly.

'We'll talk outside,' he said.

His heart jumped at the cold anger of the voice. What had he done? The door clicked behind them and they were alone in the corridor.

'You were in the school's playing field yesterday, McDonagh.'

'Yes, sir.'

'Watching the football match between Fifth Year A and a team from Scoil Sraid Ui Chonaill. There were teachers from that school present and some parents as well. You chose to treat them to a display of disrespect and rank bad manners.'

'How, sir?'

'You were cheering for Fifth Year A. How? *Come on, Cronin's*, you kept shouting. A mere guttersnipe would have the good manners to say "Brother Cronin's".'

'I'm sorry, sir.'

'You have reason. If you were one of my own charges I'd punish you here and now, but you belong to Brother Raymond. I've already told him what occurred. When you get back to him, tell him you have admitted your disrespectful behaviour and that I am leaving it to him to punish you.'

He reported back to Brother Raymond, the English teacher.

'If you were cheering at one of the minor league matches for the Peadar Mackens or the Kevin Barrys, would you keep

yelling "Come on the Mr Kevin Barrys" or "Come on, the
Mr Peadar Mackens"?' Brother Raymond wondered.

'Nobody does that, sir.'

'They'd sound damn silly if they did. However, you'd better
get me the leather.'

The leather was kept in the press with exercises awaiting
correction. When he had fetched it Brother Raymond told him
he could put it back. It was puzzling but he did so.

'If Brother Cronin happens to ask me,' Brother Raymond
said, 'I can say with truth: oh, he got the leather all right. So
can you. In this life keep as many people happy as you can.
All right, you can go back to your desk.'

At lunchtime he told Brian about it.

'Cronin is an oul droopy drawers,' he said. 'Did you ever
notice the way he talks? High up in the head. He probably has
no knackers. Have you any money?'

'Fourpence.'

'Marvelorious. Buy me a cup of tea and a doughnut.'

'I have to call down to the church.'

'It'll only take ten minutes.'

There were several small shops where they met for refreshment if they had the money or to cog an exercise neglected
the previous night. They went down wooden steps to a basement and found Cunningham struggling to finish a Latin
translation. They got two buns and two teas for the fourpence
and joined him.

'Don't talk to me,' he appealed. 'This bloody thing is as long
as a wet Sunday.' They looked over his shoulder.

' "Fabius was surrounded by the nearest soldiers and killed.
When this multitude had fled the gates of the camp were
occupied by the crowd and the march impeded. More men
perished in that place without wounds in that place than in
the battle. Neither were many absent but they were driven
from the camp. . . ." '

'That's all wrong,' Brian said.

'I don't care.'

'It doesn't make sense.'

'It doesn't have to make sense. It's all right once you can show you had a go.'

'Are you mad? You'll get clatthered.'

'Oh, shut up.'

'I have to go,' Tim said.

They left Cunningham to his fate and hurried to Stephen's Green. The church was empty and the flagged floor echoed to their footsteps.

'So this is where you serve mass. *Dominus vobiscum. Et cum spirit tu tuo.*'

The gold leaf on the inlaid walls reflected the points of candles. The bust of Cardinal Newman regarded them suspiciously.

'Wait here,' Tim said.

He crossed the altar alone, genuflected before the tabernacle and went into the vestry. As always there was the faint smell of incense. He wrote in a note to the clerk:

This morning a woman asked me to have the name of Joseph Devlin added to the list of the recently deceased for tonight's meeting of the Men's Sodality. He is a deceased member and their prayers are requested. In the hurry this morning I forgot to tell you.

He left it on the robing altar where it would be sure to be seen. He was greatly relieved. To have deprived the departed soul of their prayers through his oversight would have been a serious matter. It had been nagging him on and off all morning.

'That's that,' he said to Brian when he rejoined him. They had to run most of the way back.

At teatime his younger brother Frank was being funny and said to him, '*Tabhair dom arain, ma se do thoil e.*'

'Oh, shut up,' he said.

'Don't be rude,' his mother said. 'What does it mean?'

'It means give me a piece of bread, please.'

She buttered more bread and said to his father, 'Isn't that marvellous. Isn't he coming on great at the Irish.'

'I suppose it's polite anyway,' his father said without enthusiasm.

'You have to have Irish for everything nowadays and it'll be a great advantage to him later on. You might at least encourage the child.'

'It will indeed,' his father said, 'and very useful too when he's queuing up outside the Labour Exchange and wants to pass the time with a bit of a chat in the native tongue.'

His mother looked hurt.

'You're in a right humour,' she complained.

They were all silent until his father got sorry and explained that he was worried by rumours of more lay-offs on the job. Business was said to be going badly. It was a Protestant firm and a lot of the garage staff were Freemasons and likely to be kept on longer than himself.

'But you're there longer than most of them.'

'It hasn't happened yet,' his father said, pushing the matter aside.

III

On Saturdays during the winter season it was always the same: great waves of sound rising spontaneously from the close-packed crowd, moments of tense silence when the houses about the ground crouched in apprehension. There were the bicycles marshalled in ranks along the wall, the women peddling fruit and chocolate, the youngsters selling coloured favours, the beggars waiting to entertain with a song or a tune on the fiddle. There were the miserly or improvident who perched themselves on the hump-backed bridge where they could see the play when it centred about the goal at the river end of the pitch but not when it swung to the other end and the grandstand blocked their view. On the bridge were the unfortunates; the halt, the old, the penniless. Inside it was different. They had jobs, more or less steady. They could pay their rent. They knew where their next meal was coming from and could claim a basic respectability. The McDonaghs always went inside. When the home team travelled the McDonaghs and their relatives and pals all travelled. That was part of the unquestioned pattern, like the Saturday Each-Way Double or mass on Sunday morning.

Friday was payday, the day the Lord spoke. Saturday was football day, rashers and eggs for tea, pints up the road, post mortems on the play. Sunday was cross-channel papers, late mass in the morning, junior league games in the public parks, best suits, clean shirts and, often enough, sore heads. It was Paddy McDonagh's world, so naturally his element that he hardly noticed it as he made his way to Tobin's public house. He had been unable to go to the match that day because with Christmas just over a month away, he felt he should make a start on the job of preparing the books for the society of which he was honorary secretary and treasurer. But he had arranged to meet his brothers afterwards for a drink before going to his mother's for tea, a Saturday ritual. There were reasonable limits to a man's devotion to duty.

That there were smaller and bigger fishes in his world he acknowledged. Some were poorer, some slightly better off. There were friendly and unfriendly. He himself was better off. Or had been up to the present. He dressed better, he had a better command of language, he made intelligent use of his mind. Music and literature of sorts interested him. He would sometimes visit the theatre, not merely for revues or Christmas pantomime with the children, but plays. He could attend to his employers' needs with competence and respect while consciously and quietly preserving his own dignity. Most of the time. In his employers' world he was a servitor, someone who obeyed instructions and did what he was paid for. He bore no resentment. That was how things were. But in this world he had been born into and through which he now walked he was a free man; indeed, in a modest way, a singular one. People asked his advice. People trusted him with their confidences. In the case of the society they paid him the ultimate compliment of trusting him with their savings. It was not that he went out of his way to push himself at them. It came about according to the nature of things.

Outside the ground a line of lighted tramcars waited silently for the crowd to emerge. Already a few early leavers were coming in dribs and drabs through the main gate. A November mist, hastening the dying of the light, emphasized the mingled odours of sea and sulphur and made the air damp. Beyond the ground he could see the gasometers, the huddled roofs, and the signals along the railway embankment. On each spire in the smoky air he could put a name. It was his world, these rows of tiny cottages, these slightly better off houses, the Bottle Workers' Social Hall, the hump-backed bridge, the fishing boats on the river, Tobin's public house.

He went inside. It was still lit by gaslight because, they said locally, Tobin had shares in the gas company. And he was asked the question he had anticipated even as he pushed open the door.

'Were you at the match?'

'No. I missed it today,' he said.

'I thought you might know who won,' Tobin said.

'We'll find out before long,' Paddy McDonagh said. 'When I was passing it seemed all over – bar the shouting.'

'I'm a Rovers man myself . . .' Tobin began.

'I never met a Ringsend man yet that wasn't,' Paddy McDonagh assured him.

'I'm a Rovers follower since I was able to sit up without assistance,' Tobin insisted, 'but I'll admit this. They won't win against Shelbourne this season.'

'You're wrong,' Paddy said, 'and I'll tell you why. They're still playing Rogers at centre forward, a man who should have been dropped two seasons ago.'

'He was very good at one time.'

'The best in the business,' Paddy agreed, 'but not any longer. He's too slow.'

Tobin shook his head and said philosophically, '*Anno Domini*, I suppose. Good, bad or indifferent, age gets at us all.'

Age did, Paddy McDonagh mutely acknowledged. What was he himself now? Forty-five. Sweet Christ. He stared at his glass in sudden melancholy. A frothy residue clung in three distinct rings about the inside, the creamy head on the dark brown porter was almost halfway down. How many more to drink before the gravedigger shook his shovel? Even as he wondered the clock on Ringsend Church began to peal the hour. The sound caused the thought to linger. He counted the strokes in silence.

A little distance away his son Tim leaned against the upright of the goal post in the public park and numbered the strokes too. Five. A sea mist creeping in over the playing field was hastening the end of the November evening. It had been giving in without much of a struggle anyway. He felt the chill of it seeping through knicks and jersey, its dampness on his face and hair. Play was pinned firmly to the far end of the pitch where the ball was more often in touch than in play. Enthusiasm had died. There would be nothing much to do in goal now except wait through the last few minutes for the end. He heard Cunningham's voice calling out to him.

'Tim. Hey – McDonagh. See you Monday.'

Cunningham was already mounting his bicycle. He turned to wave acknowledgment, then leaned back again and attended with only half his mind to what little was going on. They had a lead of four to one. The game was in the bag.

Beyond the distant players and the cottages marking the park boundary the masts of ships and the arms of cranes broke the skyline. Above them, as yet barely discernible, a grey disc waited to become a moon. Sound too was oddly subdued. It was as though life had gone off without him, taking the players and the huddled knots of spectators with it. He leaned against the upright as at a tramstop and waited for the world to come back. He would be going to Brian's for tea. He was glad. There was a melancholy in the evening which made him low in spirit, a melancholy which would increase if he were left to travel alone through damp streets where people were drawing curtains and lamps were being lit. November was a sad month. Evenings closed in, leaves fell, names were handed in to the churches to be put on the List of the Dead.

When the thin note of the final whistle brought play to an end the world returned again and he joined the rest at the park wall, where; surrounded by a forest of muddy knees and sagging stockings, engulfed in odours of sweat and embrocation, he changed back into his clothes.

'The other crowd are saying they're going to lodge a protest,' Brian told him.

'What is there to protest about?'

'The light. They say the match should have been abandoned because of the bad light.'

'Sour grapes. They were already beaten halfway through.'

A foghorn on the river was calling out at measured intervals. His clothes were damp.

'Hurry up,' Brian said.

There was mud on Brian's hair and forehead. He looked at his own knees and hands.

'I wish I could have a wash.'

'Don't worry. We have running water.'

'I mean now.'

'Christ, will you come on.'

He stuffed his togs in the bag and tied it to his bicycle carrier. They cycled side by side.

'That's where the oul fella races his greyhounds,' Brian remarked as they passed Shelbourne Park.

'I've been in it with my father,' he answered. 'He goes nearly every Saturday. He's a Shelbourne follower. What's yours?'

'It's all Gaelic football with my oul fella,' Brian said. 'He follows Tipperary in the All Ireland. Otherwise it's greyhounds, breakfast, dinner and tea. Do you like greyhounds?'

'Not very much.'

'That makes you my blood brother, McDonagh. Send up smoke signals if in danger. I hate the sneaky skinnymalinks.'

They pushed up the hill and crossed the iron bridge. A tram driver behind them banged impatiently on the footbell. They moved to one side and grimaced broadly at him as he passed.

Grandfather McDonagh lay still in the half-light of the bedroom and listened to the voice of someone calling to a neighbour in the street outside. The damp air had chilled his shoulders. He was unsure of the time. Someone knocked on the hall door below, and it was opened and then closed again. His afternoon rest had gone on longer than he had intended. It would be as well to get up.

To avoid the risk of a dizzy spell from stooping he had left his boots beside him on the bedclothes. His jacket too. His hard collar and silk string of a tie were looped about the bedpost. At seventy-three putting such things back on took time. The narrow stairs creaked under his weight as he descended to the kitchen where the light was already on.

'I'll have a look at the paper, missus.'

'You won't. It hasn't come.'

'I heard the knock on the door a few minutes back.'

'That was young Byrne looking for the loan of a cupful of sugar.'

'Divil ever they're done,' he said. 'What's the time?'

He stared at the clock on the wall until he got it in focus. Half past five.

'The bloody paper's late.'

'Maybe the child is sick,' she said. 'I've often pitied him, a little wisp of a thing out with his bike and his papers in the worst of weather.'

'If he is he picked a nice night for it – Saturday. Has no one any consideration nowadays.'

'You're in a great flurry about your oul paper.'

'So would you be if you had one leg of a double up and wanted the result of the second.'

That puzzled her.

'How can you know you've one horse up when you weren't out?'

'I heard someone shouting the result of the first to a neighbour in the street a while back.'

He lifted the morning paper from his armchair at the fire and said unnecessarily, 'This bloody thing is useless.'

In an attempt to soothe him she said, 'Anthony Rowe may have the evening paper when he comes.'

But Anthony was in the same plight.

'I'm like yourself,' he said, 'waiting for it all evening. And like yourself I said to myself, Anthony I said, there's nothing for it but take the football coupon to the McDonaghs with you and get a screw at theirs. I'm at a loss to understand it.'

'The missus thinks the youngster may be sick.'

'On the only night there's a bit of news in the paper?' Anthony said, unbelieving. 'This is deplorable. What about the racing results and the football reports and the cross-channel scores?'

'It's the racing results are important to me,' Grandfather McDonagh told him. 'I have a strong interest in the outcome of the last race at Lingfield.'

They heard the key turning in the latch.

'The men of the house,' Anthony Rowe predicted.

He was a small man, about seventy, who wore wire spectacles all the time on the tip of his nose but ignored them by continually gazing above them.

The sons trooped in.

'Have you the late sports between you?'

None of them had.

Paddy said, 'I got a look at it in Tobins while I was waiting.'

'Did you happen to notice if Highland Hero won the last race at Lingfield?'

Paddy tried to remember.

'Highland Hero. Wait now. No. That was Hapless Hope at Manchester. Or was it?'

'If you can't remember,' Grandfather McDonagh begged him, 'at least don't torture me.'

'You'll get one when you go up the road,' his wife told him. She had a large plate in each hand, one loaded with rashers, the other with fried eggs. 'Now sit over – the tea is ready.'

They seated themselves in a pattern that never varied: old McDonagh at the head of the table, Charles and Christy to his right and left, Paddy and Jim to the right and left again. Anthony

Rowe occupied the bottom chair. He crossed himself before taking up his knife and fork.

'Yiz lost?' he remarked.

'Three-one,' Christy admitted, 'it was painful.'

'Nothing scientific,' Charles put in, in a resigned voice. 'All kick and rush. Football in this city has gone to hell.'

'Rogers should be dropped,' Jim offered.

'He should,' Paddy agreed, 'I said it two seasons ago.'

'He did, mind you,' Anthony Rowe confirmed, with an approving look over the spectacles. 'I remember him saying that.'

'The whole bloody bagful should be dropped,' Christy decided, 'they're making a show of us.'

There was general agreement. Jim said to his father:

'We met our friend the enemy in Tobins – old Turner.'

It had the anticipated effect. His father's face darkened.

'And what had that miserable article to say for himself?'

'He was saying the third goal was like the famous one Nolan scored in Waterford in '26.'

'Bloody liar. He wasn't in Waterford in '26.' The old man pushed his cup to the side.

'Tea, missus,' he demanded.

She fetched the teapot and poured for him without demur. Her stoop had become almost perpetual, her eyes for a lot of the time peered at something remote from her surroundings. Their comings and goings belonged to a world so unrelated to hers that she hardly noticed them. Except Paddy. His presence was always a reality, a point of contact with the material world which otherwise she seemed almost to have left. She turned to him now.

'What about you, Paddy?'

'No thanks, Mother, not yet.'

She put down the pot and withdrew again into reflection. They resumed their talk of football. Saturday consisted of little else.

After tea he took out the violin which had been left in readiness in Brian's before setting off for the match and he tuned it while Mrs Moloney lifted the lid of the piano stool and searched for the volume of waltzes. Much of what she disturbed was sheet music bought from time to time in Woolworths. She put to one side songs such as 'Ramona' and 'Lay My Head Beneath a Rose' and 'Carolina Moon'. She was musical in a sort of a way and liked to play the piano with him because in years gone by when her brother was alive, she told him, he was a violinist and they used to play together on winter evenings. Brian as usual dissociated himself and was trying to make a wireless that would fit in a cigar box, but Cornelius and O'Sheehan were expressing a polite interest prior to retiring for chess. O'Sheehan had the cat on his knee at the fire and was stroking it behind the ears.

'Here's one little creature who will pay close attention,' he said.

'The cat?' Cornelius questioned, not sure that he had understood.

'Her ladyship,' O'Sheehan confirmed. 'Animals are affected by music, though some more than others. Cows milk better if you sing to them. Horses stay quiet. I knew a blacksmith once who always made his helper sing 'The Coulin' if he was shoeing a horse that was restive. And cats have been known to beat the time.'

'What about dogs,' Cornelius enquired, 'would they run better, do you think?'

'Dogs will take music as it comes though in general they are unmusical. Some may even howl because the higher frequencies are distressing to their hearing. But cats are different. Cats prick their ears and take a close interest, at times even lascivious.'

Cornelius made a little signal at the use of the word in front of the boys and O'Sheehan went on quickly to cover up.

'And what about your own son and heir here, is he musical at all?'

Brian stopped work for a moment to throw him a look of scorn.

'He's like myself,' Cornelius said. 'He can play anything provided it has a handle.'

Mrs Moloney found the waltzes and set them on the stand.
'Can you read over my shoulder?'

'I think so,' he said.

She was a stout woman with a large bun of hair but he made
out the notes correctly most of the time. All he could do was
double her right hand. But the sound was full and the novelty
held their attention. After a couple of pieces she thought they
might try one of the songs so that she could play the accompaniment while the violin took the voice part which was
likely to be more satisfactory. While she searched Mr O'Sheehan
asked if he could play 'The Coulin'. He knew it and obliged.

'My God,' Cornelius said, 'but that's what I call music.
These waltzes and things is all very well but give me our own
Irish airs all the time. Them and the Gaelic tongue together.'

He turned to Brian and said, 'I hope you were attending well
to that ancient and lovely air.'

Brian stopped work to look up at the ceiling and said,
'*Thermeh turmoon thermeh ormold cormow dirmied ormof.*'

'And what class of gibberish is that?'

They called it the Lingo. You just put a sound like rm between each syllable and with a little practice it became dead
easy to speak and understand. Brian had said: 'The tune the old
cow died of.'

'Nothing, really,' Brian answered.

'You needn't be making a farce of your heritage,' Cornelius
said with severity, 'I don't know what sort of a child I'm rearing
or what they teach you in school but it isn't manners anyway.'

He turned to O'Sheehan.

'The young nowadays has regard for nothing. All they want
is jazz bands.'

'I hate jazz bands,' Brian said.

'You hate greyhounds too. And the Irish language. Is there
anything you don't hate?'

'Now, now,' Mrs Moloney appealed, 'is it worth all that?'

'Damn the bit of it,' Cornelius agreed, 'because it rolls off
him like water off a duck.'

He turned to O'Sheehan.

'We'll go for our game,' he said. But at the door something else struck him and he turned.

'That's another thing he hates. Chess. All he's interested in is gadgets. And Bulldog Drummond, the true blue Britisher. Cross-channel trash. That's what his head is stuffed with.'

He followed O'Sheehan who had retreated already in some embarrassment.

'Which of the songs would you like?' Mrs Moloney asked, ignoring what had happened.

'Anything really. What about "Carolina Moon"?'

She spread it out and they played. Once, when he had been ten or eleven years of age he had stood at the Liffey wall at the bottom of Ringsend Park and watched a boatful of young men and girls being rowed down the river. It had been night and the moon was full. As they lifted the oars clear of the water droplets of bright silver dripped from the blades. Some were playing ukuleles and all were singing 'Carolina Moon' with some of the men improvising harmonies. The sound drifting to him across the water seemed so beautiful that it twisted inside him into a knot of pain and pleasure. He had longed to be grown up and going downriver in a boat making music with pretty girls. Even now the tune brought the sensation back and with it the dark river, the silver droplets, the brilliant moon. With it, too, came a sense of loss. Memory always added that, as though the things you thought about were calling out: come back, come back. Time was the culprit. It stole the world minute by minute, and hour by hour. A puzzle with no answer.

'Lovely,' Mrs Moloney said. 'You sight-read so well. Do you practise a lot?'

'Most days, I suppose.'

'What pieces?'

'Studies and sonatas, mostly. Corelli or Handel but sometimes Mozart. And we have junior orchestra once a week.'

'That's the best of living in a big city. In a country town you don't have much opportunity. If you bring one of the Handel next time I might be able to get around it. Will you do that?'

He promised he would. She tidied the music and said she would leave them in peace. 'That was a great treat for me,' she assured him. She seemed to mean it.

Brian put away the cigar box when she had gone and said, 'Did you hear that oul bastard going on at me. Bulldog Drummond, the true blue Britisher. Does your oul feller carry on like that?'

'He doesn't mind about magazines. In fact he sometimes has a read of them himself.'

'I wouldn't be surprised if mine did too. A crafty read behind my back. Otherwise how would he know all that stuff about Bulldog Drummond? I hope Tipperary get the tar beaten out of them in next season's All Ireland.'

'That other man with him. I think I met him before. Years ago. Has he a screw loose, do you think?'

'Bats. He told the da once he was Oisin.'

'Who?'

'Oisin. Your man in the Fianna who went off with that fair-haired filly to Tir na nOg – what's this her name was?'

'Niamh. But that's mad.'

'Bonkers,' Brian agreed. 'Isn't that what I'm telling you. Still, he has his good points – old O'Sheehan.'

He rooted in his pocket and produced half-a-crown.

'He slipped me this when I opened the hall door to him. He does it quite often.'

He put it back in his pocket.

'Which do you vote for, McDonagh – the pictures or a ramble around town?'

'How about the Fun Palace?'

'All right. We'll speculate a bob on the one-armed bandits. That'll leave plenty for fish and chips.'

As they were going through the kitchen Brian said to his mother, '*Wermee arma gormo-irming irmin tormoo tormown. Wermee wirmill bermee barmack armabourmout termen.*'

'Hasn't there been enough upset over that nonsense already,' she complained. 'What are you supposed to be saying?'

'Tell her, McDonagh.'

He told her. 'We are going into town. We will be back about ten.'

'Very well. But put on your heavy coat. It's turned cold.'

'*Bormolormox*,' Brian said.

They talked the Lingo to each other for a bit as they walked towards the city.

'I want a screw at the evening paper, Jerry,' Grandfather McDonagh told the curate. The bar was packed with the usual Saturday crowd but the McDonaghs found room to sit down. By one means or another they always did.

'It's with a man in the back bar at present,' he was told, 'but you'll have it the minute it's free.'

'I've a double on my mind, Jerry. No need to say more.'

'Certainly, Mr McD.'

Charles took the first round. He would be followed by Christy, Paddy and Jim in that order, and last of all by his father. If they wanted a sixth Charles would pay for it but the rest would reimburse him individually. An International. If one of them was short of ready money, as might occasionally happen, they chipped in for him. Family ties exacted that collective responsibility and Time had provided a ritual for everything.

'We had a bit of a heave in the office during the week,' Jim told him. 'There was this senior grade job going and they passed over several to give it to their chosen man. Need I tell you his religion?'

'Digs with the left foot, I suppose,' Christy said. 'Sweet Christ but this country has a long road to travel before there's a modicum of equality. They tell you Dan O'Connell won Catholic Emancipation but I beg leave to doubt it.'

'We're not finished with the Penal laws yet,' Charles agreed.

'Was he a Mason?' Paddy asked.

It was a subject that came close to him.

'What do you think?' Jim said. 'And with a head on him shaped from childhood by a B.B. hat.'

'They rule the roost, the same Masons,' Charles decided, 'and they look after their own. I could name ten large firms where they'll only have Protestants for foreman or senior clerk or department head. No Catholic need apply. That's the motto when it comes to dishing out the plums.'

'I'm anticipating the same trouble myself,' Paddy said gloomily.

'Over promotion?'

'If it was only promotion it'd be bad enough but it's more serious. There's talk of more lay-offs and there's a pair close behind me, both of them Protestants and almost certainly Freemasons. If it happens yours truly stands an odds-on chance of the breadline.'

'What about the union?' Jim asked. 'Isn't it first in last out?'

'It is according to the book but there are ways around it,' Paddy said. 'All they have to do is to invent two foremen's jobs and promote the pair of them. That puts them ahead of the field and Paddy McDonagh and some other Joe Soap get the knock. It's all stage-managed. I've seen it happen in the past.'

'Bloody gangsters,' Jim said.

An injury to one McDonagh was the concern of all. But Jerry's return at last with the paper provided distraction. The old man began to search through it for the racing results.

'There's nothing but news in this blasted thing,' he complained as he scanned page after page. 'Ah, here it is. Manchester. Old Orkney eight to one. That's the first leg, Jerry. I'd half-a-crown all on to the second.'

He searched again for the Lingfield results and found them. They could read the good news in his face before he spoke.

'I've brought it off, lads, Highland Hero first in the field at six to one.'

'A tidy little win,' Jerry said, 'and a grand end to the Flat Season. Let's see. Eight half-dollars all on to Highland Hero at sixes . . .'

Christy did a quick calculation.

'You'll collect six quid.'

Jim rubbed his hands together.

'I think the rules are quite specific as to procedure on such an occasion,' he suggested generally.

'Clear and unambiguous,' Christy supported. 'The winner has the honour of shoving out the boat.'

The old man folded the paper deliberately and handed it back before complying agreeably by ordering the bonus round.

'Bring us five small whiskeys, Jerry, and have one yourself.'

'Much obliged,' Jerry said. When he had gone Jim became serious again for a moment and said to Paddy:

'I'd have it out with the boss. I mean face-to-face. No ill-temper or anything, just a firm and reasonable how-do-I-stand kind of interview.'

'I was considering that.'

'It's often the best way. Gangsters and all as they are, they don't like to appear too blatant.'

Paddy nodded. He had had the same thought. Jerry returned and they drank to the old man's good luck.

The slot machines in the Fun Palace made them two shillings richer, an event unusual enough to be worth a celebration, so they bought a packet of cigarettes and picked on a fish and chip shop which struck them as very classy and had tea and cakes to follow their chips. Music and coloured lights added some sophistication. They lit up, inhaled, blew smoke through their noses, observed the patrons at surrounding tables. Young men in their best suits held hands with their girlfriends and bought them magnificent-looking ices.

'I love money,' Brian said. 'In fact I'm crazy about it. I intend to roll in it when I'm older. I bet you do too. Own up.'

'If I can,' Tim said. 'I suppose everybody wants to be rich. I mean it's only natural.'

'The oul fella keeps saying money is the root of all evil, but to get him to part with it you nearly have to operate on him.'

'That root of all evil stuff is a cod,' Tim said. 'The rich put that sort of stuff about to pacify the workers.'

Brian stared at him.

'You sound like a bit of a Red, McDonagh. If old Quinny hears you you'll be excommunicated.'

'Brother Quinlan should be excommunicated himself. Pope Leo was in favour of the trade unions but Quinny can't stand them.'

'He can't stand sex either,' Brian said. 'That list on the wall. I mean if there wasn't sex there'd be no popes, would there? Sex is great.'

'How do you know?'

'Never mind.'

'Come on, Moloney.'

'There was this dame at a party where we were playing spin-the-bottle and she came outside with me. Very hot.'

'And what happened?'

Brian tapped cigarette ash into the tray.

'You're too young,' he said.

'Swank.'

But he looked mysterious and it could be true. Moloney would chance anything. Cunningham was worse still.

'Word of honour,' Brian said. 'Of course she was older than me.'

'Then say what you did.'

'Some other time,' Brian said.

The girl came to make up the bill and that was that.

Out in the streets the mist hung about the lamps and trailed in thin streamers above the river. Trams rattled past, their steamed-up windows filled with blurred figures. Electric signs stained the wet pavements with their colours. People brushed past them on the crowded path as they picked their way through, their hands deep in their pockets, at ease in their own city, conscious of their right to its streets, proud to lay claim to membership. They made their way back to the quays, passing the dark eye of Merchants Arch where sometimes a prostitute operated and then the Ha'penny Bridge, part of its graceful arch visible and the rest lost in mist and dark. They passed the bookshop owned by Mr Curtis. It was empty, its blinds drawn.

'Have you learned Monday's poetry?'

'A fair bit of it,' Brian said, 'but the endings mix me up.'
They began to recite together:

> 'O my Dark Rosaleen
> Do not sigh, do not weep
> The priests are on the ocean green
> They march along the deep
> There's wine from the royal Pope
> Upon the ocean green
> And Spanish ale shall give you hope
> My Dark Rosaleen
> My Own Rosaleen.'

Brian dropped out to listen. Tim continued:

> 'Shall glad your heart, shall give you hope
> Shall give you health and help and hope
> My Dark Rosaleen.'

'That's the bit I keep mixing up,' Brian complained, 'it's like trying to remember a laundry list.'

'He used to live around here.'

'Who?'

'The poet. James Clarence Mangan.'

'How do you know?'

'An old chap who lives in a flat above us told me. We passed his bookshop a while back.'

'Intellectual neighbours. Very snazzy. Carry on with the recital, McDonagh.'

They went through the rest of the poem together, faltering at times, prompting one another, singing the lines to the beat of their feet until they came to the end of the third verse.

> 'Over dews, over sands
> Will I fly for your weal
> Your holy delicate white hands
> Shall girdle me with steel
> At home in your emerald bowers
> From morning's dawn till e'en
> You'll pray for me, my flower of flowers
> My Dark Rosaleen

My fond Rosaleen
You'll think of me through daylight's hours
My virgin flower, my flower of flowers
My Dark Rosaleen.'

'That's very sexy,' Brian observed, 'don't you think so?'

'It couldn't be,' Tim said, 'Dark Rosaleen isn't a woman. It's Ireland.'

'He must have been thinking of a woman. It's obvious. You'll think of me through daylight's hours, my virgin flower, my flower of flowers. God, it's sippy.'

'I don't think so,' Tim disagreed. Brian made a derisive noise and fell silent. They were nearing his home. The street climbed steeply uphill from the river, the old houses bent over them. Tim peered into the darkness at a glimmer of words: dews and sands, fly and weal; holy, delicate, white; emerald, girdle, steel. The clammy air touched his face with invisible hands. The dampness clung. It prickled in his nose and eyelids. He wiped it away.

At closing time Jim asked them back to his place for a nightcap. Charles and Anthony Rowe agreed to go. The old man decided a late night was beyond him. Paddy excused himself on the grounds that he wanted to be fresh enough the next day to get in a bit of work on the society books and Christy simply said no. 'An early night tonight,' he told them as he went off. 'See you all on the Christmas tree.'

Jim stared after his retreating figure.

'That's a late conversion, isn't it?' he remarked.

'I think he had a skinful last night,' the old man said.

He stood with Paddy to talk with some neighbours and when they had finished Paddy said, 'I'll ramble down with you to say good-night to the mother.'

He walked slowly to accommodate his pace to his father's.

'I don't like this talk of redundancy,' the old man told him.

'It could be a false alarm.'

'Isn't there a crowd of our own to combat the Masons? The Knights or something?'

'The Knights of Columbanus,' Paddy said. 'They're for people a cut above us – business and professional men – that kind of crowd.'

'There'd be no harm in making enquiries.'

'Left-footed or right-footed,' Paddy said, 'I'll have no truck with Masonry. What's wrong is wrong.'

'I don't understand these things,' the old man confessed. 'The world has moved ahead of me.'

They fumbled in the letterbox and drew out the long string that held the key. His mother was sitting in the firelight, her hands folded in her lap.

'The double came up,' the old man told her.

'There you are,' she said, 'the news was worth the waiting after all.'

'You're sitting in the dark,' Paddy remarked.

'The fire was bright. I was saying my few prayers.'

The old man yawned and removed his jacket.

'I think I'll say my own in bed. It won't be any great harm just for one night.'

'You have the same story every night,' the old woman complained. 'Christy's gone up to say his in bed too.'

The old man threw his collar and tie on top of the jacket.

'They're all prayers, aren't they? I don't see what difference it's likely to make up above whether you pray vertically or horizontally.'

He pulled the braces down from his shoulders.

'Well, good-night, son. Good-night, missus. To bed, to barracks.'

'What did he win?' she asked when he had gone.

'About six pounds.'

'They say the divil's children have the divil's luck. Still, I might get round him to part with a pound or two of it tomorrow. I'll watch my opportunity. Will you not sit?'

'No. I've things to attend to in the morning. I brought you this.'

He handed her a Baby Power. It contained a glass measure of

whiskey. She held it against the firelight and admired its yellow gleam.

'That's grand, son,' she said. She slipped it into her pocket. 'Are all at home all right?'

'In good form. The talk is about Christmas.'

'We won't feel it,' she said. 'You'll have your hands full now the family is coming on.'

'We'll manage well enough.'

'They're the best times when you look back. I went through it myself and I know. You have the children about you.'

'There's none of us a hundred miles away,' he suggested gently.

'It's not the same, son. But you'll find that out in your own time. Where's Charles?'

'Gone up to Jim's.'

'Then I'd better leave the chain off the door.'

Paddy leaned over her shoulder to kiss her lightly on the forehead.

'Good-night, ma. See you tomorrow, maybe.'

'Please God.'

He left her sitting in the firelight, her face lit, her body in darkness, the clock that his father found difficulty now in focussing on ticking away loudly on its wall. He shut the door quietly and faced into the mist. The last trams had gone. Saturday was at its end.

IV

From early morning grey columns of cloud rode steadily before the north-east wind and rain drenched the city all day. By four o'clock when Paddy McDonagh parked outside the directors' entrance the streets were almost dark. He made his presence known at reception and announced that the car was in readiness. The uniformed attendant, moustached, tall, an

ex-Irish Guard of about his own age, joined him for conversation.

'Who's the passengers?'

'Mr Blair and young Mr Blair.'

'I'd better have the umbrella in readiness.' He fetched it and
returned.

'Where are they off to?'

'Limerick.'

The attendant looked out at the rain.

'I'd rather you than me. Still, you'll have a taste of life in a
big hotel. Upper-class luxury.'

'The driver doesn't stay with the directors,' Paddy McDonagh
said. 'They don't think it desirable. You find yourself bed and
breakfast in a lodging house.'

'Oul bastards. You might see them the worse for drink, I
suppose.'

'Not the Blairs. Strict T Ts.'

'Some of their cronies then. I wonder what's taking them to
Limerick in this weather.'

'That's a question I've been asking myself,' Paddy McDonagh
admitted.

'Is things bad, do you think?'

'I wouldn't know. But I've heard the rumours.'

'So have I. I think it's talk.'

'I hope so.'

They noted the humming of the lift. The attendant got his
umbrella ready and said:

'Prepare for Brass Hats.'

He conducted them individually to the car. Paddy McDonagh
opened and shut the door. Before driving off he passed in two
rugs from the front seat. To do so he had to open the panel in
the glass partition. It segregated the front seats from the back
to prevent him from overhearing his passengers' conversation.
Before he closed it old Mr Blair's voice said:

'The evening is very bad. Drive with care and moderation.
We have ample time for the journey.'

For a couple of hours after that there was no further communication. Paddy McDonagh picked his way through the chaos of trams and horse drays that cluttered the older city until its streets ended almost abruptly at Inchicore and the road crossed open country. Rain slanted against his headlights in silver bars that were shattered from time to time by heavy gusts of wind. The wipers kept their arc of window reasonably clear, the milometer registered steadily. Naas brought to mind, as it always did, a saying which had intrigued him all his life: 'That's the man that fought the monkey on the Naas Road.' He resolved, as he always did, to enquire about it when he got back, though he suspected he would forget. He always had. The Curragh plains reminded him of the war. He had done his first soldiering there. The town of Kildare huddled in misery as he slowed for its narrow streets. They smelled of cattle.

The journey, he reckoned, would take about four hours. Unless they decided to stop for a meal. He was hungry already himself and hoped they would but thought it unlikely. They had probably arranged a meal in their hotel on arrival; say between eight and eight-thirty. A normal enough hour for them but not for him. By the time he found digs it would be maybe half past nine. No matter. He watched his speed. He kept alert. Safety and not speed had been the old man's command. At some stage he hoped to ask directly about the redundancy rumours. The young Mr Blair was quite unapproachable but the old had his moments of informality. He would ask about your health. He might even enquire about your family. How many? What ages? A beginning would be to impress by efficiency. Evoke confidence. Create a good impression. Then he must watch his opportunity.

Two hours passed. He slowed down yet again. The panel slid open.

'What town is this, McDonagh?'

'Roscrea, sir. Did you wish to stop?'

'No, no. Keep going.'

The panel slid shut. He was isolated again. He rolled down his window to get his bearings and felt the rain on his cheek. It had emptied the twisting streets. There was the same smell of cattle. He found his road out and gathered speed once more. He was hungry and wanted a smoke too but that was out of the question. The old man would sometimes say on a long journey: 'I know you like to smoke, McDonagh. Why don't you have a cigarette.' No hope of that with the younger man present. He thought instead of his rain-sodden surroundings.

Wrapped in the rain and the darkness were the fields of Ireland which he could not see, November fields of dormant soil, flooded drains, gateways where cattle had trampled the ground until it became a quagmire. Two months earlier he had driven this way in sunlight and looked out to admire the gleam of blackberries in the hedges. Blackberrying time was over. The humming insects slept in the crevices of stone walls. Cattle were locked in the darkness of winter sheds.

The wheel in his hand had become heavier and began to pull to the left. He adjusted but it grew worse. After a moment in which he tried to wish the thought away he pulled in to the side and stopped. By then he could feel the rim making contact with the roadway. He opened the panel to explain.

'A flat tyre, sir. I'll have to change the wheel.'

He found the torch and got out to investigate. In a short while the rain had penetrated his trousers at the knees. He could feel its wetness on his skin but forgot about it quickly when he discovered the extent of the damage. Both front tyres were flat. There was no quick solution to that one. His heart sank as he broke the news.

'Both tyres, McDonagh?'

'Surely you have spares,' the younger said.

'One spare, sir, but not two.'

'And why not?'

'It isn't customary, sir. There's hardly room.'

'It ought to be customary. What are we to do?'

Paddy McDonagh reckoned the next town, Nenagh, to be five or six miles away. He said he would walk on to it and seek help.

'Can you take one of the wheels with you and have it repaired?'

'The man couldn't possibly,' old Blair said irritably. 'Have a modicum of reason.'

'Are we to spend the night here?'

'I'm afraid you must find a telephone somewhere or walk to Nenagh,' old Blair said. 'Send a taxi back for us. Then arrange to have the car put in order again. You can follow on to Limerick and report at our hotel in the morning.'

The journey took more than an hour in darkness so complete that he depended utterly on the torch. Such traffic as there was came against him. There was no telephone that he could find. Groping his way by the meagre beam of the torch, half blinded by rain that soaked to the skin so that his clothes weighed on him like a burden, he wondered if he had stepped across some invisible boundary into a tenantless world. But within a mile of the town a lorry travelling in his direction pulled up for him.

'I expected I'd meet up with you when I saw your car at the side of the road a few miles back.'

'Both wheels,' Paddy McDonagh said. 'A cautious bookmaker would give you two hundred to one against it.'

'Some bastard spilled a load of old timber and didn't bother to tidy up – rotten planks full of nails. I ran into the same trouble myself. Only one flat tyre, though, thanks be to the Seven Holy Men of Roscrea. I'm sitting in a pool of water since changing it.'

'I've had a drenching myself.'

'You should have waited by the car. Someone has to come along eventually.'

'I had two directors in the back. It was only a question of which of them would burst into flames first.'

'That's why I drive a lorry. A load of sand or cement isn't great conversationalists, but they're both very patient.'

They found a garage that was closed but the lorry driver knew where to locate the proprietor. When a taxi had been despatched for the Blairs they decided to tow Paddy Mc-Donagh's car to the garage.

'We may as well have a roof over our heads,' the proprietor decided.

The lorry driver said he'd leave them to it.

'Thanks for the help,' Paddy McDonagh said.

'For nothing,' the lorry driver assured him. 'You today, me tomorrow. I'd recommend a stiff glass of malt until you have a chance to get those clothes dry.'

They got the car on tow after another session of unremitting rain and worked without any break until it was ready for the road. By that time the public houses had closed. Paddy McDonagh resumed his journey. The walk and the work had kept him warm, but as he drove he grew cold. The search for a lodging house where anyone was still awake and in the slightest bit interested took an unbearable length of time.

In the morning he reported to the hotel as instructed but had to wait around half the day to drive the Blairs back to Dublin. His clothes were still damp and their clammy feel sapped his spirit. The Blairs seemed to think that in some way he was to blame, an inopportune time to probe for information about the future. He felt very ill when he got back to the company's garage. Nevertheless he persevered until he had managed somehow to wash the car. It was spattered with the mud of the journey and would be scrutinized first thing in the morning. There could be an adverse report. He felt in no position to risk that.

His mother's hand shook his shoulder and her voice said:

'Tim, I want you to get up immediately. I want you to call on the doctor before you go to school.'

He sat up and shook his head to waken himself and saw Frank still asleep in the other bed.

'Why can't you send Frank,' he complained. 'Why always me?'

'For the love of God don't start an argument with me – I'm nearly out of my mind,' she begged.

The tone of her voice brought him fully awake. He threw back the clothes and asked grumpily, 'What's wrong?'

'Your father has been very sick all night. I think he was delirious at times. He kept saying: "Someone answer that bloody telephone." I've been awake all the night.'

Her words frightened him. He began to dress.

'I have your breakfast on the table. Take it first. Then call on Dr Stephens. He's the company doctor and lives in Heytesbury Street. I don't know the number but you'll see the nameplate on his gate. Ask him to come as soon as he can. If he's not there himself leave an urgent message.'

He took his breakfast quickly, collected the books he needed for the day and his lunch which she had wrapped and left ready for him.

'If he's not there, make sure they take a message,' she repeated.

'I know what to do,' he said.

A white frost clung to the iron railings and lay on the pavement. The roofs of houses gleamed with it. In Stephen's Green broken twigs and dead leaves torn away by the recent gales strewed the paths, their colours kindling under a washy sun. The park attendants were not yet at work. Most of the cyclists who passed him were labourers and tradesmen. Usually they were office workers but it was too early for them as yet. He searched up and down twice before he found the nameplate he wanted and rang several times before the door was opened. The doctor was not there, they said. But they would give him the message. Yes. They understood its urgency. He was not to worry. The school bell was clamouring loudly when he got there and he ran to be in time. But he was unable to work on the geometry problem he had intended to complete before classes started, and he got two on each hand for his neglect.

'I'm disappointed, McDonagh,' Brother Quinlan said pleasantly as he drew the proffered hand into a convenient position for the blows. 'You're usually conscientious. What happened?'

'I meant to finish it this morning but had to do a message instead.' He could have said what the message had been in the hope of getting off but decided not to. He wouldn't satisfy Quinlan.

'Never put off till tomorrow what you can do today. You've heard that maxim before? A very wise one. This will help you to remember it.'

Brother Quinlan hit him hard but with great friendliness, two on the right hand, then two on the left. The sounds rang through the classroom like pistol shots.

'Finish it for tomorrow,' Brother Quinlan said, as though it were a mere suggestion.

At lunchtime no one had money so they strolled down Camden Street to the blacksmith's forge. On the way Brian said:

'What possessed Pater Pius Timotheus to let himself in for it?'

'I had to call on the doctor. My father seems to be very ill.'

'What's wrong with him?'

'I don't know. He was delirious at times during the night, my mother thinks.'

Cunningham was curious.

'What's delirious?' he enquired.

'From delirium, you uninformed thick,' Brian said. 'Seeing things that aren't there. Saying things that don't make sense. Like you, Cunningham.'

'I don't find it funny,' Tim said.

'Don't mind swallow-the-dictionary here,' Cunningham advised him. 'He likes to swank.'

'I'm sorry,' Brian apologized. 'Cunningham has an effect on me. I get carried away.'

They bickered for a while.

The blacksmith was shoeing a horse. Coal dust and the tang of smoke and the acrid smell of cauterized horn mingled in the air and robbed the forge of daylight. Except when the bellows excited the dull red glow of the coals into flame it was hard to see. The blacksmith grasped the hoof between his knees and began to hammer in the nails.

'It doesn't hurt, you know,' Cunningham explained unnecessarily. 'The horse doesn't feel any pain or anything.'

'Let's go,' Tim suggested.

The ring of the hammer, the gloom and smells, the trailing streamers of smoke about the black mound of coal and their red circle of fire depressed him. He wanted to know what was happening at home.

They stepped out again into the streets where in preparation for Christmas some shops were already displaying coloured streamers and paper chains. He was silent and morose. Cunningham and Brian left him alone. They conducted a discussion on Christmas parties and the possibilities offered through their unsettling effect on the female sex. People were shopping. The sun had strengthened since morning. It was a little warmer.

The can which the milkman had refilled in the course of the afternoon was still on the doorstep when he arrived home and his mother had left a note on the kitchen table for him. Without waiting to take off his coat he picked it up:

Tim, Doctor Stephens ordered your father into hospital the moment he saw him this morning he believes it is pneumonia and the ambulance has just been here and taken him away. I have to take some things in for him I was too flustered to put them together at the time and then I will go down to leave word at his mother's and get advice about what is best to do.

I am leaving a stew in the oven share it out among you and I am afraid to light the fire but it is all set and ready just put a match to it. Look after the others until I get home which I don't know what time it will be as I don't know if I will have to call again to the hospital as it will depend on what word they have.

Be good and turn out the gas but please God the news will be good. I have promised masses and placed trust in Our Blessed Lady and St Joseph so it is in their all-loving hands. Mammy.

He told his sister to get out the plates and his brother Frank to look after the knives and forks and distributed the food. It was all very strange.

'Mammy never gives me stew,' his sister complained. 'I hate it.'

'Shut up,' he told her, 'and eat it.'

She glanced at his face and obeyed. Frank and his younger brother did likewise. He lit the fire and after a long time the room became warm and looked almost normal. He washed the dishes. That was strange too.

'Daddy's been taken to hospital,' he explained, 'and your

mother had to go in to see him and do other business. Probably she'll be a long time so just get on with your exercises and things as though she were here.'

Then he went to the table at the window where the peacock with a read bead for an eye still guarded the photograph album, pushed it gently to one side and sat down. The curtains framed the empty street, now growing cheerless under a sky whose washed-out colours were being drained of light. When he was younger he had waited there often for the return of his mother or father or for his aunts to bring him on weekends to their house by the sea. It was not so much a seat by a window as a limbo for reflection. In it the world sat still a little while and submitted to scrutiny. It was like being in den. Nothing could happen while he remained seated there, provided he did so in good faith and on the reasonable condition that he must not sit there forever. But he remained until the room had grown so dark that he had to switch on the light. He restocked the fire and made the tea. No one came. He sent the others to bed in order of seniority, a jealously guarded right. No one came. As the hours dragged on his anxiety grew incessant and made him restless. The sound of traffic pinned his attention until it had passed and faded with distance. Footsteps drew him back to the window several times until repetition and disappointment convinced him of its futility. He thought of his school exercises and spread his books on the table. But when he opened them it was only to stare at them. To make a start was slow and difficult. Nevertheless it had to be done so he persevered until the work took hold of his attention. Some hours later he had become so deeply absorbed that the sound of an engine and the slamming of car doors startled him. He heard their voices outside and knew they had come back by taxi, a rare extravagance. It was a thought that made his heart sink. He left down his pen and watched while his mother was led in by Aunt Kate. Uncle Hugh and Charles and Christy followed. He could see from his mother's eyes that she had been crying. Her face was drawn and tired. Aunt Kate said; 'I'll hang up your coat for you, Nora. You've had as much as you can cope with for one day.'

As his mother consented he searched Uncle Christy's face, his eyes asking the question his tongue refused to articulate. Christy said to him:

'Everything's seen to. We left your father settled in and comfortable. He's in capable hands.'

'Are the children all right?' his mother asked.

'I gave them their tea and sent them to bed at the usual time.'

'You're a good child,' she said.

Uncle Christy had picked up a bag of stout somewhere on the way. That was inevitable on critical family occasions. He cleared his books from the table and got glasses and a corkscrew while they talked. Their voices reassured. He felt surrounded and protected. Uncle Christy had got whiskey too and said to the women:

'Sit down, Kate. Sit down, Nora. A drop of this will do you both good.'

'I don't think I'd be able for it,' his mother said.

'Nonsense,' Uncle Charles told her, 'a pick-me-up is what we all need. Let there be none of this prim and proper nonsense.' Aunt Kate said she agreed wholeheartedly with him. When they had sat down too Uncle Charles filled their glasses and raised his one.

'Here's to better news in the morning.'

'With the help of God,' his mother said. Her voice quavered a little as she said it.

'He's in the best of hands anyway,' Uncle Charles assured everyone. 'I've heard good accounts of Dr Isaacs from all sides. A top notcher in the profession.'

'I have great faith in a Jewish doctor,' Aunt Kate said.

'True,' Uncle Charles agreed, 'they make the best physicians. I understand there was a great wealth of medical knowledge surrounding the old Jewish faith. A priest remarked it to me once.'

'Their strong point is diagnosis,' Uncle Hugh contributed. 'I think it has to do with the artistic temperament, a sixth sense.'

'They're hard men when it comes to the money, just the same,' Uncle Christy observed.

'I could nominate many a Christian tarred with that brush,' said Charles. 'Another little drop – Nora, Kate?'

He poured unbidden.

'We've interrupted Tim at his school exercises.'

'There's not much left,' he said, 'I can finish it in the morning.'

They talked again about his father.

'He was wandering in his mind all through the night,' his mother was explaining. 'It had me frightened.'

'That would be the fever,' Uncle Charles told her.

'I suppose the job now is to bring down the temperature,' Christy speculated.

'It has to run its course,' Uncle Charles explained, 'and the fever will remain while it does so. There's a crisis point in pneumonia, usually on the ninth day. Once he's over that the fever will drop and he'll be on the mend.'

'Please God,' his mother said.

She went in to look at the children. While she was out of the room Uncle Charles lowered his voice and said in a serious tone to the others, 'Paddy is a strong and active man but there's one little detail that causes me concern. During the war he was knocked about during a gas attack. I don't recall the ins and outs but I know he got more than a whiff or two before things were rightified. Mustard gas, I imagine. It could leave a mark.'

'A little weakness . . . ?' Christy conjectured.

'It might. The lungs, you know. Or it might not.'

Tim gathered his school books from the chair and began to loop the strap about those he would need the next morning. It was an excuse to turn his back. He did not want his face to be seen.

Each night they called to accompany his mother to the hospital and each night he was left to mind the other children. That seemed reasonable. His mother had to be left free. But the hospital was only a block or so from the school, a short detour each evening when classes finished. At first he simply passed by the gates. Then he began to venture into the grounds, an easy matter in the winter half-light. On the way home he would slip into the church to pray briefly before the Blessed Sacrament that his father would be spared. Usually it was empty. At most two or three old women were his companions or a beggerman resting from the weather in the warmth and semi-darkness. He thought of it as a battle between his father and Death, to be won or lost by either within a period of nine days. He ticked them off as they went by. On the seventh evening rain was falling steadily and the hospital grounds seemed deserted. Lighted windows rose one above the other in the heavy granite walls. As he drew nearer he was tempted to climb on to one of the ledges to peep in. He had no idea what ward his father was in or even if the accessible windows gave on to a ward at all, but he edged through a dripping fringe of bushes and reached up towards the nearest ledge. He dragged himself upwards. There was barely room to stand. Nothing could be seen through the lower half of the window which was steamed up. He pressed his fingers against the woodwork and raised himself slowly, until a voice below startled him.

'Hey – you.'

Beyond the fringe of bushes a figure was gesticulating at him.

'Come down here.'

He hesitated.

'At once,' the voice ordered.

He went down unsteadily on his hands and knees and lowered himself to the ground.

'What the hell do you think you're at?'

It was a young man with a raincoat draped about his shoulders. Underneath he wore a white hospital jacket with the leads of a stethoscope trailing from one of its pockets.

'Are you going to answer me, or would you prefer to talk to the police?'

It was hard to organize his thoughts. There were too many powers to be propitiated: God and Death, doctors and the police. He managed hesitantly:

'I thought I might see my father.'

'In the nurses' recreation room? Highly unlikely.'

Speech had made it no longer possible to check them and the

tears welled into his eyes. The young man bent to peer at him and saw. That doubled the shame.

'Do you mean your father is a patient?'

'Yes.'

'What ward?'

'I don't know. I've never been to see him.'

'Why is he in here?'

'He has pneumonia.'

'Pneumonia. I see. And his name?'

'McDonagh.' That seemed too little. 'Mister Patrick McDonagh.'

'And you thought you might see him by climbing the window?'

'Yes.'

The young man regarded him for some time. His expression became gentle.

'As it happens,' he said, 'I've just been with him.'

He put his hand on his shoulder.

'And what's your own name?'

'Tim McDonagh.'

'Come this way. I may be able to let you go to him for a minute or two.'

They climbed a stairs and went along a corridor. The young doctor opened one of the doors and led him quietly between rows of beds to one which had screens partly about it. His father opened his eyes and saw him. He did not seem surprised.

'Tim,' he said after a while.

He nodded his head. The young doctor stepped back.

'What time is it, son?'

'About four o'clock.'

He stood where he was, uncertain of being allowed to move any nearer the bed.

'In the morning?'

'Oh no. The evening.'

'Have you been to school?'

'Yes. I was on my way home.'

His father closed his eyes again.

'Good boy,' he said. His forehead and face were beaded with moisture. On the top of the locker there was a glass and a napkin. He moved across without thinking, took up the napkin and wiped the sweat from his father's face. When that had been done the young doctor beckoned him and they left quietly. In the church he notched off day number seven and said the usual prayers. His anxiety had gone. He felt almost normal: not indeed a happy normality but a sort of calmness, a grim composure. He said nothing at home of what had happened.

They returned on the tenth night with the news that his father seemed over the worst and on the mend.

'I expect Tim would like to visit,' Aunt Kate suggested.

'To be sure,' Uncle Christy said, looking across at him.

Uncle Charles considered gravely as usual and decided slowly.

'I think that would be in order,' he said. 'At this stage, why not?'

They looked in turn at his mother.

'We could bring you on Sunday,' she offered. 'There's visiting in the afternoon.'

On Sunday there were so many people they had to go in in turn and were asked not to stay too long. He accompanied his mother and Charles and Christy. Each bed had its small knot of people. Fruit and mineral drinks were piled on all the lockers. His father was sitting up in bed, propped by pillows. He greeted each one and then said:

'Hello, son.'

'Hello.'

For the moment he could think of nothing to add. His father beckoned.

'Let Tim come nearer a moment.'

Uncle Charles made way and he went to the bedside.

'I had a dream about you the other evening,' his father told him. 'You were standing by the locker there and one of the junior doctors was standing behind you. You had your school books under your arm. That's all. There was nothing else. Wasn't that strange?'

For a moment he was puzzled. Then his father smiled in a way that isolated both of them from the rest. It was a brief signal of conspiracy. The doctor, then, had told. In a way he was glad.

'And how's the form today?' Christy asked conversationally.

'As you can see,' his father said, 'able to sit up and eat an egg.'

'And ready for something stronger, I'll warrant.'

'I'd murder a pint,' his father confessed.

'No doubt,' Charles said, 'that will come later on the menu.'

'There was something going through my head this while back,' his father said, 'and I can't answer it. I wonder could you?'

'We'll have a stab,' said Charles.

'You know the expression: "That's the man that fought the monkey on the Naas Road". How did it originate?'

Uncle Charles pulled at his nose and reflected for a long time.

'I should know,' he complained. 'I have something in the back of my head about a law case at the turn of the century. I think one of the defendants put up some explanation or other about meeting a monkey. Let me think about it.'

'If you find out,' his father said, 'let me know. It's getting between me and my sleep.'

They talked generally until Christy suggested it was time to let him have a word in private with Nora. As he made to follow Charles and Christy his father said:

'Stay where you are, Tim.'

He sat down again.

'What about money,' his father asked. 'Did the job make arrangements?'

'They sent it up to me on Friday.'

'That's a relief. And things are all right?'

'We're managing fine. Aren't we, Tim?'

'Yes.'

'That's good.'

His father became amused at something.

'I had a surprise visitor this morning,' he said, 'Aunt Emily.'

'I haven't seen her in an age. How is she?'

'The same as always. She's so pleased with de Valera's government you'd think she was the member for Cross Kevin Street. I told her your brother Hugh had been promoted to captain.'

'And what did she say to that?'

'It nearly killed her. She said she found it remarkable how some could get on. A captain you tell me, said she, and he never fired a shot.'

His father shook with laughter but his mother was angry.

'A bigot and a begrudger,' she said. 'Will she never forget the past.'

The laughter had made his father tired. A hectic flush filled his cheeks. His eyes became unnaturally bright, then lost their lustre.

'You're tired now, Paddy,' his mother said. 'We'll leave you to rest.'

'Yes. Do that,' he answered.

She bent over to kiss him.

'Good-bye, love,' he said, 'good-bye, son.'

They took their leave but turned again at the door of the ward to wave back. He acknowledged briefly and dropped his hand. Charles and Christy were waiting. As they walked down the corridor they could hear from some distant ward the handbell being rung to bring the visitsng hour to an end.

Monday as always brought English class and the usual stint of poetry to be memorized. He found he had regained his usual ease. He waited without anxiety to be called on, stood up, recited, sat down again, and listened as Brother Raymond picked this one and that to continue where the other had left off. There were no casualties. The class settled back with relief while Brother Raymond wrote on the blackboard:

The Objective Case may be used (1) as a Direct (2) or a Cognate (3) or a Factitive, Object (4) after a preposition (5) in Apposition (6) after the adjectives 'like', 'near' (7) as an Indirect Object.
Task: Give examples of each.

They opened notebooks and set to work. He wrote down:

(1) He met his *friend*
(2) He fought the good *fight*
(3) They made him *captain*
(4) The book lay in the *desk*

He stopped to consider number five: In apposition?

The hot water pipes had tinged the air with a faint smell of metal. Above them particles of chalk dust, visible where a weak sun slanted through the windows, were agitated by the warm current from below and swam in patterns. The pens scratched. A note passed from hand to hand came to rest on his desk. He looked around. Cunningham was making signals. He opened it. It was in semaphore:

Decoded, it read: 'See me after school. Without Moloney.'

He wrote in turn in semaphore: 'OK' and gave it to Jackser Deegan beside him to pass on. As he did so he remembered the objective case in apposition and wrote beneath the other four examples:

(5) He knew John, the *postman*.

Then he completed six and seven.

(6) He sat near *John*.
(7) John gave *Dick* the letter.

He pushed the completed exercise towards Deegan who was in difficulties. Beyond the dancing chalk dust, framed in the squares of the windows the trees spread their branches stripped bare of leaves.

The shops were full of the approaching Christmas. Holly and ivy decorated the windows. Hams and turkeys hung in rows both inside and out. For the first time he no longer felt compelled to pass the hospital.

Cunningham said, 'I kept missing you last week. It was like there was a jinx. You kept doing the disappearing trick.'

'I know. They needed me at home.'

'I was waiting to ask if you'd come to this party over Christmas. My sister's birthday. The old man caved in and said she could have one.'

'When?'

'On the thirtieth. But that isn't all. Do you remember Anne Fox?'

'Summer camp?'

'Anne there are millions sad and weary. Correct. She's coming too.'

His interest quickened.

'How do you know?'

'My sister was making out her list and the name was on it. It's the same one, all right. I asked about her. It isn't my party, and that's why I wanted to avoid Brian. She agrees I can have one friend but no more. Anyway she can't stand Moloney. Will you come?'

'Of course I'll come. Who will I know?'

'There'll be my sister's pals, mostly. I wouldn't say they'd throw a fellow into mad frenzies or anything like that but one or two are gamey enough. And there'll be Anne Fox. You were wagging your tail around her, I remember.'

'Nearly two years ago.'

'All the better. She'll have more to show. Anyway, you'll come. I'll try to work in Brian, but don't tell him for the moment.'

Cunningham fixed his three-speed in the lowest gear before throwing his leg over the saddle. He began to sing in falsetto, 'Sighing every night so dreary, won't you buy my pretty flowers.'

He waved and went off, pedalling madly.

It was the song perhaps. It was the name. He remembered the overpowering reek of perfume, the dark cave of the wings, the village under the moon. He stood again beside the bus, and they were writing down names and addresses that afterwards hardly anyone used. The sparks flew up into the night sky and were carried away by the wind. Where did things go when they had finished happening. Was Time something flowing past you, or did a person swim through Time. He went up the stone steps, crossed the hall where the oil lamp was already flickering on the hall stand and opened the living room door. The empty feeling had returned.

'Where's your mother?' he asked Frank.

'I don't know. She was out when we got home.'

He looked around. The table had not been laid. The fire had been lit but was now out. No meal had been left in the oven. He turned on his sister.

'Why the hell didn't you do something about the fire?'

'I was afraid to. When it's too low and I interfere with it I always put it out.'

'Cut some bread,' he ordered.

He broke sticks and got paper and coaxed the fire back to life. To stave off their hunger he made tea. The others washed up. It all took time. Darkness set in before everything had been attended to.

'Do you think it's Daddy?' Frank asked.

It had not occurred to him that any of the others would share his anxiety. They seemed too young.

'She may have had to go to the hospital for some reason. Or she may have gone down to his job. Or to see about his insurance. There could be lots of reasons.'

Yet he wondered that she should go without leaving their meal or even a note.

He resigned himself to the now familiar routine, saw they did their school work, sent them to bed at the appropriate time, settled in with difficulty to his own exercises. From time to time his interest flagged and he became conscious of the fire in the grate with nobody sitting by it, the clock on the mantelpiece ticking quietly to no one but him, the stillness otherwise which gave him the feeling of being watched by the vacant chairs. To break its spell he flung down his pen, stood up, replenished the fire unnecessarily and made a racket with the fire irons. Around nine o'clock, when he was about to repeat the routine for the third or fourth time, he heard the hall door opening. Feet sounded in the hall and someone tapped on the door. Though there was nothing very strange about that his heart jumped. He found with relief that the caller was Mr Curtis from upstairs. He stepped inside.

'Is your mother busy?'

'She's not here. I think she may be at the hospital. She'd gone by the time I got home.'

Mr Curtis seemed incredibly old. He was bent and much smaller and used a walking stick. But the eyes peering through his pince-nez were still alert and observant.

'Never mind. I stopped to enquire about your father.'

'Will you sit down?'

'No, no,' Mr Curtis said. 'I see you're at your homework and I mustn't interrupt. Tell her I'll call tomorrow when I'm passing.'

As he turned to go someone fumbled at the hall door. Tim followed and touched his arm to detain him.

'Just a moment,' he said, 'this may be my mother now.'

Uncle Christy opened the door and let Aunt Kate and his mother through. The sight transfixed him. His mother was leaning on Aunt Kate and seemed to find it hard to walk. When she saw him she said:

'My poor child, what's to become of us.'

Her sobs, amplified by the bare hall, drove their unbelievable message deep into every recess of his being. Aunt Kate helped her into the room. Uncle Christy came to him and put his arms about him.

'Tim, son,' he said in a voice uncharacteristically tender, 'your father took a bad turn early in the afternoon. He died a short while ago.'

He tightened his grip about the heaving shoulders. He said, 'That's it. Cry it out, son. But when we go inside, remember you're now the man of the family.'

The blinds were drawn. For two evenings the house was never empty of visitors. They sat and sympathized in low voices and drank cups of tea or glasses of sherry. Aunt Kate came to stay and looked after the housework. He remained at home from school but away from the hospital. On the morning of the funeral he sat on the chair by the window and stared at the drawn blind until the sound of wheels and hoof beats told him it was about to pass. He bent the blind a little at one side. There were flowers and he saw beneath them the gleam of brass handles. They flashed briefly and were gone. His shoulders bent under their weight of loss until his head rested on the photograph album and the red bead dug into his forehead. The bent corner of the blind, straightening slowly, resumed its shape and blotted out the street.

V

For Christmas the family retreated prudently to the house by the sea where the aunts took care that all should be muted and decorous. Festivity and merrymaking were avoided and undesired. When Brian replaced him at Cunningham's party it was a relief, not a disappointment. The aunts decorated the house with paper chains and balloons as usual, they prepared turkey and ham and made plum pudding as a matter of course. Out of regard for the day itself they even pulled crackers and put on paper hats after dinner. But that was to amuse the younger children. Neighbours who called to talk and take a drink were subdued and avoided excess. They came to offer their company, not to sing the usual songs or hammer on the piano or make fun as in other years. They sat quietly about the fire and promoted neutral conversations devised to keep the mind from introspection. Christmas was an embarrassment, unwanted but unavoidable.

There was the customary after-dinner walk from the Pigeon

House to the Poolbeg Lighthouse, a traditional exercise indulged in by strangers as well as neighbours. They strolled along the narrow arm of granite with the river on one side and the sea on the other while their dogs cavorted and scattered the seagulls. Unbelievably calm, the water wore a fixed and frosty glitter, the air came heavily into the lungs, eyes searching the width of the eastward sea watered in a short space and shed tears. On the way back icy fingers chilled the face and numbed the hands through their thick gloves. Howth Hill on one side and the harbour and spires of Dun Laoghaire on the other were already merging into the dusk. Along the shipping roads of the river the buoys, hardly necessary as yet, flashed weakly. The foghorns were at it again too. All the familiar furniture was exactly as it had always been in a world which nevertheless had become wholly foreign and which, if it meant anything at all, meant something hitherto unsuspected. There was a murderer somewhere in the heart of creation waiting to ambush. There was an invisible thief, unpredictable, but capable to some extent perhaps of being understood. The world was no longer to be taken on trust. It required vigilance. It demanded constant scrutiny. It proffered love to break the heart; the more abundantly so, the more certainly.

THREE · # The Young May Moon

The young May moon is beaming, love
The glow worm's lamp is gleaming, love
How sweet to rove
Through Morna's grove
While the drowsy world is dreaming, love.

TOM MOORE

I

Brian Moloney dared the world to surprise him. He had it taped. Perhaps it was his daily contact with the customers in his father's pub. Perhaps it was a question of geography, of contiguity, the character of his immediate surroundings. The bells of Sunday, booming over roofs and cobbles, stirred the decaying tenements of High Street and Patrick Street, Meath Street and Francis Street and the Coombe to a crowded and revealing life. The women wore shawls, the children frequently enough went barefooted. In the churches where the candles glowed in their shrines and the murmured Latin hypnotized the mind, the air was heavy with the smell of poverty. It was a world of low wages or no wages at all for many of his neighbours. And when he walked to school it was a journey through the multiple tiers of a society where tuppence ha'penny looked down on tuppence, while tuppence in turn was a cut above three ha'pence. Iveagh Hostel offered a casual night's shelter to the destitute. So too did the Morning Star Hostel down by the river. The tenements were for those who had not so utterly given up. Crowded cottages without gardens and corporation houses with tiny ones were a step higher. Respectability fringed the South Circular Road, modestly in cottages, more assuredly in two-storey houses. In Harrington Street there were even hints of residential splendour. What your father did for a livelihood was of importance. Where you lived measured your social acceptability. His own address in High Street would not have qualified but for the nature of his father's business. Publicans were solid and substantial citizens regardless of location. They had money, were influential in politics, had a reputation for supplying illustrious sons and daughters to the religious life. His own father left the newspaper aside frequently to boast that such and such a bishop was the son of a publican. Reverend Mothers of similar origin abounded.

Perhaps, in addition to contiguity, it was a matter of observing, reflecting, assessing. To do so was part of his nature. He watched the comings and goings of committee men and local politicians in the course of meetings conducted by his father who was now chairman of the Peadar O Tuaithil Cumann of Mr de Valera's Fianna Fail party. He listened when he could to what they were exercised about: no easy matter since much of their business involved conspiracies and plots and issued from the side of the mouth. Nevertheless, interesting items came his way. One of the committee advocated a campaign against a number of shebeens where prostitution was alleged to be rampant. Others took the view that it was really a matter for the clergy and advised him to go easy. Unfortunate women had votes too, as had their customers. A firm plank in their programme and one which engaged his fancy was the provision of indoor lavatories for the residents of Crescent Street. He thought it worth relaying to Cunningham. Otherwise he was unimpressed.

In between times his father pursued his interest in greyhounds and entertained his friend O'Sheehan. Through winter and summer, year in and year out they sat down to chess. Naturally their colloquy had regard to current happenings as well as domestic tittle-tattle, general knowledge, philosophical insights and observations on human character and behaviour. As a brief sample they discussed at some length the following:

(1) *In 1934*: The wisdom or otherwise of Ireland joining with Britain and France in advocating the admission of Communist Russia to the League of Nations. Allowing that it might indeed be wise, could any benefit be held to justify even temporary alliance with the traditional enemy?

(2) *In 1935*: The Irish Nationality and Citizenship Act, by which Irish citizens ceased, at least in Irish eyes, to be British subjects. It was agreed that this was a step forward on the road to the complete dismantling of the Treaty of 1922 and to the achievement of full national sovereignty.

(3) *In 1936* (A): The outbreak of the Spanish Civil War and the enlisting of 700 volunteers under General O'Duffy to fight on

Franco's side. Cornelius approved on the grounds that it represented succour and support for God and His Holy Church. O'Sheehan welcomed the translation of General O'Duffy to a foreign clime and the possibility of his early martyrdom.

(B) > The abdication of Edward VIII in order to marry an American divorcee, to wit: Mrs Wallis Simpson.

1. Cornelius denied surprise and found no more than confirmation of what he had long recognized, viz. an ever-accelerating descent towards universal moral turpitude. He predicted deplorable ill effects as a result of such example from one in a high public position (e.g. he had discovered his eldest son devouring a newspaper article which furnished intimate biographical information concerning the lady in question).

2. O'Sheehan found it difficult to become exercised about the indissoluble nature of Christian marriage but managed a polite compliance.

3. Both, however, exulted in the opportunity presented to Mr de Valera to remove the King's name from the Free State Constitution, an opportunity seized on and given legislative reality within forty-eight hours.

There were topics of less public moment, of course. The death of young McDonagh's father elicited a brief but compassionate exchange. A difficulty concerning one of the greyhounds took longer to dispose of and taxed their ingenuity. It concerned a dog with a good turn of speed but a deplorable temper.

'I can do anything with him myself but daren't let the missus or the youngsters near him,' Cornelius said.

'And he races well?'

'He has great things in him, unless he's barred for fighting with the others.'

'Was he born at Whitsuntide, by any chance?'

'How did you guess that?'

'Whitsuntide is an unlucky time. There's an old belief that a horse foaled then will grow up dangerous or kill someone.'

'Let's hope it doesn't extend to dogs,' Cornelius said.

'Talking of old beliefs,' O'Sheehan continued, 'puts me in mind of a procedure for taming a horse which was highly regarded in the old and ancient days. It might be worth trying in the present predicament.'

'And what was that?' Cornelius enquired.

'A very simple procedure. To tame a difficult horse it was the custom to whisper the creed into both ears; his right ear on Fridays and again, but into the left ear this time, on Wednesdays.'

'And did it work?'

'Highly efficacious, by all accounts, provided it was regularly practised until the brute was tame.'

Cornelius was dubious.

'The old people had powerful remedies in bygone times, I'll grant you that. Indeed, my own grandmother had her share of them, God be good to her. But for some reason they don't seem to give the same results nowadays.'

'The fault is not in the remedies,' O'Sheehan insisted, 'but in the people themselves. There's been a general change in the nature of people since the old times.'

'Besides, would what worked for a horse apply to a grey-hound?'

'It costs nothing to find out.'

'There's the clergy to be considered,' Cornelius said, troubled. 'They might be a bit put out at someone stuffing Christian prayers into the ears of a brute.'

O'Sheehan saw no objection.

'I hardly think so. Consider St Francis. Talking to the birds. Preaching to the dumb animals. It seems perfectly in order.'

Conviction straightened the hunch of Cornelius's shoulders.

'By God then, I'll give it a trial,' he decided. 'If it does no good at least it'll do no harm.'

He requested a recapitulation of the procedure. But the dog pulled a muscle so badly before the treatment could take effect that it had to be put away. The event revived the misgivings Cornelius had originally entertained. It bore the hall-mark of Divine disapproval.

There were three further matters to distract his mind. The first, the result of devious political string-pulling and colloguing was the appointment of O'Sheehan to a small committee set up for the purpose of compiling a comprehensive dictionary of the Irish language. The task would be long term and carried a reasonable monthly stipend. They rejoiced mutually in the eventual success of their joint efforts.

The second was the Constitution Act of 1937. Cornelius welcomed its ban on divorce for a complexity of reasons, among them the unshakable conviction that it was a jab at the low standards of neighbouring royalty. O'Sheehan thought the act in its totality smelled of papal encyclicals. They debated at length and with application, avoiding acrimony but forced on a number of points to reserve their respective positions.

The third, far from academic, was the growing recalcitrance of his eldest son.

'He'll do nothing he's told. He objects to everything. He'd contradict the Lord God Almighty on His heavenly throne,' Cornelius complained. 'Do what I will I can get no good of him at all. And he makes a nose rag and a doormat out of his unfortunate mother though she doesn't seem to see it.'

'It's a phase he's going through,' O'Sheehan said. 'All boys do. He's asserting his sense of independence.'

'Independence. What independence? That's a good one. Who feeds him, who pays for his education, who keeps the clothes on his back?'

'I mean his independence of personality,' O'Sheehan explained gently. 'Come now, Cornelius. If he didn't make his throw for independence he'd be lacking in manliness. You'd have real cause for anxiety then.'

Cornelius, who felt he had his fill of anxiety as it was, found it beyond him to agree.

II

Tim McDonagh leaned against the iron railings and wondered what he would do. The square behind him was ringed with trees. Already the first leaves lay yellow on the grass. In the blood-red sky above him Sunday was dragging itself to its conclusion. He was alone.

Sunday was almost always boring. In the morning he served mass, in the afternoon Devotions. The rosary came first; then the sermon with Father Fahy preaching for hours and everyone either falling asleep or wishing he'd shut up; then Benediction and that notorious oul bitch who started every hymn half a bar before everyone else and stuck to her lead to the bitter end. There was the lunch he never seemed to have the appetite for on Sunday and his mother's complaints that a boy of seventeen must eat or fall into a decline. Nearly always it ended in aimless walking or indecisive dawdling. What would he do?

While Devotions had been going on people were lying on the beaches, strolling on the promenade at Dun Laoghaire and walking the moors or among the mountains about Glencree. Now they were all on their way home. From Portmarnock and Bray, from Howth and Enniskerry. Probably they were remarking the sunset. 'Isn't it a beautiful sunset,' they were saying. Probably.

Earlier the same sunset had transmuted the city. The tricoloured flags on public buildings had fluttered defiantly against it. The Liffey caught fire from it. The bridges grew enormous. Huge shadows sprawled across lawns and squares. The statues swaggered with bronzed insolence.

Now it was act two. Regular bars of smoky cloud made the sky into a ploughed field. The colours were more various. The west was full of deep caverns and twisted paths, seas with stately ships, towers and spires and palaces. Remote, insubstantial, certainly beautiful, but not to be indulged. He began to search his pockets. What would he do?

Frank McDonagh turned for a moment from the window and said, 'Is Tim not coming home to tea, Mother?'

'It doesn't look like it.'

'I thought he said he would.'

'He promised. But lately your brother's promises are all made to be broken. I can get no good of him.'

Feeling he had landed Tim in trouble Frank said:

'I expect he's having tea with a friend.'

'If he is he might at least have told us. You were serving Devotions with him. Did he not say what he was doing?'

Frank remained silent. She began to get angry.

'It's just not good enough. This is the third Sunday running his meal has gone to waste. I hope when you're his age you'll show more consideration.'

Frank thought.

'He missed the apple pie. I bet he'll be sorry he wasn't here for that.'

She was still in a mood. Frank moved away from the window and said, 'Father Fahy was preaching today. He goes on a lot. Tim can't stand that.'

'No doubt. Is listening to God's anointed so great a trouble to him? Why didn't he come home with you?'

'I think he was a bit fed up. When he's fed up he goes off on his own.'

'It's now I miss your father,' his mother said. 'He's getting beyond my control. Going off without telling me and staying out until all hours. How does he expect to pass his examinations. He never studies. I think he's beginning to smoke too. Have you ever seen him smoking?'

The question seemed to surprise Frank.

'No, Mother. Never.'

Tim found the butt he had been searching for and lit it. It was small and lasted no time at all. When it began to burn his fingers he threw it away and resumed his walking. Beyond the square a low railway bridge crossed the road with a public lavatory beside it which he used more because it was there than from any real necessity. When he emerged he had made up his mind. He turned towards the city and headed for High Street.

Brian was stretched on his bed, a book by his side. The room was in half-light. To use the chair Tim had to remove a broken coathanger and a bottle of hair dressing. Brian watched him.

'You might have called earlier.'

'How am I supposed to know you're in?'

'Where else would I be on the last day of the holidays? Have you any money?'

'A penny.'

'One single penny?'

'One. Solitary and companionless.'

'Cigarettes?'

'None.'

'Christ,' Brian said. He turned on his elbow. 'It's a bleak prospect. I've touched the ma to the limit and I can't go near the old man because we had a ferocious row earlier.'

'What was it this time?'

'Work. I told him I'd like to become a doctor. He wants me to be a civil servant. It has me stretched out here in the horrors.'

He turned on his back again.

'Ever think of being a doctor?'

Tim had thought of many things. There was the question of money.

'University is out.'

'They make pots of money.'

'Some of them.'

'Most of them. Besides, think of all the lovely women.'

'Women?'

'Lovely women. Think of it. Dr Moloney I've sprained my ankle. Dr Moloney feel my leg. Dr Moloney I'd like you to examine my organ angelorum. My God, imagine getting paid for that.'

With Brian everything was a balloon: to be blown up.

'What about the ugly ones?'

'There are no ugly women,' Brian pronounced. He raised

himself on his elbow again and looked accusing. 'I bet you write poetry. Own up.'

'Sometimes,' Tim admitted.

'All adolescents do. It's because you've got all these sex instincts all growing up inside you but you haven't any sex outlet. So what you don't throw off in pimples you try to put into poetry. That's called sublimation. It's all in this book I was reading – the book the row was about.'

'I thought you said it was about wanting to be a doctor.'

'It began about this book. How your body works. The old man caught me. The way he went on you'd think he never entertained an unchaste thought. So I said I was reading it because I was thinking of becoming a doctor. I'd show you the book only he took it away. I wouldn't be surprised but he's got his nose dug into it since.'

'So it's back to the poetry again.'

'Not me,' Brian said. 'This sublimation stuff is no go. I'd rather have bad thoughts.'

The door opened. Mrs Moloney brought in cocoa and sandwiches. She was fond of Tim and feared he might be only half fed because his father was dead. When she had set the food before them she said:

'I saw you serving on the altar at Devotions this afternoon.'

'Hairy-looking altar boy,' Brian observed.

She ignored him.

'Was that your younger brother with you?'

'Yes. Frank,' Tim said. Now that food had been put in front of him he found he was starving. He tried not to eat too fast.

'Your mother is a proud woman, I'm sure,' she said. 'You're both such a credit.'

Brian watched her go.

'That was meant for me,' he said. He looked at him sourly. 'It's bloody near time you chucked in this altar-boy racket.'

'Why should I?'

'Because you're getting a puss on you like a bloody monk, that's why.'

The bedsprings jangled as he heaved himself on to the floor. He straightened his tie and put on his jacket.

'Let's go out,' he said with resignation. 'We'll squander that penny on some mischief.'

But at the hall door he stopped and changed his mind.

'Hang on a second. I'll have one last despairing go at the ma.'

He was gone for some minutes. When he returned he held up a shilling for inspection. Then he put a triumphant arm on Tim's shoulder and led him down the steps.

'*Sursum corda*,' he admonished. '*Ad urbem eamus.*'

The sky drama was nearing its close. Furrowed clouds now edged with black spanned a limpid ocean of modulating greens and paling golds. Housefronts and streets gave back the stored-up heat of the day. Touch a wall and it was warm. Brian said:

'Tomorrow starts the last year at school. Have you thought about that?'

'For most of the day.'

'Well?'

'I hate endings. Yet I want to be finished with it.'

'We'll have Cronin, after all.'

'I no longer care about Cronin.'

'Nor I. He's only a miserable little celibate with a squeaky voice. Did you notice we're both taller than him now?'

'Are we?' Tim smiled. 'It's not a very remarkable achievement.'

'What will you do when you leave?'

'Whatever turns up. Uncle Hugh has been talking to the mother already. He knows this man and that man and they have pull in this place or that place. It seems very complicated to me.'

'That's how jobs are got,' Brian said, 'through knowing someone or other. It's serious in your case, isn't it?'

'My mother,' Tim said, 'is doing a Novena.'

'Do you believe that helps?'

'My mother does.'

Brian dug his hands into his pockets and reflected. 'I meant what I said about giving up the altar-boy lark. It's getting bloody ridiculous.'

Tim coloured.

'I know,' he admitted. Then he added:

'It isn't simple. My mother wants me to keep on. I think it makes her feel secure.'

'Does it not embarrass you?'

'It's only for a while. You don't have to rub it in.'

His mother's attitude was part religion, part superstition. She believed his staying on brought a special flow of grace. She was also convinced it brought plain honest-to-god good luck. He got away from the subject.

'This doctor business. Are you serious?'

'Is it any use? In a few months the machine will go into action. There'll be the usual almighty bloody scramble. They'll have us dragooned into exams: for the civil service, for bank clerkships, railway clerkships, insurance clerkships. Never mind what you have to put up with so long as you land a job. Aim for the ones that are secure. If you have to use a pen and wear a collar and tie then you're respectable as well. Christ, it's appalling. Circumstances are different for you, I admit that. But so far as I'm concerned I don't think I'm going along with it.'

'What's the alternative?'

'University would give more time, if the old man can be persuaded.'

'I'd like to get started at something,' Tim said, 'asking for money at home gets worse and worse.'

'If my old man can stuff his greyhounds with brandy and eggflips he can shell out for university and look cheerful.'

Tenements lined each side of the street. Aggravated by the heat, odours of unwashed halls and overcrowded rooms flowed out to taint the air. Children were everywhere. They played hopscotch on beds they had chalked out on the pavement or chanted street rhymes and swung long skipping ropes. They were poorly clad, some almost in rags.

'How would you like to live in a tenement?'

'I pity the people,' Tim said. 'Someone should help them.'

'I pity them too. But to be honest I can't bear smells and

snotty noses.' Brian put his hand on Tim's arm: 'Do you see that shop there?' he asked and pointed. It was one of a row of tumbledown premises, some selling coal and paraffin and bundles of wood, some displaying secondhand furnishing incredibly decayed, some offering groceries and sweets.

'When I was about twelve or so I was coming home late one night and I stood to look in the window. It had spools of film in it, odds and ends cut off from larger reels I suppose and I had a projector at home. It was old-fashioned with an oil lamp in it and a funnel on top to let the fumes away. You wound it by hand and if you accidentally touched the metal casing when the lamp was lit you got the fingers roasted off you. While I was standing there at the shop window this old josser came along and began to talk to me. He told me he'd been in two wars. He was dirty and nearly in rags, and I guessed he was probably on his way to the night shelter. After a while he asked if I'd like some sweets and told me to put my hand in his trousers pocket to get them. His clothes stank and I didn't want sweets out of pockets like that, but I didn't know how to refuse so eventually I put in my hand. When I did there was no lining to the pocket at all and of course no sweets. Instead I felt this great big naked prick as hard and upright as a rod of iron. What would you do in a case like that?'

'Run like hell, I expect,' Tim said. 'Did you?'

'No,' Brian said. 'I didn't want to give him the satisfaction of having codded me. So I pretended to believe it was just an unfortunate accident and I said politely: "Oh excuse me, oh I do beg your pardon." And I walked away.'

'I've met old lads like that too,' Tim confessed. 'They're nancys, I suppose.'

'No. Just hard up,' Brian said. 'When I got home I washed my hands for about half an hour. That pock-marked oul weapon of his must have been verminous. Yet when you think of it it had a noble history. It had won its medals in the Boer War and lived dangerously among the Turks after Gallipoli. Will either of ours be able to make the same proud boast?'

'Cunningham claims to have opened his campaign,' Tim said,

'some laneway off Moore Street last winter. For the sum of two shillings and sixpence, he says.'

'Do you believe him?'

'Others brag. Cunningham does it.'

'Old Cunningham's a bit of a lad,' Brian agreed. 'Why don't we see if he's in?'

'I don't mind.'

Darkness had settled quietly. When they turned the corner at York Street the tenement smell stayed behind and the air became sultry and smelled of flowers. Horse cabs waited under lamplight by the great gate of Stephen's Green. In Grafton Street the lavender woman outside Woolworths pressed a posy on them.

'Sixpence, young gentlemen.'

They laughed.

'For your sweetheart,' she said to Tim.

'I haven't got one.'

'Then you will some day, with the help of God. Give me something, young gentleman.'

He rooted in his pocket and found the penny.

'It's all I have,' he explained. She took a sprig of lavender from her basket and put it in his buttonhole.

'For luck, young gentleman.'

He thanked her and they resumed their walk.

'You're an extraordinary nit,' Brian remarked. He meant it kindly.

Cunningham himself opened the hall door. His face looked scrubbed and shiny and his hair wet. As he was greeting them he broke off and said: 'Wait now – there's a funny smell.'

'It's Lord Lucan here,' Brian explained. Cunningham saw the buttonhole. He bent over to sniff at it incredulously.

'Merciful God, McDonagh's gone pansy.'

'You're smelling death, Cunningham,' Tim warned.

'Come and have chips. I've a bob.'

'I can't. I've just had a bath.'

'Boasting again, Cunningham.'

'Look. I'm really half naked. Why don't you come in?'

In the sitting room Tim added another smell to the list – that of stale pipe tobacco. It was a large room, heavily furnished and much lived in. There was a gramophone and someone had left records scattered about.

'Tomorrow worries me,' Cunningham confessed. 'I haven't all the books. When I was given the money to get them I nicked fifteen bob and I haven't been able to make it up.'

'What did you nick it for?'

'I nicked ten bob to put on a horse and five to try and get it back. The two lost. It was this oul fella I heard telling the da it was a cert. Why don't you get the chips and have them here.'

'Who'll do the leg work?'

'Me,' Tim said. 'You're putting up the cash.'

'My bike is in the garden,' Cunningham said.

The air about his cheeks was balmy and gentle, the sky full of stars. Night hid the suburban gardens and their scented pathways. As he pedalled the sensation of something coming to a close bore down on him again. In stealth and silence something dear and familiar was slipping away. What it was he could not define. But it was passing. It was moving out of reach. Nothing he could do could stay that movement. He closed his eyes briefly. Diurnally turning the earth turned. He pedalled. Whatever it was that was slipping away he solemnly blest it.

The hall door had been left open for him and as he entered the hall the gramophone in the sitting room was in use. There was laughter and girls' voices.

As he opened the door Cunningham rose and said; 'You know my sister Mollie. This is her friend Janet. And someone else you know – Anne Fox.'

'Hullo,' he said generally.

They had the advantage of surprise.

'We've been hiking in the mountains all day,' Mollie told him, 'miles and miles. My legs don't belong to me.'

'Don't talk,' Janet agreed.

Anne's eyes scrutinized him for some moments. Then she said pleasantly:

'Tim McDonagh – my goodness.'

The schoolgirl of his recollection had become a young woman. Slim, unselfconscious, with dark hair now down about her shoulders, she seemed even prettier than he had remembered.

'Won't you buy my pretty flowers,' he quoted. As a greeting it was hardly brilliant but at least it would convey that he remembered.

'There's an absolutely gorgeous smell,' Mollie hinted.

'Yes, let's have the chips,' Cunningham said. 'There's three bags. Who's going to share mine. Janet?'

'For God's sake,' Mollie protested. 'We have plates. I'll put the chips in the oven to keep hot and make tea.'

'I'm sure it isn't fair to deprive them,' Janet said.

They brushed this aside.

'There's lashings for everybody.'

Mollie took the chips and went off to the kitchen. The gramophone which had been playing 'At the Balalaika' churned to an end.

'What else have you got?' Janet asked.

'I don't know. They're Mollie's.'

She explored among the pile of records.

'That's something I meant to ask,' Cunningham remembered. 'What's a balalaika? Is it a sort of horse and coach or a Russian thing for making tea?'

'It's a musical instrument of some kind,' Brian told him.

'Like a guitar,' Tim added, 'but with a triangular body. I'm not sure how many strings.'

Janet was having some success.

'I love this one,' she said. 'Do you know it? "Just the Way You Look Tonight". May I put it on?'

'Put on anything you like,' Cunningham said generously.

'Or take off anything you like,' Brian suggested. 'That might be more entertaining.'

As Mollie returned with the tea and their plates of chips the music began again.

'Frank Sinatra,' she remarked, 'he's absolutely gorgeous.'

They talked about music and the films that were on in town and then about the end of the summer holidays. Cunningham had cigarettes which they shared. Then it grew late and the girls said they must go.

'We'll see you home – if that's all right?' Brian offered.

'Is it?' Tim asked Anne.

'Of course.'

At Huband Bridge they parted from Brian and Janet to continue on their own along the canal. The night was very still, the road empty. Between its tree-lined banks the ribbon of water gathered from the stars what light it could and gleamed faintly.

'Whereabouts were you walking?'

'Around Glenasmole,' Anne said, 'but don't you ask me exactly where. I'm hopeless about places and how you get to them. Are you?'

'I've been in the mountains a lot.'

'Mollie is marvellous. She knows all the roads.'

'When do you go back to school?'

'In a week. For the last time, thank God.'

'No Irish course this year?'

'That's only for the younger ones.' She smiled at him. 'You've got a good memory.'

'I haven't forgotten that concert either.'

'Neither have I,' she said openly. Then, as though she thought that too forward she qualified a little: 'We were a collection of forsaken females locked up in a nunnery in the middle of nowhere. You've no idea what a stir you all caused.'

'That goes both ways.'

'Not really,' she said. 'Boys have much more freedom.'

As they left the canal to turn into Upper Leeson Street he took her arm, but only briefly, until they had crossed the road.

'Are you staying on for Leaving?' he asked.

'There's no point,' she told him, 'unless you intend to go to university, of course.'

'And you don't?'

'No. I haven't the brains. When I leave I'll probably do a

secretarial course.' Her pace slackened and she came to a stop.

'Well – here we are.'

As she turned to face him to say good-night she became amused and started to smile.

'Do you always sport a buttonhole?'

The sprig of lavender surprised him. He had forgotten about it.

'An old woman in Grafton Street gave it to me. For luck – she said. Does it look swank?'

'Oh no. It looks nice.'

He removed it. Its spill of silver paper glinted between his fingers.

'Would you like it?'

'That wouldn't be fair.'

'For luck?'

He held it towards her. She hesitated. Then she took it and raised it to her face to breathe in its fragrance.

'It's lovely,' she said. 'Thank you.'

'When will you be home again?'

'At Christmas – a long time.'

'Could I see you?'

Again she smiled. 'Why not?'

'I know lots of mountain walks – if you'll come.'

'But of course I'd come.'

Happiness lit up inside him. 'Thank you,' he said.

They were both silent.

'Well. I suppose I must go in.'

He took her fingers lightly in his hand.

'All right. Good-night, Anne.'

She left her hand with him for a moment, then withdrew it gently.

'Good-night, Tim.'

She unlatched the gate and went up the garden path.

He set out for home, his feet sounding loudly in the empty streets. At Leeson Street Bridge the water in black and silver manes writhed and thundered through the sluices of the lock.

The spume brushed his face like silken threads. High above him the sky spread its crowded dome of stars without limit or number.

At Christmas she wore a hat of silver fur and a muff to match. They eliminated any lingering trace of the schoolgirl. She was demure, self-contained, pleasingly elegant and, as he thought, prettier than ever. They had coffee and cakes together in Roberts of Grafton Street where a piano trio played music. Metzler arrangements, he thought.

'Do you know it?' he asked.

She did not.

' "The Swan", by Saint Saëns. It's from a ballet.'

'It's nice. I wish I had your memory for music.'

'We play these things in the College of Music orchestra,' he explained, 'that's how I know.'

They offered each other first choice of the cakes and felt agreeably sophisticated. At first they planned country walks but weather and the short evenings combined against them. Instead they went to the pictures on a couple of occasions and began to hold hands. At parties seasonal games provided the licence to kiss for the first time. Lips, he discovered, had a fragrance like a flower. They were cool at first and then they became warm. In his arms she was compliant and yielding. They exchanged notes and small gifts. By the time he walked her to her gate on the last night of the holidays they had told each other they were in love. It was hard to say good-night. It meant good-bye for perhaps half of the year.

He said several times, 'I love you, Anne.'

'I love you, too.'

There was the compulsion to assure and reassure.

'How much?'

'Terribly.'

'So do I.'

They kissed again and again. In the darkness frost sparkled on the bars of the gate and told them how long a time it would be until summer. But it would come. That at least was certain.

In the meanwhile they comforted each other by declaring that what they felt would never change. Never. It was only a question of enduring through the months between, a matter of being patient.

III

Cornelius found his daughter reading at the kitchen table. She was sixteen years of age, a quiet girl who, unlike Brian, gave him little or no trouble. He earnestly hoped it would remain so.

'Where's your mother?'

'She's gone out to Devotions.'

'And that brother of yours?'

'He's in his bedroom, studying.'

'What's seldom is wonderful.'

She pushed the book aside.

'Brian has only a few weeks to the exams,' she explained.

'Don't talk to me,' Cornelius begged, 'you'll get no class of a decent job these days without the Leaving Certificate and what does he do? He cuts it fine. Very fine indeed. As per usual. The most important test in a young man's life. But you might as well talk to that wall there.'

Cornelius seated himself. It helped him to bear his troubles.

'I want you to go into the shop, Eilish, and fetch a bottle of whiskey for me. I've O'Sheehan above and there's none in the cabinet. If I venture into the bar myself someone will buttonhole me.'

Eilish rose dutifully and was back with the whiskey in no time at all.

'Good girl,' he told her. 'I've got one biddable and obedient child in the house, thanks be to God.'

He rejoined O'Sheehan at the chessboard.

'We'll have a preliminary drop,' he invited, putting two glasses in front of them and shaking the bottle carefully. As he poured he noticed a bundle of papers bulging from one of O'Sheehan's pockets.

'You'll lose them,' he warned. O'Sheehan stuffed them down.

'Notes,' he explained. 'I was working at the dictionary.'

'And how's it going?'

'A heavy labour, but a worthwhile one.'

'You're well able for it. A man of scholarship with a power of Irish.'

'The Irish is no trouble. It's the English.'

'And what has the language of the Saxon to do with the matter?'

'An Irish-English dictionary can claim little authority if it fails to show a firm grasp of both. That's what the notes are about: etymology, syntax, English grammar. I find it laborious.'

'I wouldn't be in too great a hurry, anyway,' Cornelius advised. 'While the work remains the money will keep coming.'

'No need for anxiety on that score,' O'Sheehan agreed. 'The French Academy have been working on a dictionary since 1830, I understand. Thirty-nine experts I'm told, and it's not finished yet.'

'And how many have we?'

'Four – believe it or not.'

'You're fixed up for life.' Cornelius sampled his whiskey, frowned, added more water. 'I wish I could say the same for that son of mine.'

O'Sheehan savoured his whiskey in turn.

'When does young Brian finish with the schooling?'

'In a few weeks' time.'

'Has he anything in mind?'

'He's romancing out of him about being a doctor or going to university. Any excuse at all to idle away his time.'

'You wouldn't encourage him?'

'And spend a hatful of money while he sits on his arse. No damn fear.'

Cornelius put down his whiskey, folded his arms, and was determined to be measured and reasonable.

'The career for him is the civil service. I'm sick and tired of telling him. What's the use of all my work for the Fianna Fail party if I have no opportunity to turn it to account. The party couldn't be doing better than at present and it's bound to continue in government. I have some small call on its gratitude. If he gets the civil service entrance examination, in no time at all, with a word or two from me in the right places, he'll be climbing the ladder. Is that unreasonable? Is that not plain unvarnished good sense?'

'I know you have influence and to spare,' O'Sheehan acknowledged. 'The dictionary appointment was due entirely to it.'

'Now, now. You had high qualifications.'

'You had the push,' O'Sheehan insisted sternly. 'Let us acknowledge the simple facts.'

'All right,' Cornelius conceded, 'isn't that what I'm saying. Let our would-be doctor below do the civil service entrance exam and leave the rest where it belongs.

'Youth is headstrong. It thinks it knows better.

'Don't talk to me,' Cornelius implored, this time looking at the ceiling.

They concluded, nevertheless, that if pressure was to be exerted, it must wait until the examinations were over. Conflict beforehand might interfere with study and prove disastrous.

'It suits to let it lie for the present,' Cornelius confessed, 'this general election in a few weeks will keep me fully occupied.'

'But unworried?'

'Oh, not a care,' Cornelius admitted. 'The economic war at an end and Britain handing back the treaty ports to us at long last. De Valera's the man of the moment. We're on the crest of the wave.'

In halls and classrooms throughout the city pens scratched in the silence and clocks measured off the allotted hours. Each day the set papers were distributed ritually and accepted silently, face downwards, until at a signal they were turned over and rustled in unison. The supervisors took their seats, folded their arms, fixed vigilant, disinterested eyes. June, abroad in streets and public parks, peeped in curiously and irrelevantly through open windows. In the breaks they gathered in groups to exchange notes. At evening they skimmed the textbooks in preparation for the next day. The altar rails at early morning masses bore the weight of their petitions. St Anthony, St Rita, Our Lady of Good Counsel, knew no respite. The statue of the Sacred Heart, much assailed, stared down inscrutably on bent, imploring heads. Novenas were in favour.

Brian worked diligently each evening and kept out of his father's way. Tim found his mother unusually quiet. She spoke softly. She smiled a lot. At meals small, attentive luxuries made an appearance; now a cake, now some home-baked soda bread, at another time an apple tart. His brother Frank was accompanying her to early mass, a willing conscript. Even Cunningham confessed to having become a daily, if temporary, communicant.

'Unless someone puts in a good word for me,' he explained, 'I don't stand an earthly.'

Brian stood still to scrutinize the heavens and said:

> 'Angels singing peace on earth
> Help us pass the Leaving Cert.'

'That's right,' Cunningham complained, 'put a jinks on me.

In St Stephen's Green along paths flecked with fallen petals nurses pushed afternoon prams. Cunningham perked up enough to assail the prettier ones with pleasantries. The metal plaques set here and there in the grass also helped to restore his spirits. He recited for their diversion:

> 'Please keep off the grass
> It's bound to wet your arse.'

They passed without curiosity the busts of James Clarence Mangan, Constance Markiewicz and Tom Kettle, breathed the moist air about the shining tendrils of the fountain, watched the ducks tracing arrowheads on the sunbright surface of the pond. Noticing June for the first time, Tim remembered that the hawthorn would be like snow along the foothill roads to the mountains and the air busy with insects.

'History tomorrow,' Brian reminded them.

Cunningham felt his spirits sink once again and looked at him accusingly.

'Let's move on,' he suggested.

It was always better to keep moving.

'Look up the Statute of Kilkenny,' Brian advised. 'A fellow told me there'd be a question about that.'

'How could he know?'

'His oul fella pals around with one of the examiners.'

'Even so, they wouldn't blab.'

'No harm to look it up though.'

'There's so many bloody things to look up,' Cunningham complained. Tim searched his mind. Eventually he said:

'It was signed in 1367, I think.'

'What did it forbid?'

'Keep off the grass,' Cunningham suggested.

'The intention was to stop the English being absorbed by the Irish, wasn't it?' Tim continued. 'So they were forbidden to use the Irish language, or to adopt an Irish name, or ride a horse in the Irish manner. Whatever that was. Without a saddle, maybe.'

'Side-saddle,' Cunningham said. 'Keep the legs closed.'

They ignored him.

'What else, though?' Tim wondered.

Brian knew.

'It forbade intermarriage, fosterage, and gossipred.'

'Christ,' Cunningham implored, 'what's gossipred?'

'That's a good question,' Brian agreed. 'What is it?'

'Maybe they weren't allowed to talk to their Irish neighbours,' Cunningham suggested, 'you know – gossiping.'

They ignored him again.

'It might mean sponsorship,' Tim said.

'How sponsorship?'

'To go sib. If one of them stood godfather to an Irish child he'd be going sib; creating a spiritual relationship.'

'I must look it up,' Brian said.

Cunningham decided he was going home. He said he wanted to consider which of them depressed him most: Professor Moloney or Professor McDonagh. As they watched him go Tim said:

'Poor old Cunningham – he's worried sick.

'I'm worried myself.'

'Nonsense. You'll walk it.'

'I'll get the exam. But I want a scholarship. It's the only way of getting to university. At present the old man won't budge.'

'Would a scholarship change his mind?'

'God knows. It might.'

They left by the Great Gate where the air was pungent with the smell of horses and the cabbies smoked and played cards about one of the seats. The street was busy with trams. As they waited to cross the road Tim wondered where each of them would be in a year's time. The gates of their present world were closing behind them. He could hear them moving on their hinges. He thought of Cunningham's figure receding companionless down a tunnel of trees.

After exams the next day Cunningham raced over to embrace them both.

'I couldn't believe it at first,' he said. 'Then I set to and wrote nearly three pages about it. I even knew who introduced the bloody statute.' He cocked his head in triumph. 'Lionel, Duke of Clarence.'

They walked in companionable silence until another thought struck Cunningham. He was in the centre and spread an arm about each of their shoulders.

'Any ideas about the geography paper?' he asked.

IV

The chief clerk conducting the interview, bulky and formidable in his black jacket and stiff, butterfly collar, had a waxed moustache and a bullet-shaped head.

'Eighteen years of age?'

'Almost eighteen, sir.'

'With the Honours Leaving Certificate?'

'Yes, sir.'

'The name here is. . . .' The chief clerk searched through the letter beside him. 'Timothy McDonagh. Is that your full name?'

'Timothy Philip McDonagh.'

A blotting pad and notebook furnished the desk. In a bold, deliberate hand the chief clerk committed the full name to the book.

'I have this introduction from Captain Keenan. Your guardian. . . .?'

'My uncle, sir.'

'A fine type of officer and a thorough gentleman; we are well acquainted. Have you a written application with you?'

'No, sir. I was just told to be here at ten o'clock.'

'We must have one in your own hand. It's a rule of Metropolitan Services. Later on I'll leave you on your own for a while to write it. Your father is dead?'

'Yes, sir.'

'He saw service in the Great War, I'm told. You must put it in your application. We respect that sort of background. I'm a military man myself – Boer War. How did you do in mathematics?'

'Honours, sir.'

'And English?'

'Honours. Also in history and Latin.

'*Faber est quisque fortunae suae?*'

For a moment it was unclear whether this was a philosophical observation or a request to translate. A questioning inclination of the bullet-shaped head suggested the second.

Tim said: 'Each man fashions his own fortune.'

'*Nullum tetigit quod non ornavit?*'

'He touched nothing that he did not adorn.'

'Very good. Do you know who said it. And about whom?'

'Dr Johnson, sir, in his epitaph for Oliver Goldsmith.'

The chief clerk was satisfied.

'Excellent. You've done very well.' He rose.

'I'll leave you to make out your application. Address it to the General Manager, Metropolitan Services Ltd, and see that you write your best hand. Say you understand there is a junior clerkship vacancy and that you beg to be considered. Set out the name of your school, your performance in the Leaving Certificate, your age, of course. And remember to mention your father's military service. I'll come back in twenty minutes.'

He was furnished with a pen, an ink bottle, some sheets of paper. He wrote slowly, forming his letters with extreme care. When the chief clerk returned that too was satisfactory.

'You write a clear, well-formed hand, Mr McDonagh. I am happy to offer you the position.'

It was hard to believe. Livelihood in a world that was short on it had come at the first try. He stumbled over his thanks.

'The salary is one pound per week,' the chief clerk told him. 'After a six months' probationary period you will qualify for a further ten shillings. After that you will be eligible for annual increments at the management's discretion. The hours are nine o'clock to five. The half-day is Saturday, nine to one o'clock. The Sabbath, of course, is free. The salary includes overtime should it arise, but that would be very occasional and unusual. Should it become excessive, a gratuity is considered. Is that satisfactory?'

'Thank you, sir – yes.'

'You may start almost immediately. Tomorrow morning if it suits.'

'Tomorrow suits very well.'

'Good. At nine o'clock.' The chief clerk extended a large hand.

'You are a young man on the threshold, Mr McDonagh. You are at the start of a career. I wish you success. When you are reporting this to your uncle, as no doubt you will be, be good enough to convey my compliments.'

'Yes, Mr Breen.'

The chief clerk drew himself erect. He was portly but straight-backed.

'Colonel Breen, Mr McDonagh.'

It was a correction, not an admonishment. He held open the door.

In the morning he was put in the charge of a fellow clerk who had been two years already with the Metropolitan. They sat at opposite sides of a large desk, one of perhaps twelve in the firm's general office. His companion pointed to the cardboard triangle which rested in front of him with the name 'Mr J. Ellis' inscribed on both sides of it. Similar cardboard shapes decorated the others.

'They supply everyone with these,' he said, 'because in this unwholesome kip there's every possibility of forgetting who you are. What did the Colonel say your name was?'

'Tim McDonagh.'

'Mister McDonagh. In the Metropolitan there are no Joes or Tims. Everyone is mister, except the tradesmen and the labourers. They don't mind, though, because they have a trade union to look after them and of course they're better paid. Supposing you bring your chair around this side and sit at my elbow for a while. It'll be easier to initiate you into all the devilish complexities.'

The chair was on castors that made a lot of noise as he moved it. Heads here and there were raised to stare at him.

'Don't mind them,' Ellis advised. 'A bluebottle found his way in here a few days ago and the excitement nearly killed everybody. Are you a punter?'

The word was unfamiliar.

'A punter?'

'Do you back horses?'

'Oh, no.'

'I have a tip for Cora's Mistake at Leopardstown today but there's another horse I'm inclined to fancy in the same race. I thought you might have some advice to offer.'

'I'm afraid not.'

'Never mind. I'll have a word with Jackson when I take a break for a smoke. Our smoking room is in the corridor. You'll hear the chains being pulled.'

Tim laughed.

'Don't do that,' Ellis warned him, 'it's not allowed. Well, let's start.'

He took a bundle of dockets and showed him how to enter details from them in a large book and the kind of abbreviations that could be used. Then he showed him how to code the dockets by putting on them the book page and a letter of the alphabet corresponding with the letter marking the position of the information on the page. Tim tried it for a while. It was not very difficult.

'Did the Colonel tell you he was through Trinity?'

'No.'

'Don't worry – he will. And in a way it's true. Once, when the Provost applied to us about a plumbing problem, the Colonel was sent in person to discuss it. He went in through the College Green gate and left later by the one in Lincoln Place. That was the extent of his academic career. Take the rest with a pinch of salt.'

Ellis looked up.

'Jenkins,' he said.

An attendant in the uniform of the Metropolitan said he was looking for a Mr T. McDonagh.

'He's here,' Ellis said.

'Colonel Breen asked me to deliver this.' It was yet another triangle of cardboard. Ellis indicated the opposite side of the desk.

'Just leave it down there.'

They resumed the business of the dockets. From time to time Tim glanced across and the cardboard spoke his name back at him. Mr T. McDonagh. It looked isolated and strange. In his mind the gates clashed finally to, the key turned in the lock. Ellis began to gasbag again.

The bicycle was new, a Rudge-Whitworth with three-speed gear, black in colour, obtained through the easy payment facilities of S. J. Geary of The Green. It took him in in the mornings to sign the clock between nine and ten minutes past (ten minutes' grace being the privilege of clerical staff only) and home in the evenings around five-fifteen. It took him back and forth at lunch hour. The days were fine, the Green gay with summer strollers. Sometimes there was a band in the evenings to keep him late for tea. In Grafton Street the girls wore summer frocks that exposed desirable details and drew the eye. Outside Roberts and Bewleys the aroma of coffee hung pleasantly on the air. The baskets of the flower sellers set Woolworth's front and the corner of Chatham Street ablaze. Along the coast road cyclists with towels and bathing togs wrapped about the handlebars made for Williamstown and Blackrock and Seapoint. Sometimes he joined them. Sometimes he went down to visit his aunts in his grandfather's house by the sea.

All things wore a new aspect. Once or twice he cycled by the school building, now closed and empty in the July evenings. It was strange not to be part of it. He looked up at the window he had sat at for so long and saw in imagination the vacant desks, the clotting inkwells. Sometimes at night he would dream he was back there, or that he had forgotten to go and was at a loss for an excuse to offer. Nearby, the main gates to the playground were bolted, something he could not remember having seen before. On the archway above them the clock had stopped. A pigeon searched the channel along the kerb for edibles; seeds from dried horsedung and other titbits. There would be no crusts discarded from school lunches. He sat a long time, one foot on the raised bicycle pedal, the other stretched to the pavement for support, and wondered at the sunny emptiness, the silence. Though uncertain of its precise relevance, he quoted in a low voice to the pigeon:

> 'The seas are quiet and the winds give o'er,
> So calm are we when passions are no more.
> For then we know how vain it was to boast
> Of feeling things too certain to be lost.'

The pigeon paid no attention. But when he pushed down the pedal to move off it hopped nimbly out of his way.

In the Metropolitan Ellis continued to preside over his

initiation, an experienced and disillusioned guide. He told him who could be trusted and who not; the unwritten rules which governed the number of times you could slip over to the toilets for a smoke and the tolerated limits to the duration of the coffee break which, he explained, must always be taken whether you wanted coffee or not because anyone who worked through was regarded as fawning on authority and a company toady.

'Mullins, for instance,' Ellis said. 'The arse of his trousers is so shiny from sitting at his desk you could use it for shaving.'

They were required to wear sober-coloured suits at all times except perhaps on Saturdays in summer when sports coats and flannels were tolerated though never an open-necked shirt. Saturdays were for sport: for football or tennis or rowing or going to the races.

The Metropolitan, he recognized, did no more than reflect the society it served. A clerk was respectable as to class and should dress like a gentleman. The bowler hat of the tradesman distinguished his rank and the apprentice trailing after him always carried the tool bag. Labourers were unimportant. They wore what came to hand, an assorted medley discarded by the Defence Forces, the Constabulary or the outdoor personnel of the Department of Posts and Telegraphs. They were uniformly shod, winter and summer, in the long rubber boots issued once yearly by the company which they seemed never to take off.

The casual hardly counted at all. Extreme lowliness obliged him to push the handcart, just as extreme youth made it the business of the nipper to collect the tommy cans and brew the tea. In difficult times it was the casual who was first to go. Give him his cards and farewell companions. Good-night and good luck, said the drake to the duck. He found it in no way remarkable. So it was in the world of childhood and the world at large. Except that in the Metropolitan it was all more or less under your nose. One day while searching the drawer of his desk he stuck his pencil behind his ear for convenience. The Colonel caught his eye and beckoned him over. He pointed to the forgotten pencil.

'Mr McDonagh,' he said, 'you are not working in a butcher's shop.'

His first reproof.

'What a horrible old snob,' Anne said when he told her.

'We haven't any trade union,' he explained, 'so of course they wipe their boots on you.'

'You should all join one.'

'The white collar worker is too respectable to do that. Or so he says. The truth is they have the wind-up.'

He was repeating Ellis. That surprised him.

V

Cornelius was in spate and had been for an unconscionable time. At first O'Sheehan listened. Then he fell to a study of the mountains beyond the window and the slow declension of the sun. It had been removing itself unobtrusively from the room about them, on tiptoe as it were, a step at a time with imperceptible pauses between. He wished he could do likewise. While Cornelius droned on he transferred his gaze to the chessboard which lay idle between them and began to review his steady progress with the dictionary, his study of derivations, of grammar, of figures of speech. Cornelius, he noticed, had switched from a periphrasis ('. . . stubborn and unbiddable ever and always since he found the use of his tongue to set his judgment against his father's') to an extended passage in paralipsis. The monologue began to offer interest of an academic kind.

'Far be it from me,' Cornelius was complaining, 'to divulge the trouble I've always had with that child; the peculiar books he's never done reading, his back answers to his mother, the job it is to get him to dress himself respectably or put a bit of polish on his shoes – unless his mother does it for him and more fool she. No. Others will broadcast his laziness and his bad manners soon enough. But when it comes to sneers at the

clergy and a loose attitude to religion then that's the limit and
beyond.' Cornelius drew a deep breath and resorted, O'Sheehan
noted with continuing interest, to a pericope.

'Need I remind you that the penny catechism has the answer
to that class of conduct,' Cornelius added. ' "He that will not
hear the Church, saith Christ, let him be to thee as the heathen
and the publican." ' He recollected O'Sheehan's unorthodoxy
and made apology. 'No offence, of course. I know you're going
to tell me you have your own view of such matters. That's a
different thing entirely. They are the honest doubts of a mature
man honestly held. You have a formidable intellect well able to
tease and untangle on its own account and one day who knows
the story may be different. But a whipper-snapper not yet out of
his teens denying all he learned at his mother's knee in his own
home and sneering openly at what he was taught in school by
the Brothers, by God it's too bloody much. Did I tell you he's
at the cigarettes?'

Metaphrase? Synesis? Certainly a Gaelicism: *at the cigarettes.*
Politeness and a desire to sooth drew speech from O'Sheehan.

'You might expect that,' he said mildly. 'After all he's
eighteen. Or is it nineteen? Near enough to manhood anyway.'

'And who pays for them – answer me that. Time enough
when he's earning his bread.'

Synedoche.

'I've seen him helping in the shop, I think.'

Cornelius laughed hollowly.

'Help is right. Help how-are-you. I can tell you that's the
help I'd as lief be without. Treating himself to the odd bottle
of stout when your back is turned, and hardly waiting for that to
help himself to a packet of fags. A large packet. And giving
snotty answers to visitors.'

'I've never heard him do that.'

'Not to you, of course. But to members of the Party and
such like.' Cornelius resorted to epistrophe. 'Politicians, you see,
is beneath his notice. The Irish language is beneath his notice.
The patriots dead that gave their lives for everything he has is

beneath his notice. Decency, patriotism, religion – all beneath his notice.'

'You must allow he applied himself to his studies.

'If you believe that, you're sadly misled.'

Apodosis.

'But he got the scholarship didn't he? Isn't that greatly to his credit?'

Again Cornelius laughed without humour.

'He got the scholarship right enough. Nearly blinded himself with the books after a year spent in idleness. And do you know why: bloody cuteness. He thought if he came home with a scholarship I'd have to say yes to the university business. He can think again. It's the civil service or let him find his own way. We'll see how he fares then. Of course the mother is at me now as well.'

'She wants you to relent?'

Cornelius sighed.

'Women is women.'

'But to please her . . .'

Cornelius slapped the chessboard.

'Not an inch. It's his will against mine. We'll see who's the more stronger.'

A double comparative.

O'Sheehan looked at Cornelius and saw a face rigid with determination. He gave up.

'Very well,' he said. 'You know your own mind. But I foresee plenty of trouble and contention.'

Cornelius nodded several times. He was grim.

'That's what I was thinking in my head,' he agreed.

Pleonasm.

Brian's mother said to him; 'You did so well in your exams and I was so proud; your photograph in the paper and everything. Now it's all being spoiled.'

'Whose fault is that?'

'When I promised to speak to your father for you I didn't know it would keep leading to rows week in and week out. I can't stand it any longer. And I'm beginning to see there's reason in what he says. You'd get on like a house on fire in the civil service with the good brains God gave you and your father able to put in a word here and a word there. You'd have a safe, comfortable job with a pension; set up for life you'd be. That's not to be put aside lightly.'

'Don't make me sick.'

'Sick or not, there's many a young man would give his two eyes for the chance. You must admit it. And qualifying for medicine takes years. Then you'd need to buy a practice. Where's that to come from?'

'From what he stacks away in the bank or under the bloody mattress.'

'I won't listen to language in the house.'

'Or he could cut down on the brandy flips he keeps stuffing into his bloody greyhounds. They wouldn't win in a fit.'

'I don't know what to do,' his mother said.

'Yes you do. You're going to give in to him.'

'You have my home divided on me. Between the two of you I'm nearly out of my mind.'

'Such as it is,' Brian said.

He lifted a plate from the kitchen table and let it smash on the floor. She looked at the scattered fragments unbelievingly. Then she fell into a weeping fit. He left her to it.

For a nominal membership fee the Metropolitan Social Centre offered recreation to staff. Its ample grounds provided cricket and tennis. Indoors there were billiard tables, card tables, darts and rings, a table for push ha'penny. The dance hall, which boasted a grand piano for functions and a wreck of a one for impromptu singsongs, was used by the Musical and Dramatic Society and occasionally by the Debating Society. There was a bar which did reasonable business, but caused complaint because unlike certain other club bars in the city it kept strictly to the official licensing hours. The directors' representatives were unbending in the matter. They also reserved a suite of rooms and a private bar exclusively for higher-ranking staff.

A separate and well-appointed building catered for the table tennis club. It was a sport at which the general manager had once excelled and to which he was still enthusiastically addicted. Ellis said that if you found a Catholic in the senior clerical grades you could be certain he was championship material. It was a fact that players from other clubs were offered senior clerical posts from time to time. The standard of play, naturally, was consistently high.

When the ring and dart boards were fully occupied Tim and Ellis used the push ha'penny table. Or they joined up with the debaters. The Debating Society harboured a small minority with Bohemian and even revolutionary aspirations. The rest were content to jaw with equal confidence on religion, politics, trade unionism, morality, art, history and current affairs. They passed around inside information on the manoeuvres of the Catholic Hierarchy and they uncovered scandals in high political circles. They reserved a special contempt for anyone taking anything at its face value. Their favourite activity, apart from listening to the sound of their own voices, was the illegal acquisition and circulation of books banned by the Censorship Board. They were a bit overpowering at first.

'Have you read *Antic Hay*?' one of them asked.

'No. Who wrote it?'

It had not been among the books Mr Curtis used to keep.

'Aldous Huxley.'

'Huxley?'

'You've never heard of him?'

'I'm afraid not.'

The eyes switched to Ellis in unbelieving enquiry.

'My God. Who's your friend?'

'Tim McDonagh,' Ellis said, 'a new recruit; fresh from the Christian Brothers and eighteen years of age.'

He turned to Tim.

'This gentleman bent over with intellect is Charlie Jackson,' he explained. 'Try not to be overawed. He has five years' advantage over you and he'd like you to think the bags under his eyes were acquired in the brothels and gin palaces of teeming

Dublin. You can see for yourself the pallid face and nicotine-stained fingers.'

'The Christian Brothers,' Jackson questioned. 'Do you believe in that stuff?'

'Jackson has left the fold,' Ellis explained. 'I forget why.'

'The Pope uses a gold telephone,' Jackson said. 'There's an adequate reason for a start.'

He addressed Tim.

'There's a marked streak of homosexuality in the Order. No doubt you noticed.'

'No. I did not,' said Tim.

'You were too uninformed to be aware of it, probably. Sadism too. Ellis denies it, of course.'

'Not at all.'

'You admit it?'

'Among other defects,' Ellis said.

'Really. Such as – ?'

'Such as rheumatism, deafness, senility, tennis elbow, fallen arches and St Vitus's dance.'

Ellis dismissed the topic.

'Come, young McDonagh, I'll show you the bar.'

'You'll find Higgins there,' Jackson said, 'he was enquiring for you.'

The parting was amicable, after all.

'Jackson was with the Jesuits,' Ellis complained. 'They all have delusions of intellectuality.'

Higgins, engrossed in a crossword, looked up as they approached.

Ellis said: 'You seek an audience, my son.'

'The very identical man,' Higgins greeted. He motioned with the paper. 'Sit down.'

'You know Tim McDonagh?'

'Certainly,' Higgins said. They seated themselves.

'It's the annual outing,' Higgins explained. 'We've had a committee meeting and fixed on the second Sunday in October.'

'Why must it always be at the time when a fellow is trying to get a few quid together for Christmas?'

'The directors have to vote the wherewithal at their annual general meeting, haven't they? It may be a formality by now, but it's manners to wait. The question is where do we go. Some were suggesting Wexford.'

'Too far,' Ellis decided. 'The longer the journey the shorter the time for knocking back the free booze.'

'My view exactly. I suggested Wicklow town after a bit of a tour around Woodenbridge and the Vale of Avoca – that sort of thing. Then jars and lunch in some hotel in Wicklow town and a dance or entertainment afterwards.'

'What about friends and fancy women?'

'We've allowed for two each at ten bob a skull. Coach tour, lunch, free drink and the rest. It's for nothing.'

'It's not bad,' Ellis approved. 'And it thins out the crush of hoary Metropolitans.'

'Old Dewsome and his faithful few were all for New-grange – an archaeological tour of the megalithic tombs.'

'He was feeling homesick,' Ellis sympathized.

'So I thought of Avoca. The associations with Tom Moore's poetry will occupy the culture crowd without killing the proceedings stone dead. What's your view?'

'Completely in favour.'

'Maybe you'd lobby it here and there.'

'No better man,' Ellis promised.

He suggested a drink. On his recommendation Tim tried a Cairne's Ale. Upon his further recommendation Tim tempered its unfamiliar flavour with a dash of raspberry cordial.

White globes the size and shape of footballs encased the gas attachments at each end of the counter. Brian lit them both; first the one on his left and then the one nearer the door, allowing the glass a little time to warm before turning the tap to its full. Rain, he noticed, was flecking the shop window and trickling down like tears across its view of the darkening street. He returned to uncork two more bottles of stout for the two off-duty bus conductors seated at the counter. They had been colloguing for almost half an hour. At a side table a little man with a hunchback and a grey face was dealing at parsimonious length with a pint of porter. Two women in the snug held a whispered conversation. It was early as yet for business and he was in sole charge. Later, by the time his father returned from the greyhound races in Shelbourne Park it would have improved, though only to its midweek level. Brian hardly cared. Good and bad did not matter. Until he bent to his father's wishes or found a solution of his own he would have only his pocket money and whatever could be acquired illicitly. That was the future as he saw it, dreary as the darkening streets beyond the window.

Brian placed the filled glasses in front of the conductors. Black body and white ring of a head, they stood on the counter like twin clerics, pillars of the island of the Church Triumphant, the crozier *über alles*. Put not heavy hands on a woman. Do not play host to desire. Discipline the organs of sight, smell, hearing. Do not touch, do not look, do not listen. Do not read what the censor forbids. Do not question what your pastor ordains. Check with him the procedures of the marriage bed. Do not seek radical social change, which only encourages the socialists. Respect the rights of property. Though the bishop may be wrong, nevertheless he is to be obeyed. If there is a doubt, hold on. The Hierarchy will have a chat with God about it. If you are poor, understand that you are greatly favoured. Remember the birth in the stable, the humble home in Nazareth. Salute the church when passing it. Raise your hat to all religious. Contribute generously to the support of your pastors. Be as little children, for theirs is the kingdom of heaven.

'How is the horses with you lately?' one of the conductors asked the other.

'Up and down. I lost a bundle in the Park last week. Information – so called.'

'Same with me. I pick it up at the nags and then lose it all on poker.'

The hunchback was nursing the dregs of his pint, grey-faced, forlorn, a nonentity in a world of no importance. Kyphosis. Caused by spinal injury, or tuberculosis of the bone or, as almost certainly in the case in front of him, rickets. What was the life expectancy? He would look it up. Brian lifted the flap of the counter and went over.

'That's a bit of a downpour.'

'Inclined to rain between showers, I notice,' the hunchback answered.

Brian smiled.

'Give me that a moment.'

He brought the glass with its lingering dregs to the pumps and filled it again three-quarters of the way. He brought the replenished glass back.

'That'll help to keep the weather out,' he said.

The grey face lit up. 'God bless you,' the little man said.

At half nine when his father returned the two conductors were still in session.

'Any luck, Cornelius?' they asked.

Cornelius, who was hanging up his wet coat before tying on his shop apron suspended activities to swear.

'I wanted the going to be hard and hard it was when the meeting started. But by the fourth race the bloody rain had banjaxed it.'

'I was thinking that,' one of the conductors said. 'What you want in this climate is not greyhound racing but races for Kerry Blues. They're better swimmers.'

Cornelius agreed. When his apron was in place he scrutinized the bar carefully. Brian knew he was making a head count of the customers. He also knew that the result was displeasing.

VI

Late September offered them a brief return of summer. A tram standing idle at the gates of Rathfarnham Castle looked as though it had fallen asleep and the windows along the narrow village street wore a bronze tinge. The fields which could be seen reaching up the foothills of the mountains were hazed and seemed to float. Pedalling steadily they lost the suburbs and the sound of Sunday bells. At Ballyboden they stopped to buy oranges and chocolate – soon after that the gradient became steep and the long climb began. They took it steadily, now in low gear, now walking their bicycles. At Killikee the city spread out below them and the great sweep of the bay confirmed the extent of their climb. They looked back to admire, to share their sense of conquest. But when they had gained the moors and struggled on another couple of miles Anne was obliged, almost apologetically, to say to him:

'Tim, please. Couldn't we rest a bit?'

'Why not?'

Leaving the bikes against the low bank at the roadside they clambered through bracken and heather in search of a clear place to sit. They became suddenly conscious of having wandered into a vast and primeval world. There was no longer any trace of the road they had left. Instead they were surrounded everywhere by chaotic landscape, solitary, undefined, filled by the sun's light until it overflowed. The deep silence brought them to a stop. Isolated, small, yet in their partnership sufficient, they looked about.

'Adam and Eve,' he suggested.

Their relationship, too, seemed to change as he said it. She put her arm through his in silence.

Above them the sky spread blue and fathomless. Before them rolling slopes of bracken and heather dipped down in a great sweep to the fringe of green fields about the long and narrow lake at the bottom, then lifted steeply again to climb the mountainside on the farther shore. The far slopes too were vast and sprawling with outcrops of grey and gleaming rock, occasional bony and misshapen trees, clumps of green rushes where the seepage was slow and bracken and heather vying elsewhere for supremacy. Mica on the sandy surface of the valley road gave it a sheen that rivalled the water's.

They sat down to wonder at it.

'What valley is it? Do you know it?'

'Glennasmole.'

'Have you ever been there?'

'A few times. You can get to it by Bohernabreena. Do you know the story of Oisin and Niamh of the Golden Hair?'

'She came to Ireland for him and he left Finn and the Fianna and the two of them went off together on a white horse.'

'You remember what happened to him when he grew lonely for the Fianna and came back on a visit?'

'He was to remain on horseback and not to set foot on the soil. But when he stooped to help a group of men to move a boulder his saddleband broke and he fell to the ground. Isn't that so? And he found that what had seemed like an absence of a few months was in fact hundreds of years and Finn and the heroes were all dead.'

'Well. Down below you there in Glennasmole, somewhere along that lake shore, is where it all happened. Or so they say.'

'You don't believe all that?'

He laughed.

'When a story's been told for several hundred years it acquires a kind of retrospective truth. There was a poem called "The Celts" on our school course, too. Was it on yours?'

'How does it start?'

> 'Long, long ago beyond the misty space
> Of twice a thousand years,
> In Erin old there dwelt a mighty race,
> Taller than Roman spears – '

'Yes. We did that one. I thought it a bit dreary, to be honest.'

'It's got a swing to it, though.'

He gazed down into the valley while the verse he wanted assembled itself in his mind.

> 'Oisin two thousand years of mist and change
> Surround your name –
> Thy Finian heroes now no longer range
> The hills of fame
> The very names of Finn and Gaul sound strange;
> Yet thine the same,
> By miscalled lake and desecrated grange,
> Remains, and shall remain.'

She smiled.

'Is that one of the miscalled lakes?'

'The lake of the glen of the thrushes – that sounds authentic enough. And the mountain beyond is Seefin – Finn's Seat.'

A light dampness gleamed along the slimness of her arm. Now that they were resting he felt his own shirt wet where it clung to the small of his back. He took her hand.

'You were tired?'

'A little.'

He ran his finger gently along her arm.

'And you're sweating.'

She surprised him by pulling away.

'No I'm not.'

He had hurt her. To sweat was probably unladylike. Yet he had meant it tenderly. She was beautiful to him in all her parts, in the shapeliness of fingers, her warmth and nearness, in the tiny pearls of sweat and their exuding, in all the sweet juices of her body.

'All right. You're not.'

'Then why did you say I was?'

He looked steadily at her.

'Because if you were, I'd like to drink you.'

He saw her struggling between outrage and understanding.

'You're mad,' she said at last. Her tone, however, carried little conviction. She rested against his shoulder.

'All right. You can go on telling me about the Fianna.'

Again he searched among the bits and pieces which had begun to recede almost from the day he left school. Yet once again the knack of recollection won:

> 'Their Ocean-God was Mananaan MacLir
> Whose angry lips
> In their white foam full often would inter
> Whole fleets of ships;
> Cromah, their Day-God and their Thunderer
> Made morning and eclipse;
> Breede was their Queen of Song, and unto her
> They prayed with fire-touched lips.'

She startled him by applauding, his audience of one in a vast amphitheatre of mountain and heath.

'Very good.'

'Thank you.'

She began to touch his fingers individually, her head averted from him.

'There are ten,' he told her. 'Eight fingers, two thumbs. I counted them once.'

'You're a bit gone on poetry, aren't you?'

'I suppose so,' he acknowledged. 'Does it annoy you?'

'Oh no. I like it.'

'I'm a bit gone generally,' he added. 'On you, for instance.'

'I like that too.'

He bent and kissed her. After a while she said:

'You have fire-touched lips, Tim McDonagh.'

'I know.'

'Are mine?'

'A bit. In a nice way, of course.'

'I think we should go.'

'Is there some hurry?'

'I think if we're ever to reach any destination whatever, now is the time to move.'

It was true. If they delayed any longer they would touch and kiss until nightfall. They walked back to the bicycles and in a short while the road levelled and it was possible to remount. Later again it began to descend.

Free-wheeling as the road wound downhill, dipping now left, now right as its camber alternated with each bend, they felt the wind of their movement slipping in a cool stream past their bodies. Spokes gleamed and rotated. Speed uprooted bog and mountain and sky and flung the world weightlessly past them. Then the road levelled and began to rise steeply once more. The holiday was over.

'Here we go again,' she said.

They walked the bicycles once more, stopping for breath from time to time. Near Lough Bray they turned to take heart from the sight of Glencree Reformatory. Surrounded by fields reclaimed from rock and bog and made fertile by backbreaking labour, it nestled far below them among the mountains at the confluence of small roads and shepherds' tracks.

'Are you ready for more poetry?'

'Say on,' she invited. 'This is Poetry Sunday. What is it this time?'

' "The Burial of Sir John Moore".'

'At Corunna. I know that one. It has a favourite verse –
She recited:

> 'We buried him darkly at dead of night
> The sods with our bayonets turning
> By the struggling moonbeam's misty light
> And the lantern dimly burning.'

'Sir John was in command down there during the Ninety-eight rebellion,' he told her. 'It was a military barracks then.'

'Poor Sir John. He went a long way to die, didn't he? When did they make it a reformatory, I wonder.'

'I've no idea.'

'Is it still a reformatory?'

'Not this two or three years.

She was staring down at its surrounding fields, now open and empty in the sunlight and peopling them, he knew, with bent and labouring bodies, once prisoners of the glen.

'It's just struck me how those beautiful fields around it came about,' she said.

'Sweat and heartbreak. The labour of delinquents.'

'It's not nice to think about, is it?'

'When I first saw it there was a blockhouse at the entrance gate and we used to hate passing it at night because we were told one of them hanged himself in it.'

'Why did you have to pass it?'

'We used to camp on the hill above it.'

'Camping and hiking. You have a nomadic streak, Tim McDonagh.'

'When my name makes the reference books, that's how they'll put me down. Tim McDonagh, Camper and Poet.'

'And musician, no doubt.

'I think it has to be one or the other.'

'So which?'

'God knows. Camper and Clerk, I expect.'

He turned to look uphill.

'Back to work?'

They tackled the ascent once again.

At Sallygap, now firmly in the heart of nowhere, a left fork brought them towards Lough Tay. At a tiny humpbacked bridge which dramatized the brown and erratic tumbling of a mountain stream, they left the road, carrying their bicycles and following its course across bogland until it offered a ferny shelf near some trees. The sky was still vast and blue, heather and fern reflected the sun's warmth and breathed back a hungry smell.

'Let's eat,' he suggested.

He went off to forage for wood.

The thicket, its mossy floor strewn with kindling and fallen boughs, offered an abundance. It lay scattered everywhere, the wrack of winter storms, caught here and there in a sunny shaft or bathed in green and dusky light. The trees crowded thickly. He had the feeling, as always in wooded places, of being somewhere he ought not and that he must wait passively until the woodland spirits came around to accepting him. He did so, as always. The silence engulfed him. He could no longer hear the river or see clearly for more than a few yards. The lake, he guessed, from some altered quality in the surrounding dusk, was straight ahead. They could explore to prove or disprove it later. Acclimatized at last, he broke an armful of the more manageable boughs and gathered kindling and returned.

She was making sandwiches. The wood was dry and the air warm. In a short while the billycan was simmering on its forked stick.

'It's delicious,' she remarked when the tea had been poured.

'It tastes a bit of woodsmoke.'

'That's what I like.'

'That's what I mean.'

That disposed of, he looked around him, assessing the landscape, savouring its patterns and colours.

'I can't spend my life in the Metropolitan,' he decided.

'Is it horrible?'

'Not horrible this day or that day. Cumulatively horrible. I can't bear signing a clock morning after morning at the same time. It becomes degrading. I don't think I was cut out to be a clerk.'

'But you've only started.'

'I know. That makes it worse.'

'What are the others like?'

'All right, by and large; decent elderly men doing their best to pay their bills or younger ones trying equally hard not to. The few you care to talk to are hard to catch up with, though. Have you ever heard of *Antic Hay*?'

'Whose Auntie Kay?'

'No. A-N-T-I-C H-A-Y. It's a book by Aldous Huxley. I made exactly the same mistake and I felt such a bloody fool. It happened over Henrik Ibsen too. I thought they were yakking about someone called Henry Gibson.'

'I've never heard of either.'

'Nor had I. How could we when every other book is banned or on the Index and the libraries never have anything you'd ever want to read after the age of ten.'

'I know. So where do the super-informed gentlemen of the Metropolitan get their information?'

'They smuggle in the banned books when they come back from holidays and they pass them around. It's quite a system. As well as that they know reviewers and there are booksellers who'll keep stuff under the counter. After a while in their company you begin to realize how much the Christian Brothers left out.'

'The nuns too,' she assured him. 'After the holidays they'd cross-question you about what plays or pictures you'd been to. At meals they read out passages to us from the *Life of the Little Flower* or her letters to Sister Marie of the Sacred Heart. They had chapter headings like "Little Sacrifices of the Cloister" and "More About Sacrifice". Between that and the smell of cabbage I wonder any of us remained sane.'

'I know. . . . Nuns are the end.'

'There was a rule you could only wear black knickers. White was sinful, for some reason. We used to be caught out in scores during gym class.'

As she remembered she began to choke with laughter.

'I remember the concert. You all lit on the make-up like famished wolves.'

'We talked about that for weeks. A concert with boys taking part was unbelievable. Usually it was Gilbert and Sullivan with the heftier girls trying to look like PoohBah or a troop of Grenadier Guards. Still, I liked the Gilbert and Sullivan shows. They were always just before Christmas. At one time I knew about six of them line for line.'

'I used to, too. In a little while even that will be forgotten.'

'I don't care, really. Do you?'

'It represents something, I suppose. Better than a blank mind.'

She reached up to touch his cheek. 'Dear Tim – you're far too serious.'

'I care for things that give happiness. Or that amuse you. Or things that have art or truth in them. Or that are natural and beautiful like what surrounds us. I don't see anything odd in that.'

'I didn't mean odd.'

'Or you, for instance.'

'Am I simply part of your well-stocked mind?'

She was teasing him.

'Let's tidy up.'

They washed the cups and things in the stream, then left them to dry in the sun and started off to find the lake.

Soon they were in the dusky silence of the thicket. If a stick snapped under their tread the sound startled them both. She stopped to admire an enormous web which bridged the distance between two blackberry bushes. The fruit, shaded from the sun for most hours of the day, hung red and unripe about it. Some droplets of dew still unevaporated since the morning clung to it and encased a tiny rainbow each.

'Isn't it beautiful?' she said.

He bent to inspect it.

'Don't break it,' she warned.

'I'm looking for his parlour.'

'It's only freshly spun, I think. If it gets broken the poor thing will probably starve to death.'

'If it gets broken and you hear cheering and singing, that's the flies holding a party.'

'Oh. Why did you have to think of that?'

She straightened and turned. It brought her close against him and he held her. A deep silence surrounded them and he could feel the warmth of her breasts through his shirt. He kissed her. After a while she looked about and said:

'It's so quiet. I'm sure no one has ever been here before.'

Her voice was very soft. They kissed again, this time with an urgency and passion which startled them both. Drawing back from him a little she said:

'I'd like to find the lake.'

He released her.

'It can't be far.'

Their voices had an altered quality and required effort to control. It was hard to bend the attention to anything except each other.

Beyond the thicket tangled heather and rising ground made the going slow. They climbed until they came on a valley which had been hidden by the contours of the slope, a shallow scoop worn out for itself by a stream. As they followed it grew broader and broader until it tumbled among boulders and miniature islands, froth lacing in patches its peaty brownness. Along its banks an occasional birch, stunted by altitude and weather, showed haphazardly its gleaming bark and yellowing leaves, or the berries of a rowan glowed and clustered above whirling water. Further downstream the slope on its far side became sheerer still. Floods had stripped it of its soil, outcrops of rock became more plentiful, the gradient more dramatic, until the slope gave way altogether to great crags of granite and towering cliffs. The river now bore leftwards, broadened yet again and began to tumble in a sequence of waterfalls from its high shelf to the lake below. It would be dangerous to follow further. Fringed by beaches of shining gravel, the lake spread its black waters beneath them. He shaded his eyes with his hands to take in first the reaches of the lake and then the chaos of mountain peaks that ringed it around.

'So. There it is.'

He felt her arm on his shoulder.

'It makes my head spin,' she said.

But happily. They had achieved their goal. It was highly satisfactory. He tried to put a name to each peak, lost orientation, began over again and persisted until a gentle push in the ribs brought his attention back to the present and he heard her saying:

'You have the oranges somewhere, stout Cortez.'

He dug them out of his trouser pockets.

'Imagine anyone ever living there,' she said as they sat down. She was pointing at the ruined gable of a house some distance away from them. A tree had established itself within the sparse protection of its broken walls. There was no trace of a path leading to it across the bogland, no sign of garden or fence about it.

'Somebody did – once. Until the Famine, perhaps.'

'Without cars or bicycles or even proper roads. No wireless, no electric light. You wouldn't believe it possible.'

They imagined long winter nights in the middle of nowhere; storms howling across bleak and barren spaces, snowdrifts blocking roads and erasing sheeptracks. They tried to reassemble a way of life when human beings and animals shared the same shelter, the same fireside, the same smoke-filled room and wavering rushlight. Other records of an earlier order began to reveal themselves. On neighbouring slopes they could discern the outlines of submerged walls, of mounds that had once been rough huts or the boundaries of thin mountain fields. Here and there, the drills of ancient potato patches still etched their faint imprint across impossibly barren-looking slopes. Suddenly and totally, in common with their better endowed counterparts, they had failed. Then their folk scattered about the world or died by the roadside and their hovels collapsed and fern took over. It was one thing in the history books. It was another in a sunny emptiness under a blue sky.

Looking at the faint imprint of the drills brought a saying she had heard or read somewhere to her mind. 'Three ridges will last to the end of the world.'

'That's nice,' he remarked when she told him. He repeated it after her. It pleased him. It was observant, it was simple, it was convincing. It had a metaphysical potency though why it should would be hard to explain. As a piece of information – if it was a piece of information and not merely the fruit of some philosopher's fancy – it was in material terms quite useless. But it touched the imagination and quickened the senses. Like music. Like poetry.

He found her staring ahead and her attention fixed. The figure of a lone hiker had appeared from nowhere and was crossing the moor at a distance from them. They exchanged looks and followed his progress closely, resenting this intrusion into their ownership of the entire mountain system of County Wicklow.

'Bloody people,' he remarked.

To their relief the rucksacked figure diminished gradually in size and eventually disappeared. They signalled their mutual relief.

'What time is it?'

He had not acquired as yet the luxury of either pocket- or wristwatch. She looked at hers.

'It's almost four.'

'Have we enough grub left for tea?'

'Plenty.'

'We could make a meal and still have time. So long as we leave around seven there'll be light enough for the hard part of the journey.'

'Lovely. Let's do it.'

They struck out for the ridge ahead. It taxed them. The sun had lost hardly any of its heat, the heather seemed tougher and more tangled than ever. It became harder and harder to keep lifting the feet. Eventually she stumbled and he had to help her up.

'Damnbloodynation,' she complained.

A large hole had appeared among the pulls and ladders in her already ruined stockings.

'Better take them off.'

She did so but found she had nowhere to carry them. He stuffed them in his pocket.

'You should have worn slacks.'

'My mother doesn't approve. She sees something brazen in a female in trousers. Lots of her ideas go back to the Ark.'

They splashed across marshy ground which left her bare legs covered with muddy freckles and soaked their shoes. Yet they began to make better progress and arrived less tired than when she had fallen.

'I've made an important discovery,' she confided in him when they were sitting comfortably by the bicycles again and finishing their tea. 'Wet shoes and torn stockings and muddy legs are only intolerable up to a certain point. After that it becomes marvellous.'

'You're not sorry you came?'

'Oh, Tim. How could I be sorry?'

'It's rotten when you think of it. From now on the evenings will be getting too short and the weather too cold. We'll be confined to the foothills and the lanes.'

'I don't mind the lanes.'

'They're a bit tame. Old dears with dogs and walking sticks out for what they call a Good Blow.'

Suddenly impatient, he gathered the used tea things to wash them in the stream. Her eyes followed him. She saw him delay to examine their shoes which they had left at the fire.

'They're almost dry,' he called back. The fern and the slope hid him.

He scoured the cups with sand. The plate he placed delicately on the surface of the water to see how long it would float, an habitual ritual which now in fancy he made his augurer of love's path. It stayed on top for long enough, a pleasing omen. Then, in time with and in tune with his recollection of an earlier self and a moment remote but still living, it sank through clearly remembered stages; first clean and white, then an aureole of gold, a bronze disc, a dark shape. But the wavering face with its disordered hair that looked up out of the water at him was not as he had once and long ago seen it. It was an amended version, one could say, a somewhat more detailed statement, a theme someone else was developing, another sketch from an unknown hand, to hang among the rest in the gallery of Self. Gently retrieving the drowned plate, he discovered her image beside his in the water.

'I didn't hear you come.'

'Because you were so far away. Miles and miles away. Where?'

She pretended amusement but her voice belied it. It was unsure as if he had withdrawn from her carelessly, without reason or due ritual. Had he been unconsciously abrupt, or spent longer than he thought daydreaming by the river? He took her hand.

'Sit down with me.'

They sat.

'I was thinking just then about something which often puzzles me. It's not easy to explain. Have you ever looked at a photograph of yourself as a baby, let's say. And then at the age of seven or thereabouts. Then at fourteen perhaps. Which of them is you? They can't all be.'

'But of course they are.'

'They couldn't. Especially when you consider the extremes.'

'Was the plate some kind of clue?'

'How?'

'You kept staring at it.'

'No. That was just a game. If it stayed afloat beyond the count of ten it would mean you and I would always be together.'

He began to laugh.

'And did it?'

'As a matter of historical fact – it did.'

'I'm so glad.'

'So am I.'

She touched his cheek.

'Then why would the lanes not be adequate enough?'

So that was it.

'Anne,' he said.

He drew her down and kissed her until love and tenderness isolated them from time and space and emptied the universe of all but themselves. The world was her body; her legs bare of stockings, her arms warm about his shoulders, lustre of eyes and taste of lips and fragrant odour of hair. Then they lay quietly together, satisfied for the moment, conscious of mutual and exclusive possession, conscious too of banked fern bending in conspiracy to protect them. Her lips were close to his ear.

She said:

'I can feel your heart beating.'

'And yours?'

He explored with the palm of his hand. She smiled. He touched her breasts, then undid the buttons of her blouse to kiss and fondle her. She made no resistance. He lifted her skirt and was ravished by her warmth and softness.

'Please, Tim. You mustn't.'

'Only to touch you.'

He bared himself and lay tightly against her.

'No,' she said, 'please.'

He could feel the warmth of her breath on his ear. He closed his eyes. For some unreckonable time they both lay close and still. Then he drew gently away. To have touched without barrier was sufficient. For the present anyway. It had to be. He covered himself once more, re-arranged her skirt, rose, drew her to him. They sat closely and in silence for some time.

'Have I offended you?'

'No, Tim.'

'I had no thought at all to harm you.'

'I know. I know you hadn't. And I don't mind. I love you

very much, Tim. More than I can ever tell you. But we can't – can we? Apart from anything else, think of what might happen.'

'I know.'

He put his arm about her, reassuring her, reassuring himself. Then for the first time he noticed how the light had changed. Clouds that had been white were edged with orange. The sun had dipped low in the sky.

'What time do you make it?'

She looked.

'It's gone seven.'

'Already?' He sighed. He rose reluctantly.

'Time to leave, I suppose.'

'I don't really want to go at all,' she said.

'Nor I. But we need the light.'

'I suppose so.'

She got to her feet.

'You have my stockings,' she remembered.

She leaned on him for support as she pulled them on, then delayed for a last look about her.

'Good-bye, lovely day,' she said to the stream and the thicket and the mountains generally. They returned, put on their shoes, packed, regained the road.

The journey for the most part was downhill and the light held good until they had passed the reformatory. There they stopped to rest and look back at the sunset. He touched her hair.

'You should be cycling into the sunset, not away from it. In films beautiful girls always do.'

'I'd rather stay with Tim,' she said. 'Someone else can have the sunset.'

She came to him and he held her closely. He said:

'Are you happy?'

'Deliriously.'

He raised an eyebrow at that. Merriment leaped into her eyes. And love.

At Killakee it was dark. The lights of the city spread north and south like scattered diamonds and the lighthouses at dutiful intervals swept the pitch-black darkness of the sea. A night wind crept up the slopes to them and chilled the air. They began the steep and winding descent.

'Cunningham was to be here at nine,' Brian said after a long scrutiny of the surrounding tables, 'but he's in tow lately with a voluptuous blonde from Drumcondra or some equally impenetrable backwater of the north side and he's not himself at all. He may well have walked under a tram.'

They were having coffee and cakes in the Grand Central after an hour or so of aimless night rambling along the quays. Customers coming in from the cinemas of O'Connell Street were shaking the rain from their coats.

'I haven't met her,' Tim said.

'Then in Cunningham's opinion you haven't lived.'

'I'd give a dozen of Cunningham's blondes for another cake.'

'Have it. It's on me. I told you Moloney is solvent. I managed to feck a pound.' Brian pushed the plate forward.

'Thanks.'

He also produced cigarettes and threw one across.

'I saw you with your own bawd the other evening. You were queuing for the Savoy.' He lit his cigarette. 'Have you, or have you not, succeeded in bedding that desirable little bundle? Have you even tried?'

'No,' Tim said.

'Of course I'm wasting my time asking you. You're the secretive type, McDonagh. You wouldn't let it be known even if you had.'

'No.'

'Whereas Cunningham finds it hard to resist putting it in the Personal Columns of the *Irish Times*. Why is that?'

'He seeks to be a man,' Tim said, 'by climbing up some woman.'

'That's the history of the male of the species, isn't it? Though there have been remarkable exceptions. Origen, for instance, found it disgusting: *Inter faeces et urinam nascimur*. We are conceived between the piss and the shit.'

Tim smiled.

'Why not? Life itself is plentifully spattered with both,' he suggested. 'Take your mind off it for a moment and you're up to your ears in one or the other.'

'Did you know that Origen had an unfortunate experience? For God's sake and to avoid sins of the flesh he had himself castrated. But the Fathers held it was an unacceptable procedure and an impediment to his ordination.'

'All I know about Origen is that he held heretical views – such as that the First Person of the Trinity is superior to the Second, and the Second to the Third.'

'And what is the orthodox view?'

'That the Three Persons are equal, though distinct.'

'You believe that stuff still?'

'Generally speaking – yes.'

'And you pray to the saints? And you still go to confession?'

'Yes,' Tim said.

'And you believe in hell?'

'There's no choice, is there? You can't pick and choose.'

'Anybody who can believe in hell,' Brian said angrily 'deserves to go there.'

'That roasts the entire Catholic Church at a stroke.'

'It's hard,' Brian complained. 'I'm tied to a father whose Trinity is the Pope, Eamon de Valera and the money in his till. And I've friends who'll pass their lives huddled under the sanctuary lamp.' He fixed his eyes on Tim's. 'You're the eternal altarboy, McDonagh. Your little bawd is safe.'

'And yours?'

Brian pretended surprise.

'Mine?'

'A friend of your sister's, I think you said.'

'That was a lapse,' Brian admitted, 'a fall from grace. I've forsworn birds. I haven't the money. And they take the time that should be spent in study.'

'Study of what?'

'Everything under the sun. For knowledge I'll be a eunuch, temporarily. You once vowed the same. Have you forgotten?'

No: he still remembered. One evening when they were sunning themselves on the rocks near the Half Moon Swimming Club and philosophizing at large while the salt dried on their bodies and the seaweed at their feet lifted and subsided with the water's slow swell and slow recession. There had been many such pacts, lightly made, as easily abandoned.

'I admit it. But there's no need to go mad.'

'The difference between us,' Brian said dismissively, 'is that I have stamina and you haven't.'

The difference between them, Tim guessed, was that Brian had a father to refuse his ambition to go on to university and he himself hadn't. He wondered that such a disappointment could leave so abiding a wound.

'All right. You have more willpower than I have. Happy?'

'Not happy – free. At least of superstitions. If I ever own a public house I'll call it The Three Persons.'

Tim caught sight of Cunningham. He was standing at the door, his eyes searching the room. Rain had plastered his hair about his forehead and his coat was sodden. Tim beckoned.

'Ask me is it raining,' Cunningham invited as he joined them, 'and I'll split you open.'

'You're late.'

'Oh, shut up.'

Cunningham left his coat on the floor, pushed the hair back from his face and sat down.

'Who's buying?'

'Moloney's in funds. He's been robbing the rich again to feed the poor.'

Cunningham managed to look scandalized.

'Have you no conscience at all?'

'St Thomas teaches that a hungry man is entitled to steal for bread. Bear me out, McDonagh.'

'I'll bear out St Luke,' Tim countered. 'The children of Mammon are wiser in their generation than the children of Light.'

'Just buy me a coffee,' Cunningham begged.

He dried his face and hands as best he could with his handkerchief until the coffee arrived. Then he recited his misfortunes.

'I brought Gwen to the pictures. She smelled of this very sexy scent and I was doing so well inside that I had every expectation of doing a lot better if I left her home. You see there's this very convenient laneway at the back of their house. On the way I invested in minerals and ices. I couldn't afford it, of course, but you have to put on the best show you can. We got the tram. More money if you like, but I couldn't wait to get to that lane. I could see goodtime Gwen wasn't much on for delay either. She's a real sport. To cut a long story short, we reached the laneway and we're just getting down to it when the bloody heavens opened. It was savage. If she'd had her umbrella we might have managed. But no. And there was no use sending her in for it because they'd have her certified if she ventured out again into a downpour like that. So the fixture had to be postponed. Match abandoned due to the waterlogged state of the pitch.'

He broke off.

'Hey. There's O'Keeffe.'

They looked about. At the far table a young man was drawing back a chair for his girlfriend. He proceeded to divest himself ceremoniously of hat and coat.

'Do we want to see him?' Brian asked.

'No,' they said.

But Brian continued to stare.

'He's got the Brylcreem look. Is he working?'

'He got a berth in a bank,' Cunningham supplied. 'That's pull for you.'

'Sartorially speaking, he's an elegant young man.'

'They go in for the dressy bit,' Cunningham said. 'Suède shoes and Club tie. He plays golf.'

Brian stared even harder.

'Jaysus,' he said.

'If you keep gaping at him,' Cunningham warned, 'he'll see us.'

The Young May Moon 263

Brian stopped and passed his cigarettes around again.

As they lit up Cunningham said: 'I'm starting work myself on Monday next in Thompsons.'

'Thompsons?'

'The outfitters place in Wicklow Street. Fifteen bob a week. It's not much but I know nothing at all about it so I suppose it's a bit of luck. An uncle was able to put in a word.'

Brian looked angry.

'We're shining examples of Irish manhood, aren't we? Here am I pulling pints and wiping the counter day after day. There's McDonagh pushing a pen from nine to five. His baby sister could do as much. And now Cunningham is all set to meet the country's demands for strong and reliable braces until he sinks into his grave. Come on. I'm not sitting here any longer.'

'I told you,' Cunningham warned, 'it's pissing rain.'

But Brian had risen and they followed.

The rain in fact had eased. People were beginning to re-appear in the streets. Young newsboys moved swiftly to dispose of their remaining papers. Strident after so unbearable a delay their voices topped the rumble of traffic. One of them brushed past. He was barefooted.

'There are lowlier than us,' Tim remarked.

'There aren't,' Brian said. 'We're totally without dignity. After that there are no degrees.'

'Wait now. At least we've shoes on our feet.'

'So has a drayhorse. I'm going home.'

Brian turned on his heel and disappeared almost as they heard him.

'What's all that about?' Cunningham wondered.

'He's not hitting it off at home, among other things.'

'He pinched that pound on his oul fella. When you think about it, it seems, well – '

Not for the first time Cunningham's vocabulary was unable to deliver. He gave up and asked instead:

'I mean, would you feck a quid on your old man?'

'It doesn't arise, does it?' Tim said.

'No, of course not. Sorry.'

Cunningham suffered his moment of embarrassment.

'I fiddle like the next,' he confessed, 'like forgetting about the change or spending on one thing what's given for something else. That sort of thing. I mean money is lovely. But I think if I took it out of his coat pocket or off his dressing table – he's always leaving it on the bloody dressing table– I'd feel . . .'

Again he gave up. 'Do you know what I mean?'

'I think so,' Tim said. 'I think Brian does too.'

'I don't mean sin or that kind of crap.'

'He said it himself a few moments ago,' Tim said, 'when he mentioned dignity.'

'Is that what he meant? I thought it a funny bloody word.' Cunningham shivered.

'Look, let's hit for home. I'm really soaked through.'

'You go ahead. I've a phone call to make.'

They parted.

The rain had left the streets cold. Tim turned up his collar, dug his hands into his pockets and crossed to the opposite side where the bronze elephant over the door of Elvery's, diminutive, neglected, faced the night bravely in its rose-and-gold-fringed coatlet and reminded him of childhood. Further up the street, in haughty silhouette on his towering column, a one-eyed, one-armed Nelson scorned the elements and spurned the faithless city. Tim turned into the post office and crossed the main hall to find a telephone booth. Mrs Fox answered and when he had identified himself said:

'She's gone up to bed but I can call her if you wish. I'm sure she's not asleep.'

'No, please don't disturb her.'

'She went to her sodality this evening and came home soaked so I made her hop into a bath and she went up to bed early. Indeed I was remarking to my husband just before you rang: what's seldom is wonderful. Are you sure you don't want me to call her?'

'No, please don't. It's not at all important. I'll call tomorrow.'

'Very well. What's this I heard about you? Yes. You've started working. Where's this it is?'

The grilling process was beginning.

'The Metropolitan.'

'Isn't that lovely. What as?'

'A clerk.'

'The clerical staff. I'm sure your mother is delighted. It'll be a help to her, won't it? And it's so hard to get a position of any kind nowadays. A big place like that would have its own pension scheme too, I expect.'

'Yes, there's a staff pension scheme.'

'Isn't that wonderful. I'm delighted. Especially for your mother's sake. But you worked hard and you have the brains and you deserve every credit. I wish Anne would buckle down to her shorthand and typewriting. That child walks about in a dream half the time. But she isn't under the same necessity, I suppose. Will you leave any message for her?'

'Only that I'll phone tomorrow.'

'I'll tell her that. Well, you must excuse me. I must put on the cocoa.'

'Thank you, Mrs Fox. Good-night.'

'Bye-bye then.'

He left down the phone.

The main hall of the post office encircled by counters and their protecting grills was silent and warm. If there were night staff in attendance, as there must have been, they were not visible. He stood for a while before Oliver Sheppard's *Dying Cuchulainn*, moved as always by its simple but eloquent symbolism, moved too by its physical realization, by the raven on the shoulder, the bonds that bit beneath the ribs but supported the body, the slumping form of the solitary hero whom no enemy dared to approach while a flicker of life might remain. It was a better story than anything the Fenian cycle could offer and it was hard to believe the deed it commemorated was not mythological also. Had Pearse and Connolly truly conducted their insurrection from behind sandbagged windows on the floor above? Had shells shattered and flames devoured and walls come tumbling down? And if they had, then what was now to be said? And had The O'Rahilly, that eccentric man, in his eccentric motor car, driven up to join them, angry that word of what they were about had not been sent to him:

> 'Because I helped to wind the clock
> I come to hear it strike'—

and if it all had happened, as indeed it must have, how much larger a time to live in than the flat, featureless, repetitive present.

He detoured by Moore Street where The O'Rahilly had been gunned down and the final surrender had taken place, remembering as he did so that he had walked here with his father on the night of his first Holy Communion when they had gone to visit the Fitzpatricks. Did they live hereabouts still? There had been the sightless man and his wife, and the oratorical O'Sheehan whom he still occasionally came across in Brian's house. There had been his father. Ten years ago? Eleven years ago? No matter. A lifetime ago.

The alleyways spun a web about him; dark, rain-sodden, heavy with vegetable smells and quite deserted except for the ghosts projected by his imagination. They lurked in a locked doorway, at the corner of a lane, under the weak light of a bracketed lamp on the gable of a house and were only a little less substantial than the misting rain. The maze led him back again to O'Connell Street and the four angels about the Liberator's statue: Patriotism, Fidelity, Eloquence and Courage. They all had bullet holes in their impressive bosoms which they nobly disregarded. Like Nelson they were contemptuous of wind and weather. And again like Nelson they waited for something to happen that might be worthy of their attention.

VII

Cornelius Moloney minded his shop, attended to his customers and kept a shrewd eye on the world. When things were slack he spread his paper on the counter and carefully weighed the news. If it was of little account, as often enough he judged it to be, he simply listened to the trams going by. They reminded him that life too was passing. In such moments two images from the distant past tended to return more persistently than others and for no accountable reason. The first was the whitewashed window ledge of the cottage he had been born in and two great cartwheels of griddle bread left by his mother to cool on it. The second was even more mysterious: a pair of reins lying across his father's hand and the rattle of empty milk churns behind him. These images, when they returned, moved him mysteriously. Sometimes they drew him to the door of his shop where the contrast between cobbled streets and the green fields of childhood set him wondering at the world's variety, the inevitability of change, the unpredictability of fate. What one of us, he asked O'Sheehan, could attempt to foresee the way ahead.

Sometimes the War of Independence came into his thoughts with the faces of men on the run who had shared his fireside and his table for brief nights and days before taking again to the hills. He had sheltered them. He had done his bit, thanks be to God. The Civil War was another matter and when it too came to mind he tried to dismiss it. The glory had turned to shame. Too much bitterness, treachery, personal uncertainty, a time when old friends on whatever side had been prepared to burn the roof over his head. Against memories of the Civil War he either busied himself with his shop or attended to his greyhounds. They had not yet made his fortune but he still hoped. It had happened to others. His happiest hours were those spent exercising them in the Park, his most exciting waiting for the traps to open at a race meeting. Beyond that he studied politics and plotted for the future, not so much his own but his family's. He was sixty-four or thereabouts. For himself there could not be that much future left.

He had hopes, just the same. Politically he had made the right moves. He had done his share for Fianna Fáil in the general elections and his reward was the satisfaction of their victory with an increased number of seats. The neighbourhood trusted and respected him as no man's fool but a good and generous ally in time of need. It paved his way to chairmanship of the party branch. It also planted in the minds of close cronies a thought which was beginning to attract consideration in his own.

'Has that son of yours any interest in politics or the party?' one of them asked him.

'Brian is it? He's been a bit on the young side up to now.'

'Damn the young if he has the brains and as it happens he has. I've heard him debating from time to time in the bar.'

'I've heard him at it myself,' Cornelius said. He sounded unimpressed.

'Don't underestimate him. We're inclined to do that with those closest to us. In five years' time there'll be another turn-out for a general election and he'll be that much older. We've plenty of old campaigners in the branch but we could do with more polish. The boy has the machinery where it's needed – upstairs. Think about it.'

Cornelius did. It would be too much to urge Brian to join the Cumann. He suspected the sort of answer he'd get. But he saw to it that he brought up the drinks and served them after committee meetings. He encouraged conversation. He even noted with satisfaction that after a frosty start Brian seemed to respond. In fact he got on well, how well became apparent to Cornelius when another of his cronies made a comment which surprised him.

'Chairman, you have an intelligent and well-reared boy in that son of yours.'

'He's inclined to hold opinions,' Cornelius countered, having first gripped the arms of his chair to steady himself.

'Be thankful he has a bit of spirit. It's in short supply.'

'I suppose that's true,' Cornelius said. But he had his own view of what was being admired as spirit. Bloody oul lip.

For all its devotion to rules and regulations, its emphasis on rectitude, its horror of irregularity, there were times when the Metropolitan was prepared to look the other way. The Monday after the Annual Outing to Avoca was such an occasion. Staff were unsettled. One or two failed to turn up at all. Some who did had not shaved. The rest, with the odd exception, were disinclined for work. Post-mortems on various incidents occupied their attention. Colonel Breen himself was noted to do much uncharacteristic wandering in and out. Near lunch time he told Jackson he had urgent business in the afternoon which would prevent his return. Jackson was to keep an eye on things. The Colonel's cheeks were blotched and purple. A badly executed razor stroke had gashed his chin. They were signs which had not escaped the others.

'He had a very healthy complexion,' Higgins remarked.

'Watching him yesterday,' Ellis said, 'you'd have to admire the military expertise. He put on a series of well-manoeuvred guerilla attacks that decimated the free whiskey. Now he'll spend the afternoon curing himself.'

'An example I intend to follow,' Jackson decided.

'I might do the same myself,' Higgins said.

'I have a strange premonition,' Ellis agreed, closing the ledger.

'Wait now, who'll look after the ship?'

'Tiger Tim here,' Ellis said. 'His need is least. He's more stunned than hung over.'

'I don't mind,' Tim offered.

It had been a new experience. He would welcome the chance to think it over.

'If anything awkward happens, phone the Scotch House,' Jackson instructed.

At lunch his mother wondered why he had not been home.

'We got back late. I stayed in Brian's.'

That was not so unusual. She accepted it. It was also only partly true.

When he was back again in the office the telephone rang and Jackson was at the other end.

'How are things there?'

'Everything OK.'

'Good. I'm ringing to let you know that if you want us between half two and half three you'll get us in the bar at Westland Row station. After that I'll phone again. OK?'

'OK.'

'Thanks,' Jackson said.

He had already learned enough to know what they intended. By buying a shilling ticket to Bray they became bona fide travellers in the eyes of the Law and could drink in the railway bar during the statutory closed period of two thirty to three thirty – The Holy Hour. The journey was purely notional and the privilege well worth the shilling each. Around half three they telephoned again, Ellis this time.

'Everything all right?'

'Everything fine.'

'We're heading for The Princes in Sackville Place.' That was an unfamiliar one. He wrote the name down.

'But if you have to phone and we're not there at the time, we'll be having a steak, in the Palace restaurant.'

He wrote that down too. Someone must be in funds. He checked back the information and left down the phone.

From the desk, which long ago Higgins and Ellis had partly concealed by a row of deliberately positioned filing cabinets, he could observe the area of the main office. Two clerks manned the public counter. The desks elsewhere were sparsely populated. Monday was never a busy day anyway. Ellis said it was because by tradition it was washday. Ellis also held that the depression associated with Monday was caused mainly by a cloud of invisible steam and soapsuds which engulfed the city as thousands of housewives boiled thousands of soiled garments in thousands of humid kitchens.

It felt a bit like that now. The Metropolitan still used gas lights as a supplement to electricity. They provided a background hiss which could be detected during quiet intervals and they made the air sultry. For occupation he drew the staves of an orchestral score down the length of a sheet of foolscap and wrote on the top:

Symphony No. 1 in D Major

von

T. McDonagh

He allocated the instruments to their different staves, put in the time and the key signatures, and was writing *Allegro con brio* at the top left-hand side when the thought struck him that it ought to have a dedication. In brackets between his own name and the first stave he inserted: Dem Colonel Breen gewidmet.

That settled, he spent twenty minutes or so filling the different staves at random with contrasting note patterns. They made no harmonic sense of any kind and he wondered if it were played how diabolical would it sound. Eventually he lost interest. The temperature had risen uncomfortably as it always did in the afternoon and the gas lighting whispered sleepily. He took another piece of paper and began to review yesterday's outing. He wrote down:

The Train. Carefully segregated. The manuals had their own section. The senior staff had theirs. The rest of us occupied the middle ground. There was only one Avoca and one Wicklow town though so we had to share those. Then different buses as well for the sightseeing: The Vale of Clara was beautiful beyond description. All those trees with their autumn colours and the woodlands carpeted ankle deep in fallen leaves. There was a side road leading down to a humpbacked bridge with three arches spanning the river and a whitewashed cottage beside it. I remember thinking you could live there comfortably on three pounds a week and still have enough to give your share at home. An advertisement in the paper might do the trick: 'Talented young man requires rich patron to furnish small weekly income. In return will dedicate musical scores, dramas and poetic works. Birthday odes, Christmas verses, Valentines and love poems furnished on request. Also lamentations for occasional griefs and misfortunes. Be blessed by posterity for a benevolence that fed the flame of Genius.'

If the last sentence was a quote, as he suspected, he could not remember from where. He continued:

Gorgeous Gwen. Cunningham's girlfriend made a stir: full figure, nice legs, curves in all the right places and no inhibitions about showing everything to its best effect. I don't think Ellis quite realized what he was letting himself in for when he agreed to adopt the two of them as his guests. Ellis and Higgins speechless. How is it done? A combination of the right shape and a manner suggesting it isn't going to be kept under lock and key. Anne thought her cheap. I didn't. There is nothing wrong with not giving a damn, though in Gwen's league I'd rank alongside St Anthony the Eremite, if that's the one who passed the time in his mountain solitude weaving mats and wrestling with demons. Cunningham looked too good to be true. He was togged out in the new suit his people got him for his outfitter's job, and he was extraordinarily dandified and with a pin in his tie. He reminded me a bit of O'Keeffe that night we saw him in the Grand Central. But Gwen obviously thought he was smashing.

The Hotel. Very posh in an old-fashioned style. Fires of wood and turf burning in the lounge and the dining room. Soup and sandwiches before the trip to the Meeting of the Waters, free drinks in the bar before dinner. Then speeches of course and a singsong. If I had money I'd spend weekends with Anne in places like that, walking in the mornings, having a drink before dinner in the evenings. Those woods in autumn, especially in the evenings around sunset –

The telephone again interrupted him. Ellis.

'Everything all right?'

'Everything fine.'

'Just to let you know we're back in The Princes again. Higgins is showing every sign of taking root.'

'I'd watch it a bit.'

'Don't worry. We had a good tightener. That banks it down. Why don't you join us after five o'clock?'

'I can't.'

'Just for one.'

'I'd like to but I've an appointment.' A lie. He had no money.

'The dark piece you were with yesterday? A man of discernment and taste, our Tim. Well. I'd better go. Higgins is getting weak with thirst. See you.'

He replaced the telephone, looked at his notes and found

they had lost interest. Memory was better. Memory could hear the chink of glasses. Memory could smell the smoke. Memory could set him dancing with Anne all over again, a man among men, entitled to his drink, his opinion, the company of women. In the heat under subdued lights they held each other closely, moving in unison.

'That Brian Moloney,' Anne said, 'I don't like him. He sneers at people.'

'They say he's good-looking.'

'I suppose he is. In a sneering way. To be sneery good-looking is the worst way of looking at all. Curling his mouth at you. His eyes pushed down his nose at you. Using big words. I can't bear him.'

'Someone else can.'

Across the room from them Brian was dancing with one of the firm's typists. Her interest was obvious.

Anne said, 'Some girls are born unlucky.'

'A while back he swore to avoid women. They were expensive and interfered with his study. But I suppose it's just for the sake of the occasion.'

'Typical,' Anne said.

'What do you think of Ellis?'

'Quite nice. And entertaining too. But who's the one with the moustache?'

'Charlie Jackson.'

'He's a bit forbidding, I thought.'

'His head is stuffed with information on everything; literature, history, politics. He reads the *New Statesman*.'

'Is that very intellectual?'

'A cut above *Our Boys*.'

'A cut above *The Messenger of the Sacred Heart* too, I imagine. Do you know we still get that at home. Or rather my mother does.'

'So does mine.'

The information amused her.

'I'm sure that puts us in some category or other,' she reflected.

But later, when they had gone out to breathe fresh air and were standing by the sea wall, something seemed to trouble her. The beam of a lighthouse was already tracing its measured arc on the water and the grey glimmer of the sea was giving way to darkness. Slow waves slapped and sucked on shingle. They were alone under the shelter of the wall.

'I meant to ask you this before but I kept putting it off,' she said. 'It's to do with Sallygap. Our lovemaking there – ' She hesitated. He helped her.

'Have I been to confession, is that it?'

She nodded.

'I have.'

'Was it dreadful?'

'No. I got told off, of course. But it wasn't so bad. And you?'

'Awful. I got strips torn off me. He was just simply nasty. I thought I'd die of shame.'

'Poor Anne. I'm sorry.'

'Afterwards I thought: Damn him. After all I did confess. And it was such a struggle to bring myself to face it.'

'In Ireland there's only the one sin. They have it on the brain. Even when it's been quite ordinary they want to know did you kiss passionately or did you embrace immodestly; how much pleasure did you take in it; how far did you go. You'd want a spiritual thermometer and a calipers. One thing is certain. He had no right whatever to be nasty to you.'

'I would have walked out only for all the people waiting outside. I didn't want a public disgrace.'

She looked down at her shoes, her anger growing as memory returned.

'Don't take it to heart,' he said gently. He took her face in his hands and found her gaze fixed steadily on him.

'If ever any man speaks to me like that again, I just won't take it. Whatever the consequences.'

Her determination surprised him. It was a side of her he had not encountered before.

Back at the hotel the dancing had given place to a singsong

which struggled for survival above the outbursts of laughter and loud conversation. The chairs and tables had been arranged in a wide semi-circle about the fire in the bar. One of the seniors rendered 'The Sergeant Major's on Parade' in a good bass baritone voice and as an encore gave them 'Let Me Like a Soldier Fall'. He had brought his music so the accompaniment was rousingly martial.

> 'Yes. Let me like a soldier fall
> Upon some open plain
> This breast expanding for the ball
> To blot out every stain.'

Colonel Breen was seen to listen throughout with soldierly emotion, his back straight, his waxed moustache stiff, his breast expanding. Ellis noticed and drew their attention. Then he offered to give them 'The Green Eye of the Little Yellow God' and followed its success with 'The Face on the Bar Room Floor'. The applause was still going on as he rejoined them.

'That was marvellous,' Anne told him, her good humour restored.

'We'll have a drink,' Ellis suggested. 'It's still for free.'

She consented to sherry. Tim, privately dubious, settled for gin and tonic. Brian and his typist partner who also came across to join them were already supplied. Cunningham saw them together and brought Gwen over. Simultaneously, Higgins and Jackson sought out Ellis to air a complaint. They were both less than sober.

'Jackson and myself would like to know why no one has thought it worthwhile to give us one of Moore's melodies,' Higgins said. 'After all, he's our national Bard, isn't he? I mean we've all been to the Meeting of the Waters, so what could be more appropriate? Are we Irishmen at all?'

'I wholeheartedly agree,' Jackson supported. 'Tom Moore was good enough to be the friend of Lord Byron – to be much esteemed as a friend and much admired as a poet by Byron. Is he not good enough for us? Is it some form of inverted snobbery?'

Higgins grew angrier.

'Little Tom Moore of Aungier Street. Christ. I mean is it because he was a greengrocer's son?'

Jackson, forgetting for the moment that he was in the town of Wicklow said, 'I'll tell you why. He was born in this proud and ancient city. That's why. Simple. Tom Moore's fault is: he was a Dublin man.'

Higgins grew angrier still. He fixed on Tim.

'You, McDonagh. You're supposed to be musical. Sing us one of Tom Moore's songs and put the priorities straight.'

'I don't sing,' Tim explained. 'I play the fiddle.'

'All right. Play us a bit of Tom Moore on the violin. Play us "The Last Rose of Summer".'

Ellis, who was beginning to find them tiresome, said:

'He doesn't carry the violin around in his waistcoat pocket. Have a bit of sense.'

'Christ, it'd make you laugh,' Higgins remarked generally, 'a roomful of so-called Irishmen and not one of them able to give us a song by Tom Moore.'

Cunningham sprang a surprise.

'If you're prepared to put up with what you get,' he offered, 'I don't mind trying to oblige.'

'Who – you?' Brian questioned, unbelieving.

'He has a very nice voice,' Gwen put in.

Brian looked around slowly, found her, stared at her steadily and in silence. Isolated and confused she coloured painfully.

'Now the bloody pianist has disappeared,' Higgins complained after he had searched the surrounding company in vain for him. 'It's typical. Now there's no one to play the piano.'

Anne saw her opinion of Brian confirmed in his treatment of Gwen.

'I can vamp an accompaniment for him,' she offered, 'if nobody else is available.'

They were both seized upon by Jackson and led to the centre of the circle. After a brief speech to the audience about the melodies of Tom Moore and their appropriateness to the occasion he announced the title of the song. Anne tried the piano generally, then discussed the key with Cunningham. They both looked nervous.

'Had old Cunningham much to drink?' Brian whispered.

'He seemed perfectly sober to me,' Tim answered.

'What do you bet he doesn't even know the words?'

But the performance had begun. Cunningham's voice was clear and good. He not only knew the words, he sang them with understanding and concern. He was listened to in admiring silence. As an encore he gave them 'Has Sorrow Thy Young Days Shaded'. Anne supported competently. It was a popular success.

Jackson and Higgins accepted his triumph as their own.

'A drink for the performers,' Higgins commanded, though there was no one in particular to command. Ellis got in quickly.

'What we could all do with is a sandwich or two. Soak it up for the journey home. Who says?'

They proved amenable and set off in search of extra food. Brian turned to Cunningham.

'What's this singing stuff. I've never heard you at it in my life before. Explain.'

'They used to have these family hooleys in my grandmother's when I was a kid and I was always brought,' Cunningham said. 'It was the customary Dublin thing, wasn't it You'd hear all the old songs at those.'

'You mean you've just been chancing your arm out there?'

'Not exactly. Those two songs were once my party pieces. You never forget things like that, do you' Cunningham became anxious. 'Didn't they go all right?'

Gwen, justified and determined to let it be generally known, linked his arm.

'What do you mean – went all right? You took the house down.'

She led him away.

The carriages swayed from side to side and voices scattered music in their wake as the train drew them homewards through the darkness. Jackson and Higgins linked up with Ellis and Tim's party and they managed to hold a carriage for themselves. For half an hour or so they sang. Then the rocking and the effect of earlier drinks and the reiterated rhythm of the wheels made them drowsy. Gwen curled up in Cunningham's arms. The typist let her head fall on Brian's shoulder. Jackson stretched out his legs and rested his heels on the opposite seat. Higgins, still game, sang on:

> 'We are poor little lambs
> Who have lost our way
> Baa, baa, baa.'

But he found himself on his own and gave up. A train going in the opposite direction clattered by in a halfhearted way.

'Was that the mail?' Ellis wondered.

'Hardly,' Jackson answered. 'I'd expect the mail to sound a bit more businesslike.'

He was examining with distaste a row of black and white photographs which were spread behind dust-encrusted glass above the opposite seat. Beauty spots of Ireland. Inch Strand, County Kerry; Tramore, County Waterford; Ennistymon Falls, County Clare. There were more, but he gave up reading them. They emanated a peculiar gloom.

'Railway carriage photographs,' he remarked to Ellis 'are born ancient and never die. They tempt you to the superstition that they come into existence of themselves, without the intervention of any human agency. Yet that, of course, is impossible. The inescapable fact is that in some remote age a head must have draped itself under a blanket to take that undistinguished array there and hands must have plunged the Madox and Bennett plates into a solution of sodium thiosulphate to develop them. The next inescapable fact is that that head and those hands are long since at rest in the clay.'

'Or above in Elysium,' Ellis suggested, 'persuading Jehovah to watch for the dicky bird.'

'I hadn't thought of that,' Jackson admitted, 'I'd believe it quite possible if I also believed in a hereafter. But I don't. What I'd relish now is another drink.'

'Another impossibility,' Ellis said.

Higgins shared their regret.

'The lousy thing about company excursions is that by the time you're landed back in the city you're sober again and all the pubs are closed. You're left high and dry.'

'Not necessarily,' Brian said. They looked at him.

'If you keep it among ourselves and swear to be quiet, it can probably be arranged.'

'You mean your old man will risk breaking the law?' Tim asked.

'The old man will be in bed. We can use the storeroom at the bottom of the yard. There's plenty of bottled stout and ale there. All I need fetch from the shop is whiskey and gin and maybe some sherry.'

'What about the police?'

'There's a cellar under the storeroom. It's absolutely safe. Even the old man has forgotten it's there.'

Ellis and Jackson brightened up noticeably. Higgins began to sing again.

> 'O don't go near the bee
> The bee's a nasty thing
> If you go near the bee
> He'll give you a nasty sting.'

The others joined in, except for Gwen and the typist. Gwen had wrapped herself around Cunningham in a knot that looked as though it might prove unopenable. The typist was asleep, her head still resting on Brian's shoulder, her features, which were gentle, partly concealed by her dark hair. Brian adjusted himself to her comfort from time to time. His solicitude, which was uncharacteristic, made Tim wonder.

'Could we stretch our legs?' Anne suggested.

They went out into the corridor and stood by an open window. The floor under their feet shifted and rocked.

'That's cooler,' she remarked gratefully.

'Cigarette?'

'No. I've had far too many.'

He lit one for himself.

'What do you think of Brian's plan?' she asked.

'I suppose he knows what he's doing.'

'It sounds risky to me.'

'I suppose so. It's a bit of a lark, though.'

'You'd all be better off going home to bed. Tell me something about sleep.'

He thought, then said:

> 'The cottage windows wink through twilight gloom
> And all is tranquil as a dreamless sleep –

I'm not sure I have that quite right.'

'It's right enough for me. Lovely sleep.'

The corridor was dark but the light from the carriage fell on the hedges and raced to keep pace with them and the sea gathered light from somewhere to glimmer at them through occasional gaps. In the air salt and sulphur intermingled.

'There'll be all eternity for sleep,' Tim said.

He forgot her for a moment as he thought of his father. Where now? In what dimension? How translated? If at all. Through a hollow sphere of darkness of unmeasurable immensity their tiny string of windows sped towards no reachable destination. Time and space would swallow all and not know it.

'Hello.' She spoke quietly. Her hand was on his shoulder, her face smiled up at him. A double weight of grief and love pressed on his heart. Identical twins. If he kissed her they would not be held in check. He took her in his arms, pressed his face against her hair, hoped she would not notice the inexplicable visitation. It began to melt away.

'You were off again somewhere,' she said, 'miles and miles away. Away off up on a magic carpet.'

A thunder of wheels stopped his search for a reply. Disturbed air buffeted them through the open window and the carriage lurched violently.

'The mail train,' Anne called.

Windows, seats, half-glimpsed forms, carriages, vans, couplings and gleaming brass handles rocked past in a frenzy of wheels, a procession that seemed likely never to end and yet did. Suddenly, startlingly all were snatched away. Their companionable light immediately found the hedge again and jogged along faithfully with them.

'That was exciting,' Anne said. 'I'd love to be going with it.'

'A moment ago you wanted to sleep.'

'I know. But I think of thundering away down the coast and the rails gleaming and the signals changing and all the deserted little stations slipping past. Wouldn't you find it exciting?'

'Anything would be exciting that wasn't leading back to Monday morning and the Metropolitan.'

'You'll find a way out. It takes time, that's all.'

It took more than time. Opportunity, for a start.

Confidence, the ability and the nerve to tackle something beyond pushing a pen. The mail was speeding past remote fields and lonely beaches, those desirable solitudes far from the grey and timekept disciplines. There was something to be said for being borne a pigeon or a seagull.

In the cellar beneath the storeroom in the lower yard they lit candles and seated themselves on empty crates while Brian took Tim with him into the shop to collect glasses and some whiskey and sherry.

'You're crazy,' Tim said.

'Not crazy. Cute. There's a few bob to be made out of this. I should have thought of it before.'

When he had distributed the glasses and was seated again beside Anne, she whispered to him, 'I don't think I like this. It's all a bit eerie.'

'Don't worry. I'll leave you home soon.'

He examined the cellar. Its ceiling was low and vaulted, the walls arched. It looked as though it might have been part of some earlier structure, a portion perhaps of the vaults radiating from the nearby cathedral which at some stage had been blocked off. Local tradition believed the ground between the cathedral and the river to be honeycombed with them. He remembered a story that a young lieutenant who got detached from the main party and lost while exploring them had been found with his broken sword in his hand and his body devoured by the rats. The candlelight flickering on the surrounding faces and their sprawling shadows on ceiling and walls that dramatized every movement tempted him to tell it. For Anne's sake he resisted the temptation. Instead he asked:

'Have you any idea when it was built or what it was used for?'

'For smuggling, probably,' Ellis suggested. 'The shipping once came up river this far.'

'Or for plots and conspiracies,' Higgins said. 'Didn't the leaders of the United Irishmen operate around here – Lord Edward Fitzgerald, Oliver Bond and the rest.'

'The Directory met above in the Tailors Hall. That's how they were captured,' Jackson told them.

'What about Robert Emmet?'

'Emmet came later. In 1803. He had a bomb factory in Marshalsea Lane. The Brazen Head Inn is supposed to have been his headquarters. He was executed above at St Catherine's Church. Anne Devlin saw the pigs and dogs licking his blood from the cobbles.'

'Sacred Heart of Jesus,' Gwen called out.

'My apologies, ladies,' Jackson offered. 'Historical fact, but not for womanly ears.'

'Not at this hour anyway,' Gwen said.

'Or in these surroundings,' Anne supported.

Brian looked around him, appraising the cellar with the tolerance of ownership.

'It's an odd place,' he admitted, 'I don't think the old man knows it exists. In fact my own feeling is that it only materializes when the memory of it comes into my head.'

'Isn't that what Berkeley believed?' Jackson remarked. 'If a thing was absent from God's thoughts, even for an instant, it would cease to exist.'

Ellis, searching around him anxiously, said:

'Do you think that's what happened to the whiskey bottle?'

'It's over there by the wall,' Brian told him.

Ellis found the whiskey bottle, took the pewter measure

which Brian had borrowed from the shop and poured himself another drink. He paid for it by leaving money on the crate which had been set in the centre to serve as a till.

'Anyone else for whiskey?'

Anne said, 'It's getting awfully late for me.'

'Wait now,' Higgins begged, 'a song from Maestro Cunningham while we're all together. Is that in order?'

Brian frowned but agreed.

'Keep it very quiet, then.'

'*Sotto voce*,' Higgins promised, with a look in Cunningham's direction which begged for compliance. He was still a bit drunk. Cunningham, his eyes fixed on Brian and the dark-haired girl, sang again:

> 'O 'tis sweet to think that where e'er we rove
> We are sure to find something blissful and dear
> And that, when we're far from the lips we love
> We have but to make love to the lips we are near.
> The heart, like a tendril accustomed to cling
> Let it grow where it will, cannot flourish alone
> But will lean to the nearest and loveliest thing
> It can twine with itself and make closely its own.'

He transferred his attention to Tim and Anne for the second verse:

> ''Twere a shame, when flowers around us rise
> To make light of the rest, if the rose is not there
> And the world's so rich in resplendent eyes
> 'Twere a pity to limit one's love to a pair.
> Love's wing and the peacock are nearly alike
> They are both of them bright but changeable too
> And wherever a new beam of beauty can strike
> It will tincture love's plume with a different hue.'

He reserved the chorus for Gwen:

> 'Then oh, what pleasure, where e'er we rove
> To be doomed to find something still that is dear
> And to know, when far from the lips we love
> We have but to make love to the lips we are near.'

Higgins shook his head several times in charmed disbelief and said over and over again:

'Lovely. Bloody lovely.'

Jackson said:

'That, I imagine, is one of the poems that outraged the moral sense of the *Edinboro' Review*. Little Tom Moore challenged the critic to a duel.'

'You mean they shot it out over a silly review?' Gwen asked.

'Not quite. Some music lover removed the bullets from the pistols.'

'Bloody right,' Higgins approved, 'absobloodylutely right.'

'You should give us a hand in the Past Pupils end of the school opera society at Christmas,' Tim suggested, 'would you consider it?'

'I haven't ever been asked.'

'You're being asked now. No one had ever heard you.'

'All right. If you think they'd have me.'

'What is it this year?' Brian asked.

'"The Yeoman of the Guard". Maybe you'd come – for once.'

'If Cunningham is going to doll up as a Beefeater I wouldn't miss it.'

Anne saw Ellis reaching for the whiskey bottle again and said in an anxious voice, 'Tim – I wonder could we – '

Tim rose.

'Right away.'

He borrowed Brian's bicycle but said he would be back to spend the night. With Anne on the crossbar he set off through deserted streets where tenements with lightless windows rose into the night and the cathedral was black and massive. The night air was cool and pleasant after the crowded rooms of the daytime.

'Why did you say you'd go back?' Anne asked when they were standing at her gate.

'I don't like to go home when I've been drinking.'

'But you're perfectly all right.'

'My mother has a nose in the championship class.'

'Won't she worry if you're not home?'

'No. I stay in Brian's now and then. She's used to that.'

'Well. Thanks for a lovely day.'

'You enjoyed it?'

'Oh yes. They're an odd crowd, though, aren't they? I'm glad I got round to mentioning the confession bit. It's been on my mind.'

'We're flesh and blood. I don't regard it very seriously.'

She looked surprised.

'You're a strange mixture. One time you're quite straitlaced. Another time you're unconcerned.'

'I think it's different when people are in love.'

'I think so too,' she said.

They kissed and she went in.

When he got back to Brian's the rest had left. Brian had fixed up a sofa for him with some blankets.

'I made a bit on all that,' Brian said, 'around fifteen shillings or so.'

'Will it not be missed?'

'I worked for it, didn't I? The stock can be replaced. The old man won't notice.' He smiled. 'Gwen was a bit under the weather,' he added. 'Cunningham thought they'd better shell out for a taxi. Still, I must admit it, she's quite a smasher. I used to wonder how old Cunningham gets off his mark so handy. Now I know.' Brian smiled. 'I saw it in operation today. He serenades them.'

He turned in the doorway.

'See you in the morning. I'll leave a note on the kitchen table that you're to be called.'

The clock in the main office crawled around to five, bringing to an end what lingering remnants of life remained. He closed the ledger and went to get his bicycle but was waylaid by Kavanagh, an elderly clerk who sometimes joined in the debates in the club.

'Young McDonagh. I'd like a word with you, if I may.'

'By all means.'

'Come and have a drink.'

'I haven't that much time.'

'One. It'll take less than twenty minutes.'

The man was senior. It was difficult to refuse. They found a nearby pub and sat down.

'What will it be?'

'Something soft. A lemonade, I think.'

Kavanagh had the same.

When the two soft drinks arrived Kavanagh paid and said:

'This stuff is as good anyday as the hard tack and a lot safer. Good health.'

'And yours.'

They drank.

'Did you enjoy the outing yesterday?'

'Very much.'

'That was a pretty and respectable young girl you had with you. Your fiancée?'

'Well – yes. We go out together.'

He wondered what was coming. A lecture of some kind. On what? He felt unequal to anything.

'You'll forgive an older man for offering advice.' There was little option. He composed himself to listen.

'There was a fair amount of drinking, wasn't there? I suppose it's to be expected with the Ellis, Jackson intelligentsia. That's their style. But you're a young man with the future ahead of you. You weren't averse to the hard stuff yourself, I noticed. That's how trouble begins.'

Sobriety, it seemed, was to be the issue.

'It was a day out, wasn't it?' he said reasonably. But already guilt began to stir.

'I don't imagine you drink usually.'

'Not usually. It's a bit beyond the range of a junior clerk.'

'Don't take offence,' Kavanagh said. 'I've lived long enough to have the benefit of experience. That Jackson-Ellis crowd are wayward and tricky company for a younger man.' He left down his glass to frame his next sentence.

'You're a Catholic, of course.'

'Yes.'

'And a young man with a lot of potential. At an age when the mind is reaching out to new ideas. The Jacksons of this city are either agnostics or outright atheists. I'm only marking your card, you understand.'

'Certainly.'

'You'll get plenty of Shaw and Wilde – that class of stuff – from that pair, but nothing much of Chesterton or Belloc or Knox or Maritain. Plenty of banned books too, if that's your bent – which I know it isn't. Anti-national ideas too. The other day they were eulogizing O'Casey and *The Shadow of a Gunman*. Did you know O'Casey resigned from the Citizen Army when he knew there was a danger of being involved in the Rising? Funked it. And when he wrote that play he took his room-mate as a model for Seamus Shields. A man who would make a public spectacle of his room-mate is despicable. Jackson and his crowd may see some merit in the play. To me O'Casey is a renegade. But you'll learn these things as you go along. My purpose at the moment is simply to forewarn you. No offence, I hope.'

He was hardly in a position to show offence. He was too new. He was too young.

'No offence, of course.'

'That's all I wanted to say to you. Keep an open mind. Read your own side. We suffered hard for it through the centuries and it's worth our loyalty. So finish that up and off with you. Young men are always busy. I won't delay you.'

They finished their lemonade and he got his bicycle. When he arrived home his mother was reading the *Life of Father Willie Doyle* VC to the two youngest but stopped to give him his tea. After tea she resumed. He retired to have a bath. Life, which had been promising to be new and entertaining had become flat and grey and heavy with disapproval.

VIII

Hallowe'en, as usual, saw the tea table furnished with a large barmbrack which was flanked by plates of apples and oranges, grapes and nuts. The younger children played at snap apple and dressed up in masks and odd clothes before roaming the evening streets to beg the customary gifts from door to door. He left them at it to call to Brian's house where he had arranged to play some music with Mrs Moloney before going on with the others to a Hallowe'en dance. It would be the last fling before Christmas. O'Sheehan was there when he arrived and when the fiddle was produced he asked Cornelius to delay their retiral to chess for a while so that they could listen. He asked the company if they knew the invocation addressed to his harp in ancient times by the Daghda and when they confessed ignorance he quoted it for their benefit:

> 'Come, applesweet murmurer
> Come, fourangled frame of harmony
> Come Summer, come Winter
> From the mouths of harps and bags and pipes.'

He listened courteously while they played through Mrs Moloney's small and usual repertoire. When that was done Eilish and a young Mr Dempsey who was to be her escort and Anne who had arrived during the music put hazel nuts on the hob of the fire to tell them who was to be married first. The nut belonging to Eilish was the first to explode, much to her embarrassment.

'I was sure mine would,' Anne said, 'I got the ring in the barmbrack at home.'

'Eilish got the pea,' Brian said.

'And what did you get?'

'Nothing,' Brian said, 'as usual.'

Mrs Moloney sensed trouble and put in quickly:

'When I was young we used to do all sorts of things. One of them was to look into the mirror at midnight, in the belief that we'd see the face of whoever we were to marry.'

'There was the same custom among the girls in my own part of the country,' Cornelius said, 'and I remember it being told of one of them – a serving girl in a big house – this would have been before my own time, of course – that she took the candle in her hand at midnight and after saying a prayer to a certain gentleman with tail and horns adorning him she looked in the mirror and the next thing there was an unmerciful screech out of her which woke the house. She couldn't tell them what terrible thing she'd seen and they did their best to laugh her out of it but it was no use. The next night there was the same ear-splitting scream sometime in the small hours and when they got downstairs there she was dead on the floor and the mirror shattered in smithereens.'

'Did you have the saucers too, one with clay and one with water,' Mrs Moloney asked, 'and did you burn a hazel stick?'

'Earth, fire and water were instruments of divination and very powerful on November eve in ancient Ireland,' O'Sheehan told them. 'It was the evening of the yearly death of the sun and there would be great chaos until the moon succeeded to the rule of the universe. In the disorder between times the powers of darkness were exceedingly powerful. Evil ran riot. Invocations could rouse the dead. It was highly dangerous to wander abroad in the night.'

'Right enough,' Cornelius confessed. 'When I was a child I wouldn't cross the doorstep on this night, not if you offered me all the treasure in Kelly's shop window – and there was many a fine box of sugarsticks and peggy's legs in that.'

'The young people of today are not so gullible,' Mrs Moloney observed. 'They're off to dances or to Hallowe'en parties till all hours.'

'Which they don't go to till all hours, or so it seems,' Cornelius complained.

'Brian is taking Eileen Madden and she hasn't come yet,' Eilish explained.

While they waited O'Sheehan began to tell Hallowe'en stories. Cornelius joined in. Mrs Moloney had her own store.

They were of ghosts and hauntings, spirits and strange rooms and stranger houses, spells and encounters and customs that had now passed away. When at last they were on their way to the dance Anne said:

'That was great. I could listen to eerie stories all night.'

'We used to do that when I was a kid,' Dempsey put in. 'We'd sit in the firelight talking about the banshee and headless coachmen and haunted houses.'

'That Mr O'Sheehan seems to know everything about everything, but there's something odd about him,' Anne wondered.

'He thinks he's Oisin,' Brian told her.

'Usheen?'

'You remember? The son of Finn MacCumhall.'

'My God – has he a slate loose?'

'Have you ever met a fervent nationalist that hadn't?' Brian asked.

'O'Sheehan is slightly dotty all right,' Eilish agreed, 'but in a dear, nice way.'

Tim smiled and said:

> 'The great gaels of Ireland
> Are the men that God made mad.'

'In the matter of patriotism, religion and drink,' Brian concluded, 'this country generally has a slate loose.' He considered further. 'Or more appropriately,' he amended, 'it has bats in its thatch.'

On All Souls' night Tim watched his mother leave a bowl of water and some bread on the kitchen table before they went to bed, so that if the spirits who had the privilege of being released from the pains of purgatory on that one night of the year dropped in they could cool their thirst and satisfy their hunger. That was dotty too, perhaps, but it was nevertheless touching. He lay awake and imagined the queue at the gates, the salutations and handshaking, the skies filled with their dispersal. They were descending in a silent shower from the night skies all over

Ireland to wander for a little while in once familiar places. He hoped it was true and prayed for their more lasting rest.

Then November began to bring the leaves down and mist and moaning winds marked it unmistakably as the month of the Dead. In December they pondered the financial situation and solved it, more or less, in their respective ways. Brian made a profit on three well-manoeuvred sessions in his backyard shebeen. A letter from his former music teacher asked Tim to deputize for him at six performances of a pre-Christmas musical show which netted him six guineas. Better still, it hinted at an avenue to additional, if very occasional, finance.

They waited for the bells to begin, for the hooters to wail, the clocks to strike: O'Sheehan and Cornelius at the fireside in the upper room beside their neglected game of chess; Eilish and her mother by the radio in the room below; Brian with Cunningham and Tim and Anne among the dense crowd outside Christchurch Cathedral only a short distance away. It was Saturday, the thirty-first day of December, nineteen thirty-eight, the last hour of the last day of the year. In the sky above the cathedral and the roofs and the crowd milling in the street an unseen priesthood conducted the sidereal rites of demise and rebirth. The year was changing as to number, an end was being determined, a beginning begun, a past and a future were about to be defined. So the waiting city chose to believe. The mystery was more bearable if it could be shown to be measurable.

Eilish and her mother treated themselves to port, not just to one glass but to whatever number disposition and good sense chose to suggest. The occasion permitted as much. The crowd at the cathedral sang songs, shouted salutations to each other, raised bottles mouthwards to drink, blew on mouthorgans and squeezed sounds from melodeons. Their din was a muted background to the talk at the chess table where the pieces were dwarfed by the bottle of whiskey Cornelius had planted at the side and from which he now decided to pour, remarking as he filled the glasses:

'There's another year almost gone on us now and we may as

well drink to it as not for we don't know what the new one
has in store for us.'

'You'd want to be a rare prophet,' O'Sheehan remarked.

'No harm to aim a shot,' Cornelius suggested.

'The numerology is a tangle,' O'Sheehan complained.
'What would you make of 1939?'

'Damn the nothing,' Cornelius confessed, but answering only
for himself.

'Take the first numeral – one. One is the number of the
sun, governing Power and Creation. But then we have nine, the
negative of the sun and symbol of Mars. Three is benevolence,
joy, kindliness. Then we have nine again, which indicates up-
heaval and change. Add one plus nine plus three plus nine and
you get twenty-two and two plus two make four and you know
what four is?'

'I do not.'

'Four is a rebel, a hater of order, four is an up-one-day-
down-another, an hysterical kind of number. I don't trust a
four.'

'And where does that leave us?'

'Among very powerful forces, some pulling this way and
more that. Against the good of one and three we have a nine
repeated, very powerful against the sun and favouring Mars.
Today is Saturday, isn't it?'

'All day,' Cornelius confirmed.

'A day ruled by Saturn whose number is eight and is positive
and therefore physical. It is associated with the fate of nations
and applies particularly to the Jewish race. Saturn is disagreeable
and a depressing companion, though tomorrow, being the
sun's day, should restore some element of optimism and be a
force for good.'

'You mention Mars and that disturbs me,' Cornelius said.

'It disturbs myself. I distrust the recurrence of the nine. It is a
powerful number and self-perpetuating.'

'I don't follow.'

'You cannot alter it by multiplication. Write down your
nine times tables.'

Cornelius found the back of a cigarette packet and did as he was bid. He stared at the result: 9, 18, 27, 36, 45, 54, 63, 72, 81, 90.

'Now reduce each of them to unity again.'

Cornelius began to do so: 1 plus 8 = 9; 2 plus 7 = 9; 3 plus 6 = 9. He marvelled as each sum in turn restored each number to nine again. He had lived a long time unaware of such wizardry.

'That beats Banagher,' he said.

'A druid kind of number,' O'Sheehan agreed.

On waste ground near the cathedral someone had started a bonfire. Its flames flickered on the railings and threw sparks at the stars. Brian said to Cunningham:

'No delectable Gwen with you tonight to wish a happy New Year to?'

'She's gone to a delectable New Year's Eve dance with this fellow who runs a delectable car and can afford such things – a dress dance with supper thrown in.'

'Old Cunningham's been jilted.'

'Old Cunningham has been saved the hire of a dress suit and two expensive tickets. He knows when he's outclassed.'

'Don't you mind?' Tim asked.

'Not really,' Cunningham said. 'Gwen is a decent sort but she likes to enjoy herself. I like her but I'm not potty about her, if that's what you mean. We don't curtail one another.'

'That's sensible,' Brian agreed. 'Sex relations should be rational and undemanding. The other kind is a rope around a fellow's neck.'

He surveyed the antic crowd and said:

'I wonder when I see people welcoming the New Year. It's like shaking hands with your own funeral.'

The radio played softly. At one side of the fire Mrs Moloney knitted. At the other Eilish was deep in her book. The clock on the mantelpiece ticked its way towards midnight. Mrs Moloney became conscious of it from time to time. She laid aside her knitting and regarded her daughter.

'I thought you'd have gone out somewhere tonight. Did Brian not ask you with him?'

'He did. I didn't want to go.'

'You're missing the jollification.'

'I don't like going among the crowds. All that shouting and stamping around puts me off. It's more comfortable reading a book.'

'And have your friends no interest, either?'

'Some of them. The Latimers are having a party but it's miles away past Clontarf.'

'Did the Dempsey boy not ask you out?'

'He's with his people in the country for Christmas. Anyway, I don't see him all that often. Only if we happen to meet up somewhere. Is it all right to take a little more port – a small drop?'

'Take what you fancy. Your father left it to be used.'

As Eilish poured, the bells began to toll, the factory hooters joined in, the sirens of ships at their berths along the river added their moaning. The cheer from the street penetrated the kitchen.

'There's the beginning now. You may as well pour for me while you're at it.'

Cornelius stopped his glass halfway to his lips.

'They're making a fair shindy, them buckos beyond,' he remarked.

'They're young and might as well.'

'I've known it to end in trouble.'

'Feastings and hostings are in the nature of youth. Rivalry and feats of skill and rowdy contests precede manhood. Though their gaiety is rough and foolish there is something to be said for it. Is it time yet to join the women?'

'When we've drained our glasses. But don't hurry it.'

'That would be unmannerly,' O'Sheehan said, 'with so palatable a drop.'

Someone grabbed Tim's arm and he became part of the human

chain which had begun to circle about the bonfire, slowly at the start, then steadily accelerating as the rhythm grew faster. He had become separated from the others and searched the moving line of faces. He located Cunningham first, then Brian. They materialized and faded as the firelight discovered and lost and re-discovered them. Then he saw Anne. She too was searching the bobbing line of faces. He shouted to her. The sound was lost in the general clamour. He lost her and found her again and this time their gaze connected. She smiled and called out but again nothing was distinguishable, nothing remained material for longer than a glimpse or the swell and eclipse of a flame. His hands were grasped firmly on either side, his body captive to the impetus of mass will and mass momentum. In the light of the flames he glimpsed again and again among a throng of unknown humanity the faces of Cunningham, of Brian, of Anne, more or less regularly at first, then less and less as the chain increased its links, until it became so long that the pace slackened and dragged to a stop. The hooters ended their wailing, the bells ceased to toll. The chain disintegrated, the crowd fell silent. There was a moment of respite before the first of the four quarters chimed. A cheer began and grew in volume.

Eilish and Mrs Moloney had opened the hall door to admit the New Year. O'Sheehan and Cornelius stood a little behind them. The heavy strokes resounded on the air and made the floorboards tremulous beneath their feet. On the last stroke Cornelius kissed his wife and daughter and grasped O'Sheehan's hand in friendship.

'A happy New Year,' he said to each of them. They exchanged tenderness and smiles and, in Mrs Moloney's case, for some maternal reason which was beyond the immediate and the rational, a hint of tears.

'Many happy returns,' they answered, 'many happy returns.'

He had marked Anne's finishing position approximately but only found her after long and feverish searching.

'Anne.'

She swung around. Her face which had been tensed and worried relaxed and shone with relief and welcome.

'Tim.'

'I thought I'd lost you forever.'

'Me, too. It was awful. In all this crowd.'

She clung tightly to him.

'Where are the others?'

'I don't know. And for the moment I don't care.'

'I don't, either.'

They kissed.

'Happy New Year,' he said.

'Happy New Year.'

FOUR · The Minstrel Boy

The Minstrel boy to the war is gone
In the ranks of death you'll find him,
His father's sword he has girded on
And his wild harp slung behind him.

TOM MOORE

I

The office allocated to O'Sheehan was on the third floor
of a building used almost exclusively by the Department of
Post & Telegraphs for the storage of equipment obsolete, in
need of repairs or simply forgotten, including oilskins traded
in for periodical replacements and rubber boots with holes
in their soles or gashes in their sides. The office itself was about
the size of a small pantry. It contained a table, a straight chair
and an attendance book (*Tinreamh* was inscribed on its cover)
in which he was required to inscribe his name on two days of
the week, with a record of his hours of attendance. The regulations stipulated that these should be from nine to five p.m.
with a break for midday refreshment. It was no trouble to him
to insert the figures 9–5 after his name, though they seldom
bore on the facts. At irregular and unpredictable intervals a
messenger (presumably) took away the attendance book and in
due course returned it. The same messenger delivered occasional
circulars and correspondence and removed anything which
O'Sheehan left to be collected. There was a lavatory convenient
to the office but unusable because the water supply was either
blocked or had been cut off. In the first months of his occupation
he had written about this to the Department of Post & Telegraphs, only to be informed in due course that responsibility for
such repairs rested with the Board of Works. The Board of
Works replied that the building as a whole had been allocated
to the Department of Post & Telegraphs and requests for repairs
emanating from any other source could not be considered. In
winter, even if he had a mind to, it would have been impossible
to work the required hours there because there was no electric
light. He wisely decided against raising the matter. His monthly
cheque continued to arrive at his home by post and from time
to time he sent on the results of his labours to the covering
address, whatever it happened to be. The fact that the title and

offices of whatever State-appointed body he was supposed to be working for seemed continually to change puzzled him.

'I wouldn't worry about it,' Cornelius told him. 'There are so many organizations for the preservation of the language being subsidized by the State these times and more of them springing up every day that there's a certain amount of overlapping and confusion. What matter to you so long as you get paid.'

'But the language we both love is made a football of. I have watched that happening and I find it disheartening.'

'That's human nature. This one sees the other one getting something and he gets a bit jealous. Look what happens when there's a vacancy for a rates collector or a postmaster. In politics a job here and a job there works wonders, even if you have to manufacture them at times.'

'But where are honour, nobility, the dreams we dreamed? How can you be so matter of fact, so unembittered?'

'One must live,' Cornelius answered.

Tuesdays and Thursdays were the days on which O'Sheehan visited his office in fulfilment of his obligations, though in severely inclement weather he made convenient alterations. His route lay by the City Hall and Dame Street, past the statues of Grattan and Moore, the old Houses of Parliament, the railings of Trinity College, picking his way through hordes of cyclists and rattling trams in the mornings and returning through more leisurely streets when the light had begun to fail. Under skies swollen with rain or black with the threat of snow, by narrow streets where pavements and window ledges clung obstinately to their skin of grime and frost he trudged to and fro, a microscopic detail of the January scene, an observer in a living canvas executed for the most part in greys and browns. He stopped to give precedence to horse cab and taxi. He made way for black- or brown-clad women pushing prams. He yielded for handcarts dragged after urchins with mud-spattered legs. Cyclists in sou'westers and oilskin capes and pull-ups wobbled uncertainly past him. Carters swathed in sacks for cloak and apron with pendant raindrops lacing the rims of their headgear screwed up their eyes and sat like drenched and down-at-heel Buddhas. The bars served hot whiskey and mulled claret. Steam from their ever-steaming kettles mixed with the faint smell of cloves and fed more moisture into the already foggy air. Clients believed it to relieve bronchitis. The sawdust, churned about by feet, grew muddy yellow. In the evenings, if he felt the cold in his bones, he sometimes stepped into the Stag's Head for a glass of hot punch. Here he enjoyed the status of welcome and respectable visitor, a standing inferior only to that of regular. He was entitled to affable salutation and, on occasion, to extended conversation.

'A raw evening.'

'Very severe. There could be snow.'

'So I was thinking. That north-easter isn't content just to skin a few unfortunate serfs on the Russian steppes. It has no good in its mind for us either.' The barman was consulted.

'Isn't that what I was saying, Paddy?'

'You were, captain. No better man to say it.'

O'Sheehan took the hot glass between his fingers and sipped. Better almost than the golden liquid was the aromatic moistness of cloves and sugar wreathing about his nostrils.

'I was out beyond the point of Howth on the ebb of the tide this morning and I thought the blood would freeze in my veins. Black ice on the deck too. We made no undue delay, let me tell you.'

O'Sheehan said: 'The thought of a sea trip these mornings would destroy me. Is it the lighthouse service?'

'Nothing so respectable. I skipper a boat for the corporation's Sanitary Department. The job is to transport the sludge from the settling beds at the Pigeon House Fort and dump it out to sea. The locals call us the Shit Ship. When they do I say: why blame the ship? Whose was the shit?'

O'Sheehan smiled above the warm and aromatic vapour: *Palmam qui meruit ferat.*

'A healthy life, the sea. By and large.'

'And hardy. Usually we attract a large congregation of gulls, but this morning not one of them showed up. Too cold for them. Will there be a war, do you think?'

'The signs are that way.'

'I heard the matter discussed by some naval butties a short while ago. They were of the same mind. It seems to be in fashion and it's catching. We have this latest ultimatum served by our national association for head cases – the IRA – on the British Army to get out of the North within four days or they'll declare war on Britain. Do they honestly expect Britain to pack up and decamp? Are they out of their minds? This unfortunate country is living in some kind of miasma.'

'This country has always lived in a miasma,' O'Sheehan agreed, 'and one that is largely not of its own making. But if they start to bomb innocent civilians in Britain – and that seems to be the intention – then we'll have lost our honour as well as our six counties. That would be Britain's ultimate triumph.'

It was pleasant on such evenings to climb the stairs to his room, to open the door on the warmth of the fire which a neighbour woman would have lit for him; to make his own tea and draw the blinds and settle in the dilapidated rocking chair by the side of the fire. Beyond the window the Liffey might wrinkle at the touch of chilled winds and the streets shiver cheerlessly under lonely lamps. He was snug with fire and the peopled theatre of his mind, where the pageant of the centuries flowed from present to remote past and he himself was the hero and the witness of all tragedies and all high deeds. The hunt spread across the mountain and the dogs gave tongue. The hazel tree by the forest pool dropped berries of poetry and imagination into the waters of the enchanted well. Conor MacNessa crashed through the forest and smote the oaks with grim strokes of his sword because their clan consented to the crucifying of Christ. Lightning forked from the darkness and Daithi was a dead king on a desolate mountain. Eithne lost her cloak of invisibility and could no longer find her way back to the land of faery, though they searched for her for fifteen hundred years and their voices calling her were the last she heard when death came to her in Patrick's chapel.

There was hope in that. There was hope too in the story of Tuan MacCarell. All the Parthelonians died but not Tuan. He

grew old but could not die. Then the Nemedians came to
Ireland and his soul migrated and he became a stag. All the
Nemedians died. But not Tuan, who became a black boar.
When the Fir Bolgs came he was a great eagle of the sea. The
Tuatha de Danaan took over. He remained an eagle and old age
descended. The Milesians conquered in turn and he was transformed into a salmon. Then the wife of Carell their chief ate
him one day and he passed into her womb and was reborn in
human shape as Tuan the son of Carell. He died at last in the
sixth century when he had related his strange story to St Finian
of Moville.

In his chair by the fire in the quiet hours O'Sheehan lived
in the guise of boar and otter, eagle and swan, stag and salmon.
In silence and warmth, in glow and flame flicker he climbed in
high places and across heathery slopes; he swam in bright lakes
or in the brown deeps of rivers; he lurked by weir and fragrant
bank; he bedded in thicket and forest; he soared over rich and
limitless plains and the palaced glories of kings. All seas, all
enchanted islands, all milkful herds, apple laden branches,
honeyflowing acres, mastheavy forests, and the four green
fields were his by right of race and lineage. If his eyes were less
than sharp and his bones ached at times and the stairs seemed
to leave him short of breath, that could mean the onset at last
of a tardy decrepitude, a welcome ageing: a first intimation
that his soul was tiring of his earthly shape and desirous again
for the springtide of sense, of sight, of vigour, restless and ready
for fresh adventures in new modes and other shapes. In some
other life – not this one. In some other world beyond that of
humankind. In fields of enchantment, perhaps, or up in the air
or, possibly, under the sea.

At almost all times but on cold winter mornings and especially
on Sundays Tim swore because his mother had blued and
starched his shirts so that putting a fresh one on was like stepping
into a suit of armour.

'If they had creased or floppy collars it would be another
cause for complaint.'

'Who ever complained about floppy collars?'

'You have a job to look after. At least turn into it looking respectable.'

'But it's bloody torture.'

'And you're swearing lately. You never used to.'

'No wonder. Soon I'll need a tin opener.'

'That's the thanks I get. That's the gratitude. If I worried less I'd be thought more of. I notice you're going to last mass every Sunday too. Soon it'll be the quarter past one at St Audeon's.'

'What's wrong with that?'

'It's there for the convenience of the Saturday night drunkards that won't or can't get up earlier. It's slothful and unchristian.'

'Ma – for Christ's sake.'

She crossed herself.

'May God forgive you the misuse of His Holy Name. You'll bring bad luck into my house.'

Cold, slanting rain or bitter frosts, the streets on Sundays were crossed and recrossed nevertheless by mass-going feet. Affluence and gentility worshipped in University Church. Perfumes troubled the warm air inside when the congregation rose for the gospel; at Communion Franck's 'Panis Angelicus' floated in well-behaved canon above fur coats and Sunday hats. Whitefriar Street, on the other hand, was democratic and exuberant. Shrines blazed with candles, votive lamps begged for favours, the statues mixed freely with the people. Clarendon Street stuck prudently to the custom of a less tolerant age and hid in its narrow laneway from unnecessary public scrutiny. From the gallery of the Pro-Cathedral, the Palestrina Choir under Dr Vincent O'Brien poured sixteenth-century polyphony over the heads of the necessitous poor. Other churches occasionally favoured were John's Lane, Meath Street, Francis Street, or the Franciscans on the quays. But the choice was limitless. It was a city of bells and churches.

Although Brian had lost interest in religion, if they chose St Audeon's it was so near him he might join them for companionship. Cunningham preferred it. The performance was both brief and to the point and the latest that could be got. For Tim the route to it led by crumbling tenements and the debris of Saturday nights' goings on. They smoked afterwards in Brian's now modestly furnished shebeen. Or they strolled into the city or gave brief audience to the social radicals preaching reform or revolution outside the City Hall or in Foster Place. On rare occasions they paid good money for *Torch* or *The Worker*, or Brian summarized their hectorings and the lot of the destitute in an impromptu verse:

> 'I remember, I remember
> The room where I was born
> The broken windows where the rats
> Went slinking out at morn
> They never went a wink too soon
> Or stayed too long away
> In fact I think the more infirm
> Remained throughout the day.'

Cunningham's sartorial splendour, the fruits of his job with the gentlemen's outfitters, frequently excited their comment.

'They like you to dress a bit,' he kept telling them. 'They believe it's good for business, so of course they let you have the stuff for half nothing. Why not take advantage?'

His trousers were of cavalry twill, his shirt tailormade with detachable collar and tweed tie. He was sporting a collar pin. His corduroy jacket, golden in colour, was perfectly cut.

'Am I strolling the boulevards with Beau Brummell,' Brian asked, looking from Cunningham to Tim, 'or out searching the ashbins with Johnny Fortycoats?' He scrutinized Tim's trousers.

'Are you aware, McDonagh, that your flannels are at half mast?'

'They're last year's,' Tim admitted. 'Either they've shrunk or I've grown a bit. I'm hoping to be able to rise to a new pair for the summer.'

'If you're buying slacks and things, come to me,' Cunningham offered. 'I can get you anything from ten to twenty per cent off.'

'Maybe you could feck a pair for him,' Brian suggested. 'He's a walking freak.'

'To be poor may be inconvenient,' Tim said, 'but what matter if it provides amusement.'

'McDonagh,' Brian said to Cunningham solely, 'has the sulks. If they make him look so bloody ridiculous, why does he wear them?'

'I told you. Poverty. Must you add your usual sneery remarks?'

Brian stopped.

'Sneery. That's an interesting word. That's not you talking at all. That's a woman's word. I wonder whose?'

'Enough,' Cunningham advised. 'We'll have a row if you go on. And all about nothing.'

But there were more amicable occasions. They shared cigarettes and the occasional windfall; they went cycling or walking together along country roads; they climbed deep into the hills. They lit fires to cook for themselves and sat around afterwards talking long into the night. From Easter onwards through that summer of 1939 they pitched tents on weekends and slept out. They speculated a lot about the future, including what seemed to be the renewed possibility of war. It was a subject to which none of them, including Brian, could bring more than the sketchiest of information. There were more interesting topics. There were affairs of finance; the vague quest for dissipation; the fact that already O'Keeffe was understood to be driving a car, though none of them had actually seen it happen; the all-absorbing debate on this bird and that bird, indeed the general consideration of womankind. It saw them through the days and the weeks.

Cornelius, on the other hand, weathered the same period with much on his mind, especially when the IRA campaign in Britain brought a severe response from de Valera, whose reintroduction of military tribunals and internment without trial set rumblings of revolt within the party branch over which it was the dubious privilege of Cornelius to preside.

'By Christ,' one of the committee declared, 'if Dev gets up to those class of tricks I'm not answering for my continuance in this party.'

'Are we to condone the bombing of innocent British people?'

'Not for a moment. But military courts and internment without trial are not to be condoned either. When the treaty crowd first introduced those Dev was the one who condemned them and campaigned for their removal.'

Which, of course, was true.

Cornelius explained to O'Sheehan, 'You see how hard it is to justify to members Dev's decision to use the same measures himself. If I put a foot wrong there'll be a mass defection to Sinn Fein. One of the ringleaders, need I tell you, is that bloody little plumbing contractor from the South Circular Road that calls himself Liam O Páircéir, whatever the hell that stands for.'

'I imagine it means William Parkes or William Parker,' O'Sheehan said drily. 'I wouldn't think there was much of the true Celt in the one or the other.'

'I might have guessed,' Cornelius said. 'Convert an Englishman to catholicism or Irish nationalism and he loses all sense of where to draw the line. Why can't they stick with their own?'

'What did Mr Parkes or Parker want?'

'A resolution of protest to be sent to party headquarters. Think of the meal the *Independent* or the *Irish Times* would make of that. It took me an hour's manoeuvring to substitute an amendment asking for clarification of the procedures.'

'I would have thought the procedures clear enough.'

'The procedures are as clear as bloody daylight – you lock up the boys as fast as you can round them in or you hang them and save lodging and expense. But it deflects the attack. Well, the amendment got through, thanks be to God. HQ can now promise to send on a copy of the act with notes and explanations. And forget to put it in the post, of course.'

O'Sheehan smiled to himself at the wile of the political mind.

'Then you out-manoeuvred our English-named friend?'

'By the skin of my teeth. When the amendment was carried

he left the meeting in protest after giving us a stave or two of that thing that goes: "Forget not the field where they perished".'

The lines were familiar to O'Sheehan, who rehearsed them for their mutual benefit.

> 'Forget not the field where they perished
> The truest, the last of the brave
> All gone – and the bright hopes we cherished
> Gone with them and quenched in the grave.'

'I hope he wasn't making reference to the men of 1916,' Cornelius mused. 'Pearse would never condone the bombing of civilians. He raised an army of patriots and gentlemen, not bloody savages.'

O'Sheehan concurred. Then, gravely collecting himself, he proceeded to deliver a brief lecture.

'The old style of revolution was more cultivated, more aristocratic. Your true Celt is a chivalrous fighter. I am thinking of Smith O'Brien in the Rising of 1845. When his men wanted to fell some trees along the walls of a demesne to make a road block he approved, yes: but he instructed them to get the landlord's permission first. Similarly in our War of Independence. If you were going to burn down one of the big houses you apologized to the owner before soaking the wooden parts with cans of petrol, or if you didn't you got a damn good telling off from your Brigade Commander afterwards. That spirit has gone. It slowly disappeared from the time patriotism began to be infiltrated by the thinking of these labour unions and the social reformers. You could see it in 1798. There was much proletarian unrest at that time and as a consequence great savagery on both sides. During the agrarian troubles Irish peasants roasted a landlord on one of his own gates. In 1867 we lost much of our American support through loose talk from certain elements in the movement who wanted to challenge the rights of property. Were they freeing Ireland as patriots and gentlemen, people naturally enquired, or were they simply unprincipled rogues bent on destroying the institutions of society? Where talk of that kind is rampant, outrage is inevitable and civilized procedures go out the window.'

Cornelius replied in kind and he too composed himself for delivery.

'That's very true. It was so after 1916 and throughout the War of Independence. Certainly in the beginning. You had ambushes – agreed. How else could a lightly armed force such as our own take on an empire? But there were limits. You didn't shoot an officer when he was off duty, say at a race meeting in the Park or at the Curragh, or at a town fête or a regatta. Or if he was out with the hunt. Neither did he shoot you. There had to be some kind of normality. Things would want to be very tense before there was any display of bad manners. No one would dream of interfering with a guest at a social occasion, say at a wedding or a funeral. Both sides mixed freely at things like that. But then the gutty element entered. In my own native place I saw them burning down a police station about the ears of decent men that intended no harm to no one.'

The recollection opened up another which still rankled.

'Then there was the bowsie element around during the Civil War, when the Shinners threatened to burn myself out of home and business if I did one thing, while the Free Staters offered to oblige in the same manner if I did another.'

'We are reaping the fruits of that spirit today,' O'Sheehan said. 'I can see no alternative left for de Valera but what he's proposing.'

'I'm not blaming him. For that matter I never really blamed Cosgrave. There can only be one government and one army. Otherwise your rights and my rights and all our rights go out the window. The gun is then King, Lords and Commons, Judge, Jury and Executioner.' Cornelius struggled with the difficulties in silence for some time but in the end remained as perplexed as before.

'Nevertheless,' he concluded, 'I can appreciate the confusion it causes among our members. They don't understand how the Republican party can be reduced to gaoling the Republicans.'

O'Sheehan nodded his agreement. These were baffling issues.

II

At Seapoint the bicycles ranged in unbroken lines along the railway bridge and the sea wall and the railings of Brighton Vale were a sign that weather and tide were right for the after-work enthusiasts. It was around seven o'clock. There was no wind. The sea was glass. The Martello tower by the water's edge looked towards Howth across bobbing heads and coloured swimming caps. On the beach, on the paved rampart and on the broad top of the railway wall supine bodies were toned in all shades possible between off-white and deep brown. Whenever Tim opened his eyes they could find no focal point in the vast blueness overhead. Stone and sky exuded heat. Anne sat close enough to draw a feather lightly along his cheek and neck from time to time. Cunningham, his feet dangling over the side, supplied an intermittent commentary on female comings and goings on the beach below. He kept a towel about his shoulders which were raw and peeling.

'See that long-legged one in the red bathing cap?' he asked Anne. 'She's with an elderly man. Over there to your right. That's her father.'

'Do you know them?'

'Sort of. She was here all through the season last year. I used to think she was wizard.'

'Then you met Gwen?'

'No. Not that. Her father came into the shop at the beginning of the year for underclothes and I served him. He wears long drawers.'

'What's that to do with her?'

'It put me off. A girl loses her glamour when you know her oul fella has just been stocking up on long-legged combinations. All the mystery is gone.'

'My God – the pitfalls. Suppose my father was one of your regulars.'

'Tim is too far gone to mind. Feel like another swim?'

'I've just managed to get dry.'

'Cool your ardour?'

'No thanks.'

'I will. Just in and out.'

She watched him picking his way through the crowd. Tim sat up.

'Where's Cunningham?'

'Gone down for a quick plunge. He's so restless I wonder how he sat long enough to get his shoulders in a mess.'

'That was last weekend. He was rambling in the mountains with no shirt on. It was useless talking to him.'

'I like Cunningham. Better than Brian.'

'Brian's all right. But things haven't worked out for him. He has the makings of a brilliant mind but nothing to use it on. Except what he can lay hands on to read.'

'And what about you?'

'Me? I'm not in Brian's league,' Tim said. 'I just wouldn't be mapped.'

'I don't agree,' she insisted.

Cunningham returned and stood upright on the wall to towel himself, stopping now and then to swear when he hurt his shoulders.

'God, they sting.'

'Once in should have been enough,' Tim said.

'I wanted a paddle with long-drawers' daughter. Which reminds me. I have news.'

He sat down to tell them but was interrupted by the approach of a train. It swayed past at slow speed, flushed and sweating faces peering enviously from its windows. They thought it might be carrying passengers to the mail boat at Dun Laoghaire.

Anne said when it had gone that the sooty smell reminded her of going on holidays when she was a child. 'I adore it. Don't you?'

'Not really,' Cunningham said, 'I always seemed to get a cinder in my eye.'

In his mind Tim proceeded to assemble smells he had grown up with, private odours like Mrs Curtis making toffee; public odours of activity and environment; the linseed smell of football boots, the embrocation smell of pavilions, vegetable smells in Moore Street and the odour of horses at the cab rank on the Green.

'There are millions of smells to remember,' he said. 'The smell of new-mown hay, the smell of vegetation along the banks of the canal and the Dodder, the smell of wild garlic in the lanes around Powerscourt.'

'Very poetic,' Cunningham said. He was flicking sand off his legs with deft strokes of his towel.

'Memory makes nearly everything poetic, even smells that were unpleasant, like the smell from O'Keeffe's the knackers. Have you ever passed it when they'd just finished hosing it out and the channels were full of chandlers, all small and white and wriggling?'

'Ugh,' Anne said.

'Ugh from me too,' Cunningham supported. 'Spare us the lifesize oil paintings.'

'In Dublin a blind man knows where he is by the smell. The smell of chocolate from Jacob's factory – he's in Camden Street. The smell of roasting malt – Guinness's – he's in James' Street or Thomas Street. The smell of burnt metal – the tram depot in Ringsend. The smell of fresh bread – that could be Boland's Mill in Ringsend or Johnston Mooney & O'Brien's at Ballsbridge.'

Cunningham stopped de-sanding himself to recite a street rhyme.

> 'Johnston Mooney and O'Brien
> Bought a horse for one and nine
> When the horse refused to go
> Johnston Mooney bought a hoe
> When the hoe began to break
> Johnston Mooney bought a rake
> When the rake was forced to stop
> Johnston Mooney bought a shop.'

He broke off.

'Do you know the rest?'

'No,' Tim said.

'Thank God. Now the news. I have every chance of getting

the loan of a hut on the cliffs near Bray for the remainder of the summer. This chap who owns it is a civil servant but he's in the army reserve and he's going for special training soon. Would you care to share it?'

'Of course.'

'And Anne?'

'Me too? That'd be lovely. But will they allow me at home?'

'My sister will come along to take the harm out of it,' Cunningham said. 'And Gwen, of course, from time to time.'

'But what about getting to work?'

'We could get up a bit earlier to cycle in. Or go in by train. It'll cost us a bit buying grub, though.'

'Not if we club in.'

'What about Brian?' Tim asked.

Anne's face betrayed her disapproval. He ignored it.

'If he can come,' Cunningham agreed, 'and the girlfriend.'

Tim was surprised.

'What girlfriend?'

'I don't remember her name, but I've seen them together here and there. The girl he met on that excursion. She works in your place.'

'Barbara Sheehy – he couldn't be.'

'But he is,' Cunningham insisted. 'Master Moloney has been holding out on us.'

He flicked the last of the sand away and began dressing.

'You never mentioned it. I can't understand that.'

'Nobody asked me.'

'Come off it. You were holding out.'

'All right. I was holding out.'

'But why?'

'I don't know. After the outing I forgot about her for a week or so. Then I found I was thinking about her – a little at first, then quite a lot. So I telephoned her. I found she wasn't the usual bit of stuff you run into. She doesn't just look interesting. She *is* interesting.'

'But why did you keep it so quiet?'

'I had decided birds were out, hadn't I? Then I found I was wrong. I don't like being wrong. Maybe that's the reason. Apart from that, life at present isn't very entertaining. It's mainly pulling pints and listening to political small talk. There doesn't seem to be much ahead either. Barbara is about the only bright spot there is. Apart from people like yourself. What bothers me now is that she should tell you. I asked her not to for the present.'

'But she didn't. Cunningham saw the two of you together here and there. He mentioned it the other evening.'

'Oh . . . I'm glad it wasn't Barbara. And I'm sorry for holding out.'

The apology was uncharacteristic. Did it mean he was going under? That would be unthinkable.

'You're going through it a bit.'

'I don't intend to give in, let me tell you. Having Barbara around helps there too. I don't have to explain to you.'

No need at all. He had Anne. He knew all about it.

In July and August the city sweltered. When at five o'clock they locked the filing cabinets and left the typewriters and the telephones to mind themselves they stepped out almost always into sunshine and often enough into torrid heat. The young men removed their jackets and carried them across one shoulder. The girls wore their sleeveless frocks and looked their best. On O'Connell bridge the photographers clicked indiscriminate cameras at passers-by and thrust tickets at them offering three walkabout photographs for half-a-crown.

The hut became a constant retreat, sometimes housing Cunningham and Tim and Brian, and on occasions when the girls decided to go, sleeping up to seven – the males on the floor in the living space, the females in the only bedroom. A small kitchenette was saturated in the mixed odours of frying pan and primus stove. Cunningham, the custodian of the key, was in charge of arrangements.

They cycled into work together in the mornings and back to it in the evenings. Or, if affairs kept them in the city until late, they still usually managed to get out to it, a hazardous journey on the main road by the light of a bicycle lamp, but mysterious and full of a new freedom when the lanes were reached and the air became heavy with summer hedgerows and the smell and sound of the sea.

It stood on the cliffs, its face to the sea, its back to the railway line which crossed a wide landscape of undulating fields. Sometimes they wandered the cliffs to Bray for the slot machines and late-night bags of chips. Sometimes they were content to mess around on the beach. There were a few sultry nights that tempted them into midnight swims. If it rained they sat in lamplight and talked. If the women were present they wandered the beach or the fields in pairs. Gwen came several times; Barbara rather less. Anne was able to stay three or four times, but most times she had to get the late train home. Usually the small platform with its gas lamps hissing in the silence of the summer's night was solely theirs. He would bring her to the station on the crossbar of his bicycle, a bumpy journey along lanes that were winding and protective and all their own.

'It's a pity you've got to go back.'

'I know. But if I seem to be suddenly overwhelmed with invitations to spend a few days with devoted friends they may decide at home that they'd like to see who they are.'

On such nights of leavetaking, tenderness and isolation translated them into a world that had slipped the nets of everyday space and time, a world fashioned by some inward artificer from imagination and emotion alone, even to the red glimmer of the signal arm above them, the vague outline of the bridge behind it, the muted patches of silver that gleamed here and there on the surface of the rails like the night sheen on a silent river. Above them the tips of the trees were hung with stars, the air itself so still and weightless that they themselves might have been figures breathing and whispering in a painted landscape.

Then the train approached and the parts began to move. First the click of a signal changing, a faint trembling along the glinting rails. Then the sudden rush of steam, the clatter of wheels, the slow succession of lighted windows gliding past and abruptly coming to a standstill. A door wrenched open, a door banged shut, short gasps of steam, the clink of couplings as they took the strain, the lurch of wheels. In no time at all it had come and it had gone. Only the ghost of their leavetaking might endure a while, their words, flung towards and from an opened window, hanging in the air and on the ear to delay briefly the return of silence.

He would climb again the steep archway of the railway bridge and think of distance growing moment by moment between them, the fields, the gates, the trees, the houses, the winding roads and the curving rails lengthening all the time and the spaces filling in with all the paraphernalia of landscape. Mingling odours of summer still haunted the lanes. Above him branches interlocked to hide the sky. Along the length of their winding and leafy tunnel the low hum of wheels kept company with his thoughts and provided their own commentary on the mysteries of presence and absence, of space and of time, until the lane in its turn came to an end and divided into two tracks: one bending right through the gate to the cliff field, the other descending steeply to where the gap in the cliffs made a frame for scattered rocks and the pale glimmer of sand and sea.

On one such night when they dismounted and she walked beside him as he wheeled his bicycle, they lingered too long and she missed her train. On the way back to the hut it was too much for both of them and though she said No you mustn't you really mustn't Tim they lay close in the darkness and he did. He had not meant to because there were all sorts of grave reasons and she had not meant to for even graver ones but she too found it harder and harder and so they both did. When it was over they lay in mutual tenderness and told each other they thought it would be all right. Which, indeed, mercifully as they admitted, it later proved to be. He made up a bed for her in the living room and used the bedroom himself because Cunningham was already asleep in it. In the morning Cunningham betrayed no surprise but when Anne had got her train and Tim and he were cycling into work together he began to brush the back of Tim's jacket.

'What's all this?'

'You had hay on it,' Cunningham explained. His face was expressionless.

'Oh, shut up,' Tim said. But he didn't mind.

I've something on my mind this while back,' Cornelius said. His wife, who had been knitting by the window, glanced across at him.

'It concerns Brian. It's been nagging at me on and off.'

She left down her knitting and waited. Cornelius looked very solemn. With deliberation he said:

'I suspect that boyo has given up going to Sunday mass.' His words shocked her. She waited.

'I've been watching him closely this while past. At first I put down all his oul anti-clerical guff to bravado. Now I think it's more serious than that.'

'But he's always out in time on Sundays.'

'So are the dogs and cats of the neighbourhood. That doesn't mean they go to mass. Have you ever asked him?'

'It wouldn't cross my mind.'

'It crossed mine. Once or twice I've seen him come out of the quarter to one with his couple of butties – young McDonagh and that other chap. But that's about the size of it. Most of the time he just takes himself off on his bicycle.'

'Maybe he gets mass elsewhere.'

'There may well be mass to be had after one o'clock some place or other. But there's none in this city.'

'I don't know what to say.'

'I talked to Eilish. It's a ridiculous idea, she said. Of course everything their father says is ridiculous these times. She was lying to me.'

'Eilish wouldn't do that.'

'Eilish is a good daughter – I'm not faulting her. But you'd get nothing out of the one of them about the other so I suppose I was a fool to attempt it.'

'You'll have to talk to him.'

'It isn't always wise,' Cornelius said. 'It could turn a temporary fad of his into something much more serious.'

'I blame those books he's forever dug into,' Mrs Moloney asserted. 'They're never done sniping at the Church and the clergy.' She began to cry.

Cornelius rose and went over to comfort her.

'That's what I didn't want to do,' he told her. 'Upset you or put a burden on you. But what's best to be done?'

'You'll have to talk to him. But don't for God's sake fight with him. You always lose your temper when he answers back. Talk to him quietly. I wonder should we get Father Ryan up to him?'

Not unless he agrees to it himself, Cornelius thought. It could do more harm than good.

He returned to his chair and churned the matter over.

'You rear them up as best you may. You teach them a right way of living and you give them what example you can. They couldn't have had a gentler or more patient or Christian-hearted mother, and I did my own best such as it may be. It fails me to understand it.'

'You'd grieve for any poor creature that loses the faith – never mind your own flesh and blood – for what hope is left for them?' Mrs Moloney reflected. 'I'll start a Novena the coming Friday.'

Cornelius approved and agreed.

'Poor hope indeed,' he confirmed. 'As well as that I was expecting that some time or other he might be nominated a candidate for the constituency. The hint has been dropped in my ear by a few of the members already – some of them more than once.'

He sat back and chewed gloomily on the situation.

'Poor hope of that either in this Christian country,' he told her, 'if the word gets about that he doesn't go to mass of a Sunday.'

Tim watched the incoming tide feeling out the contours with delicate tendrils. It crept around rocks and trickled in thin streamers across captured patches of sand, cloaking a ruthless and inexorable advance in a show of innocence ànd diffidence. The sun had gone, a light breeze from the sea played along the deserted beach. Cunningham, loading the airgun from time to time to take potshots at the tin can which was serving him for target practice, was having difficulty with the light. A long pause and a flow of bad language followed three or four shots that had gone wide. Then the gun cracked again, the tin can lifted into the air and clanked along the stones when it fell.

'Got it,' he shouted.

'Why don't you give up. It's getting too dark.'

'Twenty square hits out of twenty-five shots. Not bad.'

'It sounded more like fifty than twenty-five.'

'The others were not at the tin can,' Cunningham broke the gun finally and joined him.

'Did you know you can win up to a fiver at those shooting competitions they run in the Fun Palace during the winter? I'm thinking of putting in a couple of hours' target practice a day.'

'The pellets alone will cost you a fiver.'

'You think so? I must work it out.'

They began to walk back towards the hut. With dusk the breeze was freshening and lifting fine particles of sand from the embankments. Seaweed popped and burst when they trod on it. It was the lonely hour between evening and darkness.

'I wish I hadn't to go in tonight,' Cunningham said.

'When will you be out again.'

'Not until Sunday morning – worse luck. These relations are coming, and they don't leave until Saturday. A whole bloody week – and more.'

'When I was a kid,' Tim said, 'a week was like forever. Now it passes quickly enough.'

'If you're on holidays. But not if you have a toothache. Or you're stuck with stuffy relatives.' Cunningham paused.

'Who owns the bicycle?' he wondered. It was leaning with their own against the side of the hut. 'Is it Brian's?'

They found him stretched out on one of the beds. The air in the hut was still and warm. Cunningham propped the gun in the corner.

'We were down on the beach,' he explained.

'I heard the target practice.'

'Why didn't you come down?'

'I watched the pair of you from the cliffs. Billy the Kid and King Canute.'

'You're supposed to be working these nights,' Tim said. 'Didn't you say so?'

Brian sat up.

'I've had an almighty dust-up with the old man. He's discovered I haven't been going to mass.' His mood was unusually subdued.

'There are three mortal sins in Holy Ireland,' Cunningham reflected. 'Not going to mass, sexual activity of any shape or make, and eating meat on a Friday. Anything else is all right, so long as you don't go around bragging about it.'

'You walked out?' Tim asked.

'It wasn't so simple. I told the old man my beliefs or lack of them were my own affair. If it had been just him and me that might have finished it. But then the mother took it up. It was unbelievable. If she'd been abusive or in a temper I could have coped with it. But instead she just seemed to collapse. I walked out and wandered around for about an hour but I couldn't get the sound of this unbelievable wailing out of my ears. It was awful, I can tell you. Obviously the thing was breaking her heart. In the end I went back and said all right, I'd give it another trial just to please her. But I told them I was getting out of there for the weekend. I had to. They were both so relieved about the mass part of it the old man didn't dare to object.'

'Had you anything to eat?' Tim asked.

'In that atmosphere? Not likely.'

'I'll make some tea.'

Cunningham trimmed the wick of the oil lamp in silence before lighting it. Time retired to the kitchenette to put on the kettle and cut the bread. There was some cheese left to make the meal a little less than spartan. They sat over it and talked until Cunningham decided it was time for him to go.

'You'll have the moon with you,' Tim said. They could see it through the window, a full, golden disc suspended above the sea.

Cunningham smiled.

'I remember we were doing *Hamlet* in school one day when oul Quinlan had to stand in for Brother Raymond. There was a bit in it I was waiting for him to skip over and he did. Just before he came to it he stopped suddenly and told Cummins to open a window. When he'd watched him doing it he took up reading again further down the page.'

He stood up to mimic Brother Quinlan.

> 'The chariest maid is prodigal enough
> If she unmasks her beauty to the moon.'

'Who was that?' Tim wondered. 'Was it Polonius?'

'Laertes to Ophelia.'

'That's right,' Cunningham confirmed. 'He was advising her to keep her legs crossed.' He sighed. 'Well – time to get along.'

They walked part of the laneway with him, delayed a while seeing him off, then returned through a small wood and moonlit fields. Without him the hut seemed unusually quiet.

'He forgot his gun,' Tim said.

It was still in the corner. Brian remained subdued and settled down to read. Tim busied himself with the washing up. To-morrow Anne would be out for most of the day. He wondered about Barbara but decided against asking. He sensed that Brian had no present desire for small talk. Yet Mrs Moloney's feelings were understandable. She would regard neglecting Sunday mass as the straightest route to hell, an accumulation of mortal sin upon mortal sin Sunday after Sunday from which there could be no redemption. Which was what it certainly would be, if you accepted the Church's teaching, though there were the possibilities of Divine Mercy and the mysterious workings of Actual Grace. But her generation set little store on such refinements. They were hardliners. A Catholic could only mean a practising one. Otherwise he was a renegade and almost certainly damned. He returned to the living room.

'Feel like a walk?'

Brian shook his head.

'I'll take a turn on the strand,' Tim decided.

The sea had covered the sand and was lapping about the stones on the upper part of the beach. It curved under the moon for almost a mile ahead, undulating near the shore, calm and luminous in its outer reaches. Music drifted across it from the esplanade at Bray where the holiday season would soon come to its close. When the coloured lights along the sea front were in sight he stopped, remembering that his father and mother had spent their brief wartime honeymoon in a hotel somewhere near the promenade. He tried to visualize it. A hotel that was not too dear, it would have been. Neither of them would have been comfortable in anything too grand. They would have gone on outings to Wicklow by train perhaps, and by the landaus that still operated from their rank near the pier to Glendalough and the Seven Churches. They had paid to be taken across the lake to visit St Kevin's Bed, an event his mother still used to talk about when he was younger. Had they sat on the sea front on those evenings over twenty years ago listening to the band below them on the green? And what happened to such an evening and such a moment of living? And to the bandsmen and the music. To say it had all passed was inadequate. What had been real could never become unreal. If it had been there it must still be somewhere. It was a thought which had troubled him from time to time ever since childhood. As always he had to leave it unresolved.

Brian had left the book aside.

'I'm glad you're back,' he said. 'Sit down for a moment.' He found difficulty beginning.

'There's something about the row at home which I didn't care to mention in front of Cunningham. I find it hard to speak about it now, so don't be tempted to laugh. When my father had finished and my mother started I said some pretty harsh things to her and she began to cry. That wasn't unusual so I didn't budge. Then this incredible thing happened. She got down on her knees to plead with me. Can you believe it? My mother. And she meant it too. It was worth any measure of humiliation to her to save me from burning forever in hell. I felt ashamed.

Not for me. For her. At the same time it was bloody heart-rending. I'm deeply fond of my mother. It still upsets me.'

'You promised to go. That's all you could do. Do you intend to keep your promise?'

'I intend to pretend. If they want to be misled then I'll oblige them. What horrifies me is the training that could reduce her to such a state. She was terrified.'

'To a believing Catholic, after all,' Tim said, 'hell is a reality.'

'My mother is not simply a believer. She's a slave.'

'And your father?'

'To be fair to him, though he's a stickler for practice, I don't think he regards everything he was told as literal.'

'Men take the omissions a bit easier, generally speaking. They rely a bit more on mercy and forgiveness.'

He found Brian staring hard at him.

'It's like listening to a gramophone. How can you go on spinning out the clichés?'

'Some regard the clichés as part of a rich message. Many millions believe as I do.'

'Many millions more do not.'

'You find most of them believe in something,' Tim suggested reasonably. 'It comes as naturally to man as eating a meal or taking a wife. Why get exercised about it?'

'My mother, for a start. Is that a desirable outcome? Myself too. Its clerics did their best to terrify me when I was too young to know better. Ordinary human activity was suspect. Don't look, don't say, don't listen – that's the rich message they had for me.' Brian stood up.

'You too,' he continued, 'a lot of the time you're just a cold, self-contained, religion-regulated automaton. And you do yourself a disservice, because beyond the piosity there's a courageous and aware person.'

It was hard to know what to say to that, except to dismiss the whole thing. As they went into the bedroom Tim paused to gaze through the seaward window. He said:

'The moon is doing great things.'

It was high in the sky. Beneath it a track of silver traversed fluorescent acres of water, a glittering highway to legendary islands. If Tir-na-nOgue existed, it surely led to it. Brian joined him at the window to appraise it in silence.

'A bit theatrical,' he decided at last. Tim drew the curtains.

But they were inadequate. A shaft of moonlight slipped through the chink between them and divided the darkness with its narrow and wavering ribbon. Tim lay for a long time watching it. He was neither awake nor asleep. Drowsy sensations and half-formed images troubled him: Brian's mother kneeling in grief's abandonment; Christ's Presence brooding among crowding stars; the crack of an airgun and clank of a can; the salt and afterglow of laving waters; Anne and the throbbing moistness when he drew down her panties, sweet odours of sin. Sensations too of persistent sway and sweep, the pearshaped earth measuring its pace to rhythms predominantly lunar but also solar and sidereal. Time and the Spirit searching and stumbling.

A week later Cunningham returned as promised. Bad weather had kept them indoors the previous evening and a thunderstorm woke both of them in the early hours of Sunday morning. They were lying late and he had to rouse them.

'I'd a rough time getting here,' he told them. 'Lots of the streets are flooded.'

His cycling cape, which was leaving pools of water on the floor, corroborated.

'You chaps probably don't know it yet but the whole city is in a frenzy.' He looked from one sleepy-eyed face to another. 'A few hours ago Britain and France declared war on Germany.'

Late in October they boarded up the windows of the hut and prepared it to weather the winter. The grey light in the sky made the sea look like gruel but the day was mild and the air thick with odours of salt and decaying seaweed. The lanes, in their rich autumn colours, offered rosehips and blackberries. There was nobody else about. All was silent. Lanes and fields had resigned themselves to their season of desertion.

III

It was late evening when Brian telephoned. Almost time to lock the desk and sign the clock. He sounded odd.

'Has Cunningham spoken to you?'

'Cunningham – what about?'

'Obviously he hasn't. Can you drop by on your way home?'

'Not this evening. I've things to do.'

'Later on, then. About nine.'

'Where?'

'Call into the bar.'

'You know I don't like going into the bar when your old man is there.'

'He won't be. He'll be off at the dogs. That's why I can't get out to you.'

'All right. About nine.'

Wondering what could be so urgent, he replaced the telephone.

November fog drifting along the river stung his eyes as he cycled towards his aunt's house. In Thorncastle Street coke fumes from the gas works made the air more acrid still. The streets were bleak and damp. Tramlines and greasy cobbles were a hazard which kept his mind on the road.

He had tea with Aunt Kate and then helped her to paint the hall and the kitchen in preparation for Christmas, a task they had shared over a couple of weeks. Her talk was sad. His grandfather, she remarked, would be two years dead in a few days' time. November, the month of the Holy Souls, had brought it freshly to her mind. Everyone had to go to purgatory, she believed, even saints and little children, though it might only be to pass through it on their journey to heaven.

'Who told you that?' he asked.

She had been taught so in school.

'I'm surprised you should ask,' she remarked, as though it were defined dogma. Probably, he thought, it had been the private conclusion of some cracked and elderly nun, turned by prolonged and excessive piety into God's little hatchet woman. Piety, unlike holiness, could end up bloodthirsty. But he said nothing.

'I've masses arranged for the anniversary,' Aunt Kate told him. 'One for my father and one for the most forsaken poor soul in purgatory. Not that your grandad would have much need. He was the kindest man I've ever known.'

The thought made her brighten up.

'I had a very funny letter from your Uncle Hugh about the goings-on in the barracks. Imagine being called back to the army and him almost fifty.'

'I had a letter from him too,' Tim said. 'He sent me a quid. It seemed rather a lot.'

Aunt Kate, now worldly-wise, dismissed such misgivings. 'Take all you can get, son. Like myself, you badly need it.'

Then she talked of the war and wondered if neutrality had any hope of lasting. Uncle Hugh, she knew, had serious doubts about it.

At half past eight he decided he had to go. 'I'll be down again tomorrow,' he promised.

'Neither of us is much of a hand at it,' she said, looking at their handiwork. 'But tomorrow should finish it.'

She stood at the door to see him off, her back to the empty hall and silent house. Once it had been busy with daily comings and goings. Now her father and mother were both dead, her sister married, Uncle Hugh away except for occasional weekends. There were no more young men calling in the evenings, no more gossiping over tea, no more card playing at a halfpenny a and, no more musical evenings on Sundays where 'Ramona' and 'Lay My Head Beneath A Rose' brushed shoulders with Tom Moore:

> Oft in the stilly night
> Ere slumber's chain hath bound me
> Fond memory brings the light
> Of other days around me.

So with Aunt Kate. It occurred to him that it was not the

approach of Christmas that had set her painting the house. It was a means to having company by seeking his help. He resolved to drop down more often.

A bottle of Cairne's ale filled in the time while he waited for Brian to be free. At the bar two bus conductors, familiar figures in spite of his own infrequent visits, were engaged in a conversation that had been going on for some years and seemed likely to continue for several more. The warmth was welcome after the damp and fog of the streets. A notice on the wall above the conductors' heads announced that the Ireland's Own Football and Hurling Club were making an all-out drive to collect funds for a set of togs and a new pavilion. Tickets were threepence each: first prize one bottle of stout a day for a year. Large print along the bottom drove the message home:

> Do you want –
> 365 bottles of stout for 3d?
> Buy your ticket now.

While he was trying to reckon how much it would mean in cash Brian beckoned him into the snug.

'I wanted to talk to you about Cunningham,' he said in a low voice. 'He's in trouble.'

'Trouble. What kind of trouble?'

'Deep trouble. Gwen thinks there's a baby on the way.'

It took a while to make sense of it.

'A baby. You mean she's pregnant?'

'That's what I said. Pregnant. Expecting. Up the pole. Call it what you like.'

'But are they sure?'

'She hasn't been to a doctor, if that's what you mean. But she's overdue, in spite of gin and hot baths and all the other indispensables of the emancipated life.'

It couldn't be. Not because it was by any means impossible, but simply because it was unthinkable.

'But I've been seeing him about twice a week at rehearsals for "The Yeoman" and he said nothing about it.'

'He wasn't sure, I suppose.'

'Is he sure now?'

'Ninety-nine per cent.'

'What can be done?'

'The first thing is to find a doctor. Not just any doctor; one who'll do an examination without too many personal questions. I don't know of any offhand and I doubt you do either, but we can enquire. Equally important is to have the money to pay him. Again, I don't know what such things cost so we'll have to find out. Do you think any of the crowd in your office could help – Ellis, for instance?'

'I could ask.'

'I've been going over the customers here but they're mostly married and middle-aged – not a very likely bunch. One or two just might have some information but I don't think I'd trust them.'

'I don't mind trying Ellis,' Tim said quietly.

'The thing is – would he blab?'

'No. Ellis is all right.'

The situation sunk in deeper. 'Poor old Cunningham. What a mess. Poor Gwen too.'

Brian was sceptical.

'It wouldn't occur to you, of course – it mightn't even occur to Cunningham – but I've been wondering on and off about Gwen and her baby. Can we be sure about it being Cunningham's?'

Ellis, sympathetic and more knowledgeable, came along to meet them. He dismissed the idea of approaching any of the pub's customers.

'If they know anyone at all,' he decided, 'it'll be some scruffy operator in some two-pair back who sets to work with a knitting needle. If he doesn't kill the woman in the process he'll try to blackmail the man. What about the usual home remedies?'

'They've all been tried,' Brian said, 'but it's no go.'

'I needn't have asked. In the job we run a kind of first-aid service, a sort of sinners' co-operative. They use douches, syringes, the lot. I think the list even includes horse-riding and cycling up steep hills. I've never seen any of it work.'

'Cunningham was wondering if there was a doctor of the right kind.'

'At one time there were quite a few – all you needed was the money. Then for a while there were too many and it became a racket so the authorities clamped down. The usual charge was about a hundred pounds. Has our friend any hope of that kind of money?'

'Hardly,' Brian said. 'Still, if we had a contact – who knows?'

'You realize it's risky – a criminal matter?'

They did.

Ellis thought it over for some time.

'May I mention this to someone else?'

'If you can trust him.'

'I can. He mightn't want to be involved, though.'

He hesitated yet again.

'Cunningham. I met him, didn't I? The well-dressed chap who sings?'

'That's him.'

'Right.' Ellis decided at last. 'I'll let you know the outcome.'

When he had gone Brian turned to Tim.

'You kept very silent, McDonagh. Why?'

'The ramifications,' Tim said, 'among other things.'

Conscience, the predictable meddler, was demanding its say.

When they met again Cunningham was present. Ellis gave him a note with a name and address on it.

'You make an appointment for an examination, nothing more,' he told Cunningham. 'Then you go along with the girl and you discuss the situation. After that it's up to the three of you. You understand – yourself, the girl, your man.'

'That's clear,' Cunningham agreed. 'I'm obliged.'

'I hope it works out,' Ellis said.

A week later Cunningham brought them up to date.

'He's willing to carry out an examination for the usual fee. If there's a job to be done we go over to some contact in London and we bring a hundred and twenty quid in cash with us. But in that case the fee for the examination plus extra attention is thirty quid.'

'Sweet Christ,' Brian said.

'So there isn't much hope, is there? Where would Gwen or I get that kind of money?'

Their gloomy silence answered him.

The gloom remained during the ensuing days; on Cunningham who found it harder than ever to address his mind to the demand of gentlemen's outfitting; on Brian endlessly ransacking his mind for a possible solution; on Tim cycling through streets that seemed themselves to be infected with uncertainty and apprehension. Vows of love, declarations of war, devastation awaiting its hour, compassion brooding on the plight of the most forsaken soul in purgatory – among such incompatibilities his thought groped and sought to rationalize.

The chessboard had made its seasonal migration from window to fireside and the hospitable whiskey bottle its golden gleam to the flames. Cornelius, who had a personal interest in the immediate future, approached it deviously.

'What are the hopes for the poor Finns? Do you foresee any chance for them at all?'

'What small country could hope to ward off the Russian Bear,' O'Sheehan answered.

'Unless Britain can help them.'

'At the moment it's doubtful if she can help herself.'

'Then what are the Germans up to? Both sides just squat on their arses looking at one another. Are they serious about the war at all?'

'In winter a wise general likes to sit still.'

'I'm glad you think so,' Cornelius admitted. 'I was greatly afraid Red Russia's attack on Finland would shake things up. That wouldn't suit at all. I have Bruree Bookall at the top of his form and on Saturday next I intend to plunge on him. I don't want black-outs and that class of nonsense interfering with the meeting. You might care to have a little stake yourself?'

O'Sheehan fished out pencil and paper,

'How was that you spell it?'

'B-R-U-R-E-E B-O-O-K-A-L-L.'

'Bookall?' O'Sheehan repeated, greatly puzzled.

'It should be B-U-A-C-H-A-I-L-L of course.'

'Ah, Buachaill – a boy. Masculine noun of the third declension. Why do you mistreat our Gaelic tongue?'

'Our Dublin bookies are no great scholars. It's better to make sure they know how to pronounce it.'

O'Sheehan wrote with reluctance and examined the result with distaste.

'However necessary it may be, the result is barbarous.'

'Never mind the barbarosity,' Cornelius answered, 'but have a flutter on the dog himself. I've been coaxing him like a devoted mother this while back and although he'll start off in the books at four or maybe five to one get in early because he's going to romp home. I intend to clean up.'

There was a knock on the door and Brian entered. Cornelius frowned.

'Andrew O'Boyle is below. You asked me to tell you if he came.'

'So I did,' Cornelius rose. 'This won't take a minute but it's important.'

He left them together. Politeness required a little conversation.

'Andrew O'Boyle,' O'Sheehan questioned. 'Isn't he on the committee of the Cumann?'

'The treasurer,' Brian said.

'An important office. High policy is at issue, no doubt.'

'High or low is all the same to my father. He has politics on the brain.'

'Your father is a dedicated party man,' O'Sheehan conceded, 'but he has other, less weighty interests. His dog racing, for instance. We've just been discussing it. No doubt you take a filial interest?'

'I prefer the horses. You get a longer race for your money and the odds are usually better.'

'Your father expects four or five to one. That seems reasonably good to me.'

'I'd wonder where he expects to get that,' Brian remarked.

'At next Saturday's meeting,' O'Sheehan answered, rooting for the piece of paper and consulting it. 'Yes – Bruree Bookall. A certainty, he assures me.'

'A certainty. Is there such a thing?'

'You're a sceptical young man.'

'I'm afraid I am. But please don't let me put you off.'

'If I did,' O'Sheehan agreed, 'the animal would certainly win. It's one of the laws of Fate, isn't it? No. I'll have my flutter.'

'Perhaps you'll be lucky,' Brian said.

He returned to the bar where his father was deep in conversation with O'Boyle. The clock promised closing time in less than an hour. While he served his customers his mind returned persistently to O'Sheehan's conversation. By closing time he had decided to contact Tim and Cunningham.

The paraffin lamp spread its miserly light about the backyard hideout and the oil stove battled unsuccessfully with the cold. They crouched about it while Brian outlined his plan. He intended to withhold fifty pounds from the week's takings when he was lodging the money on the following Friday. If the dog lost he would be in trouble but there would at least be a few days' grace before his father got to know. If it won, the money could be replaced and there would be nothing to worry about. The surplus should be enough to take Gwen and Cunningham to London. If in fact London was really the place in question. He suspected, he said, that it would turn out to be somewhere in Dublin, with the talk of London being used only as a cover-up.

'Suppose the dog loses,' Cunningham said. 'Think of the fix you'll find yourself in. I can't let you risk that.'

'If it loses I'll think of something – either that the bank made a mistake or that the money just disappeared on my way there – after all things like that do happen. Anyway I'm reasonably sure about the dog's chances. If the old man's going to plunge he's been up to some doggyman's trickery. Probably he's been stuffing it to slow it down over its past outings. By now it'll rank as an outsider and he knows if he leaves it alone this time out it should do better than anything else in the race. So he wipes everyone's eye at long odds and then comes home to lecture me about going to mass.'

'It may be sharp,' Tim commented, 'but it's kids' stuff compared with certain gentlemanly racketeers in the medical profession.'

'Young Lochinvar is beginning to learn,' Brian remarked to Cunningham.

'We're all beginning to learn.'

'Cheer up,' Brian told him. 'I'll have the fifty quid by Friday evening. Someone else will have to handle the bet, though. It wouldn't do to risk the old man spotting me or even to see either of you two. Any suggestions?'

'Ellis might help again,' Tim suggested.

'Will you ask him?'

Tim said he would.

'That's settled, then. Anything else?'

They thought it over but nothing suggested itself.

Cunningham remained glum. 'Win or lose, I'm eternally grateful.'

'We'll win,' Brian said, 'the gods will it.'

Brian got the money to Tim on Friday evening. Tim in turn passed it to Ellis, who removed the wad of dog-eared notes from their envelope with reverence.

'Fifty pounds. How many months' work at your salary?'

'Nearly six,' Tim calculated.

'It makes you think, doesn't it?'

It did, but not wholly in Ellis's terms. Strictly speaking, it had been stolen. To accomplish what? He avoided formulating an answer. There would be time for that if and when Cunningham and Gwen got clear of their trouble. Ellis as reverently replaced the notes, sealed the envelope and raised it to his lips.

'God send you back to us,' he prayed.

God might. God might not. His ways were peculiar. Having created a being, was He willing to allow the outcome to be determined by the performance of a greyhound? It would seem so. His will appeared to encompass its own negative. Had He

willed that this all-powerful will could be all-powerfully un-
willed? Was there, in fact, such a thing as Chance? If there was,
then it was uncontrolled by God and therefore more powerful
than the All-Powerful.

'I'll see you in Flahertys as arranged,' Ellis promised.

'It's good of you to help.'

'Young men will do it, if they come to it,' Ellis said. 'We
are flesh and blood.'

Waiting in Flahertys for news was hardly bearable, though
better, they agreed, than each on his own. They sat in the
upstairs lounge where the uncurtained window kept them in
touch with the street below, or what could be seen of it by the
light spilling out of shopfronts and the windows of passing
trams. Driven by a light breeze, raindrops flecked the glass and
depressed Cunningham.

'I wonder will it affect the racing,' he said.

'The rain? Hardly. It's only a sprinkle.'

'Doesn't it make them skid?'

'Only when the dogs are using their cars,' Brian said. 'Tonight
they're racing on foot. Take your drink and forget it for a while.'

'Easier said than done.'

'What time should Ellis arrive?' Tim asked.

'Anytime after a quarter to nine.'

They all looked around at the clock.

'Christ. Nearly an hour,' Cunningham lamented. Brian
frowned at him.

'You're undermining the morale,' he warned, 'and that's no
good for any of us. I've fifty quid of the old man's cash sweating
on the nose of Bruree Bookall and I don't want my mind
riveted on that painful fact every thirty seconds.'

'Sorry. I have the jim-jams.'

'And you're giving them to me.'

Tim attempted a diversion.

'It's a peculiar name for a dog.'

'Bruree Bookall? It's the old man's tribute to de Valera –
Bruree Boy. Dev grew up in Bruree.'

'I always thought he was born in Spain,' Cunningham said.

'No. In America. But he was sent to live with his grandmother in Bruree when he was a small kid. The old man says he was known locally as Eddie Coll.'

'He escaped execution in 1916,' Tim remarked, 'by claiming his American citizenship.'

'Bloody cuteness,' Brian decided.

'Fair play,' Cunningham said. 'If somebody was going to execute me I'd claim to be the only surviving descendant of Oliver Cromwell if it'd do any good. Or an illegitimate son of Jack the Ripper.' He reviewed what he had said. 'That wasn't a very happy remark.'

'Not at the present state of the play,' Brian agreed, 'but please go on.'

Cunningham stood up, emptied his almost full glass in one long, deliberate swig and said:

'We'll have another.'

'Keep that up,' Brian warned, 'and you'll be on your ear when Ellis comes.'

'Or on my arse. What is it to be?'

Tim asked for a Cairne's ale.

'That's right. Help him on his way.'

'Oh, for Christ's sake be human,' Tim said, goaded by the tone.

By the time fresh drinks were before them the gloom had settled again. Brian addressed himself to Cunningham solely.

'If I may ask you a personal question without McDonagh here biting the snot off me – '

'Ask away. I'm beyond caring.'

'Were you and Gwen – or are you, or do you think you're, in love?'

'Love is a difficult word. I don't think we ever talked about it. We got on well together. Too bloody well you'll say in the light of tonight's carry on. No, I don't think we were in love.'

'She went out with other chaps, didn't she?'

'Quite openly. Neither of us minded about that.'

'Has it ever occurred to you – about her pregnancy – if that's how it is – '

'You mean that it's not mine. Yes, it has. At the beginning it could have been. But more recently one of our travellers smuggled in a package of FL's for me and I've been using them. Of course I know they're not always a hundred per cent foolproof.'

'Have you talked to her about it?'

'Not really.'

'Don't you think you're being a bit noble?'

'We mayn't be in love – whatever that's supposed to mean – but I'm very fond of her. I think I should stand by her.'

'Up to a point certainly. But there's a sensible limit.'

'Are you trying to change my mind?'

'If I wanted to do that I wouldn't be sitting here, would I?'

'Isn't that the answer?' Cunningham said. 'We stand by one another.'

'But you're wide awake to the possibilities. That's all I wanted to be sure of.'

Not for the first time Tim wondered at the unpredictable, almost clinical mixture of shrewdness and concern. Cunningham too was a puzzle; in one matter unscrupulous, in another honourable in a way that was almost too simple and unquestioning.

The glasses were almost empty. He stood up to offer his round.

'The same again?'

The crowd at the counter had grown. He elbowed his way through and waited his turn. Again the thought of what the three of them were actually engaged in seeped up from the recesses of his mind and began its demands for attention and clarification. He pushed it away. It was at once too late and too early for that. The only present recourse was to close the ears and eyes to considerations which seemed to trouble the others not at all. Yet the nagging refused to be entirely stilled. It preoccupied him and made him sweat. The smell of cigarette smoke and the buzz of conversation seemed to belong to some separate world. The barman, coming at last to give him attention, was not wholly real, his own voice not really his.

'I'll have them sent over,' the barman said. He turned and his heart almost stopped. Ellis was at the table. They were waving to him, excited, urgent. He went quickly across.

'The dog won,' Cunningham said.

'Keep it quiet,' Brian warned. He stood up. 'We'll talk about it outside.'

'But I've just ordered drinks.'

'No panic,' Ellis advised. 'Just all sit down and we'll talk quietly.'

'All right,' Brian agreed. 'But let it be quietly.'

They waited until all had been served. Then Ellis slipped the roll of money to Brian.

'I got fours,' he said. 'There's just under two hundred and fifty there. You can count it.'

'Sweet immemorial Jesus,' Cunningham said. 'I just can't believe it.'

'No need to count it,' Brian said, 'but we'll peel off a fiver to share with thirsty friends. You're a bloody brick.'

'I got on early,' Ellis said. 'The price took a sudden tumble, I can tell you.'

'Down to what?'

'Down to even money.'

Brian shrugged.

'I'm sorry for the old man, but at least he got evens.'

He turned to Cunningham.

'You'd better get moving as fast as possible.,

'Right away. I'll get Gwen to our medical Al Capone to-morrow. I've then got to think of some way of skipping work for a day or so.'

'Can't you travel on a weekend?'

'A weekend mightn't be long enough. We'll see.'

They drank their way through Ellis's account of the race. It was hard to believe it had come off. It was more difficult still to accept the sudden acquisition of so much hard cash. Even Brian felt unconsciously at his pocket from time to time to check that the wad of notes was actually there.

Cornelius said nothing either to wife or family. It was not his habit to share the ups and downs of his greyhound breeding with them, still less to feed them with information which might leak out subsequently and be seized on by other wily and wide-awake punters. But for some days he went about his business with a face like a thundercloud. To O'Sheehan alone he bared his soul.

'You only got evens too.'

'My own fault for leaving it too late. I could have had fours.'

'I found this much out. Some cute whore plunged fifty quid, that's what caused the tumble.'

'Perhaps he had a pre-vision,' O'Sheehan suggested. 'Some have the gift of sensibility and discern vibrations of coming failures and successes. Cathbad the Druid, for example – '

'He had information, that's what he had. But how the hell did he get it?'

'Or Fedelma of Croghan – '

'On the animal's previous showing he didn't stand an earthly.'

'One thinks of Morann of Usna.'

'He'd be out of his mind to lay fifty pence, never mind fifty quid.'

O'Sheehan sighed.

'There is the possibility of genuine error,' he said. 'It's such a large sum it looks as though he meant to back on shorter odds but in the fuss of the moment confused the two names.'

'Highly unlikely and fifty smackers at risk.'

'What was the favourite's name? It escapes myself.'

'Every detail is engraved in my brain,' Cornelius answered. 'Brooklyn Baby.'

The name hung in the air. Cornelius stared hard at it until he believed he could see it.

'There's the breath of a chance,' he said eventually, 'that you've stumbled on something.'

'They are not dissimilar.'

'You think they could be mixed up?'

'I believe so. Over-anxiety or a drink or two too many might help to tip the scales.'

'Brooklyn Baby. Bruree Bookall. You could be right,'

Cornelius conceded. 'I hope to God you are. I was beginning to wonder if I'm starting to talk in my sleep.

Dear Des

You'll be surprised to get this so soon after my last but I've been thinking more clearly in the few days between and really I don't know what I was going on all depressed about. I'm sure I depressed you too and I'm sorry. I felt sad about everything even though everything went so smoothly and the worry was all over. I even feel sad now for all sorts of reasons but it will pass the way everything does. You were a brick to come over with me and I'll never forget that to you. For a start I'd never have found my way about on my own. I still take hours to work out how I'm to get from point A to point B but at least I've done it successfully a few times which is a real step forward.

What I am really writing for is to say that I'm going to stay on here. There's absolutely no bother getting a job and although this may make you think I'm not quite right in the upper storey (maybe I'm not, either) I find London a cheerful place. The talk we always heard about English people being unfriendly and stuck-up is nonsense. Everyone talks to everyone else at the slightest excuse.

As for Dublin who'd want to go back there. O yes the people are nice enough I mean one's friends are and O yes there's the mountains and the sea you talked to me about that once I remember and I agree but it's so bloody dreary and dull and rosarys with every meal and priests going on about C-H-A-S-T-I-T-Y and not keeping company with bad companions and did he touch you intimately and where and how many times. The old ones you can take it from but there's something morbid about those young fellows and tell me why do they smell faintly of something is it lace and silk vestments or starched collars a sort of haberdashery smell? No Des not for me. Here they're even looking for women to drive lorries and nobody cares much what you do certainly everybody doesn't think its her business like they do in Dublin.

So I'm off job hunting any day now. The money you left with me is plenty and I didn't say a sufficient thank you for that either, but of course it wouldn't last for ever. Thank Brian for me as well.

You know I didn't really like him at all and I thought he was a contemptuous would-be intellectual which in a way I suppose he is but he turned up trumps for both of us just the same. I remember being angry when you told me you'd told him. It shows the state of mind I was in. You had to tell someone I can see that quite clearly now.

Well Des we've weathered the storm and I for one am off for a new life here even if Hitler does start eventually to drop his bombs on us. People are saying there'll be rationing in the New Year. When I was coming back here to write this workmen were taking a public statue away, I suppose for safe keeping. Who he was or where it was I have no idea but there were notices everywhere saying – always carry your gas mask. I knew the kind of twist you'd give to that if you were with me and I laughed to myself. It makes me laugh now too.

Dear Des I'll miss funny things like that which you would say if you were around. Say a prayer for me. You might think that contradicts a lot of things I said earlier but it doesn't really.

Yours dearly
Gwen

IV

Rain lashing the city from early morning cleared the streets of cyclists and Christmas shoppers. A pre-dawn gloom loitered in the sky and refused to be budged. Tim, rubbing a clear patch in the fog that clouded the tram window to keep in touch with where he might be saw it louring over the drenched statues in St Stephen's Green. Brian read for hours in an empty bar. Cunningham, the morning dragging interminably, sorted and stacked anything that offered. He telephoned Brian about the letter. He also offered to return a five-pound note he had been holding in reserve in case Gwen ran into financial trouble. It was now unlikely to be needed.

'We should all have a bash,' Brian suggested. 'Phone Tim and we'll blow it.'

'I'm on.'

'Ask Ellis too. We ought to stand him a night out.'

'When?'

'Tonight if we can.'

'But the weather is foul.'

'I know the weather's foul. All the more reason for a bash.'

Their meeting in Nearys at half past eight was ceremonious, a victory celebration. Cunningham solemnly handed over the fiver. Brian waved them elaborately to chairs. He ordered drinks. When they came with his change he distributed one pound note to each. Only Ellis hesitated and expressed embarrassment. His protests were pushed aside. Had he not placed the bets and collected the money, a man's part in their concerted effort? Tim's support was canvassed.

'A maxim, McDonagh.'

'To every cow its calf,' Tim suggested.

Brian beamed at Ellis.

'Our Tim,' he explained proudly, 'spoken of even in boyhood as The Sage of Synge Street.'

He raised his glass and proposed the health of their esteemed guest and companion. Ellis, owning that he was now wholly reassured, thanked them simply but promised to reply formally when he bought the next round. He did so. Cunningham in his turn insisted on calling for five hot whiskies and expressed his appreciation and best thanks to all there assembled. Tim called his round in due course and offered, in view of the fact that the previous speakers had said all there was to be said in the way of mutual congratulation and esteem, to sing a song. The offer (as he had rightly anticipated it would be) was declined regretfully on the grounds that the management barred singing on the premises and it would be unfortunate to find themselves so early in the proceedings and on such a filthy night, flung out. Perhaps later, in some less orderly house, when they were more fully fortified with the right stuff.

'I feel great,' Cunningham told them. They were all feeling great. The shadow that had been hanging over them had lifted. Christmas was around the corner, a time of licence and an excuse to live beyond their means without attendant guilty anxieties. Along the counter gas lights enclosed in their round, white-frosted globes glowed elegantly on brass fittings and the busy handles of the pumps. Tiny, blue-flamed bunsens kept the water bubbling for the punch. Lemons and cloves in packets were in readiness nearby. From the street for the first time since their arrival, the voices of carol singers drifted faintly. The rain, they realized, must have stopped at last.

'How about moving on?' Cunningham suggested.

'Where to?'

They thought they'd try the Crystal.

In Chatham Street sawdust clotted in the channels and turkeys hanging from skewers filled the shop windows. Smells of fish and poultry and smoked ham clung as always in the air. The carol singers invited them in uncertain stanzas of church Latin to come and adore.

'*Venite, venite,*' they urged again and again, '*in Bethlehem.*'

Brian, the first to change his mind about going so far as the Crystal suggested an alternative.

'*Neque in Bethlehem neque in Crystalo bibemus, fratres, sed in capite stagii.*'

'Amen.'

'What's all that?' Cunningham asked.

'He wants to go to the Stag's Head instead of the Crystal.'

'All I could ever remember of Latin,' Cunningham recollected, 'was that Julius Caesar had a calico belly.'

Over drinks in the Stag's Head Brian returned to the matter of the carol singers.

'If they must fling pious exhortations at us they might at least equip themselves to do so in two or more parts harmony.'

'Part singing was never in our tradition,' Ellis said. 'The best we can manage in that line is a drone.'

'Yet we're a highly musical nation,' Cunningham said, 'or so I was always taught to believe.'

'A large part of what we were taught was bloody lies,' Brian said, 'and that's the hairiest of them.'

'We have a folk culture in music,' Tim suggested, 'not a classical one. Given our history, how could we?'

'What has history to do with it?'

'It cut us off from the development that went on in Europe, I suppose,' Ellis supposed.

'The Normans brought their court poetry with them and we copied it. Surely they brought some kind of polyphonic music too. If they didn't – the English would have.'

'As I understand it,' Cunningham said, 'we were seriously engaged beating the bejaysus out of each other by then, not swapping serenades.'

'We were sitting on our backsides, satisfied as always that the way Finn MacCool did it was the only way and the best way and anything new or different was no concern of ours,' Brian concluded. 'And inferior, anyway.'

'I've forgotten what started all this.'

'The carol singers,' Tim told Cunningham.

'O yes. *Venite, venite.*'

Ellis excused himself as he got up. Cunningham rose with him to protest.

'Wait now – it's my turn.'

'*Non in locum bibendi eo,*' Ellis explained, '*sed ad lavatorium hominis.*'

Cunningham, much to his own surprise, rose to the occasion. '*Ite. Et pater omnipotens tecum.*'

On his return, having placed his order and still awed by his achievement, he said, 'It must have been the whiskey.'

The carol singers were at it again, a different group with a more extensive repertoire, their voices drifting in faintly over the hubbub of the now smoky and busy bar, their collection boxes jingling from time to time as footsteps sounded on the pavement and receded. A group at a table nearby who were tending from time to time to drift into song also were being quelled at ever-decreasing intervals by the management.

'You have a low opinion of our fellow countrymen,' Ellis said to Brian, 'and I agree up to a point. But I would imagine Tim is right and that history has something to answer for.'

'All right. History has. So too have obscurantism, pietism, moral cowardice and a nationalism gone demented. I suppose we are not entirely to blame. We are turned out to face the world with very little. A little Irish, a smattering of latin, a nodding acquaintance with Shakespeare and hardly any litera-ture after Keats and Shelley and the poets of *The Nation*. Nothing in the public libraries that mightn't be read to a Reverend Mother on her deathbed. That's the extent of our armoury. And you can't blame that on the Saxon.'

'Yet in the townland I come from. . . .'

'Where is that?'

'A small cluster of houses lost in the rocklands of Clare.'

'How long are you in Dublin?'

'It must be five or six years. I came here to work with about three quid in my pocket, to tide me over until I got settled in. I was being paid a pound a week in the Metropolitan and so ingenuous that it was a few weeks before I really understood that I wasn't going to be able to keep on meeting the twenty-five bob I needed to pay for my digs and my keep. When the truth dawned on me I moved in with the older sister who works in the civil service, though neither of us fancied the arrangement much. We thought the neighbours suspected we were living in sin.'

'And about your homeplace in Clare?'

'It's cut off from everything and yet comes up with surprises. I don't mean it's claim to a number of bishops in America, which is understandable enough. I'm thinking of an aunt of mine who became a governess with some branch of the royal family; a neighbour whose brother is president of a firm of famous French distillers; and a lad I played with as a child who was back from teaching in Spain last time I was home and who knew Lorca and could quote his poems.'

'Does that prove anything of importance?'

'Only that regardless of what's doled out to us some of us make our way.'

'When we emigrate,' Brian said. 'When we break clear of the native straitjacket. Not all of us can do that. Besides, in

Clare you're almost the next parish to New York. You hob-nobbed with the Spanish armada. You got away with the wild geese to France and the Napoleonic wars. You were probably talking European politics when the rest of the country was grovelling about in the usual fog of petty nationalism.'

'We elected O'Connell.'

'Precisely. And the nationalists have been deploring it ever since.'

'There was a song we used to have as kids,' Cunningham remembered. 'And it had a couple of lines that went:

> "To hell with the Queen and her oul ghibileen
> And hurrah for Dan O'Connell".

What does *ghibileen* mean?'

No one knew.

'Of course it might have been *gibereen,*' Cunningham amended. 'You never really know with kids' songs.'

Tim had a thought.

'It may be a corruption of jubilee. Queen Victoria's Diamond Jubilee, I think, was just before the Boer War.'

To their surprise, the barman began to call closing time. Ellis, a veteran, rose like a shot and disappeared among the scrum of drinkers about the bar. But he returned empty-handed some minutes later.

'It's no go. They've stopped serving.'

'But they only started shouting a moment ago.'

'That's always the way coming up to Christmas,' Ellis said. 'They get too much custom and can't cope.'

'What about your hide-out?' Cunningham asked Brian.

'There's nothing laid in, but we could sneak something down from the bar, I suppose.'

'Why not do the bona fide?' Ellis suggested. 'If we leave immediately we'll get ahead of the rush.'

The bus took them clear of streets and shops past remote suburbs and darkened houses in which people of temperate habit were already respectably asleep, and deposited them near winding lanes under a now clear and incredibly star-crammed sky. Thin ice covered the wayside puddles. The air was sharp and smelled of winter fields. They groped after Ellis into almost total darkness.

'I've gone blind,' Cunningham announced.

'Just ahead,' Ellis encouraged.

A trickle of light from a window and again from under a door raised their hearts. They knocked.

'Who's there?'

'Travellers,' Ellis said.

The door was unbolted for them.

'From where?'

'All from Fairview,' Ellis said. They were scrutinized briefly, admitted, and duly provided for.

'Why Fairview, for God's sake?' Cunningham whispered.

'It's on the other side of the city. To be legally a bona fide traveller you have to have slept the previous night more than three miles away. Or maybe it's five miles. Kevin O'Higgins initiated it, I think.'

'His Intoxicating Liquor Act of 1927. The old man keeps it and its amendments at his bedside with his missal and his rosary beads. It kills him to have to put up the shutters at ten while pubs like this can stay open until twelve. Are we, in fact, legally bona fide here?'

'I don't know. It's always safer to have a false name and address ready. Stick to the Fairview area though. Well, *slainte*.'

'*Slainte 'gus saoghal*.'

Small groups knocked and were admitted from time to time. As the place filled up Tim looked more closely about him. They were at the foot of the Dublin mountains, he knew, somewhere near Tallaght, in what could have been a country kitchen. Oil lamps hung from the walls and stood on the rough counter. The fire blazing in its wide grate had turned the surrounding whitewash yellow and brown. Blackened pictures above it portrayed subjects that were no longer discernible. The owner, bringing a tray with their next round, withheld it for a moment to interrogate them. He was a small, worried-looking man.

'All over eighteen?' he asked. He seemed to have singled out Tim. They looked at each other in surprise.

'I have to ask that. There was a sermon in the church this week against under-age drinking and the guards around here like to be seen to do their duty.'

They assured him that all was within the law.

'Good, good. That puts me in the clear. The question was asked.'

When he had gone Brian said to Ellis, 'You see what I mean?' Ellis took it easily.

'The law is the law, I suppose.'

'And the parish priest is the Pope, as well as being both the temporal power and the chief superintendent of the police.' Brian turned to Tim. 'He was looking very hard at McDonagh here, I thought.'

'He was,' Tim admitted. 'Next time I'll bring along the birth certificate.'

He resented the interrogation. The rest did too. It questioned their adulthood.

'I told you Gwen finds London a cheerful place,' Cunningham said. 'The funny thing is I did too. Everyone is beavering around digging everything up and putting sandbags and things in one another's way. I mean, things were going on.'

'Would you think of going over?'

'I might. There's plenty of work. I might even join up.'

'If you do,' Tim said, 'I bet you won't be asked whether you're eighteen or not.'

'No. If I knew where he lives, I'd go and piss at that parish priest's gate.'

Ellis, secure in his seniority, smiled and ruminated on the subject.

'Dublin sadly misses its Red Lamp quarter. It used to be concentrated around Mecklenburg Street but the clergy and the Legion of Mary succeeded in killing it off when the British left. Have you heard about it? It was known as Meck Town in Gogarty's time. When he found it reduced in the end to one derelict hotel he wrote a lament:

> 'Where are the great Kip Bullies gone
> The bookies and outrageous whores
> Whom we so gaily rode upon
> When youth was mine and youth was yours:
> Tyrone Street of the crowded doors
> And Faithful Place, so infidel?
> It matters little who explores
> He'll only find the Hay Hotel.'

'My grandfather, I now remember,' Cunningham said, 'always maintained that things were never the same after the British left. I'm beginning to understand what he meant.'

With their wholehearted approval, Ellis continued:

> 'There's nothing left but ruin now
> Where once the crazy cabfuls roared,
> Where new-come sailors turned the prow
> And love-logged cattle-dealers snored.
> The room where old Luke Irwin whored,
> The stairs on which John Elwood fell:
> Some things are better unencored
> There's only left the Hay Hotel.'

At a nearby table someone, encouraged by his assembled companions, was about to succumb to song, though discreetly, to avoid possible reprimand. Only the opening line was clearly intelligible:

> 'In an ancient Irish Chapel, St Patrick took his stand. . . .'

Brian winced and appealed to Ellis:
'More Gogarty, for God's sake.' Ellis again obliged:

> 'Fresh Nellie's gone and Mrs Mack
> May Oblong's gone and Number Five
> Where you could get so good a back
> And drinks were so superlative;
> Of all their nights, O man alive
> There is not left an oyster shell:
> Where greens are gone the greys will thrive;
> There's only left the Hay Hotel.'

Ellis, finishing, discovered his glass gone low.

'We have time for another?'

'How do we get home?' Tim asked.

'By phoning a taxi – no bother.'

'Then I'll do the honours.'

'You're out of order.'

'I've come to my drinking majority, a comparatively recent dignity. Let me have the pleasure of exercising a lawful right.'

Tim went to the counter and ordered. No comment good, bad or indifferent issued from Authority. It had said its say. When the drinks came Brian raised his glass.

'The Hay Hotel.'

They toasted it. No one was sober, though no one was drunk.

During his wait at the counter Tim had been thinking.

'I've been working out the seven stages of the life of the Irish male, chronologically and in order,' he said. 'At zero we are born. At seven we are responsible for our trespasses and must give an account of our sins, confessing to the priest and receiving the Eucharist worthily within the appointed times – Ash Wednesday to Trinity Sunday. At twelve we are confirmed and the Bishop strikes us on the cheek to indicate that if called upon we must willingly bear stripes for Jesus Christ's sake. At sixteen we are free validly to contract marriage, though the privilege for obvious reasons remains theoretical rather than practical; at eighteen we may order and consume fermented beverages on production of satisfactory proof of age – a written certificate or physical evidence such as a blue chin or premature baldness; at twenty-one we can claim our vote and the key of the hall door; at sixty-five we are retired and may die without any feeling of disgrace. That's seven – I think.'

'He's right. I was counting them,' Cunningham said.

Ellis, who could see the door, had his attention fixed elsewhere.

'Names and addresses, lads. We have visitors.'

He spoke softly and Cunningham missed it.

'What did you say?'

The sergeant and the garda were already on their way to the counter. They paused at intervals to slowly scrutinize various groupings of customers.

'Thermink urmup arma fermalse nermane.'

'Armand armadrermess.'

'Rermight.'

The process of individual interrogation began, the sergeant attending to one side, the garda investigating the other. He quizzed Ellis first.

'John O'Donnell.'

'Address?'

'7 Crescent Terrace, Fairview.'

'Have you any proof of identity?

Ellis gave the matter deep thought, then rooted through an inside pocket to produce a battered envelope in corroboration. The guard examined it closely and returned it.

'And you?'

'Noel White,' Brian said, '6 Crescent Terrace. We're next door neighbours.'

The guard turned to Tim.

'Chris Carroll,' he said, '10 North Strand Road – top flat.'

'Are you a student?'

'That's right. B.Mus. First year.'

'Anything that would identify you?'

'I'm afraid not. I was playing for a concert earlier and changed my jacket for it.'

'Me too,' Cunningham said. 'We've both come from the same concert.'

'What's your name?'

'Douglas Corrigan.'

'And what do you play?'

'I'm not an instrumentalist, just a singer.'

Cunningham's sartorial get-up, splendid as usual, proved psychologically convincing. Checking the names and addresses individually again in the hope of some lapse of memory, the Law quizzed Tim and Brian and Ellis and forgot to ask Cunningham to furnish an address or give his name again.

'Where did you get the envelope?' they asked Ellis when the Law had departed.

'I always carry two. One with a northside address, the other a southside. It saves trouble.'

'While he was talking to the rest of you I was desperately trying to fix on a name – one I'd remember,' Cunningham confided. 'Then I thought of the fellow who flew the Atlantic by mistake – Wrong Way Corrigan. How did you arrive at yours?'

'The season that's in it,' Brian said. 'White Christmas – Noel White.'

'I followed Brian's lead,' Tim said, 'Chris Carroll – Christmas Carol. I couldn't forget that.'

'You acquitted yourselves nobly,' Ellis conceded. 'I take off my hat.'

They had a last round to mark the success.

'To John, to Chris, to the bold Douglas here.'

'To Noel,' they said. Then they telephoned for a taxi.

The night sky was star-studded still. Faint blue light glimmered back at them from the icebound puddles. The cold air made their heads spin as they clambered into the taxi.

'Where are youse for?'

'The Hay Hotel,' Cunningham suggested.

'Where's that?'

'Never mind him. High Street will do us all.'

There was covering enough in the hide-out to bed them all for the night, Brian had told them. For Tim and Cunningham at least, it was better than facing home. Ellis agreed to join them too.

'Sing us a song and shorten the journey,' he asked Cunningham.

Cunningham obliged. His voice mingling with the pulsing of the engine had a disembodied sound. They listened engrossed. The taximan added his personal approval.

'It's a good song that. My own father often sang it. "O List to the strains of the old Irish harper." There's not many of us left. I wonder how long the petrol supplies will last.'

'We never died of winter yet,' Ellis said by way of comfort.

'Maybe not. But if it's rationed yours trewly here can pack

it in. I might even go across the other side and join up. This war is a Bobbie's job, I'm told. Each side has a gentleman's arrangement with the other. You just clock in at the front line at nine o'clock and you clock out again at five. No shooting or anything unpleasant in that line. A fella could do worse. Did youse hear the rumour at the start that Dev and Frank Aiken had been executed above in Arbour Hill? Who the hell puts things like that about?'

'A band of disaffected Leprauchans,' Brian thought, 'bent on recovering Ireland for the Tuatha de Danaan.'

'Led by Walt Disney,' Ellis suggested.

The taxi driver had not been listening.

'Not that I'd shed any tears if they had been executed, one at a time or both together. I've no love for any of their kind. What did they ever do except bleed the unfortunate country.'

'The voice of the Firbolgs,' Ellis whispered to Tim, 'a bag-carrying race, resentful of the soldier-Milesians.'

They told him to pull in some distance from the door so as not to disturb the slumbers of the household. Brian rationed out the available coverings when they were safely in the hide-out. They pulled two ancient palliasses together and decided there would be room for the three of them if they squeezed up a bit. Cunningham said he was not due in until after lunch and could sleep on. Brian agreed to call the others and to leave a note for his sister in case drink caused him to oversleep. Then he wished all good-night and put out the light.

Almost immediately Cunningham began to snore, a rhythmical rasp that rose and fell in the intense darkness.

Ellis listened for a while. He remarked:

'Wrong Way Corrigan is sailing above the clouds.'

'Full throttle, by the sound of him.'

'I think he enjoyed himself.'

'We all did.'

'Except when you were challenged about your age.'

'That gave me a bit of a jolt. I admit it. Why me?'

'These things keep happening in this life. The trick is to grow an extra skin.'

'I thought I'd made a start on that a long time ago, when I was twelve or thirteeen. It doesn't seem to have been altogether successful.'

'What happened at twelve or thirteen?'

'My father died. People I'd loved seemed to pop off like flies from the time I was ten, but that put the lid on it.'

'You were very close to him?'

'Too close. He left a great hole in the world. In fact when I forget not to look it's there still.'

It was there now. A void vast and empty in which anguish stumbled and cried out. Ellis was silent for a while. Cunningham continued to snore, but with less gusto. Ellis said:

'Probably that's why you're unsure of yourself.'

'Am I unsure of myself?'

'Not of yourself, perhaps, but of what's around you.'

'I take people and things at their face value. I don't pass judgments.'

'And you are constantly deceived?'

'That is to be expected.'

Ellis considered and said:

'One way to be happy remembering your father is to think of some special and perfect moment, some moment of complete mutual acceptance of each other. That's what I do myself.'

'Your father is dead?'

'Five years ago. We were always very close and grew nearer as the years passed. I had been home for holidays as in every other year and had only got back to the Metropolitan when the news came.'

'And what do you remember most happily about him?'

'My last trip home. He had met me at the train as he always did. He was a man who took a drink and he knew damn well that up in Dublin I had started to take it too. Nevertheless I had kept up the fiction still of not being a drinker. I didn't want to embarrass or hurt him and I simply went on the dry whenever I was at home. But on that occasion as we were driving through the village in his pony and trap he pretended to have a sudden thought and said to me: "Son, here it's your fourth or fifth visit home and I never thought to ask did you take a drink." He said it as though it had simply been thoughtlessness. So I said, as a matter of fact, I did. The result was we had two pints and chatted over them together among his friends in the pub that had been his regular for years. I knew it was his way of acknowledging my manhood. He was a simple man and I know also, foolishly perhaps, that he was taking pride in my pride. Does that make it sound riduculous?'

'On the contrary. Sacramental.'

There was a brief silence. Then Ellis, reflectively, said, 'Sacramental is an apt word.'

They were silent again. Cunningham, his snoring stage long past, was now breathing rhythmically and serenely.

'Corrigan is home and safe,' Ellis said.

'And his mind at ease,' Tim agreed. 'It's probably a long time since he last slept sound.'

'I suppose we should follow his example.'

'I suppose so.'

He heard Ellis turning on his side and drawing the covers more closely about him, child of Clare's cold rock and strand, a memory of its low-ceilinged, lamplit pub and of two pints of porter taken on an evening with his father locked forever inside him. Like the wet touch of dripping leaves and the cold feel of a hospital window against the nose. Keys, surprisingly, to unlock the impalpabilities of the heart.

In the morning Cunningham woke up to find Eilish bending over him. She had tea and bread and butter to offer him. The other two had already gone.

'Brian asked me to bring this.'

He looked at the cup and then up at her.

'Aren't you taking a chance?'

'No. My mother and father are both at ten o'clock mass.' She smiled. 'Do you feel dreadful?'

'Not dreadful. Numb. Brian told you, I suppose.'

'Yes. He was looking a bit bloodshot himself. Aren't you very foolish, all of you.'

It was a woman's view. He took the food.

'It's very decent of you.'

He had met her with Brian on only a handful of occasions. She was a fairhaired, gentle girl and, as it seemed to him for the first time, pretty. He wondered at not noticing before.

'When you've finished, just leave the things on the floor. I'll come for them later.'

'Do you have to dash away?'

'I'm afraid so. If they come back they'll wonder where I am.'

'What time is it?'

'It's nearly half past ten.'

'That late? And I still feel drugged.'

She smiled at him again.

'Your eyes are all puffy. But the tea will perk you up.'

'I'm very grateful.'

'For nothing. Don't let it go cold.' She hesitated. 'Well – see you.'

'I hope so.'

His eyes followed her to the door and remained on it for some time after it had been closed.

When the curtain descended for the first interval Tim left his instrument on his seat and went backstage to see Cunningham. He found him sitting before the mirror in his dressing room. His jester's cap and bells lay on the dressing table.

'How was it?'

'Marvellous. Brother Raymond says your Jack Point is the best thing we've ever had.'

'I'm nervous as hell in that bloody finale. There's so little for me to do in it and it goes on so long I'm never quite sure where I come in.' He rooted from pocket to pocket under his costume. 'Now I can't find my fags.'

Tim gave him one and said:

'Brian is here.'

'I didn't see him.'

'In the third row. He's with his sister.'

'Eilish?'

'He's only got the one.'

'Maybe he'd drop round afterwards.'

'I'll tell him.'

On his way back Tim found Brother Raymond.

'Brian Moloney is here with his sister and Des Cunningham would like to see him afterwards. Is it all right if I bring them backstage for a cup of tea?'

It was characteristic of Brother Raymond to say:

'Bring them to the staff room. There's something better there than tea and cakes.'

After the final curtain he did so, picking his way through the younger boys who had made up the chorus and who were still filing down the corridor. They were fitted out as young maids, their cheeks unbelievably crimson, their lips painted, their eyes plastered with mascara, their gowns trailing carelessly along dusty floors. Some of them kicked a paper ball in front of them. Others, unable to get near it, jostled and pushed. The din was earsplitting. Inappropriate cosmetic odours smothered the air. Their world was still only separated from his by a handful of years.

'Does it bring it all back?' he asked Brian.

'It does, though I don't particularly wish it to.'

'Some of them look ravishing,' Eilish remarked.

Brother Raymond was already installed in the staff room, the door of which had been furnished with a card which said PRIVATE. Bottles and glasses filled the cabinet behind him. Crates of Guinness were stacked on the floor. He rose.

'Brian Moloney – you're welcome.'

'My sister Eilish.'

'Delighted, Miss Moloney. And where's the Merryman himself?'

'He's changing,' Tim explained. 'He'll be along shortly.'

'Close over the door, Tim, like a good man. We don't want the world gaping in. Now, Miss Moloney, I don't have to ask those two rapscallions what they'll take, but I'm not properly instructed in the taste of charming young ladies. Some whiskey, perhaps, or some port. We have also, I hope, something or other in the line of minerals, though they're not what you'd call heavily in demand.'

'Some port then, if you please.'

While he saw to their needs there was a knock on the door. 'Yes?'

A Brother Flanagan stuck his head around it.

'Come in, Joe. You weren't long finding us.'

'I was looking for Brother Cronin.'

'He'll be along, you may be sure. Help yourself. There's fags as well in the second drawer. You know the company, I hope. The young lady is Miss Moloney – Brian's sister.'

Brother Cronin arrived almost immediately and after him Cunningham and Brother Clancy, the conductor.

'The maestro and the Merryman himself. Brother Flanagan – you'd better do the honours. Anything about Brother Superior?'

'Gone back to the house with company – some government ministers, I understand,' Brother Cronin said.

'We can rest easy so,' Brother Clancy said and flopped into a chair. When he had been supplied he fixed on Cunningham.

'Here's to the hero of the hour. A grand performance.'

'Everybody says so,' Brother Raymond agreed.

Brother Cronin, who had never been popular with them, looked oddly at Cunningham and said, 'It puzzles me how he slipped your net all those years.'

'It puzzles me too,' Brother Clancy agreed.

'Full many a flower,' Brother Raymond suggested. 'If we remember our Gray's "Elegy".'

'I meant to ask you,' Brother Cronin recollected, still looking at Cunningham, 'where are you working at the moment?'

'Thompsons, the outfitters.'

'That's on our list,' he informed the others. He had a special responsibility for finding employment outlets and liked to remind people. 'We have very good connections there. Is it satisfactory?'

'I find it all right.'

'And you, Tim – the Metropolitan, isn't it? That takes a bit of pull. The Freemasons are in the saddle there, I'm afraid. Nothing

above clerical grade B for the Catholic – isn't that the way?'
'I'm afraid it is.'

Brother Cronin looked meaningfully at the others. You see – his expression said.

'And can the Knights do nothing?' Brother Flanagan asked – indiscreetly, it seemed to Brother Cronin, who continued:

'Still, the Metropolitan is very good, even in the lower clerical grades. And pensionable, I believe.'

'That's so,' Tim said.

'We've been doing exceptionally well with the civil service in both the clerical officer and junior ex. grades. What's this the figures were this year?' He failed to bring them to mind and when nobody else seemed to remember either he went on: 'We do well too with the insurance companies, the railways, the shipping concerns. And you, Brian? I'm told you're working in your father's business, and that surprises me. I expected you'd go for a profession.'

'The professions are overrated,' Brother Raymond said. 'Very often the first step to emigration. Miss Moloney, your glass?'

'You're kind – but, no, thank you.'

'Come on, Jack Point, you've earned it. Tim, Brian – ?'

Brother Flanagan looked after the company once again. He lavished cigarettes all round. On excursions, at major school football matches, and in the week of the end-of-term concert discipline was always informally relaxed and the senior men among the Brothers took advantage. The cigarettes made the rounds, the whiskey glugged into glasses, the Guinness popped at short intervals, but only behind closed doors and, it seemed to Tim, in the most innocent of ways, to which they set prudent limits. As they became excited and talkative, Cunningham contrived to isolate Eilish and engage her in conversation. She had very much enjoyed the show, she told him, and praised his performance.

Then she said, 'Except that I always feel so sad for Jack Point at the end when Elsie chooses Colonel Fairfax, instead of him. It doesn't seem fair. Of course the music makes it seem sadder still.'

' "O thoughtless crew, ye know not what ye do",' Cunningham quoted.

'Yes – that's the bit – it's very moving. And then the song.'

Cunningham smiled and in a very soft voice for her ears only sang the line: 'I have a song to sing-O.'

She sang in response: 'Sing me your song-O.'

'Elsie's line,' he remarked. Then he said: 'That's odd. They're very alike.'

'Alike?'

'Elsie and Eilish.'

'Oh.'

She coloured a little but they both laughed together. Then she became grave and said thoughtfully:

'There seems to be this rule, doesn't there – that if people are rich and handsome they ought to have everything else as well. But why should they?'

'Things like that bother me too, but I can't pretend I know any of the answers.'

'When it comes to the point, who does, really?'

'That's what I think too,' he agreed.

Her smile and the expression in her eyes conveyed her approval. He had won her interest.

The cold air of the street was welcome when they got outside. Tim went off home but Cunningham walked some of the way with Eilish and Brian. She thought the Brothers had been very kind. And very tolerant too, when you thought about it. Cunningham explained that they were quite decent on special occasions. Brian conceded that they had their moments, though they were few and far between. They walked and talked their way through late streets that were quiet and almost deserted and by rows and rows of houses in which not a light showed.

The greeting cards stood once more on the mantelpieces, the decorations reached from wall to wall. In crowded, smoke-filled pubs, deplored by the discommoded and hardened regulars as that inevitable seasonal nuisance, the Holly-and-Ivy drinkers, they gathered boisterously and drank to the time-that-was-in-it. They shouted compliments at one another across bobbing heads and jostling shoulders. Or they went shopping through chaotic streets; Tim with Anne, Brian with Barbara. With so much coming and going to lay the way open for him, Cunningham contrived to make Eilish's better acquaintance without exciting much attention. But he was aware that recent circumstances must cast their shadow and it made him diffident enough at first to feel he should say something to Brian. Brian told him it was up to Eilish and dismissed it, though when Eilish showed herself to be agreeably disposed it surprised him, not because of Cunningham, but because she was usually withdrawn and slow to respond. Her mother noticed too.

'She's been out every other evening,' she remarked.

'Why shouldn't she?' Brian answered.

'It's not like her, that's all. He dresses very well though, doesn't he? I've often remarked that.'

Cornelius was less indulgent. There were nights when he looked at the clock and then at his wife.

'Where is it that daughter of ours is, would you mind telling me?'

'She's out with the Cunningham boy.'

'Till this hour?'

'She has to have her bit of freedom.'

'I have one nightwalker in the family. I don't want two — especially a daughter.'

'It's Christmas. Don't spoil it for her.'

'You give them an inch,' Cornelius complained, 'and they take a yard. And a lot of them think Christmas is for blackguarding and drinking. You know where that leads.'

'Eilish is sensible.'

'Until she has three of them Pimm's Number One under her stays or some other of them fancy drinks the young ones nowadays is going in for. Or until some young blackguard with a flat slips her a Mickey Finn.'

'A Mickey Finn? What sort of a thing is that?'

It was a word that had been mentioned in the course of

vague scandals reported to Cornelius across his counter. He had no idea at all what it was.

'I won't amplify the subject in a decent household,' he answered.

Christmas Eve fell on Sunday so they celebrated on the Saturday instead. Eilish went to the evening show in the Royal with Cunningham and then on to Nearys to join the others. Barbara and Anne, conscious of what was currently the thing to do, were both having Pimm's No. 1.

'It's gorgeous,' Barbara told her. 'A work of art really. Look at all the odds and ends. They give you a cherry on a stick-thing too, but I've just eaten it. Anyway I'm travelling home for Christmas tomorrow and there'll be no fun at all so tonight I'll drink and be merry.'

'Is it awfully strong?'

'It's more a meal than a drink,' Cunningham told her.

She turned questioningly to Brian.

'You've heard the voices of emancipated womanhood. Why look at me?'

Cunningham joined the battle for service and returned successful. Barbara, scrutinizing the packed lounge and the animated faces, said:

'I love Christmas Eve but I hate Christmas Day. You have to stay at home and talk to aunts and uncles. It can be so dreary. And this year with Sunday in between it's going to be twice as long.'

'I don't mind staying indoors so much,' Anne said, 'it's the family walk after dinner that gets me. I'd rather listen to the wireless.'

'That's exactly what I don't like,' Cunningham said. 'We get the Pope in the morning doing his *Urbi et Orbi* routine. Then the King's speech in the afternoon.'

'This year the King's speech is just what I'd like to hear,' Eilish confessed.

'You should suggest that,' Brian said. 'I'd love to watch the horror on the old man's physiognomy.'

'I know. He'd hit the ceiling.'

Tim said, 'This is the first Christmas Eve we've had the cash and the freedom to go out on the town. Have you considered that it could easily be the last?'

'I wish you hadn't said that,' Anne told him.

'But it could be true,' Barbara said. 'I see what Tim means.'

'You mean you think the Germans will invade us?' Cunningham asked.

'Or the British. They must be feeling pretty sick about giving us back the ports.'

'In that case Barbara has the right idea. We should eat, drink and be merry,' Cunningham said, looking from one to the other. 'Did someone say he was buying?'

Tim spent Christmas Day in Aunt Kate's with the rest of the family. She had asked them down because Uncle Hugh's army leave had been cancelled. She herself had refused his mother's invitation for Christmas dinner. It would leave their father and mother's house empty on Christmas Day, a thing that had not happened in over fifty years.

'No. We couldn't have that,' his mother had decided. Tim, when he had considered it, found it quite unthinkable too.

Cunningham, accepting a cigar and a couple of glasses of sherry from his father while they waited by the fire for dinner, took the opportunity to ask him to subsidize an evening for the entertainment of his own and Mollie's friends. He found his father agreeable.

'On Saturday your mother and I will be visiting the Mac-Dermots – if that would suit.'

'Thanks. That would be great.'

He told his sister.

'How do you do it?' Mollie asked. 'I've been dropping hints like iron plates all around him for a fortnight and not a bloody twitch of a muscle from him.'

'I think I'll slip up to Brian after dinner and tell him.'

'You'll have mother giving out. On Christmas Day the place for any respectable person is in his own home. I can hear her at it in my head. Yak, yak, yak.'

'She'll lie down after dinner. I'll slip out then.'

He found Eilish alone. Brian had gone out to walk for an

hour. Her father and mother were both sleeping off the effects of their meal.

'It's the same at home. The whole city is horizontal. And they talk about a Merry Christmas.'

'Won't you sit down? I can offer you a drink – there's port and sherry. Or whiskey?'

'If your old man won't object to his stuff being lashed around to all and sundry – ?'

'Of course he doesn't mind. Some whiskey then?'

'It's uncanny the way you read my mind.'

He sat down. She brought him a liberal measure and the jug of water which on social occasions was seldom far from wherever Cornelius's liberal elbow had rested.

'Aren't you having something yourself?'

She filled a glass with sherry and joined him at the fire. He looked around. The piano was open. A book of carols sat on the stand. On top of it a fat, red candle burned, its base dressed in ribbons and sprigs of holly. On a side table the wavering tips of three smaller candles formed a crescent above their gilded stand.

'Brian shouldn't be long,' Eilish said.

He smiled across at her and raised his glass:

'So far as I'm concerned, Brian can be as long as he likes. What I called about was to ask if the two of you will come to my place on Saturday next. It's not a party, exactly, but the old man will leave out a modest supply of the right stuff.'

'I'd love to.'

'I'll ask Barbara too, of course. Then there's Mollie – you haven't met her, I think?'

'Who's Mollie?' she asked. Her voice had changed a little.

'My sister,' Cunningham explained. 'She'll have some friends along too, but they're all right. I'd forgotten you hadn't met Mollie.'

'You hadn't mentioned her before,' she explained, smiling again.

'She's a bit mad, but good gas. Intellectual in a way. She buys records and goes to plays. Of course lots of girls go in for the highbrow stuff. You do yourself – a bit.'

'Not really.'

'You should hear McDonagh. He'd bury you in chat about C sharp minor and opus ninety ten.'

'I know. He sometimes plays with my mother.'

He looked at the piano again and the music open in readiness.

'I thought it might be you. Is she very good – your mother?'

'Well – old-fashioned. She plays things like "Lay My Head Beneath a Rose". And Moore's melodies, of course. But my father likes to sit and listen to her an odd evening.'

'What sort of music do you like yourself? I mean apart from Gilbert and Sullivan.'

'Songs from films, mostly. Not classical though. Well – except Gounod. I love Gounod. I suppose Gounod is classical?'

'I don't think he ranks very high,' Cunningham told her. 'In fact, he couldn't because I like him too.'

'And Puccini, perhaps – *La Bohéme*?'

'Yes. *Bohéme*. I've been to it a couple of times with my people. In the Gaiety.'

He left down his glass and spread out his arms towards her and burst into song.

> 'Your tiny hand is frozen
> Let me warm it in mine.'

Then he broke off as suddenly and looked anxiously at the ceiling.

'My God. Have I wakened the house?'

She dismissed that and said, 'You really do have a very nice voice.'

'McDonagh makes a bit of money from time to time with his violin. Apart from the school show he plays for others and knocks down a guinea a night, I understand.' He looked at his watch. 'Maybe I should go.'

'You don't have to.'

'I'd rather not be around when your father and mother come down. They'd think I'd a bit of a cheek, coming uninvited on Christmas Day.'

'They wouldn't mind at all.'

'No. I'd find it embarrassing.' He rose. 'Thanks for the drink.'
'I'll see you out.'

She followed him into the hallway.

'You'll tell Brian. He could drop in on me if he wishes.'

'Yes. I'll tell him.'

They were face to face in the half-light. He looked about him.

'Don't you hang mistletoe in the hall?'

'Not a scrap.'

'Could we assume it, do you think?'

She hesitated. Then she raised her face. He drew her to him and kissed her. She held him closely for a while. Then he said:

'See you on Saturday.'

'Yes. Saturday.'

She stood in the doorway and watched as he mounted his bicycle. He waved back at her as he was cycling away. She waved in return.

For Tim and Anne the party ceased to be an unqualified success about halfway through. Cunningham, who was smoking Turkish cigarettes to heighten the occasion, had offered one to Tim. It was oval-shaped and thin.

'What's this?' Tim asked.

'Pasha. Very classy.'

'Those bloody things,' Mollie complained. 'He has the house smelling all day like a sultan's tent.'

'I like the smell of them,' Cunningham said. 'There's something sinful about it.'

As Tim lit up Mollie's attention removed itself to a conversation near her. They had begun to talk about the war and a number of firms that were closing down because of it.

'There's quite a lot of them,' Mollie said, 'and some others are transferring their senior staff. Gretta Furlong's father is being called back to England.'

'I wouldn't like that,' Eilish said.

'They were talking about that at home today,' Anne put in. 'My father thinks he may be called back to their head office.'

'And where's that?'

'In New York.'

'Would the family go too?'

'It's more than likely.'

'Lucky you,' Mollie said. 'Don't you find it exciting?'

But Anne was looking across at Tim. His eyes were fixed unbelievingly on her, his expression shocked and hurt.

'I'm sure it won't come to anything,' she said quickly.

There was no opportunity to say anything more until they were alone and on their way home. Tim walked in stony silence until she touched his arm and said:

'I've made you very angry, haven't I?'

'How would *you* feel if there was some likelihood of me going away, and I didn't bother to mention it to you?'

'They only talked about it today.'

'So you just blab it all out in front of a roomful of people. How do you think I felt?'

'I know. That wasn't fair. I could have cut out my tongue.'

'I honestly can't understand.'

'I'm sorry. Truly. I feel miserable about it.'

He remained frozen and withdrawn. They walked in unhappy silence until once again she touched him on the arm. 'Tim?'

He stopped. 'When is it likely to happen?' he asked.

'I don't think it's likely at all. They were only wondering about it.'

'And you'd go with them?'

'Not if I'd any choice. I don't even want to think it could happen.'

'Neither do I. The last couple of hours was enough of that.'

But his mood continued. It kept them separate from each other even as they said good-night.

V

It was the coldest winter, according to the newspapers, in fifty years. At Boulogne, they reported, the sea froze. It was one of the few items of solid information to get past the new press censorship, which was seriously interfering with the dutiful attempts of O'Sheehan and Cornelius to keep up with the march of events. It affected meetings of the party branch too, where the school of thought which regarded England's difficulty as Ireland's opportunity still fought for its place in the formulation of policies.

They argued it out under Cornelius's chairmanship in the smoke-filled room above the bar and later in rented accommodation without him when his health was not the best and his doctor ordered strict rest in bed. It had begun when he was shifting crates and had an attack of dizziness and temporary blindness. It recurred when the steep hill from the river over-taxed his strength and he had to sit on a doorstep to recover. But it in no way deflected his attention from the activities of the party. O'Boyle made it his business to call after each meeting to enjoy a late-night drop at the fireside or the bedside while he brought him up to date. He had disturbing news of the number of times their common enemy Mullevins, who had his eye on chairmanship, succeeded in manoeuvring his way into the chair in the absence of Cornelius. There were recurring manifestations of a pink tint in the contributions of one of the younger members, a recent comer called appropriately, as Cornelius noted to himself, Newman. He was inclined to take it lightly at first.

'If he's one of these Reds a word dropped with the clergy will soon have him in his box.'

'Not young Newman,' O'Boyle said. 'He's as cute as a bloody fox. One minute he's spouting this leftist oul lingo of his – it'd make your hair stand on end. And the next, begod, he's talking about Aquinas.'

'Is it Saint Thomas?'

'Some class of a saint or other all right, and one I don't mind confessing I know sweet damn all about. It seems this Aquinas decided private property wasn't very respectable and that things should be held in common.'

'He's a bloody liar. I can't see any bishop sticking his Imprimatur on that.'

'Nor can I. But that's the tune he's playing. A great saint and doctor of the Church taught it, he says: "All things are for all men".'

'They are too, I suppose,' Cornelius allowed, 'provided they can pay for them.'

He turned the matter over.

'And what's Mullevins doing while all this is going on?'

'Studying the football medals on his watch-chain. Mullevins is no match for these college-educated young fellows. That's why I've urged you time and again to get young Brian to come forward. We need youth, and we need education. Brian has both.'

'I'd have to be very sure.'

'He wouldn't be attacking private property – you can be sure of that.'

Cornelius was suddenly tired.

'With the young nowadays you can be sure of nothing,' he said.

O'Sheehan, though as a non-believer he laid claim to no comprehensive mastery of the subject, did his best to elucidate the Aquinas puzzle.

'If I remember rightly, Thomas taught that the right to private property cannot be considered absolute. There are higher rights that must control appropriation. For instance, one man can't be allowed to corner all the wheat in the world and so deny bread to the rest of mankind. It's lawful to acquire a thing and control its use, up to a point. But in certain circumstances, and in situations of grave need, anything may be regarded not as any one person's property but as common. A starving man, for instance, may take a loaf of bread without guilt.'

'You mean he can't be clapped in gaol?'

'He can be gaoled, certainly, because he has broken the law. But in the eyes of Thomas and, as I understand, the Church, he has committed no sin.'

'And could he rob the till below and off with him with the week's takings?'

'Presumably. In certain circumstances.'

Cornelius was astounded.

'That's not what they taught me in school.'

'The man's situation would have to be grave – *in extremis* – you understand.'

'My own situation would be bloody grave too,' Cornelius objected. 'The week's cash gone and John Jameson & Co. and the rest of them banging on the door wanting their bills paid. It doesn't sound like religion to me.'

'That, unless I'm wrong,' O'Sheehan insisted, 'is the Thomistic viewpoint. But you could get a theological opinion.'

Cornelius thought he would be better without one.

'The members wouldn't swallow it,' he said. 'There was none of that stuff in the penny catechism.'

But the need to reassure the members personally or to confront young Newman's unorthodoxies was postponed indefinitely by the state of his health. There came a night when he waved away the packet of cigarettes held out to him by O'Boyle.

'I'm off the fags,' he explained. 'Doctor's orders.'

And then an evening when besides the whiskey bottle near the chessboard a second stood with, to O'Sheehan's eye, an unknown, gaudy-coloured liquid in it. Cornelius, having poured whiskey for his guest, helped himself without enthusiasm from the second bottle.

'The hard tack is out,' he explained, 'for the present anyway.'

'Is that some kind of medicine you're having?'

'No, indeed. A mineral. "Vimto" I think they call it.'

'Is it unpleasant? I thought from your face . . .'

Cornelius held it away from him, the better to examine it. 'It's nothing to write home about,' he confessed.

Being confined to the house more he became better acquainted with its coming and goings. Young McDonagh dropped in to see Brian and sometimes to play music with Mrs Moloney for an hour or so. He judged him to be a quiet, decent boy, though it was hard to tell with the younger generation of the present: then the dark-haired young one called Barbara who was in and out with Brian, especially at the weekends and who, he gathered, lived in her own flat or bedsitter – he hoped they weren't up to any tricks such as bottle parties and the likes or even more peculiar and dangerous goings-on; and then young Cunningham who seemed to be perpetually hanging around Eilish and whom his wife seemed determined to encourage.

'The family are very respectable. He's a good-looking boy too,' she remarked.

But Cornelius grumbled. 'Handsome is as handsome does.'

'And he dresses so nicely.'

Too nicely. Cornelius's inclination was to knock off marks for that. 'He's a bit of a Mickey-Dazzler all right,' he allowed.

What he was not aware of was that on Fridays, his wife's night for going out visiting, if he himself were confined to bed, his daughter was likely to be entertaining the young man to cups of cocoa and occasional bottles of stout at the fire in the kitchen which they transformed into their quiet haven for courtship, for bantering, for long and solemn explorations of things near the heart. She was reticent and shy at times, Cunningham soon noticed, about her more personal interests and hobbies. When she admitted to keeping a scrapbook, he had difficulty persuading her to show it to him.

'It doesn't mean much to anyone except myself,' she said. But he persisted and she did.

It was a ragbag of things: drawings and scraps that went back to childhood, cut-outs from papers, odd photographs, poems culled from magazines, half-finished compositions of her own in different coloured inks. She was right. It made little sense to anyone else.

'How long have you been keeping this?'

'Since I was seven or so. It was a way of passing dull evenings.'

A photograph of Brian at about that age caught his eye, then one of herself, but younger, mounted on a donkey. Joyce Kilmer's poem about a tree turned up and he read out the first two lines:

> 'I wonder if I'll ever see
> A poem lovely as a tree . . .'

'When I first came across that,' she said, 'I thought it was super. I still do, in a way.'

In his hands he held a world that had been happening long before he had known her, a world in which he had had no part.

He thought that strange. On the front page, under her name and address, she had inscribed:

> 'When I am dead and in my grave
> And all my bones are rotten
> This little book will tell my name
> When I am long forgotten.'

The doggerel was all too familiar. Taking a pen from his pocket he thought for a moment and then wrote underneath it:

'Mine too – Des Cunningham.'

'Thief,' she complained. But her eyes meeting his, contradicted.

'Why shouldn't it tell both?' he asked.

'Why not,' she agreed, her voice suddenly soft.

Throughout January and February, while Cornelius continued to be confined to the house and an early bedtime, the kitchen remained one of the few places they could enjoy being alone together. Then he was up and about more but forbidden to work in the shop or resume his duties as chairman. O'Boyle, however, continued his reports and the party branch tottered along without his firm guidance and his experienced control, a loss which O'Boyle never stopped deploring.

'And how did things shape tonight?' Cornelius inevitably enquired, ready to spend as long as needs be to untangle every nuance and implication. Inevitably he poured a generous measure of whiskey.

'Easy there, chairman, easy. You're not joining me yourself?'

'Still strictly taboo, Andrew, strictly taboo.'

And then the business for consideration.

'Mullevins got into the chair again tonight. Moran proposed him.'

'I've concluded that that fella is a plant from the national executive.'

'But why would he want Mullevins in the chair?'

'Trying him out. Watching what he favours and what he doesn't and taking his measure just in case,' Cornelius said. 'By God and I could tell them in five seconds. Number One, that's all Mullevins ever favoured. Number One first, last and all the time. What was Newman up to?'

'Absent. He has the flu, it seems.'

'That's something, anyway.'

'Oh' Páircéir was the star turn this evening. He was on about Nelson's pillar again – a monument to imperialism, he calls it, and an insult to the men who fought in the General Post Office. Did you know he claims he was in there himself?'

'If he was,' Cornelius said, 'he was buying stamps. Who does he want in place of Nelson?'

'Wolfe Tone. And he gave us a verse or two into the bargain of "In Bodenstown Churchyard there is a green grave". Then Mullevins interrupted to say he had heard a number of suggestions that Father Mathew would be more appropriate. The Apostle of Temperance, he kept calling him – "Ireland sober is Ireland free". It took me nearly twenty minutes to get the floor and point out there's already a statue of Father Mathew in O'Connell Street.'

'He was having a dig at me and the public house here,' Cornelius concluded.

'I suggested to the meeting that two statues in the one street to the Apostle of Temperance could give visitors the idea we're a nation of boozers.'

'I'd have shut their mouths for them quick enough,' Cornelius said, 'I'd have proposed a religious statue – St Patrick, let's say, or the Blessed Virgin. That'd put a flea in the bed, I can tell you. Could you see any man jack of them with the guts to stand up and oppose a statue to Our Blessed Lady?'

O'Boyle could not. He shook his head sadly but admiringly several times before he found the words: 'There you are, I'm always telling you. That's the touch we miss of late. That's your rare and personal gift – tactical instantivity.'

Winter, Brian remarked, seemed to bring a cash shortage as well as bad weather, partly because they were clearing debts accumulated around Christmas, partly because the entertainment available was mostly indoors and had to be bought. On weekends particularly the lean times irritated him. They searched about for something to do.

'How about the pictures?' Cunningham usually suggested.

'No. It costs money.'

'Let's just go for a ramble,' Tim said.

'I've done nothing else in this town but ramble since I learned to walk.'

'Why not take the bikes?' Cunningham offered.

'Why the bikes?'

'Well – they're faster. And you get further.'

'Where further do you particularly want to get?' Brian asked, 'and why do we have to get there faster?'

'All right. What do you two want to do?'

'You heard Tim. Just ramble. If you hadn't been born on a bicycle you'd know that to ramble is the inescapable destiny of your citizenship and class. You'd know – '

'Christ. Look what I've started.'

At weekends they could usually bring the girls to the pictures and drink coffee in small restaurants afterwards. Early in the week they might even have the price of a drink at night. But midweek usually saw them cleaned out. That meant aimless rambling through dark streets, prolonged conversations and occasional railing against their penurious condition. Then the German invasion of Norway and Denmark in April gave a sudden impetus to the war and in May the attack on Holland and Belgium and France brought it closer and occupied much of their discussions. But by then too it was possible to wander in the mountains again and to think of the sea once more.

'Are we going hutwards this summer? I can get the key again.'

'I'm on,' Tim said.

'Me too.'

'When we were there last year,' Cunningham remembered, 'I used to wake up sometimes at night to go out for a piss. I'd smell the sea and see the stars and maybe the moon. It was bloody wizard. I don't think I was ever so happy before. Then, of course, the Gwen thing happened.'

'How is she?' Brian asked.

'I haven't heard. But knowing Gwen, she won't be lonely.'

'When can you get the key?'

'In a week or so. I'll write about it tomorrow.'

'Meanwhile, how about Saturday afternoon?'

'If we go out Ballinascorney way,' Tim suggested, 'we could have a look at that German spy's house in Templeogue.'

'Or maybe come across another parachutist,' Cunningham said. 'Someone in the office told me the mountains are thick with them. There's plenty of money in being an agent, I imagine.'

'Drop a note to Dr Hempel about it,' Brian suggested. ' "Respectable young man willing and able for any skullduggery. Possesses Leaving Cert. and several merit badges from the Boy Scouts. Skilled in semaphore, bridge building, map making and first-aid. Very nice singing voice." '

'Except for the last bit, it doesn't sound at all bad.'

'The snag is the IRA are there before you.'

'What's left of them,' Brian said. 'Dev has most of them locked up.'

Saturday was fine. They followed the road around Glenasmole lake until a track on their right offered easy access to the mountain side and they could begin the long climb. Shoots of fern were curling already among the rocks, a scattered carpet of young greenery that accompanied them along the steeply rising ground. It took them almost an hour to reach the summit where they stretched full length to rest and get their wind back. The mountains of West Wicklow spread their jumble of peaks and shapes before them. A river curved and gleamed in the valley below. Cunningham broke the silence. 'Hey – look.'

'What's the matter?'

'He's spotted a parachutist,' Brian guessed.

'No. A huge beetle.'

They rose and gathered around. On a rocky shelf a beetle lay helplessly on its back, its legs gesticulating wildly in its effort to right itself.

'How did he manage that?' Brian wondered.

They bent closer to inspect it. The exposed belly was multicoloured and there seemed to be tiny parasites moving about on it.

'Are they young beetles?'

But no one knew. Meanwhile the feet had stopped threshing about and were curled up tight to the rest of the body.

'He's cottoned on we're watching him.'

'Anticipating execution,' Brian said.

'You mean you're going to kill him?' Cunningham asked. 'Why do that?'

Brian found a twig and poked it until the beetle was again right-side up.

'Nature slipped when it made beetles. Sheep too. If they fall over on their backs they're banjaxed.'

They watched for some minutes but the beetle never moved.

'I bet he's feeling he could kick himself,' Cunningham told them.

'Beetles are spared that sort of self-criticism,' Tim remarked.

'The vegetable Is. The beetle Is and knows that it Is,' Brian recollected, 'but man has the edge on both. "I Am; I know that I Am; I know that I know that I Am." So he goes through life deploring himself. Let's move.'

They began to descend, a long journey over rocky outcrops and tangled heather, aiming for the bridge over the river. A tiny and blurred image gradually assumed outline and shape until they jumped at last from the green bank onto the road and looked down at the brown swirl of water and the foam trapped among the rocks. It was almost six o'clock. They were ravenous. Cunningham filled the kettle while Tim and Brian collected wood. They found shelter and lit a fire. The light had almost gone by the time they sat around it to eat and then to smoke.

'We'll pick up a bus at Brittas,' Brian said.

'How far is that?'

'Almost five miles, I think.'

A light breeze was scattering sparks from the fire.

'What chance we're going to be invaded?' Tim wondered.

'They're too busy with their own problems at the moment.'

'I was thinking of joining this new local security force, just the same,' Cunningham told them. 'Would you join with me?'

Tim said he probably would. Brian wasn't interested.

'Have you thought of the British army?' he asked.

'Sort of,' Cunningham said. 'If I thought nothing would happen here.'

'Nothing ever happens here,' Brian said.

'I know. Here I am, twenty years of age and likely to spend the next forty fitting oul codgers with long combinations. Have you thought about that?'

Tim said he had. 'I won't stick the Metropolitan indefinitely. I doubt I'll stick it for as many weeks.'

'Why don't you pick up your fiddle studies again? Isn't there money in it?'

'If I could qualify as a teacher. Or for the symphony orchestra. I think it's a bit late in the day though.'

'It's never late if you buckle down,' Brian told him. 'If I were you I'd work at it day and night.'

'I can see myself,' Cunningham told them, 'the shoulders stooped, the hair gone grey – what's left of it – the false teeth in the tumbler at the bedside at night. Oh yes. And the barman saying when I go into the local around nine, "The usual, I suppose, Mister C." Why is it always this Mister M, Mister C, Mister Mac stuff?'

'It preserves a decorous anonymity,' Brian said, selecting his words nicely.

'I'd have my own special seat at the bar too and get mad if I found someone else planted on it. Christ. It's frightening. Don't you find it frightening?'

'I find what will follow more frightening still,' Tim said.

'You mean death?'

'Yes.'

'So do I. How about you, Moloney?'

'It's not so much death I mind,' Brian said, 'it's the blatant insult.'

It was almost dark The sound of the river seemed to have grown louder, the wind so much cooler.

'Better kill the fire,' Brian said.

They filled the kettle and emptied water over it and waited until the burst of steam and ashy smoke had died to a persistent, complaining sizzle. Brian reckoned they should reach the bus route in about an hour and a quarter. It was a downhill journey under a dark and starless sky. As they walked the sound of the river died away behind them and the beat of their boots on the road took over.

Though he said nothing about it to Anne, nor she to him, Tim wondered from time to time about confession. It had been strange to miss communion on Christmas morning for the first time ever. He had neglected to make his Easter duty too. The rule book assured him he was earmarked for hell. Yet it was not that which bothered him. It was the surprise of feeling cut off, of being locked out. An invisible barrier had descended between him and a sequence of procedures which had become second nature. How culpable was he in the Cunningham–Gwen matter? Heinously? Moderately? Only a little? Whatever the degree, he acknowledged there was guilt. The Anne thing was quite different. Grievous sin, the rules said. He was not at all convinced. If it was grievous it ought to be plainly felt to be so, but he had no sense of guilt whatever. On the contrary; it made the situation almost impossible. He could see little sense and even less honesty in promising – as in confession he would certainly be required to do – to avoid occasions of temptation in the future; or to promise not to be alone with her or not to touch or to kiss, or other equally unthinkable and even ludicrous disciplines of the same kind which seemed so plainly to be a denial of love and even life itself. The only way of conforming with that would be to abandon the whole affair, to avoid any meaningful contact at all with women, to save up for marriage and then off to the markets to select a mate, duly guaranteed, for delivery undamaged within a reasonable time. That system may have worked in some differently functioning society in some long-gone age, when marriage was simply marriage and love largely extra-territorial, if none the less a fact of nature. To explore love while avoiding temptation was a contradiction in terms.

Religion's view of the matter seemed to make love itself a state of temptation, though of course much more besides. And if he went to confession and explained that he had difficulty about making impractical promises, he would be told he must pray for grace and trust in God and do his best. And that he must go frequently to the sacraments. And be sorry for his sins. And to do penance and exercise prudence. He could be prudent up to a point; penance he had no objection to. Reasonable efforts at restraint and self-discipline were part of the conduct of living. But empty promises and praying to be denied what he knew to be proper, and professions of sorrow for acts which seemed nothing less than fitting in their tenderness and intention, would be an insult to faith, not a submission.

He debated with himself constantly but could see no solution. The parts refused to fit. Theory had no bearing on truth. The answer, at least temporarily, was to take life on trust, to put up with the locked-out feeling, to submit to the pull of the changing currents. There was no basic slackening in his belief. If anything, the more he bent his mind to the clashes and contradictions, the more it seemed to contract into focus. He took life as usual. Except that he inclined more to silences. As Anne noticed.

VI

The sea was there and the beach curving at the foot of the cliffs, the crowding trees and the meandering, intimate laneways all, as it seemed, just as they had been a summer before. That was at first when Eilish joined them for the new season; no longer simply as Brian's sister but as Cunningham's girl-friend, a subtle change in status. They went about in pairs or groups doing the usual things; wandering the fields and lanes, swimming when the weather allowed, or playing the gramophone and talking and looking out at the rain when it kept them indoors.

They talked about the war, which last season had been a vaguely understood threat, but now was a reality. They looked eastwards from the cliff top at times and wondered what threatening cargoes the sea might be hiding or what might be brewing unsuspected beyond the poker-faced horizon.

It was funny, Cunningham remarked on one such occasion, not to know what was going on. They agreed that that was how they felt. In turn they lifted eyes to the easterly distance and in turn they forgot about it. Or looked a brief question one to the other and forgot about it. Forgetting about it was so easy. The urgent things were near and about them.

When Barbara returned from her two weeks' holiday in her parents' house in the country, she spent only the night in her flat and then hurried out early next morning to the hut because that was what his letter had asked her to do. She found Tim there already with Anne and Eilish with Cunningham. They welcomed her noisily and she was glad to see them. When what politeness required had been observed, Brian, who was mending some fault in one of the window latches, said: 'Why don't you go down to the beach for a swim and I'll join you when this is done?'

But instead of swimming she changed and lay alone on the warm sands and listened to the surge and eddy of the water. To be so early on the beach was a novelty. In the freshness of the morning, rock and sand and sea looked as though they had just been made. To pass the time she took out his letter again and read it. It was curiously mannered and had been written in one of the many odd moods of his which had puzzled her early on in their relationship but which she was now increasingly able to share.

My Darling

You will be back (hopefully) almost as soon as this reaches you and there is little further to say except to ask you to come out to see me here as early as possible – Saturday if you can. It seems very important at the moment that you should do so, perhaps because I've been all on my own all day – pleasantly so – and now it's evening and I'm still alone and looking across a millpond of a sea at Dalkey Island. No one around that I can see. Everything silent, time standing still. I am savouring, as someone said (Hopkins I think) the taste of myself, of I and me above and in all things. Earlier I have been wandering both in the flesh and in the imagination, first to the ruins of old Shanganagh Castle and then, uninvited and unnoticed, to the new one, the seat of General Cockburn, a mansion of a place. It contains many paintings of merit, several antique bronzes, tables of mosaic and Egyptian granite, numerous slabs of Greek and Roman marbles, volcanic specimens from Mount Vesuvius and Etna, with other collections concerned with natural history. In the hall is a marble sarcophagus and in the ceiling of the library is inserted a copy of Guido's *Aurora*. The room itself commands splendid views of the sea and mountains. In front of the house the proprietor has erected a pillar composed of Grecian marble to commemorate the passing of the Reform Bill in 1832. (What was that? I wonder. Probably something to do with the extension of the franchise.) In the grounds are the ruins of the church of Kiltue.

I have also this evening established that the island of Dalkey is two miles east of Kingstown, separated from the mainland by a narrow sound of about 300 yards in width and perhaps 1200 yards in length and that it contains about twenty-five statute acres. To have these details to hand at last is a great ease to the mind.

And did you know that within the memory of many a society was formed, which elevated the island to the dignity of an independent kingdom, the monarchy being elected by the same society as are also the high officers of state, including His Grace the Archbishop of Dalkey Island and the commander of the fleet who is known as Admiral of the Muglins. Yet the only inhabitants, I understand, are two or three artillery men, who are in charge of the small battery which mounts three twenty-four pounders. There are also, of course, a Martello tower and the remains of an ancient church dedicated to St Benedict.

These are wonders which I cannot wait to explore again and share with you and that is why you must make no avoidable delay. You won't, will you? Already outside the hut my masons are erecting a column composed of green Connemara marble to mark the occasion. And God has agreed to switch on all the stars of heaven for the festivities on that night.

> I love you
> Brian

She folded it and put it away and stared across at Dalkey Island, wondering if the artillery men were part of the war situation, though two or three seemed highly inadequate for any purpose whatever, or if they were simply part of his rambling imagination. She wondered as well how he had managed to get into Shanganagh Castle. A while later she heard his feet on the rocky, upper shore and turned to greet him. He squatted beside her and surprised her by saying:

'You were reading my letter.'

'How do you know?'

'I watched you earlier from the cliffs.'

'Is that a nice thing to do?'

'I found it very agreeable.'

'And how do you know it was your letter?'

'Because when I asked you, you were surprised and said how do you know.'

He scrutinized her closely.

'You haven't changed at all.'

'Nor you,' she said. 'Do you think it's eternal youth or something?'

'That could be it. And we share the same old fault still.'

'I've forgotten what that was.'

'We talk too much.'

'Yes. We do – don't we.'

They felt the slight strangeness which their separation of two weeks had created between them and came to each other urgently to dispel it. It ebbed away quickly and easily. When she sat up at last she said:

'Did you feel it was a long time?'

'Interminable.'

'Me too. But it's over now. And we have today and tomorrow before I go back to that bloody old office.'

'What would you like to do?'

'Anything at all. Did you really get into that castle?'

'Not really.'

'I thought not. And the antique bronzes and the marble sarcophagus and the tables of mosaic were simply imagination?'

'Not altogether. I set it all down more or less verbatim from *A Guide Through Ireland* by a James Fraser published in 1843. I'd been reading it most of the afternoon.'

'And the artillery men on Dalkey Island came from that too, I suppose.'

'I'm afraid so. They're hardly over there still. Nor their three twenty-four pounders. But the king of Dalkey Island continues to be elected from time to time – which is a consolation. And for all I know the antique bronzes and the copy of Guido's *Aurora* may still adorn the seat of General Cockburn.'

'But not poor General Cockburn himself.'

'In all likelihood, no. He may be in heaven. If there's such a place I imagine that's where a man who erects a marble pillar to a Reform Bill would probably be found. If not, then he sleeps with his fathers:

"General Cockburn, he is dead
All his friends are lapped in lead." '

'Now we're becoming morbid. It's time for our swim.' She waited for him to change and let him test the water for her.

'How is it?'

'Affable,' he said. His dive sent splashes everywhere which soaked her and made her scream. But the worst was over and the water was mild after all. Late that night God kept His promise and the sky was a sieve of stars.

Eilish surprised Cunningham by turning out in a two-piece swim-suit.

'It lifts up the heart,' he told her, with unaffected enthusiasm.

'Are you making fun of me?'

'God, no. You look wizard.'

'You think so? I bought it specially for coming out here.'

'For me – I hope.'

'Yes,' she said simply. She looked down but could feel his eyes fixed on her.

'You're very lovely, Eilish, you really are.'

'Thank you.'

She was at ease again and looked up.

'You don't think it's a little bit brazen?'

'Call it alluring,' he suggested.

'Oh God. You do.'

'I don't. Honest. It's absolutely right.'

'My mother hasn't seen it yet. She'll probably have a fit.'

'Mothers are always having fits. I wouldn't mind.'

'No. Whose life is it, after all? Though she's not a nag. In fact we get along quite well.'

'Does Brian?'

'With my mother, yes. But my father and he don't see eye to eye.'

'I know. Does it bother you?'

'A bit. I get pulled in two directions. But a lot of the time things are fine.'

'It will pass,' Cunningham predicted.

'I think so. Basically they're fond of one another.'

He stood up.

'Let's christen the new swim-suit.'

'Can't we just sit still a while,' she asked.

'If you wish.' He sat down again.

'You're such an old Jack-in-the-Box at times.'

'I know. Does it make you unhappy?'

'Not unhappy. Just a bit out of breath.'

'Everything is very short. The weekends, holidays, the summer. Life too.'

'I know. It's all so sad.'

'You're thinking of your father, aren't you?'

'You knew?'

'Has he been worse lately?'

'I don't think so. A bit better if anything. But at times you catch a glimpse of what has to come.'

'That's what I have against sitting still,' he told her.

She laughed and stood up. 'All right. Come on.'

He chased after her and passed her. By the time she reached the water's edge he was already well out from the shore, his head disappearing and re-appearing as the gentle swell lifted and lowered.

Tim and Anne made the most of it. Although nothing more had been said, the momentary hint that she might have to move abroad had been enough to show that their future together was not altogether beyond question. They could agree it would not happen and decline to discuss if further but it never entirely went away. They kept it at bay by making plans for the far future. She encouraged him to take up Brian's suggestion and start working at the violin again. She felt if he was good enough for the casual engagements he had been getting around Easter and Christmas and for amateur opera seasons then there was the possibility, however far ahead it might be, that something permanent would offer.

'You keep saying you don't want to spend your life in the Metropolitan,' she told him, 'so why not have a try?'

As a result he dug out his books of studies and exercises again and began to bring them with him to the hut. When the others had gone off swimming or walking he sometimes stayed in to practise. She grew used to reading on the grass in the evening light with the sound of the sea mixing with a Kreutzer study or the endless reiterations of a series of Sevcik bowing exercises. At first it seemed odd and incongruous. Then it became simply part of the day.

'It sounds awfully good,' she told him.

'It isn't really. I'd need a teacher to get anywhere.'

'What's to stop you going back to the one you had?'

He smiled and said, 'For a start – I'm getting a bit hairy.'

But he enquired and found there was no obstacle at all.

'He'll take me on again when the summer break is over. There are Extern scholarships and he thinks I've a fair chance of one. If I got that I wouldn't have to stump up any fees.'

'How long would it all take, do you think?'

'Two years. Three years. Or not at all. It's unpredictable.'

'Was he encouraging?'

'Well – he didn't burst out laughing.'

She smiled at that.

'So I've three years, perhaps, to learn how to starch a white shirt and iron a black bow.'

'Or hold out the hat while we try our luck with the theatre queues.'

'I wouldn't mind,' she said.

They went walking on the beach in grey, evening light which had started its long and imperceptible fading.

'It's made you happier,' she said.

'You think so?'

'You don't disappear into yourself so often. It's not nice when you're all locked up and inaccessible.'

'I don't mean to be.'

'I know.' She hesitated. 'May I ask you something? I mean, it affects me too.'

'Of course.'

'I don't want to pry.'

'Please.'

'Have you been to confession? I know you hadn't up to Christmas because you didn't go up for communion. But have you since?'

'No. It's all a bit complicated. Have you?'

'No. I keep remembering what happened the last time I went. A repetition of that and me and Holy Mother part company. And I wouldn't wish that to happen. Is that what bothers you?'

'Not really. I don't mind what they might say. It's simply that I can't fit the rules on the subject to the facts of the situation. How could I pretend to be sorry for something so beautiful and fitting – or promise it won't happen again? That amounts to denying you.'

'I thought it just has to be a sort of intellectual sorrow.'

'Intellectual or emotional, it's all one. Not possible. Not justified. Two people in love are by the nature of the situation drawn to each other. I don't say there should be no restraint. I only say that total restraint is impossible. St Thomas described the underlying reality; delight, he said, is a kind of movement. Love is the same. A drawing towards.'

'I wouldn't suspect him of knowing much about it.'

N

'There were no flies on old Thomas.'

'There are thousands of people in love who seem to get by.'

'They either don't know or they're cheating.'

'You can be over-scrupulous. Priests will tell you that themselves.'

'I could be. But I'm not. Abelard's answer was mad too. He held that the truths involved in man's final end are not the truths of nature but contrary to them. That's absurd. It shows there's something wrong somewhere.'

She looked at him oddly. Then she put her arm through his and said, 'You're quite extraordinary – do you know that? You won't do what they tell you to do – '

'What they tell me I should do is simply not possible.'

'And in the course of a few minutes you'll quote two or three saints either to back up what you say or to demolish what they say.'

'I'm no disbeliever. You mustn't think that.'

'I don't. It's very much the other way round.'

She stopped to look squarely at him.

'There are times when I feel like a temptress or something. Do you ever think of me in that way?'

He took her in his arms.

'You mustn't say things like that.'

'I don't mean to be flippant. Or mocking. Or even upset,' she explained. 'It's just that sometimes it's so hard to understand how you're feeling or thinking. Are you angry?'

'No. You asked me something and I answered you as honestly and precisely as I could. I love you very deeply, Anne. Totally.'

'The same goes for me, Tim.'

'And have I answered?'

'Yes. I don't altogether understand. I don't really have to. You were keeping some part of yourself from me, I thought. Now I know you're not. Now everything is fine.'

They reassured each other with embraces and tenderness until, not much noticed by either of them, the grey evening had declined totally into darkness and it was time to pick their way cautiously back over seaweed and faintly gleaming sand.

Then in August they talked of the blitz that had begun in England and when bombs were dropped in Wexford and people killed they wondered if it was going to spill over and what it would be like to endure, especially in a country so far without air-raid shelters or adequate defences. The government's recruiting drive began to seem not quite so mindless, after all. And on the last weekend of the same month, while they squatted around a bonfire they had lit on the beach from driftwood, they heard the droning of engines from the east and stopped their talk to look up at the sky. The stars looked back at them and gave nothing away. They waited. The droning grew in volume until the night air throbbed under its weight. They knew from the heavy, pulsing sound that it was a bomber. They remained silent, conscious of an unfamiliar menace and their own helplessness. The throbbing reached its peak and began to fade in volume as it moved inland, becoming at last not audible as sound but hanging as a silent tremor in the dark air. Cunningham looked at the circle of grave faces lit by the glow of the fire:

'What I find unbearable,' he told them, 'is having nothing to fling back at the bastards.'

'Precisely,' Brian said. The cold emphasis in his voice caught Barbara's attention and made her frown. But she repressed the impulse to look at him and kept her eyes on the flames leaping upwards from the fire.

'Was there any mention of this Wexford business?' Cornelius asked O'Boyle.

'I raised it myself. Mullevins was inclined to push it under the carpet, but I refused to let him. Three unfortunate Irish souls gone to their Maker, I said. And it wasn't the British done it, either.'

'How did they take that?'

'There was a majority vote for a protest from the government to the German embassy.'

Cornelius expressed satisfaction.

'That'll soften Páircéir's cough for him.'

'Which was my studied intention.'

'You done well. The people wouldn't stand for us going in with Hitler anyway – excepting the usual handful of diehards.'

'They would not. In fact, if I read the popular mood aright, there's more than a sneaking sympathy with the traditional enemy.'

'There must be no appearance of siding with the British,' Cornelius warned. 'That's be enough to ruin us. No. Neutrality is the card to play. Dev has the head screwed on the right way, and we back him. Invasion will be resisted from whatever source.'

'That's the ticket.'

'And this young fella Newman. How was he behaving?'

'At it again. Though this time it was Páircéir he was after. He says the plight of the working classes must have precedence over both partition and the revival of Irish. There's this slogan he yells out of him when he gets over-excited. "Social Reform – not Shamrocks".'

'Social reform – is it?'

O'Boyle had another thought. 'Oh yes – and he wants to nationalize the banks.'

'There'd be no trouble at all to a man with a heavy head cold to get the commy whiff off of that. Can Mullevins not see the harm it could do to the good name of the party?'

'Mullevins is no match for the college education. I told you before.'

O'Boyle studied his whiskey and hunched under his burden of disillusion.

'We're in queer times, chairman. The young whippersnappers set aside the old ideals of nationhood. And Mullevins, who never heard a shot fired in anger, tries to chisel his way into the chairmanship in place of a man that went through it all.'

'I weathered my share,' Cornelius owned.

'A man that shot it out with the Black and Tans.'

'Wait now,' Cornelius corrected. 'I make no false claims. I was never a fighting man in that sense. I harboured the boys on the run, certainly. I passed on despatches now and again. If bomb and bullet were hidden under my roof I made no remark. But I wasn't a shooting man, and I was never out on my keeping.'

'And suppose word of harbouring them that was had got out in the wrong quarter?'

'True. I'd have been in the height of trouble. In that sense, I suppose, I wasn't far from the front line.'

'No more than myself,' O'Boyle agreed, 'and damn the bit of thanks for it now.'

'Eaten bread . . .' Cornelius said and shrugged to dislodge ingratitude from his shoulders.

O'Boyle, having lowered another mouthful of whiskey, tilted what remained in the glass back and forward while he composed his next enquiry.

'We'll have a general election to face in a few years' time – if not before it.'

'I'm aware of that.'

'In circumstances of unusual difficulty, with shortages of this and shortages of that,' O'Boyle pursued. 'The electorate won't be in the sunniest of moods. It'll take tricky manoeuvring by any government to keep their goodwill. They'll expect Brains, not Mouths.'

'You're back on the subject of Brian again?'

'I am, chairman. He'd be an asset to us as a candidate, and being the son of Cornelius Moloney would stand to him in the neighbourhood.'

'It's his being my own son that makes it hard for me.'

'It's not the reason for my suggestion, which is on his merit, though of course it's to his advantage. Besides, there's another important aspect.'

'There is?'

'The state of your health has kept you away from the meetings for a good while now and even our friends can have short memories. Mullevins is hell bent on getting the chair. But if Brian was at the meetings you'd be there by proxy, so to speak. And you'd have an additional ally.'

Cornelius looked hard at O'Boyle.

'That's the soundest reason you've put up so far,' he conceded.

'Then you won't object to me putting it to the lad?'

Cornelius considered deeply. Not only was he being drawn two ways, but he was not at all sure how Brian would react.

'I'll neither object nor encourage,' he decided at last. 'Let it lie strictly between the pair of you.'

'That's very sensible,' O'Boyle assured him.

Cornelius reached for the whiskey bottle to refill his guest's glass but paused briefly before pouring.

'Remember. Strictly between the two of you,' he emphasized.

VII

A decision arrived at and acted upon, one more in the long chain that stretched back link by link to some remote beginning, O'Sheehan moved the chesspiece ponderously and deliberately, then unclasped the leash of concentration and lay back in his chair.

'Your move,' he said.

Though September was in its third week the chess table was still in its summer position by the window overlooking the cobbled street and the electric wires which accommodated the comings and goings of the No. 21 tram.

'I'm in a pucker,' Cornelius confessed.

O'Sheehan's eyes brightened briefly in friendly triumph, then without his permission transferred their attention to the world outside. There was little to look at. A dog wandering aimlessly on the opposite pavement stopped from habit outside the shop of James Byrne & Son, Victuallers, to sniff the sawdust, but it was Sunday evening and it found nothing of interest. The street was full of shadows, the mountains beyond the city were dark, the jumbled roofs in between caught in isolated patches a last gleam of the sun.

'I think I'll leave it until next time,' he heard Cornelius say in a voice so tired that it compelled his attention. Cornelius seemed grey and drawn,

'You overtax yourself and it's my fault. We should have stopped an hour ago.'

Cornelius reached for the whiskey bottle.

'Be a good man,' he asked, 'and fetch a glass for me from the cabinet.'

'Isn't it taboo?'

'Taboo be damned. I can live without whiskey. Or I can live without chess. But what life is there for a man without either?'

O'Sheehan did as he was bid.

'In the old times,' O'Sheehan said, 'the whiskey was a cure for heart trouble provided you added sugar and a little grated bread to protect the brain and the liver.'

'We'll have it unadorned.'

'As you will.'

He poured for both of them, drank a little and rested back in his chair. O'Sheehan watched closely but tried to disguise the fact. A while later Cornelius sat up and drank again.

'How is it now?'

'I'm feeling better already.'

He looked better. The tired lines had softened out. His colour had improved.

'A man can be over-abstemious,' O'Sheehan remarked, 'a nice moderation is often more beneficial.'

'I'm having my troubles – with the committee, you understand.'

'So you were saying.'

'And I'm stuck in the bloody house while they intrigue against me. If I had the full use of myself, there'd be a different story, let me tell you.'

'That time is coming, never fear. But you must be patient.'

'I keep thinking about Mullevins.'

'You do yourself wrong. That man's not worth a *cumall*.'

Cornelius looked puzzled.

'A *cumall*?'

'A measure of value in Celtic Ireland. Don't you remember? It meant the price of a woman slave.'

Cornelius stored it away for possible use when the hoped-for confrontation arrived. His thought changed their theme.

'The British are taking a terrible pasting these times: London, Liverpool, Bristol, Manchester. That's not war – bombing innocent civilians. And there are a lot of Irish there too. Supposing they do the same to us. Have we half-a-dozen planes in the air corps or even an anti-aircraft gun itself?'

'I gravely doubt it.'

'I'm of like mind. The most we can do is trust in God.'

'No trouble to the Gaelic temperament. The early Celts would lend money on a promissory note repayable in the next world. The practice is mentioned by Valerius Maximus. Rolleston records it.'

Cornelius looked uneasily on the domed forehead that could accommodate without splitting itself apart the lore of the Celts, the observations of Roman rhetoricians and the Thomistic system of philosophy. Not for the first time O'Sheehan puzzled him. How had he come by his assortment of information? Who (he never allowed the question to formulate itself too frankly) might he really be? He reached again for the whiskey bottle and answered the frown on the other's face.

'A thimbleful for luck. Then it's the waterwagon for me for another spell.'

Brian was on duty in the bar when O'Boyle finally approached him with the suggestion that he should join the party. Neither it nor the assurance that it would lead to a political career within a few years meant anything at all to him, but he had always found O'Boyle to be a well-disposed and gentle-mannered man, and he promised to think about it. Cunningham, who in some mood of the moment was sitting on the roof of the hut, nearly fell off it when he told him. Barbara looked sensible and suggested it was at least worth thinking about. Brian was scornful.

'Can you see me on a platform at the chapel gate, being asked where I was in 1916?'

'Under the bed,' Cunningham suggested from his perch.

Barbara ignored him.

'Don't be silly. You weren't born in 1916.'

'They'd ask just the same. They always do.'

'There was this political meeting I saw once in the country,' Cunningham told them from the roof, 'and to rig up a platform they had laid planks over some pörter barrels which some fool had left lying on their sides instead of upright. This fellow mounted it and began as usual: *"A cairde Gael"* then – cross my heart and wish to die – he stepped forward and went on: "What this misfortunate country needs is more shtability". But as he moved the bloody barrels began to roll under him and the platform collapsed.'

The recollection convulsed him. Barbara refused to be amused.

'I agree there are plenty of damn fools of politicians,' she said, 'but there are brilliant ones too – great statesmen.'

'She sees you at an Easter parade – an Taoiseach Brian Moloney and his cabinet taking the salute as they march past.'

'Will you come down off that, Cunningham,' Brian said, irritated. 'You're making me dizzy.'

Cunningham obliged.

'One thing you could do,' he suggested when he was safely restored to earth, 'is fix us all up in good jobs. That's what politics is mainly about.'

When they were alone Barbara returned to the subject.

'Are you really so set against the idea?'

'I haven't even thought about it.'

'But you ought.'

'Ought?'

'Cunningham is right. Politicans have influence. Good politicians have a good influence. Doesn't that make sense?'

'Perhaps so,' Brian said, 'but supposing I turned out to be a corrupt one?'

'That's ridiculous.'

'Not a bit. Thanks for the good opinion, just the same.' He stopped. 'What's so funny?'

'You,' she said, 'you said that so solemnly.'

'It's a serious possibility.'

But she continued to be amused.

He forgot about the matter altogether for some weeks. Then the days shortened and high winds and heavy seas sent the breakers surging beyond the summer tidelines, and it was time once again to board up the windows of the hut against winter storms. The three had tea by lamplight when the work was finished, their shadows making restless movements all about them and the air cold and damp. Under their feet the floor-boards quivered at times to the crash and tumble of surf. In the darkness beyond its thunder German and British craft were patrolling the lines of their double blockade. Beyond that again Britain awaited yet another assault in the so far unbroken sequence of night raids. When Tim pumped the primus and set it in action for washing up, its incessant buzzing drowned out the conversation of the others. He felt alone in a narrow shed on the brink of menace. Eventually they had everything tidied away and took the final look around.

'That's that,' Brian said. They stepped outside.

The wind beat in hard from the sea and though it was not visible they knew there was a moon somewhere because a faint light suffused the sky.

'I'd like to walk into Bray and get the train from there,' Cunningham said.

'You're mad.'

'Why mad?'

'The beach isn't passable.'

'Not the beach. I mean across the golf course.'

'Oh,' Tim was dubious. 'Well – all right.'

'Not me,' Brian said. 'I'll get back to town. See you tomorrow, if you don't break your necks.'

In no time it became a distinct possibility. It was darker than they had anticipated. The walk, so pleasant during the summer with its cropped grass and wide views of the sea, became an eerie battle against wind and treacherous terrain to the incessant beat and thunder of waves. It was unexpectedly difficult to know where the links ended and the cliffs began. A broken bridge with a couple of planks intact, which they had crossed with unconsidered dexterity many times during the summer, loomed up out of the darkness, a dim outline spanning a channel of turbulent water that brought them to a standstill. Tim weighed their chances and shook his head. The planks looked far from stable, and the wind seemed likely to blow them off balance if they attempted to cross. They bore inland instead, groping over unfamiliar ground until a distant light caught their attention and they used it as a landmark. It turned out to be a signal box. On the boundary of the railway line they found a small thicket which they recognized and which temporarily established their bearings. They sheltered there and considered.

'I'm not sure this was such a good idea,' Tim remarked.

'Neither am I.'

'There's a swamp somewhere ahead.'

'You're reading my thoughts.'

'We could walk along the line. There's a disused station further on towards Bray with a lane leading, I think, to the clubhouse. Should we chance it?'

'Better that than a watery grave.'

'If we're not mown down by a train.'

They searched and found a way through the wire paling and on to the tracks, where the force of the wind half stunned them. Great gusts made sound at times that were like approaching expresses. It became a nightmare of blind blundering forward, interrupted by sudden stops and tense listening until, much shaken, they were able to climb at last on to the platform they had been searching for. The ticket office was barred and shuttered. So too were the waiting rooms. Though they knew the world of people and their comings and goings could hardly be much more than a mile away in one direction or another the deserted little station denied that it continued anywhere at all. They searched for an exit and found themselves in a laneway which led after an interminable time to a clearing among trees where the bulk of an old mansion rose in front of them. If it was the clubhouse it showed no lights and gave no hint of human activity. A driveway curving away to the left offered hope of a kind. Though it too was almost impenetrably dark, it was wide and easy to negotiate and their pace became confident.

'That's better,' Cunningham said.

It led at last to the main road.

Bray, windswept and gale-torn, its hotels and guest houses full of empty rooms, clung by its teeth to survival. The railway station, deserted under gas light, denied any possibility of a train. Yet eventually, as in a dream, one came. They climbed in. In a while the wheels had adopted a familiar rhythm, the coach swayed gently, the windows reflected their faces back at them.

'Only a few weeks ago I was courting Eilish in that thicket by the signal box,' Cunningham said. 'It was a warm night with thousands of stars – you know what I mean. It was marvellous. I could have stayed there forever. Tonight that bloody same thicket gave me the willies. I thought I'd never see civilization again.'

'Such as it is,' Tim said.

He stretched out his feet to rest them on the opposite seat.

'What's wrong with civilization?' Cunningham asked. 'This is like being back from the dead.'

He pressed his face against the glass to peer out.

There was nothing to be seen except the light from the carriage window which fell on the hedgerows and raced to keep up with them. Occasionally, but only for a moment or so, it disappeared. The disappearances and reappearances began to amuse Cunningham. It was as though it had difficulty keeping its grip.

As he came down the steps of the station Brian turned up his collar and fixed his hat firmly against a wind which was making sudden onslaughts around Harcourt Street corner. Squalls of rain, spasmodic and unexpected, stung his face. He put aside the temptation to make a chance call on Barbara. Winter was ahead, the basic pattern waited to be resumed. Resigning himself to what was no longer avoidable he headed for home. The walk there was as predictable as ever. At Harrington

Street Church, Saturday's trickle of penitents, dark figures in the light spilling from the porch, shuffled in and out, the doors thudding after each as the wind whipped them closed. Beside it the school he had once journeyed to daily lifted rows of blank windows that let the light of street lamps in on empty classrooms and bare, untrafficked stairways. Heytesbury Street hid behind drawn curtains. It, too, had been part of the routine trek of schooldays. Above Long Lane the windows of the Meath Hospital spilled light from wards and corridors where Death, among odours of medicine, ambushed and laid siege. The cathedral, an amplitudinous mother hen, nested unproductively on vault and gilded slab. In Iveagh House they had the beds made ready for the night's paupers. Lost winds in the maze of lanes off Nicholas Street continued their search for Mangan and Zozimus. And in High Street, flanked by the neighbours of a lifetime, the licensed premises of Cornelius Moloney conducted its lawful business. All were present, all correct, their sameness a blight on the spirit.

The lower rooms were in darkness, the slacked-up fire in the kitchen a sign of careful preparation for limited absence. It seemed he was to be relieved of the ritual of making conversation, but as he climbed the stairs to his bedroom a bar of light showed under his father's door and his father's voice called out to him:

'Is that you, Brian?'

He retraced his steps. His father, a shawl draped about his shoulders, was in session with Andrew O'Boyle. The fire blazed in its grate. Behind him the bed had been freshly made.

'I knew your foot on the stairs,' his father said.

Precisely.

On the table the whiskey bottle held its place of honour surrounded by letters and scattered memoranda of some kind.

'Your mother and Eilish went out to confession.'

'That's the women – God bless them,' O'Boyle remarked, edified.

'I'd wish on me for a *smahan* of punch, if you wouldn't mind?'

'I'll heat up some water.'

'Get the cloves too if you can find them,' Cornelius instructed, 'and the sugar bowl. Don't overlook the sugar bowl.'

The cloves involved a search through presses until he located them. He remembered also to bring a couple of spoons to keep the hot water from cracking the glasses. As the steam rose it spread benign odours.

'Make a glass for yourself, why don't you?' Cornelius invited.

For politeness' sake, he consented, taking care to pour the hot water on to the spoon.

When all was ready O'Boyle, always conversational, enquired, 'It's hardy outside?'

'Blowing a gale.'

'And wet into the bargain – I heard it on the window. Were you far abroad?'

'Out by the sea. We were boarding up a friend's holiday hut against the winter.'

'I was a great lad for the sea myself at one time,' O'Boyle remembered. 'Every evening in summer a crowd of us would be down at the Half Moon swimming club. You know it, I suppose? Out past the Pigeon House.' O'Boyle scrutinized him closely. 'You've had your share of sea yourself, I'd say. Isn't he looking fit, chairman?'

Cornelius, unimpressed, said:

'Small wonder. The young have it soft nowadays.'

'Because they won't put up with the hardships you and me endured. And more power to them.' O'Boyle turned again to Brian. 'Am I right?'

'I don't know what those hardships were.'

'Nor never will, please God.'

O'Boyle sipped cautiously at his punch, testing its temperature. 'I'm delighted you came in while I was still here because I've been waiting to ask you something this long time.' He put his glass down with care. 'Have you given thought at all to what I had to say to you?'

'Say to me?'

'Now, now. About joining the party?'

It was unexpected. Brian glanced across at his father and saw him pick up a document which seemed all at once to require his undivided attention. The face had become a mask, blank and immobile. He sought about for an evasion.

'I don't seem to hold much in the way of political views.'

'The political views can safely be left to the higher-ups. You're the son of your father and concerned for your country. That's the true and only test. Am I right, chairman?'

Cornelius raised his head only long enough to make his position clear.

'I warned you, Andrew,' he said curtly, 'this is solely your concern.'

He resumed his study.

O'Boyle was confident of his ground. He returned again to Brian.

'You needn't be nervous at all,' he continued. 'All the new recruit needs to do is to support the party line – whatever it happens to be. After a while you'll get to know the ropes yourself. Then, in no time at all, given your education and good family name, you'll win your nomination as a candidate.'

'Wouldn't I be expected to make speeches?'

'A few, well-chosen words, as they say. There's always plenty of others to do the real talking. It'll all be worked out in advance for you anyway when the national executive plans the campaign.'

Brian, in the hope of avoiding confrontation, studied his punch. O'Boyle judged he had gained ground and pushed his case.

'Does that make it easier?'

'It could happen on occasion, I suspect, that I wouldn't see eye to eye with the national executive.'

'Highly unlikely,' O'Boyle assured him. 'We stand for republicanism and the ideal of a united and Irish Ireland. You'd hardly find fault with that.'

The note in O'Boyle's voice told Brian it was no use. They were looming nearer and nearer; the worn repetitions, the mesmerism of glories past, the worship of dead oracles. Voices from that locked-in world of patriotic fantasy had been singing about his ears since childhood; in classrooms, at home, in public-house arguments, commemorative ceremonials, in endless spates of articles in Sunday newspapers.

O'Boyle, their present mouthpiece, went on compulsively: 'We stand for the things good men died for, the men of ninety-eight, the Fenians, the men of nineteen sixteen. Emmet, Pearse, O'Donovan Rossa.'

'And the Four Glorious Years,' Brian suggested, the temptation now too strong. O'Boyle missed the note that made Cornelius glance up briefly, his face displeased, his eyes hardening.

'Now you have it. Well spoken.' O'Boyle's approval was ingenuous and trusting. His points, he felt, were persuasive.

'They are not for me,' Brian said, as inoffensively as possible.

'I don't understand?'

'The men you talk about. If I have to look back, I'd rather look to people like George Russell.'

'George Russell.'

'Otherwise A. E., the poet. He was a patriot too in his own way but he saw things differently:

> "The worship of the dead is not
> A worship that our hearts allow"

He wrote those lines. I like them.'

'Our heroes and patriots, is it? Surely every decent Irishman honours our martyred dead?'

'Not any more. That's part of my difficulty. To my mind our politicians only exploit them. They use them to rubberstamp everything from *gombeen* morality to book censorship. That's not for me.'

His father's voice cut in from behind his back: 'And what *is* for you, if the question isn't too presumptuous?' It was heavy with sarcasm. It was girded for battle. Brian, too, squared up. He was not going to be intimidated.

'Russell, among others. I've already told you.

'George Russell is it? The Hairy Fairy.'

'Hairy or not, he had a piece of good advice to pass on, if I can remember it. It was in the same poem – ' He paused to think.

'No blazoned banner we unfold
One charge along we give to youth,
Against the sceptred myth to hold
The golden heresy of truth.'

'Now we'll have the powtry flung at us,' Cornelius explained carefully to O'Boyle. 'Matter a damn whether he or anybody else has the slightest notion of what it's all supposed to mean, we'll have the powtry spouting out of him by the yard.'

'It means an end to political ambition, anyway,' Brian said sadly.

Cornelius ignored him.

'By the yard, Andrew, for further orders. And I'll tell you who this George Russell was, though you should remember him yourself. At best he was a hairy-looking eejit with a bush of a beard that went about hearing voices and searching for the fairies here, there and yonder and then painting peculiar pictures of them and writing even more peculiar powtry about them. At his worst he was cycling about the country helping to spread co-operatives and communism among decent farmers on behalf of Sir Horace Plunket, Unionist MP for Dublin, until Cosgrave made bad worse by sticking him into the Senate in twenty-two. That's the stud book for our Mr Russell.'

But O'Boyle was near to tears. He appealed to Brian.

'Russell – a Unionist's lackey. You're not in earnest, son?'

'Too bloody true he's in earnest,' Cornelius said, raising his voice almost to a shout. 'I've lived long enough within earshot of his oul guff to tell you that.'

'If he was a lackey,' Brian said, 'he'd an odd way of expressing it.'

'A lackey,' Cornelius repeated. 'Trust Andrew to put his finger on it. Drinking cups of tea with Protestants and backing up Willie Yeats on divorce. That's Mr Russell for you. They got off soft to have their books banned. They should have been burned.'

Brian pushed his glass aside and stood up.

'Persuade him to stop shouting,' he said quietly to O'Boyle, 'it can't be good for him.'

'I've caused trouble,' O'Boyle said. He was deeply distressed. Then he turned to Cornelius.

'For God's sake calm yourself, chairman. The boy couldn't mean it. You hurt him by attacking him.'

'He could and he does,' Cornelius insisted. 'Always and ever he's sneered at his own country. They all do, because everything they have was handed to them on a plate.'

'It's quite a plateful, isn't it? 'Brian remarked, 'with a war next door for good measure. There's more than enough on the same plate, whoever handed it to us.'

Cornelius said, 'And what would Russell propose you should do about it?'

The contempt was no longer to be endured.

'I don't know what Russell would advise if he were alive,' Brian answered, speaking slowly, 'but I can tell you what I've decided myself. I'm joining the RAF.'

There was a stunned silence in which he himself shared. A notion had become a decision in the act of announcing it. It surprised him. Nevertheless he was quite sure of it. He looked around. The information had paralysed all movement. O'Boyle's expression was of utter disbelief. He was the first to speak.

'Are you out of your mind, son? Is it kill your father you want to? Have you given a thought at all to his name and what he stands for?'

'I'm over twenty now. Am I not entitled to stand for something too?'

'By giving his enemies weapons against him, is it? Have you any notion what Mullevins and Páircéir and their ilk will make of this when word reaches the party that the chairman's son is off to wear the King's uniform?'

His father found his voice again. It cut through O'Boyle's plea.

'You're wasting your time, Andrew.'

'But how will I answer the committee when the matter is raised?'

'Tell them the truth. Tell them my son would serve under any flag but his own. Like many another I could name. Tell them he despises his own country, Andrew, that's the be all and the end of it. If I was younger, though, he'd swallow his words – '

'Calm yourself, chairman, calm yourself –

'You'll leave this between him and me – '

'I wish you were younger. You'd know what it was like to be brought up in this happy homeland of hypocrisy.'

'You'll leave the room, mister.'

'Very well.'

'And from the moment you join the British Army this is no longer your home – understand me clearly.'

'I understand.'

'No longer your home. No longer my son. A renegade.'

The word struck like a blow, drawing from O'Boyle an involuntary puff of breath. Brian nodded stiffly and left. The remains of his punch cooled on the table, the sugar crystallized in a ring about the bottom of the glass.

It was still early enough, not much after nine. He pulled on his overcoat again, threw his pyjamas and razor and toothbrush into a bag and got out his bicycle. Rain was falling still, the wind buffeted about him, making it hard at times to keep the handlebars under control. Cunningham, opening the door to his knock, found him bedraggled and out of breath. He stood in the hallway to wipe the rain from his eyes and face.

'Is something wrong?'

'Can I stay here tonight?'

'You've had a row at home?'

'Well – can I?'

'Of course. I'll tell the mother to rig up something in my bedroom. Give me your coat.'

Later they drank cocoa together at the sitting-room fire while Brian told his story. They explored what they knew of the procedures, who to contact, what were the choices. When that had been covered Brian fell silent, the earlier scene rehearsing itself in his thoughts. He regretted the confrontation. In spite of himself his father's words hurt. In spite of himself also, he felt the rub of guilt. There were Eilish and his mother to be considered. There was Barbara.

'Do you think I was a fool?' he asked Cunningham.

'You could be.'

'I don't usually act on impulse.'

'You don't. Sometimes it's best, though.'

'I've been thinking about my mother and Eilish. Barbara too.'

'So have I.'

'You feel I'm being unfair to them?'

Cunningham realized he had been misunderstood.

'Sorry. I meant I've been thinking about my own family. Eilish, too, need I say.'

'What has that got to do with it?'

'This RAF thing,' Cunningham said. He smiled. 'I'm going with you.'

They could enlist in Belfast. There was a depot in Great Victoria Street, they were told, which catered for all three services. Some kind of identification was all they would need. And, of course, some money. Cunningham decided to work his notice. Brian borrowed from Eilish and in the meanwhile avoided contact with his father by sleeping downstairs. The house was sunk in gloom. Eilish said little. His mother, her attempts to dissuade him fruitless, wept at odd times as she went about her housework. The night before he was due to leave Barbara ignored her landlady's rule about entertaining young men by having him to a meal in her flat. She lit the fire in the grate for the occasion, and he brought along two bottles of wine, one for the table and one to take as they sat together at the fire.

Barbara said, 'I suppose, when you make a decision like this, it's because you must. But do you know why?'

'Not really.'

'It's going to be so lonely all over again.'

'I know. I'm sorry.'

'Eilish called in to see me in the office, did she tell you?'

'No. What made her do that?'

'She was upset, I suppose. We had coffee and she showed me this charm thing she'd bought for Des Cunningham. It had a five-pointed star on one side and on the other this scraggy little monkey. She's going to ask him to wear it all the time. For luck.' She paused. 'Do you believe in things like that?'

'No more than in Holy Water.'

'I thought you'd say that.'

He poured wine and handed the glass to her.

'I'm not sure I should have any more.'

'Why not? Eat, drink and be merry.'

'And I wish you wouldn't say things like that. It isn't lucky. It isn't . . .'

She began to cry and he said:

'Please, Barbara. You mustn't.' He took her in his arms. After a while she wiped her eyes and decided to take the wine after all.

'Poor Brian. First your mother and Eilish. Now me. How does it feel to be a weeping wall?'

'Unworthy. I love you, Barbara.'

'That's all that matters, isn't it?'

At Amiens Street station next evening they gathered in November fog under inadequate lamps to make their farewell. The clock dawdled, the train waited, luggage carts trundled by them and vanished in the gloom which enveloped the farther reaches of the platform. Conversation grew more and more irrelevant but they kept the talk going. Brian kissed Barbara and then Eilish and then Anne. He turned to Tim.

'*Sgarúint na gcompánach* – the sundering of companions.' He embraced him.

'*Pax tecum*,' Tim said, returning the gesture.

'Wishing peace to someone bound for war seems a bit odd.'

'The peace of Self, not of situation.'

Cunningham embraced him too and said, '*Pax tecum.* They sing that in the mass, I remember.'

'They're always singing,' Brian said. '*Sanctus, sanctus. Alleluia, Alleluia.*'

'*Venite, venite,*' Cunningham added, his mind offering a sudden memory. 'Why, I wonder?'

'To keep the truth at arm's length,' Brian answered.

For a moment they ran out of things to say. The women, too, were at a loss. Then Tim said, 'I feel I should be going with you.'

'Someone has to stay,' Brian answered. 'The oul sod may have to be defended too.'

'Against whom, though?'

'A conundrum. Will McDonagh be shooting at Germans or Russians, or at Moloney and Cunningham?'

'Please . . .' Eilish said.

To cover her distress Tim remarked, 'Conundrum. That's a great word of your father's, I remember.'

'So it is,' Brian turned to Eilish. 'Thank him for the loan of it when you get home. And give him my love.'

Too distressed to judge his altering moods, she wondered if he was in earnest.

'Do you mean it?'

'Yes, seriously. Give my love to both of them.'

His troubled thought showed for a moment in his eyes. Eilish was crying now, though soundlessly, two large tears welling and spreading on her cheeks. Somewhere in the gloom and distance a whistle was blown. It was time. He kissed her a second time.

'My sweet sister,' he said tenderly.

He joined Cunningham and closed the carriage door.

Smells of steam and smoke saddened the air. The carriages shuddered and couplings groaned and the wheels bit on the rails before moving into rhythm. Coaches undulated gracefully as the train glided forward. Clack-a-clack, clack-a-clack, the wheels said. Their waving forms receded. They were soon lost in the darkness.

FIVE · Farewell Companions

Bold Robert Emmet, the darling of Erin
Bold Robert Emmet will die with a smile
Farewell companions both loyal and daring
I lay down my life for the Emerald Isle.

TOM MAGUIRE

I

As the flags on the map in the window of Combridges of Dame Street spread out and multiplied, the Bovril sign above College Green ceased to splash its colours against greybricked buildings and evening skies. The streets themselves progressively altered. Taxis were restricted, motor cars few. Signposts had disappeared altogether. Trains were said to do the same on occasion. They set out for remote destinations and neither arrived nor returned. The poor quality of the coal, it seemed, was to blame. In city grates turf replaced it and smouldered for hours before consenting to burn, colouring the air with its distinctive tang. Bicycles proliferated, horse traffic returned and with it an upswing in the supply of manure. Aunt Kate, for one, approved. With her vegetable plot and her few roses in mind, she kept a sharp eye in her head on journeys about the neighbourhood and returned with bucket and shovel to gather any offerings she had spotted. Occasionally she asked Tim for his help. It was an embarrassment, of course, but he never refused. He was deeply fond of her and her loneliness touched him. At least two nights in the week he slept in the house to keep her company, though he found sleeping in it uneasy. The only rooms in use were the sitting room on Sundays and the kitchen on weekdays. The rest were cold and silent. If he opened a door for any reason he found a space trapped in the past, unfriendly to intrusion, empty, yet in some odd way, inhabited. Even the sitting room brooded on memories. The picture of *The Gambler* still moralized on the wall, the wickerwork lady in her crinoline still occupied the top of the piano and quivered delicately if he struck the keys. Ware behind glass in the china cabinet corroborated old decencies. On the work table photographs flanked the needle box, and the cover trailed frondlike tassels almost to the floor. Sheet music from Woolworths which filled the piano stool offered, in addition to voice line and keyboard accompaniment, some simple fingering for ukulele *obbligato*. It smelled of damp. Neither these nor the gramophone cabinet, nor the undisturbed records stacked on shelves below it had anything further to add. They were defunct, they merely awaited dispersal.

Aunt Kate seemed one with them. On wintry mornings, her voice floating up to him from the kitchen told him she was on her knees, a kerchief about her hair, rubber gloves on her hands, cleaning out the kitchen grate. Her small but sweet voice rehearsed an out-of-fashion song.

> 'What will I do
> When you
> Are far away
> And I
> Am blue –
> What will I do?'

What indeed? It could have been childhood again. He lay and watched the unseasonable sun streaming into his grandfather's room. It cast delicately stirring curtain patterns on the white walls and made a ghost of the halo on the ceiling above the votive lamp and the statue on the altar to the Sacred Heart. He listened, timelessly suspended, a bird observant in the branchy tree of memory, until her voice called up the stairs.

'Tim.'

Despite the sun the air struck coldly.

'I'd have let you lie on only the gas will go off in twenty minutes if you want toast or something fried for you.'

Fuel short and gas rationed: these were the daily considerations.

'No. Just bread and butter.'

On dry evenings she cooked in the garden on a drum filled with sawdust, operated on some draught principle, an ingenuity of the army's introduced by Uncle Hugh on one of his rare visits home.

He remembered: 'I have my own tea and sugar somewhere.'

Bring it with you, these days, or let social life collapse.

'Never mind. So far I'm well enough stocked with both.'

The Black Market. Aunt Kate, veteran housekeeper, understood the imperatives of supply.

Eilish, when she called to the Metropolitan to share her news with Barbara, would come over to talk to him. Her father, she said, was much the same. Her mother, though, was down in herself and lonely. He should call in some evening for a talk and a session of violin and piano. She had always so enjoyed that. Was he persevering with his studies? And doing well?

'Not bad. I get odd weekend engagements. If I could get off from here for afternoon rehearsals now and then it would be a lot better.'

'And won't they let you?'

'A Metropolitan man,' he told her sadly, 'dies at his post.'

It was a shame, she thought.

'Count yourself lucky not to be a wage slave,' he said.

'But I am. Or will be next week.'

That was news.

'Your first job. Where?'

'A solicitor's office,' she said. She hoped it wouldn't be like the Metropolitan.

Bombs fell here and there and damaged buildings but nothing else. An outbreak of foot and mouth disease which entailed the wholesale slaughter of cattle and sheep was more serious. O'Sheehan suspected Hitler.

'They sprinkle it from the air,' he told Cornelius.

'Sprinkle what?'

'A class of virus. From their aeroplanes.'

'What would they do a thing like that for?'

'To put a stop to our cattle exports to Britain.

Cornelius would never have suspected such blackguardism, he said. After close, mutual consultation they concluded it was in breach of the Hague Convention.

In Grafton Street on Easter Saturday the flower sellers' baskets blazed with tulips and daffodils. People smoked their first cigarette after six weeks of Lent or swallowed their first drink. The sun itself came out to smile. Eilish met Barbara for coffee in Roberts and presented her with an Easter egg.

'How lovely.'

'They were displayed everywhere in Woolworths. I just couldn't resist.'

She ordered coffee and said:

'Thank God I can have sugar with it again.'

'You gave it up for Lent?'

'Mother and I always do. I don't mind tea so much, but coffee without it is nearly undrinkable. Did you give up anything?'

'Nothing,' Barbara confessed. 'I'm just deplorably weak-willed. Except that I cut down on smoking.'

'That's a lot harder, really.'

'Laziness. They're so scarce most of the time. And the bloody females betray you and keep them under the counter for their good-looking men customers. I had a letter from Brian. Had you?'

'Not this couple of weeks.'

'They've passed him to train as a pilot. He's up in his hat. What about Des?'

'He's to be a rear gunner and wireless operator.' She looked grave. 'It sounds awfully dangerous.'

'I know,' Barbara said, frowning and picking at the tablecloth. 'But that's what war is about, isn't it? Do you worry a lot?'

'I'm afraid I do.'

'Me, too.'

The café trio, returning refreshed from hidden quarters, picked up their instruments and began to tune them.

'I wonder Tim McDonagh didn't go with them. He can't bear the Metropolitan.'

'He's working furiously at his music,' Eilish said. 'He wants to become a professional eventually.'

'Is he good enough, do you think?'

'He sounds awfully good to me,' Eilish said.

'Lucky Anne.'

'Yes. Not like us. All on our own.'

'I know. A couple of old war widows.'

They both laughed. The trio began to play softly. Barbara examined the Easter egg with renewed pleasure.

'On our way out,' she said, 'I must buy *you* one. I insist.'

II

Cornelius, ears alert, eyes fixed on the faint glimmering of the bedroom ceiling, concentrated his attention.

'Are you awake, missus?'

'Yes. I can hear it.'

'Another of them tonight. What time is it?'

'Past three o'clock.'

The air in the bedroom was unusually still and warm. Dawn was not far away.

'I hope he doesn't do what the other did – empty his bombs over innocent neutrals.'

'God forbid. Should I see is Eilish awake?'

'What good will that do? Anyway he seems to be heading off. What the hell do they want over here?'

'They say it's German planes. They lose their way.' Cornelius relaxed a little.

'German or English, he seems to have found it again.'

'You're not sleeping these times.'

'I worry about the party. There are a few imbeciles, and I'm not there to deal with them.'

'Is that all that troubles you?'

'Isn't it enough, woman?'

'Have you no thought of Brian?'

Cornelius hardened his voice.

'Brian chose his own way.'

'And no thought for me? Every time one of them crosses in the night I lie here and think to myself: is it my own son that's away up there in the darkness.'

'I've done nothing to turn him against me. What I taught him were the true things; to respect his religion and his country, to love her language and cherish his inheritance. Is that too much to expect?'

'Have the children always to think the same thoughts as their father?'

'He doesn't have to join the army that shot his own country-men.'

'He doesn't see it that way.'

'There's a hell of a lot of them don't see it that way – the cosmopolitan brigade with their bottle parties and a sneer for everything decent. They can't even stand two minutes in a picture house to pay respect to their own national anthem.'

'If something happens to him maybe you'll change your tune.'

'It was his own choosing. I've heard enough.'

'That's how it always ends: you've heard enough – '

'Whisht, woman – '

The sound had returned. Mrs Moloney said, more to herself than to her husband, 'Whoever he is, he's some poor mother's rearing.'

'He's very near this time – '

'German or British, friend or enemy.'

'Over the park, by the sound of him.'

'Bits of children – that's all they are – doing as they're bidden.'

'I hope the fools don't open fire on him,' Cornelius said. 'That's what persuaded the last fella to ditch his cargo.'

'Children – '

There was an outburst of heavy fire.

'The fools – ' Cornelius said.

More gunfire blasted the air. Mrs Moloney, gripping her husband's shoulder, breathed: 'Sacred Heart of Jesus.'

Cornelius sat up the better to hear.

'That's the anti-aircraft battery above in the park,' he told her. He shouted his anger: 'Can't you let him go about his business, damn you – '

As he shouted the plane released its bomb load. The bed heaved ceilingwards, pictures clattered from the walls; the roar of the explosion was deafening. It threw Cornelius off balance and flung him to the floor. He raised himself and groped about for the light switch. It had no effect.

'Christ, that was near.'

Eilish came in.

'It can only be a few streets away,' she said. 'There was a sheet of flame.'

'Wherever it is, it's blown the lights.'

Mrs Moloney, who had got out of bed to find the font, was sprinkling holy water about the room. She stopped to say to Eilish:

'There are candles in the back of the press in the kitchen, child. Do you think you could find them?'

Cornelius was pulling on his clothes and swearing when he failed to locate missing odds and ends. Eilish returned with the candles and lit them.

'You're getting dressed?'

'There may be something I can do.'

'Are you out of your mind?' Mrs Moloney asked him. 'A man in your state of health.'

She appealed to Eilish. 'Talk sense into your father, child.'

'The brigades and ambulances are already out,' Eilish said. 'Leave it to them. You can see the fires from my bedroom. It seems to be over near the custom house. Go on up there and I'll bring up a cup of tea.'

They did so. The glow filled the sky and they could hear the ambulances plying to and fro but there were no more bombs. They sat silently most of the time until dawn whitened and spires and roofs were assembled again in their usual patterns. It was the North Strand that had got it. Dead and injured were being dug out of the rubble.

Dear Mother

Just a line to let you know the books I asked you to send on have arrived at long last. It's extraordinary how much more complete it feels to have them within arm's reach again. There are others still on the shelf by my bed which I've been tempted to ask for too but space is strictly limited and anyway they would create a problem if I have to move. (As I may – there's talk of completing training outside Britain – Canada perhaps.)

Tell Eilish I saw Des Cunningham a few days ago. His course is wireless etc. so we've been separated for quite a while. Needless to say we had a hell of a night together, although Cunningham did hardly anything else except talk about her which got a bit monotonous for me, need I say, but will please her to hear, need I say – (two need I says – never mind).

I'm sorry my father is still not prepared to be on talking terms. What have I done that I have not in all conscience a perfect right to do? Nevertheless please remember me to him, and give him my love and sincere wish that his health will return quickly and wholly.

My love to you too and as much of it to Eilish as can be fitted in edgeways beside Cunningham's soulful contributions. Keep well.

Ever, Brian

P.S. Will write more fully later. Just wanted to acknowledge books. Please don't send cigarettes anymore. We get all we need in the canteen here. And at the right price. Brian.

Tim resumed his letter to Brian.

– So much for the news, if you can call it that. The bombs fall from time to time, but nothing as bad as the North Strand which I told you about some months ago. When I think of the loss of life such a comparatively small operation caused, I can see how utterly crazy the people are (only a few, admittedly) who think we should be in it. Churchill, for one, is soapboxing through his imperial and commodious arse. We have no protection of any value against air attacks. The Germans could wipe Dublin off the map in a couple of nights. On the ground we might last a bit longer – people talk of holding them for five or six days, long enough for the British to come down from the north. Probably the safest place to be is in the army.

Apart from the bombs and shortages of all kinds (the bread is eighty or ninety per cent extraction and tastes like a sponge filled with wet sawdust, though Uncle Hugh sometimes pinches a few white loaves for us from the army stores where the fare seems to take the refined tastes of officers and gentlemen into consideration –

what was I saying? Yes,) apart from the bombs nothing seems to happen and has not happened for so long that I've forgotten if anything ever used to. Things seem to shrink and petrify. I told you about Aunt Kate's house which has opted out of time. My other grandparents' place is much the same – the same photographs, the same meaningless pictures, the same shell cases polished on the mantelpiece, my Uncle Joe's service medals still on the wall and his citation for bravery, dated 1917; which seems a bit ancient until you look at what's hung beside it and find yourself reading Robert Emmet's speech from the dock. But at least it feels lived in and the uncles still bring the parcels of stout back with them on Saturday nights and argue football into the small hours. I called to Aunt Emily's after being nagged for ages by my mother to do so (she can't bear Aunt Emily herself but feels the family 'must keep in touch'), and it was the same. The picture of Uncle Freddie (the Republican who was shot in an ambush or something in 1922) remains on display, with an Easter lily stuck above the frame and a poem beside it written in a prison cell and all about freeing Ireland and saying the rosary. Aunt Emily is in her seventies now but as bitter as ever. There was one change though. Dev's picture has been taken down since he let some Republicans he had gaoled die on hunger strike. He has now joined Aunt Emily's ever-lengthening list of the turncoats who have betrayed Ireland. When I mentioned that a couple of my friends had joined up she blasted off in regulation fashion. Your father, you see, is not unique. But that's the Ireland we've inherited. Hurricane, famine, earthquake, volcano, even a world war have no real impact. Kathleen *ní* Hoolihawn won't cast a glance beyond her four green fields.

I'm finishing this in the office here, which more and more I can't stand the sight of. Otherwise though, things are shaping better. I get a steady flow of engagements playing for amateur productions of opera and musical comedy and the odd professional job. I keep on studying too, in the hope of going full time if the opportunity turns up. There's talk, I understand, of building up the radio orchestra. One tip I got is to switch over to viola, which only involves learning the clef – the technique is the same. Viola players, it seems, are few and far between. That's quite understandable. Most parents see music for their kids exclusively in terms of either piano or violin.

Since I wrote above about Aunt Emily I've had a look at the

paper – one of Ellis's minor extravagances. A man who staggered into the police station wearing chains and things has turned out to be Stephen Hayes, head of the IRA. It says he was kidnapped by some of his own crowd last June and held prisoner since on charges of some kind. So it still goes on. Why should anyone seek to harm us? Leave us to it, and we'll have each other for breakfast.

Answer when you can. I have a standing instruction from Barbara to send her love whenever I write, so I do so now. Also Anne's. She's going to fencing classes these times. That's us. Armed to the teeth.

Regards,
Tim

The wind tore ragged scrawls through the grey and black clouds massing above O'Connell Bridge and made rents that let through the angry light of evening. It set white wavelets streaking across the dark tide of the river. The man manipulating the barrel organ on the bridge used his free hand to wipe away the water it kept drawing from his eyes. It blew away whole chunks of the music which was already battling for a hearing above traffic and passing feet. As O'Sheehan crossed the bridge he felt the chill force of the wind on his cheek and forgot for a moment the voice that had been struggling to make intelligible speech inside his head. He paused to drop a shilling in the green baize bag. It was more generous than his wont, but then his whole attention was not on what was going on about him. Even the reedy tune, gapped though it was and despite the evidence of his eyes, seemed to emanate from a source inside him. He hurried on to his room, where the fire had been lit for him and the table laid as always.

Through his meal he debated whether he should call on Cornelius. His company would be welcomed, of that he was confident. But it might also be tiring. It was the duty of friendship to be prudent as well as companionable. His friend was far from well. Rest, even if it involved a measure of boredom, might be the better option.

He drew his chair to the fireside but left the window drapes undrawn and sat so that he could observe the sky. Without the

wind to harass him it had features of enchantment and beauty to
be pondered and explored. It was a place to soar into, on bird
wing or by arts of levitation or astride a steed with adequately
magical properties, procedures with which he was reasonably
familiar since he had had recourse to them, though infrequently,
in the past. The time for some such experience seemed near at
hand – comparatively: a year, two years, five years, something
of that order.

The voice returned; it was a woman's, very beautiful. It was
familiar, though from many ages ago. Here in the solitude and
warmth and quietness, with the chiaroscuro of the sky to
sharpen the antennae of the spirit, it became more and more
easily intelligible. And then identifiable. Niamh. How long
now since she had appeared so suddenly before him, her hair
no less golden than the diadem that encircled it, her eyes no less
brown than her dark brown mantle with its embossed stars of
gold, her steed white and shod with silver? The trees and hedges
ringing the lakeside were fragrant with blossom and shimmering
under the mist of morning.

'What is your country and race, lovely maiden?'

'I am Niamh of the golden hair, daughter of the king of the
land of youth.'

'What seek you here?'

'The love of Oisin, if he will journey back with me to my
father's kingdom.'

'That I will. And to the end of the earth.'

On horseback then through corridors of cloud and colour,
the billows heaving below and ahead, the forests and headlands
of Ireland receding behind. A hornless doe passed at one stage,
pursued by a white hound with one red ear. And again, as he
remembered, a maiden on a brown steed with a golden apple in
her hand, followed by a youth on a white horse with a gold-
hilted sword. What had they meant, these airy visions? He had
never found out. But the land of youth had been as they had so
often heard; flowery places, melodious fowles, fruit-heavy
branches. And in clusters by brown streams the airy, delicate
tree of the Druids, the rowan with its berries. The noble willow

too, unfailing ornament of poems. There feast cloyed not, chase tired not, never faltering the enchantment of music. No agony of limb either, no sickness of body, no waning of intellect, nor withering of spirit nor decrepitude of flesh. Why then had he wished to re-visit the old ways? An old answer; the human heart and its inescapable yearnings. Love of homeland drew him and the cherishing of dear companions who, as it turned out, were dead long centuries and in their clay. Gone too the white-walled dwellings from the Hill of Allen and the ramparts all crumbled and nothing but grassgrown mounds and grazing cattle. No Finn, no Oscar, no Caoilte, no Diarmuid; he himself an airy horseman forbidden under pain of instant age to set foot on the green sod of home, yet fated to do so because, as he stooped from his saddle, the bellyband broke and he tumbled to the ground. He watched his youth bounding away from him with the freed steed as it bolted.

For the best, perhaps. Mortal nature hungered to die as well as live. Who knew it better than himself, for whom death came tardily and then only to transform? Shape and species might alter, but all resumed as before, bringing again the boon of youth and comeliness and young lustihood, all the sweet delirium, burying but never obliterating the low murmur of loss. Allan, Cualann, Leitir Lee. Finn, Oscar, Conan, Caoilte.

The window undraped framed a night-blue sky with a single star. He had slept. From remote depths in the echoing cavern of memory the faint voice still called: come away, come away. . . .

III

The voice at the other end of the line sounded right, yet it was hard to believe. Ellis, who had his drawer open so that he could scan the racing news in the paper concealed in it, looked up curiously at his note of surprise.

'Is that Tim McDonagh?'

'Speaking.'

'This is Des Cunningham.'

'Des Cunningham – ?'

'My God – he's forgotten me.'

'Where on earth are you?'

'Here on earth at home. I'm on leave, got back yesterday. Can I see you? How's tonight?'

'Tonight – I'm playing for a show.'

'Tomorrow night?'

'I'm playing all week, damn it.'

'Then I could go to it, couldn't I – or are the public not admitted? What is it?'

' "Faust".'

'Oh – cheerful stuff. I'll take Eilish. I'll take Anne too, if you like. We'll go in style.'

He was as good as his word and paid for a box. Tim could see him from the orchestra pit, Eilish and Anne on either side of him, the ritual box of chocoates perched in front of them on the upholstered ledge. He was in dinner jacket and bow tie, and the girls were in evening dress.

'Doesn't he look awfully well?' Eilish remarked to Tim when he managed to join them briefly in the bar at the first interval.

'Splendid,' Tim agreed. 'The finery takes my breath away.'

'He insisted. It's fun, really.'

Cunningham explained, 'What I like about opera is you can shout things like "encore" and "bravo" – '

'I heard you,' Tim said.

'So the least it deserves is a black tie. That wasn't the fiddle you were playing, was it?'

'The viola. I switched some time ago because there's a shortage of viola players.'

'Crafty McDonagh.'

'He's getting a bit of sense,' Anne said, defending him.

He had seen her in evening dress perhaps once before. She looked very beautiful, he thought – so beautiful, in fact, that his pleasure had in it an inexplicable twinge of pain.

He said to her, 'You look marvellous. You too, Eilish. You've no idea how impressively superior the three of you look from that pit.'

The first bell began.

'When can you join us again?' Cunningham asked.

'Not till the final curtain, I'm afraid. But the bar stays open for nearly an hour.'

He spent the intervals in the bandroom. As always it depressed him, though more so tonight for some inexplicable reason. As always he felt young, inexperienced, ill at ease, a tyro facing difficulties the professionals had forgotten had ever existed. Some of them were amiable and talked to him about conductors they had played under and singers who were great or deplorable and their eccentricities. But the residential core of the orchestra stayed apart. They were elderly and going bald and wore jackets that passed for black only in the dimness of the pit. Exposed to any light at all they became a mouldy green. During the intervals they gathered immediately into the card school about the large props basket commandeered long before for use as a table and resumed where they had left off in a game that continued night after night for the run of the season. Each occupied the place immemorially his. The game was central, the music an interruption, as tolerable and as interesting as getting up to wind the clock. They had seen too many lovers estranged and re-united, too many maidens betrayed and husbands deceived and heirs reinstated on the uniqueness of a birthmark. While students rollicked in cafés or populaces revolted, whether duels were fought or assassinations were plotted or poisoned cups changed hands, their business was simply to saw or blow as indicated by the notes in front of them and keep an eye on the conductor to see whether he wanted it loud or soft or somewhere in between – provided he entertained any strong feelings in the matter – and what tempo he desired, assuming he had made up his mind.

The fire drill procedures, which he had read through at least twice without becoming much enlightened, were listed in detail on the wall, flanked by trade union notices long out of date, and photographs and holiday postcards. The photographs mixed variety turns, opera stars and circus acts. The postcards devoted themselves to seaside promenades, fat women and sex. They were curiously depressing. He was always impatient to be back in the pit and getting on with the job. In spite of the moments of uncertainty and technical anxiety, the music dispelled the drabness and at its least offered diversion. At special moments it even swamped through him and raised him as on a tide. Yet he was glad when it was over to pack up his instrument and store it with the others in their cupboard. When he made his way to the bar the second curtain had already been lowered. It was gaudy with advertisements: 'Say it with flowers'; 'Guinness is good for you'; 'Wine and dine after the show at The Cremona'.

An aroma of coffee clung on in the bar which was by no means crowded. They were waiting for him.

'Are you exhausted?' Anne asked.

'Only deafened. The brass are right behind me.'

Cunningham pushed a drink towards him. 'I like the brass when they lift you out of it,' he said.

'But not six inches from the back of your head.'

'I've got used to noise,' Cunningham said.

They waited with interest, but he said no more. Eilish broke the short silence:

'It's always a surprise how much one knows about an opera already: the Jewel Song, the Flower Song, All Hail Thou Dwelling –'

'Pure and lowly. Or is it poor and lowly?' Cunningham asked.

'Pure.'

'And that march,' he continued. 'It lifts you up by the hair when the chorus and orchestra bash it out, and yet it's spoiled by that bloody stupid parody we used to sing – you remember it:

> 'Old
> Soldiers, like the leg of a duck
> Most
> Soldiers, never get half enough – '

'Thanks,' Anne wailed. 'That's ruined it forever.

'It's given me an idea. I'm in funds – loaded. Why don't we go and eat?'

'Extravagance.'

'My sweet Eilish, why not?'

Anne looked at Tim.

'It's too expensive,' Tim said.

'I've money, I told you,' Cunningham was suddenly in high gear and not to be dissuaded, as though whatever was inside him must be let out or it would buckle something. Tim wondered if it was simply a reaction to disciplines temporarily relaxed, or if it was something more meaningful – a throw against imminent menaces, a screwing up of mettle. They finished their drinks and waited at the back of the empty theatre while the two women went to the cloakroom. The second curtain had now disappeared behind the last, asbestos-grey and slablike. It had no place for nonsense about wining and dining or saying it with flowers. Two painted words simply said: Safety Curtain. Little bodies were frail and combustible.

'How do you find things over there?' Tim asked, now that the women were absent.

'Tough enough. They use you pretty hard.'

'A wireless gunner, isn't it?'

'That's it. I expect you know Brian qualified for the pilot's course.'

'Yes. He wrote. When will you be listed for active service?'

'Pretty soon.'

'Does it bother you?'

'That's what I joined up for, isn't it?

'And the prospects?'

'As at now – not great. I'm told they reckon a gunner's survival expectancy at about twelve flying hours.'

Tim said nothing. Unease stirred inside him. But the card players in the bandroom had had the same effect. And a while ago, just as oddly, the grey expanse of the safety curtain.

'But what are statistics?' Cunningham pursued. 'One poor bugger may have had it before he gets upstairs at all. Another lasts forty-five minutes. Another stays aloft until someone notices he's losing his teeth. It's not at all like the statistics say: twelve hours – bingo; twelve hours – bingo. Only the mathematicians believe that.'

They heard a door opening and closing. Cunningham warned, 'That's not for mixed company, need I say.'

'Of course not.'

In the Cremona candles flickered on the tables and the steaks were so good that he insisted on buying them a bottle of wine to toast the rich pastures and strong farmers of Ireland. Britain currently seeming to be a bit short on both.

'Which reminds me to ask,' he said to Tim, 'how are the mountains? I often think of them.'

'The gorse is in flower.'

' "The Gorse in Flower". That could be a jig or a reel. Like "The Blackberry Blossom" or "The Wind that Shakes the Barley". Anyone know any more?'

' "The Bush in Bloom",' Tim said.

' "The Field of Daisies",' Anne offered.

Eilish said, ' "The Mountain Lark".'

'That could mean another thing,' Cunningham suggested. 'And the camp. What's that like?'

'All Nissen huts and runways, but I don't mind that. There's the sea near it and a few irregular bumps that do for hills if you use a little imagination. What waxes me off is the communal centre. They slap a mug down in front of you among the breadcrumbs on the counter, and no matter what's on your plate it smells of vinegar and chips. On evenings off I go down to this little teashop in the village. Lots of the others do too. It's to have a teacup instead of a mug and a tablecloth instead of scrubbed boards and someone to serve you the scones and toast. It feels odd even now to be out of uniform. De Valera said he wouldn't let me home if I didn't take it off.'

'Why is that?' Anne asked. 'Is it the IRA thing – or something?'

'The wages of neutrality,' Tim said. 'It saves embarrassment when he wants to walk past the German embassy.'

Anne said she hadn't thought of that. They had another bottle of wine which Tim insisted on buying. It made them laugh at very ordinary things, and they began to feel, yes there were times when the world was a wizard place to be in as at present, yes when it was warm and gently glowing with love and altogether dreamlike. Candlelight fell on bare arms that moved gracefully, bracelets glinted, and perfume breathed from young and vibrant bodies. Then Eilish and Cunningham were holding hands and she was leaning her head on his shoulder at more frequent intervals, and Tim and Anne were exchanging unspoken messages of tenderness, and the hour was growing very late indeed.

'How are taxis?' Cunningham asked, as though it hardly mattered at all.

'Not a hope,' Tim said. Nevertheless, he dragged himself to his feet and consulted the waiter. A horse and cab might be possible.

'Perfect,' Cunningham enthused. But while they were waiting in the foyer he amended it. 'Nights like this shouldn't be let end, should they?'

'Think of it as a pause for breath,' Tim suggested.

They were informed that, in fact, two cabs were available, which was more convenient. The clip-clop of the first reached them faintly from the street.

'Your privilege,' Tim said to Eilish and Cunningham.

'Right. I'll see you on the weekend – yes? The mountains, maybe.'

They went out to the steps. Hailstones were falling lightly and soundlessly, to nestle in clusters at joins in the harness and melt silently on the sleek coat. Cunningham waved and the cabman flicked the reins. They waved. The hail whirled in thick but noiseless squalls into which the cab vanished.

'It was a lovely night, wasn't it?' Anne said.

He was very conscious of muted streets, the peaceful alchemy of snow.

'Great,' he answered.

But later in the cab he confessed that he had been uneasy at times and for no apparent reason.

'That's odd.'

'You too?'

'Yes. And I couldn't tell why. I hope it isn't premonition or something. I'm thinking of Des.'

'Mine started ages before. In the bandroom, as a matter of fact.'

'What sort of a feeling?'

'That nothing was really very interesting. That everything grew stale and old. I think it was those bloody card players. I probably transferred it to you.'

'That's probably it.'

She lay against him and they listened sleepily and silently to the clip-clop of hooves until she stirred again and said:

'What bloody card players?'

He explained.

It was while Cunningham was still on leave that the unthinkable happened, all, as it seemed, in a moment. He was waiting in the street for her and thinking of comments he might make about their weekend outing with Eilish and Cunningham when he caught sight of her. Her appearance alarmed him. She was pale, even stooped. Clearly something was wrong. He went forward towards her and took her arm.

'Anne – something's wrong?'

She told him. Her father and the family were returning to the United States. It had been announced quite baldly to her the previous night, all decided, all irreversibly fixed. America's entry into the war had finally tipped the scales. Young men were being called up, staffing rearranged, the Irish branch closed down.

'He was talking with my mother about it most of last night. It was dreadful.'

'But you don't have to go with them.'

'I tried to suggest I shouldn't. They wouldn't hear of my staying.'

'Tell them to go to hell.'

'Tim – please. Don't be angry with me. It's too much. Last night I couldn't sleep at all.'

Her misery was plain even through his own despair and anger. He told her he was sorry. They were to have gone to the cinema, but they both agreed it was now out of the question. They decided to go walking instead. He put his arm through hers and she leaned against him for comfort, so closely that passers-by looked curiously at them. He hardly noticed or cared.

'You could stay here on your own.'

'I've thought about that, but it isn't possible. Not on what I earn. You must know that.'

He did. That was why they had both pushed the idea of her having to leave so resolutely out of mind in the first instance.

They talked it over and over. They walked with it through street after street between rows of uninterested houses and by railinged gardens that were preoccupied with the hint and stir of spring, until the grudging light of the March evening faded altogether and the lamps strewed their cold sheen on damp footpaths. When there seemed no aspect of the situation left to explore they decided a drink might help them in some way or other to find a solution.

But they only sat huddled together in growing hopelessness and dejection, so that the barman glanced across at them from time to time convinced that they were having a quarrel.

'It may not be for very long,' Anne said. That raised his hopes for a moment.

'Did your father say that?'

'No. But the war can't go on so very long now, can it? I mean with America in it now as well.'

'Perhaps.' he said. But it was a long way from being convincing.

'You remarked we both had that moody thing the other night. Do you think it was because this was going to happen?'

'No.'

'I think it was,' she said quietly.

'It wasn't,' he said, raising his voice, 'because it isn't going to be let happen.'

But it did. The days passed and the reality became plain

and inescapable. They adjusted as best they could. It might only be for a year, they decided. They would correspond regularly and watch every opportunity to be together. If he succeeded in getting a better job they might even be able to be married fairly soon. They talked a lot about that possibility, especially on the day before she was to leave when they had gone out in a mood of sentimental pilgrimage to the hut. It was still boarded up and damp, but it was somewhere to be alone together for their last day. It was a sunny afternoon in May, not yet warm enough for swimming, but pleasant for walking on the beach. The small islands were clearly visible, the waves sparkled and broke among the rocks as though nothing at all in the world was astray. When they returned to the hut they made tea and had sandwiches and lingered so long afterwards that they had to leave the cups unwashed and the teapot unemptied while they rushed for their train. The next day she had gone. It was hard to believe. Nevertheless, it was so.

Returning to the hut a week later to tidy up, he found the two chairs still drawn to the table, the cups and plates and spoons lying as they had left them, and scattered crumbs about the table. He moved a cushion back to its proper place before putting the crockery into the basin. Dregs of tea smelled strongly when he removed the lid of the teapot. Above the level of the deep brown liquid, leaves had dried out where they clung to the sides. A week ago she had poured for him from it, and they had shared it.

He moved quietly about in the dimness. It was eerily silent. Where was Anne now? In some apartment he had never seen, in a strange city an ocean and more away. The leaden weight in his breast ached with longing to follow. He washed up slowly, rinsed the teapot and put it on its shelf. It gleamed in the dimness. Everything he handled seemed weightless. Everything he touched or moved was charged with absence. When all was in order he closed the door and locked it.

There was nobody about. The sun shone, the islands nestled in the afternoon haze, the sea smiled and stretched without sail or sign of life as far as the eye could take in; a vast space of sun and cloud and sky which still, it seemed to him, was not ample enough to match the emptiness and loneliness inside him. It made him long to cry out. Its smiling, undulating unconcern stripped him of hope. She was not only an ocean and more away. She was lost to him. The thought seemed likely to tear his heart out.

Eilish and Barbara met as usual for coffee. They talked about it.

'So Anne has gone away,' Eilish said.

'Yes. It's some weeks ago now.'

'Is Tim very down about it?'

'I imagine he is,' Barbara said, 'but our offices are different, and I don't see him all that much. And he's not exactly talkative, is he? – not like Des or Brian.'

'I like him.'

'But so do I – don't misunderstand me. Only he's a bit far away in himself a lot of the time. I suppose regular doses of that highbrow music he plays does things to a person's head.'

'And I remember sitting here saying how lucky Anne was.'

'I remember that too. Well – you never really know, do you? Des was back?'

'For ten whole days. It was marvellous. It was hard to settle back after it. Only for the job I'd go mental.'

'You like it?'

'It's all right. There's not all that much to do. My main chore for the boss seems to be to queue up at Hafners for sausages for his wife after I've been to the bank on Fridays. Then on Saturdays to get her books from the library. She's struck on Frances Parkinson Keyes.'

'At least it gets you out. Not like me. It's nine to five day in, day out. The boys have the best of it. They get around – France, Italy, Africa – just imagine it.'

'They have to join the army first.'

'Who'd mind joining the army?'

'And get killed,' Eilish reminded. 'You wouldn't see much then.'

'I'd see the next world, wouldn't I?'

'We'll all see that. All you have to do is wait.'

'And rot,' Barbara said.

Eilish, scrutinizing her closely, began to smile.

'What's funny?'

'The way you said that. It was just like Brian.'

Aunt Kate had something to say too. She was, as always, sympathetic.

'You miss her,' she said, 'and that's very natural. And you miss your two pals that's away in the army. It's been a big change in a very short space of time. But you're young and you'll get used to it. To be young and lonely is not the same as to be growing old as well as being lonely. Your life is ahead of you and you have your health – two great blessings, so don't overlook them. Time will pass – you'll climb the ladder and things will be possible then that are not so now. Your holidays should be coming along soon – ?'

'Next month.'

'And where are you going?'

'I don't feel like going anywhere.'

'You'd be wiser to do so. Pick somewhere where there's company of your own age and a bit of life going on. None of this walking all on your own in the mountains getting your end maybe from the rain and the loneliness. Sure that's no holiday at all.' She remembered something else. 'Did you see the paper a couple of mornings ago? There was something in it about them wanting musicians.'

'No. I didn't see anything like that.'

'I thought you mightn't so I cut it out for you.' She rose. 'If I can think what I did with it – '

He watched her searching the kitchen dresser and the work boxes and the knick-knacks which were everywhere. To her the answer would be to get used to their several absences. But the whole point was he did not wish to get used to them. He did not wish Anne to grow used to being without him, and he did not wish to grow used to being without her, an unlikely eventuality anyway. And he wished to continue to miss Brian's company for one set of reasons and to miss Cunningham's for another, because they were, simply and unsentimentally, his friends. Without them life limped along at half cock, something he might shrug off, or become resigned to, or learn to tolerate. But get used to? No. That would be to surrender the centre and the essence.

Aunt Kate was making sounds of incredulity. She had discovered the clipping in an egg cup. She denied to him that she had put it there herself. Never, under any circumstances, would she store such a thing in an egg cup.

'It must be the fairies,' she said.

She brought the clipping to him.

'Is it of interest?'

The radio orchestra had vacancies for instrumentalists, including string players. Application forms would be sent on request.

'Yes, indeed,' he assured her.

'It might be your first break, so don't let the chance pass. And say a prayer for success. There's nothing like prayer.'

'There's practice,' he suggested. He spoke mildly.

'Practice makes perfect,' she agreed, 'but prayer is very powerful. You're not getting cynical about it, I hope, like so many nowadays.'

'Of course not. I'll pray too.'

The salary scale, he noticed immediately, was a lot better than his own. Even at the start it was just about enough to get married on. It was, of course, a very long shot.

When he wrote to Anne she was enthusiastic and urged him to work hard for it. It was a tender letter which continued to regard their separation as very temporary – a lie neither believed. Still, though there were times when he had little heart for it, he did as she had asked and practised evening after evening. As a prop against loneliness it was not very effective. The need was not just to fill in time but to fill up the wound in himself. But at least it helped to make him feel he was doing something practical, and that he was not entirely powerless.

Aunt Kate said, 'You'll have the fingers worn off you.'

'Is it getting on your nerves?'

'Indeed it isn't. It brings life to the house and stops me talking to myself.'

There was another matter he felt might as well be attended to in the new circumstances, so he settled for a weekend's enclosed retreat in Tibradden Priory, going in on Saturday afternoon and remaining until after six o'clock mass on Monday morning. Strict silence was the rule, in between lectures and meals. They walked and meditated in the grounds during their free time or made appointments for special guidance and consultation. He thought: why not?

Father Purcell, his stole laid out in readiness for confession on the locker beside him, the window at his back framing harvested fields and autumn-coloured mountains, listened carefully and then said:

'And if there were difficulties until now, why do you feel you can now undertake there will be no repetition?'

'It's very simple. The other person has gone away.'

'And you felt no sense of sin, you say?'

'None.'

'In that case, how do you propose to be contrite?'

'An intellectual sorrow. I'll accept what I am told and wish to be sorry. Is that enough?'

'Provided you are sincere – yes.'

'I'm sincere, I assure you,' Tim said.

'When you love,' Father Purcell suggested, 'it's difficult to understand the teaching on such things. Often enough I think it's not put over sufficiently clearly or even accurately on our part. Too much generalization, too many don'ts and not enough positive thinking. But staying away is not the solution.'

'I'd have come if I hadn't to promise there'd be no repetition. That seemed hypocritical.'

'You have to promise to try. That's quite different. As to guilt, it's the pattern of behaviour one judges, not the isolated act, which in certain circumstances may not be gravely sinful at all. Love, of course, will seek its proper food. Was it Yeats said that? Anyway it's very natural. The trouble is there's a definitive element in sexual acts which makes them disturbing until a permanent relationship is possible. You know also what is said: "We are not our own".'

'Quite.'

'And you acknowledge that?'

'I belong to God. That's beyond question.'

'Yet you stayed away from His sacraments.'

'I've explained why. It's been a lonely experience.'

'I know,' Father Purcell said.

'You do?'

'Yes. Well, I think we can do the job now. There's no need to kneel down.'

'I'd rather, if you don't mind.'

'As you please.' Father Purcell took the stole from the locker, kissed it, draped it about his shoulders. 'We've talked at length and you've been admirably frank so a simple and formal mention will do now.'

'Very good – '

Tim crossed himself and began: 'Bless me father for I have sinned . . .'

Father Purcell listened with bowed head and closed eyes.

They met again on Sunday evening. Father Purcell invited him to his room again and offered tea.

'Now that the winter is coming on,' he said, 'we'll be resuming our classes in Thomistic philosophy. They're intended for the intelligent layman and of course they're free. Would you be interested?'

'Certainly.'

'I thought you might. They're on Thursday evenings – a course of twelve. I'll send you the literature.'

'Thank you.'

'They may throw some light on certain matters that you find puzzling at present. Such as the recognition of grave sin. I've remembered what St Alphonsus Liguori said on that subject, by the way. Did you know?'

'About recognizing grave sin? I don't think so.'

'He said: when an elephant comes in – you notice at once.'

Tim laughed. Father Purcell allowed himself a worldly wise kind of smile. Then they both gazed out the window at a sky which was filling with sunset.

The stillness of evening rested on the fields about, on trees in their autumnal shades, on unstirring ferns which dressed the mountain slopes, on heather aglow under the sunset. So it was over the whole of Ireland, as far as Cork in the south and Donegal in the north and Galway in the west; all the fields of Ireland becalmed and silent, preparing patiently for night. It would come in an hour perhaps, but later in Galway because it was so much further to the west. It would move across the islands beyond Galway, and the ocean beyond the islands, to abide eventually over Anne and whatever happened to be occupying her until it was time over there to switch off the light and the waking world and retire into sleep. Evening would pace the waste of waters between them and paint them mile after mile in sunset colours. As he stared into the western sky he sent in the wake of the sunset a token of himself, a spiritual particle which would reach her unerringly and mysteriously through the homing multiplicities of their love.

IV

At his best Cornelius enjoyed a slow and undemanding walk through the streets or a visit to his shop premises to talk to old customers. When not so good he sat either in his bedroom or at the kitchen fire and endured with detachment the collapse of the world. Food rationing and fuel shortages were his wife's concern and of academic interest only, except in so far as they interfered with the running of the public house. His foreman's regular difficulty in finding adequate stocks touched him more nearly. To surmount the worst he sometimes found it necessary to use a bit of political pull, but at least there was gratification of a kind in proving he still had some left. Selling off his greyhounds was another matter. He was no longer fit enough to train and exercise them and it was unavoidable, but it hit him hard. When his wife had cleaned up the yard with unconcealed relief, he stood alone in it and saw in its empty and tidy unfamiliarity the pointlessness of existence. Had he built a livelihood and developed interests and acquired a little honour in the community only to be stripped of them at the end? Had he raised a family to have them scorn his principles? And were we all, whatever we might choose to believe from time to time, born simply to die?

O'Sheehan told him that all things are so ordained; they just pass away in the end into that from which they took their rise, an answer, as he explained, in accord with the Milesian view. Andrew O'Boyle, more practical, suggested that a little outing of some kind before the winter set in would adjust his spirits. He arranged an excursion by horse and cab which took them all, himself, Cornelius, Mrs Moloney, O'Sheehan, even Eilish, on a drive through the park and by the strawberry beds. It was a moderate success. Even Eilish enjoyed it, though at first the horse and cab brought back memories. But the sky was blue and the river sparkled on the way out and they had an excellent old-style lunch near Lucan and its once fashionable watering place. Eilish and her mother admired the deer in the park and wondered at the growing supplies of turf which were accumulating in high banks along the verges of the roads. Cornelius was critical of its quality. O'Boyle expressed the view that if the department of supplies failed to improve on its performance it would affect the government's chances in the general election due to be held in the following June. Their minds began to run generally on the preparations to be made.

'The thing to watch from now on,' Cornelius suggested, 'is the chapel gate collections.'

'That was my own thought,' O'Boyle agreed. Cornelius referred back to old times.

'In my own younger days,' he remembered, 'the organizers would gather a number of the lads in the village around them to whip up an interest. Then they'd get people down to address them, preferably a couple of high-ranking men with a good national record. We all felt we were doing something for Ireland and helping to make the country a better place to live in.'

'True,' O'Boyle said, 'and we never thought of it simply as a political party. It was *The Organization*.'

'And we must follow on in that spirit,' Cornelius agreed. 'We must study respectability and decency in all that we do; at the same time being careful not to let the other crowd get their foot in the door.'

'I'm thinking we'll have our work cut out for us,' O'Boyle said gravely.

'Where do you see the threat?'

'Larkin may win a parliamentary nomination from Labour.'

'They could well split over that.'

'Perhaps. The other challenge will come from this so-called Farmers' Party. They're all substantial men and there seems to be a distinct swell of discontent in the rural areas.'

'The signs are that way – unfortunately.'

Eilish studied in silence her father's grave face and wondered that two so utterly alien worlds could exist in so cramped a space. Her own thoughts wandered some twilight landscape seeking remembered words and moments, or promises of reunions uncertain and yet to be. It was a world in which she was isolated and companionless, where the landscape was as melancholy as the parkland gliding past the windows, fraught with multicoloured branches, sentinel trees and the undulating sadness of great, flat, autumnal vistas.

'I would have thought Larkin had done enough for this city to have his place in politics assured,' she heard O'Sheehan say.

'Only for the Transport Union he himself founded it probably would be,' her father answered. 'They're his bitterest enemies since the split of 1923, and they're afraid of their lives he might assume leadership once more. That wouldn't suit their book at all.'

He thought about it further and added: 'You're right, Andrew. It'll be a hard campaign for ourselves. I wonder will I be fit and back in the chair again for it?'

'With the help of God,' O'Boyle said.

But he was not. The party machinery stirred into life early in the new year without him and by May the campaign was well under way. The posters began to appear, the slogans were scrawled on walls, but the most he was allowed to do was walk a while in the streets, and the closest he could get to the party campaign was through the loyalty of Andrew O'Boyle and his frequent reports.

'You were right about Larkin,' he was told. 'Some of the top union brass are after him. And after the son too – he got nominated with him. It appears the young fella attended the Lenin-Stalin school in Moscow.'

'I wouldn't play it up. Our own crowd was sending telegrams of congratulation to the Soviet crowd around the same time. That sort of stuff can blow up in your face.'

A short while later O'Boyle was reporting that Mullevins and his followers were taking part in the smear campaign too. Cornelius disapproved strongly and advised against it, but it had no effect.

'They're on to the communist angle in a big way,' O'Boyle reported. 'They figure it should put them on the right side with the clergy.'

'It'll put us on the wrong side with a lot of decent workers.'

'And they're for playing up this Lenin-Stalin school that young Larkin is supposed to have attended.'

'There's another school he attended – St Enda's. Paddy Pearse kept himself and the brother there all through 1913. Where does that leave us?'

'I'll make that point at the next meeting.'

'Do. Talk sense to them, Andrew.'

'I'm hoarse talking to them. I've passed on all you've had to say. They won't listen.'

'Then I'll go down and talk to them myself.'

But it would fly in the face of all advice, and he put it off. He knew he would not be equal to it. The thought depressed him and filled him with resentment. In committee rooms and on the streets the toughest election in five years was being fought and he could only potter about and participate at second hand.

He saw the manifestos being posted and the painted slogans appearing on walls. The folders and the exhortations were pushed into letterboxes without any effort to consult him. Influence had drifted away from him. 'Out of sight, out of mind' he told himself as the papers reported the speeches and the campaign built up to its climax. As a last resort he wrote to the branch deploring their part in the smear campaign and predicting that it would work against their interests instead of for them. Though O'Boyle reported that the letter had been discussed, he got no reply. And when the votes had been counted and it was found that Labour had gained at the expense of the government, he wrote once more, again deploring the campaign and suggesting that it was in some measure responsible for the loss of the ten seats which now left the government in a minority in the house. This time he got a reply which he showed to O'Boyle without comment of any kind.

A Chara

I am directed by the committee to refer to your recent letter and to repudiate the suggestion that our opposition to the bid by communism and communistic elements within the Labour party for political power adversely affected the outcome of the recent general election.

I am to point out that James Larkin (Junior) stood openly as a communist candidate in the elections of 1927 and that he is a product of a well-known Soviet revolutionary school where he studied for some years. James Larkin (Senior), as is well known, has, in the past, been lionized in Moscow where the Third International invested him with a one-twenty-fifth share in the rulership of the earth. Larkin, of course, is not alone in the campaign of national disruption to which we drew attention, as was our plain duty as Christians and Irishmen. Nor are we questioning the constitutional right of Labour, as such, to take their legitimate part in the democratic process. The question which must continue to be asked, however, is what is being done to remove the communists and communist influence from the Labour party. The committee have therefore unanimously adopted the following resolution: 'We, the committee members of the Peadar

O'Toole Cumann of the Fianna Fail Party, though we are not opposed to the Labour Party as such, nevertheless feel it our duty to draw public attention to the success in the recent general election of the extreme communist elements in that party.

'Communism is condemned by the church and has no place in our national life, being deplored by Christians of all denominations as an atheistical creed which would undermine our Gaelic traditions and our national heritage. We call on all true Irishmen to be vigilant against the spread of this pernicious doctrine of godless materialism.'

The above will be released to the press in due course.

I am to add that in the opinion of the committee, the known enlistment of the son of one of our most senior and prominent officials in the forces of the traditional oppressor, is unlikely to have influenced the electorate of this constituency in our favour.

Is mise le meas
L. Páircéir
Runai

O'Boyle handed the letter back. Though hardened for half a lifetime to politics, its tone shocked him. He took care to keep any hint of that from his voice. He spoke quietly and with sympathy.

'That's Mullevins and his clique for you. And you mustn't let them upset you. Do you think the electorate knew or cared where your son was? Half of them have sons in the British Army themselves and the other half have them working in British factories. It's the usual jockeying for power.'

Cornelius too remained quiet and controlled.

'There are two things which distress me,' he said. 'The first is to see a good man slandered. Larkin is a good man, whatever they say about him being a Red, which I don't believe anyway. The second is young Brian. What they say is true. For the first time in twenty years they have something they can use against me. And there's a third thing, now I think about it. It's time for me to resign.'

'You're out of your mind.'

'Not one bit. If they're set to choose Mullevins as the alternative, they'll not find Cornelius Moloney standing in their way.'

O'Boyle said nothing. That, it now seemed clear, was the dignified way; to recognize the end of the line and accept it. Unemotionally.

From then on, it struck him afterwards, the change began in Cornelius. In himself too, for that matter, though its precise nature was not easy to define. There was the consciousness of being discarded, naturally, and the initial bitterness; then adjustment of a kind, a sense of inevitability, as with the process of simply getting old. He mentioned the letter to O'Sheehan for the relief of deploring its cruelty.

'After a lifetime of service, they could do that to him,' he said, 'knowing well he was too ill to fight back. And all for the sake of position.'

'I know he's been sick a long time and absent,' O'Sheehan answered, 'but I would have thought his grip still firm enough.'

'In politics it's your enemies and their manoeuvres you must watch. You can't afford to be missing,' O'Boyle said. He shrugged. 'That's the game it is. You're up, then you're down.'

'It will go hard with Cornelius,' O'Sheehan remarked.

There was sadness in his voice.

V

Evening had crept into the street outside. Tim could see it from the table by the window, where the peacock on the photograph album, alert as always behind its glass bead of an eye, had been pushed aside to make room for his notebook and his letter to Brian. He was alone. Warmth and silence wrapped both the room and the deserted street. After a while, taking up his pen, he set down the words 'Ionic School' in the notebook and underlined them. Underneath them he wrote:

Thalles: 625–550 BC
Examined nature of the visible world. Held –
(1) Water the principle of all things.

(2) The earth a flat disc floating on water.
Anaximines: Held fundamental substance is air.
Anaximander: Believed world composed of indefinite matter.

Without any commentary he wrote down: *Pythagoras,*

Parmenides, Monism.
Zeno: Held motion impossible. Everything static.
Heraclitus: Had the contrary view. Pantu Rei – all changes.
Nothing Is. Everything is Becoming. ('You cannot step twice into
the same river')

The clash of views that had agitated the search for wisdom
five hundred years before Christ cast up before his imagination
an archaic and classical landscape, sun-filled and timeless, where
Pythagoras exhorted his disciples to abstain from beans and
Empedocles leaped into Etna to prove he was a god. Diogenes,
who lived in a tub, wandered through the streets and carried a
lantern in the daytime so that he could offer to the curious the
explanation that he was searching for an honest man. Old gods.
Old fables. Peripatetic wisdom. He wrote in the notebook once
more:

'All is motion,' said Heraclitus,
 As the shadow on the sundial moved in silence:
'All is rest,' declared Zeno the Eleatic,
 And smiled to see the Discus thrower transfixed on his pedestal.

The conceit pleased him. He pushed the notebook to one side
and resumed the letter to Brian.

Over the winter, as I told you, I did this course in Thomistic
philosophy – not very deep or exacting, more a sort of layman's
guide – but I intend to go on with it later in the year, so I'm
doing a bit of a review on my own account of what we've gone
through up to now. I'm not sure that I have much talent for it;
there are many things now obscure which I thought I had grasped
quite clearly. Who was it said the dog had gone, tail and all, but
he was still left with the wag?
I look forward to your being back on leave next month. Don't
devote it entirely to Barbara. I went out to Seapoint after tea for a
swim and it got a bit unbearable for a while when I was sitting on
the railway wall drying off. It was thronged as usual and the bikes

were stacked all along the way but it was as lonely as anything. Anne going away put the tin hat on things, I'm afraid.

No word yet about the orchestra vacancies. In a way it's just as well. More time to practise. I won't write again between now and when you get home. Instead I'll concentrate on music and philosophy (that last bit reads splendidly, I think) – see you.

As ever,
Tim.

He gathered the sheets together, closed the notebook and restored the photograph album to its customary position. The street beyond the area railings was untrafficked and peaceful still. War seemed a long way away.

As they had cycled, high summer had travelled with them: an exulting warmth, a fluffiness of cloud, a tangle of growing things along crowded hedgerows. Now as they rested it lay all about them. It rose odorously from the profusion of grass and fern. It lay on the roofs and spires of the city jostling together on the plain below them. It was a web of haze over the arms of the bay and its expanse of water.

'Marvellous,' Brian said.

He was lying back against the grassy bank. Sweat beaded his forehead still and trickled down each temple. He looked older, Tim thought, though not physically. It was in the eyes, a new seriousness, even gravity, which replaced from time to time their confidence and sudden humour.

They shared oranges and a little chocolate, neither easy to come by of late and likely, it seemed, to fall out of circulation at any time.

'I've missed this,' Brian admitted.

Tim remembered the last time he himself had rested and admired the same view. It had been with Anne. How long ago now? He pushed the matter away.

'Is it very rough beyond?'

'At times,' Brian answered. 'Mostly it's routine, even plain dull.'

'You mean you don't want to talk about it?'

'Not just now. I'd rather make the most of this. Where are we heading for, by the way?'

'Sallygap, for a start. If that's all right?'

'There are three possibilities when you get to Sallygap,' Brian remembered. 'Straight on for Glenmacnass; left turn for – Lough Tay, isn't it? Or right turn for Coronation plantation and Brittas?'

'Right. I'd rather not Lough Tay, though. I spent one very special day there with Anne and I don't much care to be reminded now.'

'You miss her a lot?'

'You understate it magnificently.'

'Yes. That was insensitive. What do you find to do, these times?'

'What I told you in my letter. Mostly I practise. I keep old Aunt Kate company a bit more than I used. And I've gone on with this philosophy thing which brings me out to the priory fairly regularly. There's a Father Purcell there I've become friendly with, a man with a bit of intelligent conversation in him. Then the odd time I go out drinking with Ellis or someone else from the Metropolitan.'

'That's a modestly full programme.'

'They are not exactly activities that fulfil the heart. But they have to do. By the way, I did an audition for the radio orchestra since I wrote you last.'

'How did it go?'

'Well – it wasn't disastrous.'

'I'd watch those holy monks – '

'They're not monks, they're friars – Dominicans.'

'Monks or friars, they're your Achilles' heel,' Brian sat up straight. 'If it's to be Glenmacnass,' he said reluctantly, 'I suppose we should get on with it.'

'I think so.'

Their journey took them across the high table of bogland where turf stacks marked the roadside for mile after mile and the smoke of numerous cooking fires puzzled Brian.

'Allotment holders from the city,' Tim told him. 'You rent

a plot for ten bob for the season and cut your own turf. It helps against the fuel shortage.'

A man pushing a wheelbarrow some distance away stopped to rest and waved a greeting to them. They waved back.

Brian said: 'There stands a man puffed up with his own virtue. He believes he's saving the missus a small fortune.'

'The likelihood is, however,' Tim remarked, 'that the country is going to run out of petrol altogether before he can get the stuff as far as the household grate.'

'Is it that bad?'

'It couldn't be worse, I understand.'

They climbed to the gap. It was steep and put an end to idle talk for the best part of an hour. The lonely crossroads seemed like the top of the world. The surfaces, they found, were badly out of repair, especially the Glenmacnass road, which looked almost impassable.

'I wouldn't chance it,' Brian decided.

Instead they turned right and went steeply downhill until the road levelled off to follow the winding course of the young Liffey. It was wide and shallow and scattered everywhere with rocks. Anna Liffey at her outset, Tim thought, all life before her, her maidenhead still intact. If young goddesses were so endowed. The storm-battered trees on the far bank were stragglers from Coronation plantation, mavericks from the rest that clung to the upper slopes and brooded on the fate and the far-off royal visit which had landed them in so weatherbeaten a spot. Yet a little sun and it became a place of wild beauty, a place to clamber in and explore, or peer into the brown river in search of its small but indomitable trout.

The sun burned again on their backs. To the left, down a sandy road, an iron bridge spanned the stream which widened on one side into a deep pool. They stripped and got in, gasping at the cold sting of the mountain water. But as soon as they had dried off and were sitting on the bank again it was as warm as ever. They were the tiny hub of an amphitheatre ringed about by mountain summits.

Brian watched a large black beetle which was negotiating

the gravelly hazards of the river shore a few inches from the toe of his shoe. It had the drugged gait of an old inhabitant sleep-walking in the sun. He pointed to it and said:

'Do you remember climbing in the mountains and Cunningham finding a beetle on its back with smaller things crawling on its belly – whether parasites or not we couldn't decide?'

'I do. You talked about Aristotle's three states of awareness, I remember: the vegetative, the animal and the rational.'

'That's right: I am, I know that I am, I know that I know that I am.'

'That same memory had come into my mind about two seconds before you spoke.'

'Had you seen the beetle?'

'No.'

'Perhaps you had seen it unconsciously,' Brian said. 'Still, why should that particular moment persist? It was of no importance whatever.'

'It's seldom the important things we remember. The odd thing is I wrote some verses about the beetle quite a long time afterwards. What made me do that?'

'Verses? Let's hear them.'

Tim cast about in his mind. They were difficult to re-assemble.

'I'd have to write them down, he said, 'otherwise I'd lose half of them.'

'Then write them down.'

'Not now – next time we stop. If you still want them.'

But that was a long time away. The road took them over the mountains into the remoteness of West Wicklow. Here again were fern-covered mountain slopes, brown streams spreading across rocky shallows or lancing on either side of isolated boulders. Yet the mood was not that of the east or the south. There was a brooding air, a feeling over the landscape of some old epic sadness. They remarked on it as the miles and the hours passed and they penetrated more and more deeply into a countryside that seemed only barely present, if present it was at all, in the consciousness of God. A solitary cottage with brown-stained walls on the point of collapse under their rotted thatch emphasized remoteness and loneliness, though a few hens scratching near the gate were evidence that someone still lived there. Coming to a crossroads just beyond it, they stopped. Brian looked at his watch: 'I make it nearly half five. How far are we from base?'

'Four to five hours, I'd reckon. Shall we eat?'

'Let's slog on a bit first.'

They knocked another hour off the return journey before rest became imperative. When water and a supply of wood were to hand they made a fire and boiled tea and had sandwiches which Tim had asked Aunt Kate to prepare for both of them. Brian was staying in a small hotel and found such things difficult to organize. The sky by then had lost its blue though the evening remained warm. Grey mist which had settled here and there on the upper slopes of the mountains was reaching downwards with exploratory fingers. Brian remembered the beetle.

'Let's hear those verses, McDonagh.'

'If you really want them. But you'll have to hold on.'

He struggled for quite a long time with pencil and paper, pondering, then writing down. He could feel Brian's mounting impatience. In the end, however, he had it all.

'What did you call it?'

' "The Beetle on his Back".'

'I don't think much of that.'

'Shall I skip it then?'

'After practically saying a mass over it? Not on your life.'

'As you wish.' Tim found a flat stone where he balanced his cigarette to prevent it rolling away somewhere. He turned his attention to the piece of paper. He read:

> 'That beetle we encountered on our stroll
> Above the leafier ways of Glenasmole
> You recollect – he lay upon his back
> And you remarked what brute and beetle lack.
> Reflect, you said, he seeks no heavenly goal
> This horny case holds no immortal soul.
> He is, but does he know he is, suppose

> He knows as much – but does he know he knows?
> Taut and alone and waiting for that stroke
> Which ends the ruminative walks, the flights
> To sultry bliss on dark, connubial nights
> He bunched himself together, curled up tight
> Feeling in bowel and belly's knot for sure
> First shock, then terror loose and in career
> And every tremor delicately spoke
> Abandoned hope's surrender to base fear.
> There on his back he waiting felt as I
> Waiting will feel when Death for me is nigh;
> I am, and have sparse knowledge of the cause
> And know I am, but shall I know I was?'

Brian made no comment, but held out his hand for the piece of paper. He examined it at length before handing it back.

'How long did that take you to do?'

'Three or four weeks – on and off.'

'It's bloody good.'

'I bet you say that to all your poets.'

'Seriously, damn you,' Brian said, raising his voice. 'In fact I demand a copy of it.'

'Have this one.'

Brian scrutinized the verses thoughtfully again before putting the paper away.

'You're an extraordinary bloody man. You have this facility for poetry – '

'For verses.'

'Very well – for verses. You have also an unusual aptitude for music – gifts of intuition and self-expression which are creative and precious. But instead of valuing them you take up this scholastical bloody algebra which passes for analytical thought, most of it about as useful as the Pope's balls – '

'Thomas holds you can find truth by reason alone.'

'Thomas has his saintly glue.'

'He admits, though, the process takes so long that revelation is a practical necessity for the overwhelming majority of us.'

'All philosophy is a cod,' Brian decided. 'When nothing much is happening it doesn't arise. In times of crisis it either fails or changes.'

But for Tim the subject had lost all interest. He had noticed as they talked that the mist had been thickening and guessed that when they began to climb again on their way home they would find themselves in the thick of it. That would mean a lot of walking.

Brian, his mood changing, used his foot to push the half-burned boughs towards the centre of the fire.

'This philosophy thing is your hedge against loneliness, as well as a search for an explanation of some kind,' he said quietly. 'I realize that. The verses are the same thing – a way to fill a hole. You let yourself ponder too much.'

'Possibly.'

'Too much of that is not good. You must devise other ways of coping with absence or loss.'

'I dwell a lot on the past,' Tim admitted. 'Recently, for instance, I've been living much in my father. That's loneliness. Or distrust of life. Or something of the kind. I find myself rooting about at home and looking at things he left: a pipe – say; an unfinished tin of Three Nuns tobacco; a military tunic – once I put it on and looked at the effect in the mirror. Or I sit still to savour the taste of myself – like that bit you used to quote from Hopkins – the idea of I and Me above yet in all things. Increasingly there's this feeling of being alone and getting lost.'

'And you imagine philosophy will find you an answer?'

'Not at all. The philosophy bit is pure accident. Indeed I doubt I have very much talent for it. It has meant companionship of a kind, though. And that isn't so dismissible as you seem to believe.'

'I didn't dismiss it,' Brian was unexpectedly mild. He brooded for a while. Then he said: 'My father, as you know, refused to see me this time home either. I find that hard to understand.'

'He's always been stubborn. Now he's ill as well. I thought you honestly didn't mind.'

'I didn't when I believed there was time enough to let things work their own slow way round to a reconciliation. Now the situation is very much changed.'

It was the first reference of any kind he had made to the war. Tim kept silent.

'You asked me what it was like over beyond. Routine, a lot of the time, as I said. Operationally though, two things worry me. One is navigational, the thought of getting lost on a night operation and being left fat-arsing around and clueless away up there in the dark. Action is one thing; being lost and without bearings is something else. The second thing is my father. I think he was wrong about the university business, partly of course because he was quite incapable of understanding why I should want it. But a lot of it was me – me giving smart answers and being fond of hearing myself talk. Basically I've a deep affection for him, and I'd like him to know that.'

Brian broke off. He seemed to feel he had said quite enough. But thinking again about it he added: 'Very simply – I'd hate to die while he still doesn't know it.'

Later, on their way home, the mist crept downwards and spread outwards until it enveloped the whole of the mountain area. They walked a lot to be on the safe side and cycled only when visibility made it comfortable to do so. It was long drawn-out and tedious. On the final descent dusk had so reinforced the mist that at first they failed to notice the uniformed figures spread across their path. The voice ordering them to halt surprised them. It was the Local Defence Force, complete with rifles and equipment. They were efficient and sticklers for the procedures and questioned them closely. But when they were satisfied they became friendly and told them there was a report that paratroopers had been dropped in the mountains earlier. There were also rumours of a pending general alert. They waved a farewell before dematerializing again into the mist.

'It follows a fellow around,' Brian complained.

Tim found it spooklike and unreal. 'Like something out of "Macbeth",' he remarked.

They had hot whiskeys in Brian's small hotel and talked earnestly and intimately together. They talked of women and love, good and evil, plans and possibilities. They argued, not for the first time, whether the universe was the accident of chance or the artefact of an Omnipotent God. Tim accepted the second. Brian concluded that whatever the ultimate truth might be, the possibility of its being palatable seemed unlikely. As they talked the night passed and another warm summer morning slipped through the window to whiten on the walls. There was birdsong. It seemed prudent eventually to resume the routine world.

They met two or three times after that. On one of them Tim had good news and said to Brian, 'Things are looking a bit hopeful. I've been short-listed for the radio vacancies. I had a letter in this morning's post.'

On the last occasion when Brian had called into the Metropolitan to say good-bye, he said, 'I was talking to Eilish the other evening and it seems the old man is going on at her now as well. About Cunningham, I mean. His disapproval of the RAF has extended from sons and heirs to the daughter's boyfriend. It started a few weeks ago when the political crowd accepted his resignation as chairman.'

'What did he want to do that for?'

'Some row about policy. And also because one of his rivals blamed the branch's poor showing on the fact that the chairman's son was busy winning the war for King and Country.'

'Some political thickhead. There are plenty still around.'

'Needless to say, he persisted with the not seeing me bit. I was in the house though, so at least my mother knows I did my best. Eilish worries me. She's not one who mixes easily, and it's a lonely sort of set-up for her. I was wondering if you would think of looking her up the odd time?'

'Of course.'

'I'm sure she'd appreciate it. I would too. Well, time to move.' He held out his hand.

Tim took it and said, 'Until next time.'

'Until next time.' Brian moved away but turned back for

a moment to say: 'By the way – good luck with the music.'
'Thanks.'

Tim watched until the glass doors closed again behind him.

VI

The second audition took so long to come about that he
thought they had forgotten him. But it was fixed eventually
for November, and he felt afterwards that he had done well.
To celebrate he asked Ellis to join him in taking Eilish and
Barbara out somewhere. It seemed a good idea to include Barbara, both on Brian's account and because she was one of the
few friends Eilish saw with any frequency.

They went straight from the office to the cinema and treated
the girls to high tea afterwards in the restaurant attached to it.
The raw November night with its light fog suspended above the
streets and condensing on the pavements disheartened them
when they got outside. Ellis felt like a drink.

'If you care to,' Barbara suggested, 'you could come to my
flat. The landlady is away visiting her sister or something of the
sort. I can't offer you very much, but I can light the open fire,
and it's quite cosy when I do that. I have some coal put by.'

'A talk would be nice,' Eilish said.

'We'll have a drink and bring something away with us,'
Ellis said.

They got stout and port and when the girls insisted on
sharing they found they could rise to a half-pint bottle of
whiskey as well.

'We're on the pig's back,' Ellis remarked.

'We must remember to be quiet,' Eilish said when they were
standing at the hall door.

'No need. I told you – she's away.'

'But if the others see us and tell?'

'My sweet innocent. Shout out "Fire" and a male will hurtle
through every door.'

'Making hay while the sun shines,' Ellis explained.

'Some would call it that,' Barbara said agreeably.

Tim thought the flat cosy and welcoming when the fire got properly under way. It was a desirable kind of living. You could be solitary or gregarious as you wished, and there was the extra freedom of being away from family. You could shape a room about you in a personal way.

'Now – glasses.' Barbara was frowning and wondering if there would be enough. After an extended search there were. They opened the bottles and settled themselves about the fire. Ellis, elaborately comfortable, sighed his contentment.

'Some music? I can switch on the wireless.'

'No. Let's talk a bit.' Eilish suggested.

They talked for a while about the film they had seen and then, for some reason, about the odd-looking balloons that had begun to appear on the roofs of cars since the ban on petrol for private use. They were supposed to be filled with gas, but Ellis was sceptical that there was anything at all in them.

'Black market petrol,' he told him. 'We might go short of a lot of things, but never cute customers.'

'The *Mé Féin* brigade,' Tim agreed.

'Have you heard from Des lately?' Barbara asked.

'I haven't had a letter for over a week, but I've had a card to say everything is fine. He'll write properly in a few days.'

It meant, Tim guessed, that Cunningham was on operational service. Barbara had the same thought.

She said: 'Brian has moved into new quarters. He had to share for a long time but now he's got a billet or whatever you call it of his own, and he wrote this usual crazy description of it. I think I have it here.'

She searched in her bag and found his letter. There were several sheets which she scrutinized quickly before she detached one and folded it so that only the relevant part was exposed. They passed the extracted bit from hand to hand. When it came to Tim's turn, he read:

'. . . or nearly so. I've made some alterations suitable to my rank and taste. Particularly, I wish you could see and admire the great fireplace constructed at my orders and the iron pot hung by a chain above an artificial bivouac. This detail will suggest the rest: The Turkey carpet, the brass harem lamps, the Japanese screen, the pieces of drapery, the oak chairs covered with red, Utrecht velvet, vases with foreign grasses, palms in corners . . .' The page ended there.

'He's a bit cracked,' Eilish said. 'Always was.'

She spoke with sisterly detachment and was smiling. The smile was very special. Whatever it was had slipped into her thoughts to produce it, Tim felt, she was on a sudden unusually happy. He passed the page of the letter back to Barbara.

'How long is it now since Anne went to the States?' she wondered.

'Almost eighteen months.'

'No! How time flies away.'

That was not how it seemed to him. But time was at once measurable and relative. Wondering once more at the mysteries of moment and place, he saw the four of them drinking about the fire as prisoners of both. Everyone everywhere was. Those they were now talking about were prisoners likewise, whether in canteen or dormitory or corridor or by the glow of instruments in a few cubic feet of darkness hundreds of feet up in the air. Mysterious in the same way were the permutations of chance and encounter. And interesting to review. He goes to visit Cunningham and meets Anne again after some years. Cunningham sleeps in the hide-out, and Eilish brings him tea. Brian meets Barbara on a firm's outing he would never have heard of if Uncle Hugh hadn't had influence in the first place with old Colonel Breen. And in what distant roots had that influence had its beginnings? And where, if the seeds of that influence had not been planted in such a place on such an hour, would he himself now be?

Eilish talked intimately to Barbara. Ellis, sitting at his ease, was more or less leaving them to it. How old, then, was Eilish? The youngest of them, certainly. Nineteen? Twenty perhaps. Barbara was somewhat older – say twenty-one. Ellis had weathered more of it than any one of them: was he twenty-six?

Whatever he was, his future remained, like theirs, about as predictable as that of a ball bouncing along a rough-surfaced road.

'By God, just listen to that.' Ellis said.

Eilish and Barbara broke off. Tim crossed to the window and drew back the corner of the curtain. Rain was rebounding in great splashes under the lamplight on the pavement below.

'Cats and dogs,' he confirmed.

'Damn. I meant to bring an umbrella,' Eilish said.

'Don't worry. I can lend you one.'

For a long time, however, it continued so heavy an umbrella would have been next to useless. It persisted and kept them housebound long after the time they should normally have gone.

Barbara offered supper of cheese and bread and butter, but not tea, because she had only the remains of her ration, so they had it with their drinks and talked. By the time the rain eased off public transport was finished and taxis, as they knew almost certainly, were unavailable. Tim said he would walk Eilish home.

'It was a lovely evening,' she said as she was leaving. In a quiet and unspectacular way, it had been, they felt. She borrowed Barbara's umbrella just in case and put her arm through Tim's so that he might shelter under it.

'I wonder where Brian and Des are just now,' she said.

It was a question he did not care to pursue so he said, 'Sitting on the Turkey carpet in front of the great fireplace, very probably, smoking their opium pipes under the brass harem lamps.'

She laughed. 'That's right. Surrounded by those oak chairs in red, Utrecht velvet, wasn't it? I can see the pair of them.'

Gutters gurgled noisily all along their way and flood pools were spread about, but the rainfall itself had become negligible.

'Brian tells me you're doing terribly well at your music, and I'm very glad. Mother too. You should call the odd time to play with her. I know she's very limited in comparison, but she loves it.'

He promised he would.

'I often think of the sound of you practising those studies inside the hut – fiercely difficult they were too – and the rest of us just lazing outside in the sun.'

They had just reached her hall door.

In a sad voice she said, 'Those were lovely summer days. I enjoyed them so much.'

'We'll do so again.'

'Please God,' she said.

She put the key in the door and opened it.

'Good-night Tim. Thank you for such a nice evening.'

'My privilege and pleasure.' They both smiled.

'Good-night, Eilish.'

The hall door dragged on its hinges as it always did. The hall was unlit but the kitchen door at the far end, slightly ajar, admitted overspill enough for negotiation.

Her mother's voice called: 'Is that you, Eilish?' She was sitting in the kitchen by what remained of the fire. 'You're late, dear.'

'The rain held us up until the buses were all off. Tim Mc-Donagh walked me home.'

'A nice boy,' her mother approved. 'Do you want supper?'

'No. We had some.'

'There's a letter for you in the hall – '

'From Des probably. I was expecting one.'

'No, it's from Brian. I recognized the writing '

'That's odd. He always writes to you.'

'I expect he felt you'd like a letter for yourself, once in a while.'

'What a nice surprise.'

Going out to get it she realized that Barbara's umbrella was still in her hand and went to put it away. But the stand, a long time rickety and unreliable, let it slide and fall. It made a lot of noise at so belated an hour. Her father's disgruntled voice came from upstairs:

'Isn't it nearly time you thought to come home, miss?'

'I'm sorry, father, I was held up by the rain.'

From the kitchen door her mother called back to him.

'She'll be up shortly. There's a letter for her, and I want her to glance through it.'

'On His Majesty's service no doubt. That's what I've reared in the end of it all.'

Eilish pretended not to hear. She opened the letter. She would never, her mother knew, be insolent or give back answers. It was not her nature. She said in a low voice:

'Just look over it quickly to yourself and then tell me what it says that might concern me.'

'It's Brian,' Eilish confirmed. She began to read aloud, but in a low voice:

'Dear Eilish,

I am writing to you directly and immediately in the hope, at least, of saving you from getting the news secondhand, probably through Des's parents . . .'

She stopped reading aloud but continued for some seconds in silence.

'Mother – '

'Child, what's the matter?'

She attempted again: 'Mother – '

Cornelius raised his voice:

'Letters. That's all that's thought of. That and gallivantin' when respectable people are at home and in their beds.'

'Mother,' Eilish said, 'Des is dead.'

'My poor, poor child – '

The voice from upstairs cut across her:

'I reared one to be a renegade and another to keep company with a renegade.'

'Mother – '

Mrs Moloney screamed up the stairs: 'Stop it. For the love and pity of Jesus stop it. You don't know what you're saying.'

'The one a renegade,' the voice returned, louder now than ever, 'and the other a disobedient bitch. But when God sees fit to return me to my health there'll be a change in this house.

There'll be short shrift for the khaki-cocking heroes and the Rule Britannia brigade.'

Eilish was white.

'Mother,' she begged, 'ask him to stop. Please get him to stop.'

Her mother hurried up the stairs. For a moment or two their voices contended loudly one with the other. Then they ceased. The house became still.

It was a silence in which the pictures on the wall watchfully regarded her, the furniture stood isolated, piece by piece. She became aware of the drip of a tap and the measured ticking of the kitchen clock. A violent trembling seized her. Looking about for something to focus on that would help to arrest her mounting hysteria she saw the worn sofa they had occupied together so many times on Friday evenings during their first winter together when they used to have the house all to themselves. She edged towards it. Drawn by its associations and the reassurance of its bulky materiality, she reached out to touch it.

When her mother came downstairs again some minutes later she had flung herself across it. It quivered under the onslaught of her grief.

Mollie Cunningham telephoned the news to Tim. How she told him or what he said in response he could never afterwards bring to mind. Yet he remembered clearly that Ellis on the opposite side of the desk was conducting a prolonged though polite telephone argument with some customer or other and that the hands of the office clock, which had been crawling snake-like through the tedium of the November afternoon, stood at ten minutes to four. The clock particularly seemed to lodge in his mind. It materialized several times in his thought over the weeks that followed, an unbidden and inexplicable intruder, the hands offering the same simple yet inscrutable information. The wet streets, too, he remembered, where the traffic moved with an irrelevant and aimless air, and the church in Clarendon Street where he stopped to pray. November had invaded it with all its darkness and fog and despair. The sanctuary lamp, a tiny sun in its rose of glass was a pendulant question. How to approach Him? How should he pray? What was there to be said?

He knelt and bowed his head and reviewed in order the accumulation of loss, a list stretching from Cunningham through his father and back to his grandparents, all deeply loved, his faithful departed; all, it was to be hoped, everlastingly at rest. He prayed also for Aunt Kate, who was in failing health and he included Anne, convinced in his shock and sense of loss that he would never see her again. He was conscious of something inside himself that was wilting and withdrawing even as he prayed. Hope, was it? Trust in being? Regard of any kind for so unpredictable a world.

The following evening he called on the Cunninghams. They received him in the sitting room with its scatter of gramophone records and its clinging odour of pipe tobacco. Mr Cunningham looked haggard and old, Mrs Cunningham was distraught. Mollie took his hand at first but then, her feeling overflowing, embraced him and wept.

Later he called on Father Purcell. They spoke together at the fire in the small reception room which was reserved for confidential interviews.

'Did you learn how it happened?'

'Either over Berlin or on the way back. There's very little detail.'

'He was one of a bomber crew, you said?'

'The rear gunner and radio operator. It seems he was killed in the air. Later the plane itself crashed. It was in flames as it went down.'

'We'll pray for him – that's all that can be done,' Father Purcell said. 'I'll offer mass for him. You might like to serve it.'

He selected the thirtieth day after death which, as it happened, was the twenty-second of December, the shortest day of the year and the beginning of winter. At a few minutes to six he preceded Father Purcell up the stone steps to the tiny chapel hidden in the tower and there helped him to robe in customary order in amice, alb, girdle, maniple, stole and chasuble. The

stone flags chilled his knees when he knelt to make the responses
and when he rose for the gospel the glimpse of sky beyond the
narrow window was pitch black still.

'*Sequentia sancti Evangelii secundum Joannem.*'

'*Gloria tibi, Domine.*'

He heard nothing beyond the first sentence: 'At that time:
Martha said to Jesus: Lord, if thou hadst been here, my brother
had not died . . .'

Not then, perhaps, but thereafter. Inevitably. At communion
he bowed his head but could find nothing by way of prayer
except to repeat silently: If you are really God, let me know it in
some way or other.

He had breakfast in the priory before leaving. It was still
early, with no hint of morning as yet in the December sky. The
light of the street lamps fell for the most part on untrafficked
streets. The pathways, wrapped in some reverie of rock or
mineral, were hardly real. All had receded from him in some
way and remained so for weeks. He wrote of it to Brian.

Nothing has very much savour any longer and of course the
dark days and the wet mornings don't help. Often I find myself
hesitating in the door of the office when I see the monotony of
another evening spread out before me. Have you ever experienced
it? You look up at the sky and out across the crowded street with
people rushing for buses and meals and there's no sense or meaning
in it at all. Books or music should fill the gap but these are things
that fail for me over lengthy periods. Sometimes I crawl in for a
drink and talk that never gets anywhere either. But at least it
brings one nearer to bedtime. I suppose it means trying to find
something better than sleeping at night and getting up in the
morning. Something that makes a little sense. For a start,
something better than Death. At present it is impossible to be
certain of anything. For Christ's sake, that's enough, you'll say.
And so it must be – though it's not the half of it. . . .

Then he tore it up, disgusted by the note of self-indulgence.

'Are you telling me you've lost your faith?' Father Purcell
wondered.

'More my hope than my faith, I think.'

'There is a paradoxical thing about hope running low,' Father Purcell told him. 'It sometimes means God is going to show you something or ask something of you.'

Why should God have to ask, when He had shown Himself so well able to take?

'There isn't much left to give, is there? Except my life I suppose.'

'There are devotion, love, service,' Father Purcell said, 'many things. For instance – have you ever thought of the Church?'

To be a priest? He smiled, though not at the suggestion, but because he had visualized on the moment the reaction it would draw from Brian.

'I'm too conscious of certain shortcomings. A sort of natural depravity, for a start.'

'We all share in that,' Father Purcell said. 'What you possess that isn't so common is a religious disposition and a kind of natural virtue.'

Tim looked embarrassed.

'In my very humble opinion,' Father Purcell added, smiling.

That, too, became intertwined with the phantom of the office clock, the often insubstantial streets, the brooding puzzlement and hurt as he re-discovered the childhood truth: there was a thief unceasingly at work in the world who made use of love to break the heart. In a void vast and empty and somewhere inside him anguish still stumbled and cried out. Something was needed to do or to know.

VII

The long gospel of the Passion on Palm Sunday began as was mandatory, without lights or incense, without the blessing of the deacon or invocation or response. Cornelius and Eilish rose together for it, she with a branch of palm in her hand, he with a sprig fixed in the buttonhole of his coat. At the Consummation they knelt together to reflect on the words: 'And Jesus, again crying with a loud voice, yielded up the ghost.' Then they rose again and stood through the concluding verses and the creed that followed. Tim, watching them from his seat some rows back, wondered if he should try to join them when mass was over. But it was so long since Cornelius had spoken to him, he was unsure of his standing with him and decided against it. As he stood to look after them when they were outside, he noticed Eilish seemed to have difficulty walking and wondered what could be wrong.

After that Holy Week was an intangible presence in every street and devotion saturated the city. The sacrament was removed to its place of repose, the altars were stripped, the candles quenched, the feet washed in public, the bells ceased to ring out and the streets were regularly astir with the coming and going of feet. He attended what ceremonies he could. On Holy Thursday, while he was doing the round of the Seven Churches, he saw Cornelius again, this time with Mrs Moloney. On Good Friday he took part in the adoration of the Cross, then queued as usual for hot cross buns at Bewleys for his mother and bought some himself as a treat for Aunt Kate. Holy Saturday had the coffee shops and the public houses buzzing again as the season's austerities came to an end. The street barrows burst into their seasonal riot of tulips and daffodils. On Easter Sunday he saw the Moloneys at mass again. This time he approached them outside. Mrs Moloney seemed happy and Cornelius was in affable humour.

'Come back to the house for a glass of sherry on the day that's in it,' he invited.

'Yes do,' Mrs Moloney pressed. 'We haven't seen you in ages.'

'Let him go ahead with you, Eilish,' Cornelius advised, 'I'm a bit slow on the pins these times.'

As they walked together Eilish said confidentially, 'Did you notice my mother? She looks like a new woman.'

'She seemed pleased.'

'It's about Brian. My father told her to ask him to write to him when he can. That means he's letting bygones be bygones. It's such a weight lifted.'

'When did this happen?'

'He was hinting around for some weeks. I think the news about poor Des brought him to his senses. Then he did his Easter duty last week, and I expect he had one or two things pointed out to him in confession. Anyway it all seems mended.'

'Brian will be pleased.'

'You don't think he'll be stubborn?'

'No. He told me so.'

'I think you're right. After all he called to the house a few times when he was on leave. Father was the one who kept it up.'

She let him in to the sitting room and helped him to sherry. As always in their house when there was an occasion to be done justice to the glasses were in readiness on top of the piano for any casual call on hospitality. The lid, he noted, was closed. He thought he knew why. As he raised his glass and wished her good health he remembered:

'That reminds me. I saw you after mass last Sunday. Were you limping badly?'

She flushed slightly. 'You'll laugh if I tell you why.'

'Try me and see.'

'Well – it was the Long Gospel. My mother used to say that in her own young days the people believed that if you stood absolutely rigid for the whole length of it you could get a soul out of purgatory, so I decided to try to do it. I could hardly walk after it and when I got home I had terrible trouble to sit down.'

'And am I laughing?'

'Not on the outside – whatever about inside. Do you believe things like that?'

'I don't disbelieve them. I think a lot depends on your own earnestness.'

'You mean faith?'

'Faith, if you like. A kind of all-or-nothing faith.'

'That's what I wanted to have. I know you know who I had in mind –'

'In your heart.'

'Yes. In my heart. That's where I meant.' Suddenly she asked: 'Are you very much astray, Tim?' She spoke softly.

'Yes, I am. Are you?'

'Desperately.' She was near to tears.

'I don't think I've ever seen the lid of the piano closed before.'

'No. But father being ill and refusing to see Brian. He was railing at me for a while too. And then Des. Mother and I hadn't the heart. But at least things will be better for mother from now on.'

'And you – ?'

She said gently: 'What is there for me, Tim; Just week-come-in, week-go-out.'

He pitied her and took her hand. But he could think of nothing to say to her that would be of any use at all.

She said, 'Some people say God tests you.'

'Perhaps He does.'

'I know this. It isn't God who starts the wars. Neither does He want bitterness or hatred. It's quite the opposite. But I'm being selfish. You were very close to Des too. And Anne so far away and for so long. Brian as well. I'm sorry, Tim.'

'It's a pig of a world, Eilish.'

'What does one do?'

'Defy it. Find something better.'

'Where does one look?'

'I'm not sure. But you begin with that question.'

They heard a key turning in the door. He released her hand. Eilish dabbed hastily with her handkerchief about her face and her eyes. They could hear the heavy breathing of Cornelius even before he entered the room but when he was seated awhile it became easier and he was able to say:

'You thought we were lost, I suppose.'

'They had plenty to talk about, I'm sure,' Mrs Moloney told him.

'Any bit of exertion and I'm out of puff,' he explained to

Tim. 'Eilish, give the boy another sherry. Or something stronger if that's his fancy. I'll take a sup of brandy myself.' He indicated his chest and turned again to Tim: 'Strictly medicinal – the ticker.'

Mrs Moloney wanted him to stay for lunch but he explained that he was expected home.

'I'm taking a week of my annual leave as from Monday and there are things to be seen to.'

'Isn't it very early?'

'I don't mind. I simply wanted to get away. Somewhere in the mountains. Or anywhere, really.'

'Footloose and fancy free,' Cornelius remarked with envious admiration and sighed heavily. 'God be with the days.'

Yet for all his desires to get away he let Sunday pass by idling at home and on the Monday he dawdled so long that the Bank holiday traffic of walkers and cyclists was already returning as he set out and the mountain road, which ran due west, was aimed when he reached it straight into the heart of the sunset. He was on foot. A sky of arrogant bronze and crimson found a mirror in each bogland pool. Later, by the time he began the descent, an almost full moon was riding above the outlines of mountains and a frosty smell hung in the air. It had the feeling of a world projected from his own imagination. In the valley he moved between the silvered foliage and slanting shadows of pine trees, the air cold on his hands and his face. A deep silence gripped road and rock and lichened wall. There was no one in the hostel except the warden who had had his fill of the earlier Bank holiday bustle and kept to his quarters. That suited. He wanted silence. He wanted solitude. Not just exteriorly. He wanted them inside him, a deep and, if possible, abiding stillness of spirit.

In the mountains in mid-April they were not difficult to find. He moved from hostel to hostel along empty roads and mountain tracks, passing or lingering at old haunts he had been to with Brian and Des Cunningham and other companions throughout boyhood. It became, in a way, a sort of pilgrimage into boyhood, though this time companionless. In forest

clearings where primrose and cowslip dotted the grassy banks
and trees spread their still bony arms, he searched in the lee of
rocks for dry twigs to start his fire and remembered the routines
of years before. When he searched out hollows for shelter from
the wind to boil water and make food, the taste of woodsmoke
on the tea conjured up long-forgotten ghosts. At intervals he
leaned over bridges or rested by unnamed streams to find a
child's enjoyment once more in the hypnosis of unceasing
sound and unceasing movement. Two thoughts, mutually
incompatible, seemed to become isolated from all the rest as
the few days passed; that he should seek contact with reality
again in violent action by following the path of the others into
war. Or by entire withdrawal into some positive kind of
contemplation and searching of self. He spent the end of the week
in the priory talking several matters over with Father Purcell,
including the puzzling contradiction between universal suffering
and the idea of an all-loving God. On Tuesday he was back
again in the Metropolitan where everything was as colourless
as usual. His idea of taking a week's annual leave at Easter, he
found, had qualified for embodiment in its catalogue of remarkable eccentricities. It was a measure of how little was
needed to divert it.

A few weeks later he returned home to find that, in terms of
its lethargic performance in the past, the government board
had been galvanized into action. Their letter, which addressed
him as *A cara*, was pleased to inform him that he had been
successful in his audition with the orchestra. However, due to
the national emergency and the uncertainty as to the duration
of the continuance of the situation obtaining in consequence of
it, his full-time appointment would be temporarily shelved.
Meanwhile, however, he would be called on from time to time,
if available, for public concerts and other occasions for which it
was considered desirable to augment the string section. It ended
Is mise le meas and was signed in Irish.

He put it aside and said nothing about it. Later on he went
out to have a quiet drink. For the second time inside twelve
months the city was in the grip of an electioneering campaign,

this time brought about by the resignation of Mr de Valera following a narrow defeat of his government in the House. Posters were tied about lamp-posts and badly scrawled slogans disfigured the walls. The issues involved wandered in and out of the conversations that went on around him. At closing time he took the long way around Stephen's Green on his way home.

The house was quiet and the others all in bed. He went to his room and read the board's letter over again. It was a mere formality, he remembered clearly what it had to say and he knew precisely what he was going to do. When he had read it to the end he reflected briefly and then tore it up. He did so without any indecision whatever.

He found the writing pad and began a letter to Anne. It was tender and hard to phrase and took over an hour and all his new-found determination and conviction to write. When he had finished he reviewed it minutely, line by line. Then he turned to the pad again and wrote in the top, left-hand corner of a fresh sheet:

Rev. Fr. B. Purcell
Tibradden Priory

He wrote:

Dear Father Purcell –

After that he searched a long time before finding a simple but adequate way of expressing his decision and making his request.

Father Purcell replied within a few days. Anne delayed, then wrote:

Dear Tim

I've kept your letter by me night and day for over two weeks now and it is nearly time to face saying what can no longer be avoided. I hope I can do so without causing any more heartbreak to either of us.

At first the notion of your having a vocation seemed unbelievable, and I half expected to get another letter saying you had been emotionally upset and mistaken, but now on thinking back over things – and I don't seem to have been able to do much else except that since your letter arrived – it has slowly come to me that the decision is not so very much out of the blue as it seemed at the beginning. There are many things you said and many things you did from time to time that looked back on now seem to have been hinting in that direction. Or so I told myself when the thought of never evermore being together with you became almost too hard to bear as it so often did. At other times I was angry that you should put our love of one another in second place to anything in the world but then I thought of what you told me about the prospect of the orchestra vacancy and turning it down and I knew what that sacrifice must have meant to you and what you were giving up also, and it helped me a bit to bear my own hurt because I could see a bit more clearly what was involved for you. Tim, it is very hard to write this, and I hope I am not saying anything that could hurt or be misunderstood. It is still very hard, and I still love you so deeply. I know I always will. You will think of me too in the months ahead, won't you? No god and no religion could want to stop that.

My parents talk sometimes of getting back to live in Ireland and it used to fill me with hope to listen to them. Now, whether they do or not, I'll stay on and make my life here. I don't think I could bear to look at those hills again and that sea and those lovely skies and be without you there. Here I won't turn every corner expecting to see you.

You will write, won't you, and tell me what you are doing and what is happening? That will be something to look forward to at the very least. So you will, won't you?

Good-bye, my darling. You'll be in all my thoughts and all my prayers.

My deepest love,
Anne.

It was June in the fields surrounding the priory when he received it and read it, a serene and sunny day. In the world beyond it masses of allied ships, troops and aircraft had established the Normandy beachhead and the invasion of Europe had begun.

VIII

Cornelius followed the invasion move by move with both O'Boyle and O'Sheehan. Politics he had finished with. Politics, he told O'Boyle, who had made some reference to Mr de Valera's resounding victory the month before, was all a bloody cod.

'Never mind politics,' he said. 'It's riddled with dishonesty. Young Brian was wiser than either of us when he refused to have hand, act or part in it. He had his head screwed on. The young sees through things in a way the old can't or won't. The old patriotism and the old love of race and language had gone out the window and neither of us tumbled to it though it was right under our noses. But the lad did. I'll hand him that. The lad had the whole bloody bunch of them taped.'

He said much the same to O'Sheehan, who was careful to keep an expressionless face. Both were more interested in any case in the march of events, which they plotted on a map where familiar names re-appeared and accumulated: Cherbourg and Caen, the Mannheim line, Warsaw, Arras, Dieppe, Verdun, Antwerp, Brussels, Mons and Abbeville. The campaign against Hitler successfully concluded, they gave their attention to Japan, about the outcome of which Cornelius admitted to some doubt. He had in mind, he explained, St Columcille's prophecy, made in the sixth century, that the Oriental races would one day over-run the world – the Yellow Peril. When the bomb at Hiroshima looked after that, Cornelius expressed a genuine horror. O'Sheehan speculated on the possibility of consequential climatic changes on a global scale, involving in the case of Ireland specifically, the danger of permanent diversion of the Gulf Stream.

'You might tell me what you think of him,' Mrs Moloney suggested quietly, when she had led O'Sheehan to the foot of the stairs. He frowned at her anxious tone and nodded gravely. Cornelius was seated in front of the fire, a blanket about his shoulders, the curtains closed against the gloom of the November evening.

'Draw up a chair,' Cornelius invited.

He had been nodding. His face was grey and drawn. O'Sheehan did not like what he saw.

'Aren't you the stubborn man,' he suggested, as though to a child, 'not to be resting in comfort in your bed.'

'There'll be plenty of time for the bed,' Cornelius answered. With obvious effort he raised himself. 'I'll trouble you to fetch the sup of whiskey for yourself and a drop for me too while you're at it. You know where to find it.'

O'Sheehan went to the press.

'In your own case,' he said, 'a taste of brandy might be wiser.'

'A taste of brandy will fill the bill nicely.'

O'Sheehan charged and distributed the glasses.

'I don't think I'm up to the chess this evening,' Cornelius admitted.

'The mind needs its rest too. You must take care of yourself.'

They drank. O'Sheehan, after closer scrutiny, found his misgivings stronger still.

'I had a letter from the boy,' Cornelius said.

'From Brian. And how is he?'

'In good form, it seems. Waiting to be demobbed and enquiring about the chances in civil aviation here.'

'He'll do well. You may be sure of it.'

'He will. He knows his job. There's not many could come through all that without so much as a scratch on him. But that's him. Cool head – clear judgment.'

'A chip off the old block.'

Cornelius shook his head, disclaiming the compliment.

'No. I myself am one of the old stock. We let the heart rule the head. That was ever our weakness. Mind you, we were blest in our priests and our teachers. They taught us the true things. What was missing was opportunity.' He became pensive. 'I sit here and spend a lot of time going back over those young days, the sport we had then and the good companions. A summer's day was never long enough for all the things we had in mind to do. Not that the education was ever neglected. Do that, and you were in for a damn fine larruping from the teacher or your father. Or both. It never done a ha'porth of harm.'

'Indeed it did not,' O'Sheehan supported stoutly.

'It's sad to look back.'

'Better to look forward. You'll have Brian coming home, remember.'

'If I'm here to see him.'

O'Sheehan pretended outrage.

'What way to talk is that?'

'I know inside me.'

'Then you must get the doctor again.'

'Doctor be damned.'

There was a stalemate during which each pursued his train of thought.

'Pour yourself another.'

'And you?'

Cornelius said he would, then changed his mind and thought he'd like a helping hand to get into his bed. There was much puffing and blowing until he sank among bedclothes and pillows, a very sick man.

'Sit by me while you finish your drink. Maybe I'll have another small taste of the brandy after all.'

With misgiving, O'Sheehan re-charged the glass. He said, 'Be a sensible man and let me tell herself to get in touch again with your doctor.'

'If that's what you want,' Cornelius agreed at last but without much interest. 'But there's something better you could do while you're at it.'

'Certainly.'

'Tell her we were talking about the boy. Tell her to write to him. He might even manage a few days' leave to come to see us. She could let him know I was enquiring, anyway. And that I'm not – well – in the best. You'll do that?'

'To be sure.'

Cornelius rested with closed eyes.

'Here's a strange thing for you – a thing from old God's time that keeps coming into my head. It's a little picture, nothing more. I see these two hoops of griddle bread on a window ledge in the sun that the mother must have baked and left there to cool. Why should I keep recalling such a little thing as that?'

'It's one of memory's tricks. To make little, wordless poems.' Cornelius was pleased.

'You put it very well,' he said. 'Little wordless poems.'

Then he looked as though he might sleep.

'I'll leave you to rest.'

'Do that. I'll sleep awhile.' But he opened his eyes. 'You won't forget about the boy.'

'No. I'll attend to that.'

Mrs Moloney saw him out. Above him in the murk of the November night a sliver of light escaped through a chink in the curtains that masked Cornelius' room. It looked strangely unreachable.

With careful encouragement his own fire flamed into warmth and cast grotesque shadows on the walls. He gazed into it. On a table near him sheets of notes for the Irish–English dictionary were scattered haphazardly. What they were about he was unconcerned to remember. Death hung above his friend Cornelius, a delicate and discernible odour, a portent of perilous, far-ranging journeying. Cornelius must go to the land of shadows by way of the plain of ill-luck, the perilous glen, the bridge of leaps, beset by treacherous quagmires, wild beasts, gorges of bottomless depth. There would be ice-cold winds in the bare trees of woodlands, snow drifts on the steep shoulders of mountains, wolf music in the deserted glens, a long journey; inevitable though, the fate of all. Death was as natural as life, perhaps ultimately as desirable. He himself would welcome it as a friend. It was all far too long, all the time between – Niamh a mistake, however glorious. Youth rode a horse whose belly-band, sooner or later, broke. Then the loss of companions, the long vain search, the lustreless minds of pygmies and churls.

'I am Oisin, son of Finn, and I pray you tell me where he

now dwells, for his *dún* on the Hill of Allen is a desolation, and though I have searched diligently I have neither seen him nor heard his hunting horn from the western to the eastern sea.'

'Of what Finn do you speak, old man? There are many of that name in Ireland.'

'Of my hero-father. Of Finn MacCumhal MacTrenmor, captain of the Fianna of Erin.'

'But Finn, son of Cumhal, and all his generation have been dead these three hundred years, old man. At the battle of Gowra Oscar, son of Oisin fell. And Finn at the battle of Brea. No man knows the manner of Oisin's death, though our harpers still sing his lays at the great feasts. But Finn and his Fianna, with their feasting and hunting and their songs of war and of love, are not as reverenced among us since Patrick came to preach us the One God and Christ His Son.'

'Is he a great poet – this Patrick? Can he make a poem according to the rules of the Imbus-for-Osna, palm-knowledge of enlightening, every second line rhymed and every other line assonanced and with three alliterations in every line?'

'Not a poet, but a great priest. The monks and virgins of Holy Patrick send up psalms and prayers daily to cleanse us of sin.'

'Is he priest-prophet then, with gifts of divination and other-sight who might tell me where Finn and his Fianna are to be found?'

'He would tell you that, certainly, old man. In hell for all eternity, with all who were unrepentent or unbaptized.'

Pious, pygmy hearts, not to understand the glory of hell if Finn's flag were planted there, a golden sun half risen from the blue floor of the sea.

'In hell then, not heaven, must I seek.'

The fire creaked. Its flames withered back to a flicker. In the silence inside him the familiar voice, now insistent, was calling to him over and over. To come where: to Niamh on the lake-shore with its fragrant hedges, was it? To Angus Ogue, god of love, at the flooded ford?

The telegram, when Brian eventually got it, was two days old. He left almost immediately but travelled with a growing feeling that he would be too late. Eilish opened the door to him, and he knew immediately that he was. Her subdued manner, her solemnity, the hush in the house itself told him. He went into the kitchen with her.

'When did it happen?'

'Early this morning. We were watching for you all the time.'

'I was away when the telegram arrived. They didn't know where. I came immediately.'

'He had priest and doctor and went peacefully enough. Nothing more could have been done. He was asking about you a lot this past while. You got mother's letter?'

'Yes. I wish I'd come then.'

'You were not to know.'

'And mother – how has she taken it?'

'Fairly well, by now. She's above with O'Boyle and some neighbours. She was terribly anxious about you.'

'I'll go up to her presently.'

He was taking off his coat when O'Boyle entered.

'Miss Moloney – Brian, you're here. I didn't see you.'

He came across to shake his hand and say with genuine concern, 'I'm sorry for your trouble. It's a sad, sad blow.'

'You'll miss him as much as any of us, Andrew.'

'Sorely. We were brother and brother to each other. He used to be asking very hard after you.'

'Eilish has told me. I was late getting the word.'

'What's God's will is God's will so don't fret yourself.' He turned to Eilish. 'I spoke to your mother just now offering to make the arrangements for you. But now Brian is here he may wish to look after them himself.'

'No, Andrew,' Brian said, 'in your hands all will be done as he would have wanted it.'

'I appreciate what you've said. I do indeed.' O'Boyle considered for a moment. 'I should send word first of all to the Old Comrades Association.'

'Certainly.'

'There'll be the flag to be looked after.'

'The flag – ?'

'For draping the coffin.'

Brian stole a glance at Eilish. She too looked puzzled.

'They'll want to have a guard of honour, of course, and arrange a firing party.'

'Is it usual?'

'In the case of someone with a national record, yes. Your father was a veteran of the War of Independence.'

Brian kept his mouth shut.

'And they'll have someone to sound the last post.'

'We'll leave all that to you, Andrew.'

'Also – if you approve – there'll be a short graveside oration. I can get someone of more public importance without the slightest trouble, but if you think well of it I'd like to deliver it myself.'

'No one more suitable, Andrew.'

'You're very kind. Well – I'll take leave of you now and see you first thing in the morning.'

Brian saw him to the hall door. When he got back Eilish was as puzzled as before.

'Was father involved in the War of Independence?'

'I'm morally certain,' Brian said, 'that he never fired a shot in anger in his life.'

'Then what was all that about?'

'That, my dear, is one of the offshoots of Irish politics. So much time is spent dredging up the past they end by believing that in some way they played an active part. With party members it's an occupational hallucination.'

'I feel it's not right to let them go on with it.'

'Why not? Father would have liked it. Himself and O'Sheehan spent a large part of their lives re-living old glories. Besides, he gave service all those years as chairman of the party branch, which is probably a lot more than most of the others. No, I wouldn't worry.'

The mention of O'Sheehan reminded both that word should be got to him, but when Brian called to his flat the next day the housekeeper told him that he had been gone for almost a week. It was very mysterious, she said, as she showed him the tenant-less room. She had found the bed unslept in, the fire unlit, his papers and belongings all in their usual places. He had said nothing to anyone. There was no indication either as to where he had gone.

On the morning of the funeral it rained, though not heavily. Brian looked after his mother. Barbara stood beside Eilish. O'Boyle, with perhaps a dozen or so elderly and bemedalled men, supervised the proceedings which, with the exception of the volley of shots, omitted at Mrs Moloney's expressed wish, went ahead as planned. O'Boyle, in his graveside address, spoke quite eloquently on the early life of Cornelius in his native Tipperary, something that at first hand he knew nothing at all about. But nobody else, Mrs Moloney included, did either so it hardly mattered.

Brian, despite his sorrow, was conscious of unintended comedy. Eilish maintained her quiet and reserved control until they began to sound the Last Post. Though not very expertly played, it struck through to her heart. As the tears came she felt Barbara's comforting arm tighten about her body.

IX

The novice who delivered the letter found Tim surrounded by a litter of personal possessions, most of them books and all of them scattered in disarray about the floor of the new room he was in the act of moving into. There was a low bed in one corner of it with a locker beside it on which stood a crucifix. The window looked out on green fields and nearby mountains, a welcome improvement on the view from the room he had just quit. It was early June out there, sunny and still. Empty shelves awaiting the books he was sorting, a press for his clothes and a straight-backed chair completed the furnishings.

He opened the envelope. It was an invitation to the wedding

of Brian and Barbara. It was formal and not unexpected; Brian had already spoken to him about it. But it meant seeking permission, and he was by no means certain of obtaining it. The Master of Novices, he decided, was the first person to consult.

He found him at last in the library, his attention fixed on an ancient-looking volume which he pushed to one side while he read the printed invitation card. He was a man of easy humour, shrewd, but approachable.

'You've been with us – how long now – two years?'

'Almost two years.'

He examined the card again.

'Is either of them a close relative?'

'No. Just very good friends.'

'Moloney – he visits you quite a lot.'

'Both of them do.'

'In uniform once or twice – a commercial pilot, I remember. Lucky man. Ever been in a plane yourself?'

He had not. The fact, now that he actually thought about it, was oddly surprising.

'It's marvellous,' the Master of Novices told him, 'like hobnobbing with cherubim and seraphim.' He handed back the invitation. 'I'll talk to Father Prior about it later, but I can't make promises. In fact I would expect a refusal. However, I'll do my best. I'll explain they're both very close friends.'

'Thank you. I understand.'

The Master of Novices was in companionable mood. He pushed the volume towards him.

'You haven't seen this, I expect. It's quite rare and valuable. We usually keep it among our special treasures.'

Tim examined it.

Divers Voyages touching the Discovery of America, by a Richard Hakluyt. The date inside was 1582.

'I expect you haven't seen this before either,' the Master of Novices said. He went to one of the bookcases and felt behind it. It swivelled silently away from the wall, revealing an opening behind. The Master of Novices switched on a light and led him inside.

'The priests' hidey hole,' he explained. 'It dates back to the penal times.'

Tim was aware of an assortment of objects, not very plentiful, and not very identifiable either, in the inadequate light.

'This is from the penal days too,' the Master of Novices said. 'A chalice. It's made of pewter, as you can see.' He replaced it. Beside it was a silver cross and a little further away, to Tim's astonishment, a rifle. He thought it might be a Lee Enfield.

'The weaponry is unliturgical,' the Master of Novices remarked. 'I must tell you the story behind it some time.' He put the book back on a shelf. 'Hakluyt, though the name is odd, was an Englishman. He drew Sir Philip Sidney's attention to the academic dignity Spain had bestowed on her master pilots. It was still an age of romantics and philosophers, but Hakluyt realized the supremacy of technology. That makes him a modern.'

He led Tim out again and returned the bookcase to its usual position. They left the library and accompanied each other down the corridor.

'Hakluyt felt that the Spaniards, and what he called the *Portingales*, were grabbing an unfair share of the New World, though he believed their original intentions were honest. In fact he wrote to Sir Philip Sidney to that effect and I am very much taken with what he said.' The Master of Novices interrupted their progress while he sought to bring the words to mind.

'Yes. I now remember. "The desire to reduce their gentile people to Christianity was the cause that Bresilia was first inhabited by the Portingales." '

Tim laughed.

'I thought that would please you,' the Master of Novices said. His mood was one of informal geniality. Tim put it down to the warm and sunny weather and returned to his litter of books.

They lay all about in the silence of the June afternoon in which nothing at all made a stir. The fields outside seemed asleep. The mountains at a distance raised their coloured shapes through a light haze to an unclouded blue sky. The gorse on their slopes would be beginning soon to fade. The thought made him wist-

ful. It drew him unaware along little roads and was joined by
others that begged silently for his attention. He cycled with
Anne once again by Killikee and Glenasmole. They sat in
shelter on heathered slopes and under broad blue skies she
touched his fingers gently, one by one. Hedges by a lake shore
were fragrant with blossom and shimmered in the light. Never
and forever. Was it so? Could he bear that? He frowned, not at
the wistfulness, which was familiar, not at the ache – he was
used to that – but at the new and unexpected unease. He pushed
it away and returned to his books.

The one first to his hand he had not looked into in years
though he had never let it out of his keeping. Opening it he
found himself gazing once again at the picture of Pegasus, the
winged horse. He turned over the flyleaf to find there the
inscription in finely formed characters:

From N. CURTIS

to

his young friend

TIMOTHY McDONAGH

Wishing him a very prosperous career

2nd June 1927

An insect was buzzing in the warmth and isolation of his
room. The sound was far away. He saw in faint outline the
insolent peacock and heard the ghostly music of dancing milk
churns. There was a smell of treacle in the still air. A bird in its
cage listened closely, its head to one side. On an insubstantial
wall the pictures of two young men in uniform, separated
one from the other by an artificial poppy, gazed down at him
from their gilt frame.